THE HELLFIRE CLUB

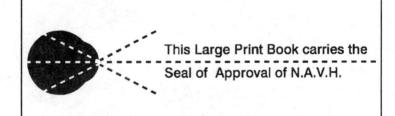

This Large Print Book carries the
Seal of Approval of N.A.V.H.

THE HELLFIRE CLUB

JAKE TAPPER

THORNDIKE PRESS
A part of Gale, a Cengage Company

Farmington Hills, Mich • San Francisco • New York • Waterville, Maine
Meriden, Conn • Mason, Ohio • Chicago

Copyright © 2018 by Jake Tapper.
Thorndike Press, a part of Gale, a Cengage Company.

ALL RIGHTS RESERVED
This is a work of fiction. The events in this novel are imaginary, including those featuring historical or public figures, except for the events and quotes specifically noted at the end of the book.
The publisher is not responsible for websites (or their content) that are not owned by the publisher.
Thorndike Press® Large Print Thriller.
The text of this Large Print edition is unabridged.
Other aspects of the book may vary from the original edition.
Set in 16 pt. Plantin.

LIBRARY OF CONGRESS CIP DATA ON FILE.
CATALOGUING IN PUBLICATION FOR THIS BOOK
IS AVAILABLE FROM THE LIBRARY OF CONGRESS

ISBN-13: 978-1-4328-5363-1 (hardcover)

Published in 2018 by arrangement with Little, Brown and Company, a division of Hachette Book Group, Inc.

Printed in the United States of America
1 2 3 4 5 6 7 22 21 20 19 18

To Jennifer,
my lodestar

We are not reformers. We are reporters. As such we will take you with us through a metropolitan area of 1,500,000, living in what should be a utopia, but which is a cesspool of drunkenness, debauchery, whoring, homosexuality, municipal corruption and public apathy, protected crime under criminal protectionism, hoodlumism, racketeering, pandering and plundering, among anomalous situations found nowhere else on earth.

— Jack Lait and Lee Mortimer,
Washington Confidential, 1951

CHAPTER ONE:
FRIDAY, MARCH 5,1954 —
DAWN

Rock Creek Park, Washington, DC

He snapped out of the blackness with a mouth full of mud.

Charlie Marder coughed up grime and spat silt, then raised himself on his elbows and tried to make sense of where he was.

Sprawled on the leafy banks of a creek, he wore a tuxedo that was insufficient to combat the March chill. A wispy fog hovered; sporadic chirping came from nearby families of wrens rising with the sun.

A stone bridge and paved road lay in front of him. Wincing with the effort, he hoisted himself onto his knees and turned. Behind him, a semi-submerged Studebaker sat in the creek's muddy bank, its driver's door open.

He squinted and could just make out, downstream, the recently restored old Peirce Mill and its waterwheel. He was in Rock Creek Park, 1,754 acres of woods, trails, and road tucked in Northwest Washington, DC, far from his Georgetown brownstone.

How did I get here?

Charlie said it to himself, first in his head and then as a whisper and then repeating it aloud: "How did I get here?" His voice was gravelly. He stumbled as he tried to stand, and realized that he was drunk. His mouth was parched. Where had he been drinking?

He looked at his Timex, adjusting his wrist to catch the light: 4:55 a.m. Memories began to emerge — a party, a celebration, a club of some sort. Frank Carlin, the powerful House Appropriations Committee chairman, encouraging a young, attractive waitress to do something. *What was it?* She poured ice water onto a sugar cube held on a flattened perforated spoon over a glass. And the glass contained absinthe. "This is how the French do it," Carlin said. And from there the night went dark.

Charlie staggered forward. Looked back at the Studebaker. Muddy tracks traced the car's path from the road to its final resting place on the riverbank. *Okay. I skidded off the parkway.* This was a problem. But nothing insurmountable. An accident. Maybe he could just walk away. He didn't recognize the car, had no recollection of being behind the wheel. "Absinthe," he muttered under his breath.

He took stock of the situation. This was not even a ripple in the ocean of atrocities he'd witnessed in France during the war. He was not a person of poor character. He was someone who tried to do good; he was currently fighting for his fellow troops from the turret of his congressional office. In the grand scheme of things, would it be so wrong to just leave the scene and spare himself a litany of questions he might not be able to answer?

And then he heard it: a low din, a car's motor heading toward him. *Ah, well,* Charlie thought. *Fate is making the decision for me. I'll stand here and face whatever happens.* He exhaled, steeling himself.

With relief, he recognized the spit-shined baby-blue Dodge Firearrow sport coupe. It belonged to someone he knew, a friend, even: well-connected lobbyist Davis LaMontagne. It was a car perfectly suited to its owner, glossy and stylish. LaMontagne pulled the car to a stop at the side of the road and rolled down his window.

"Charlie," he said, "Jesus Christ."

He opened the door and emerged, looking as though he'd just stepped out of the pages of a magazine ad for cigarettes or suits. His hair slicked back, his blue hip-length bush jacket hanging loosely from his broad Rocky Marciano build, he briefly surveyed the scene, then began to negotiate his way carefully down the rocky, muddy decline toward Charlie.

"Davis," Charlie said. "I have no idea —" He spread his arms to finish the sentence for him.

Before LaMontagne could respond, they heard a sound in the distance.

Another car.

Its windows must have been open despite the morning chill; as it drew closer, they could hear the bark of a radio newscaster. LaMontagne didn't move, as if he were freezing the action in his world until this problem took care of itself.

And it did. The sounds of car and radio changed pitch, suggesting the car, off in the distance, was now driving away from them.

Unruffled, LaMontagne continued his approach and arrived at Charlie's side. Charlie was hit with a whiff of his smoky, woody cologne.

"Are you all right?"

"Fine," Charlie said, though his head was throbbing and he would have given his left arm for a glass of water. "Do you have any idea how I got here?"

"Last I saw you was at the party," La-Montagne said. "You were snockered. Then you made an Irish exit." He raised his hand and made an elegant illustrative explosion with his fingertips: *poof.* "You okay? Jesus. Thank God you're alive." LaMontagne looked over his shoulder at the Studebaker. "Whose car is that?"

Charlie suppressed a wave of nausea; when it passed, he rubbed his chin and shrugged. "I have no idea."

LaMontagne pulled on his black leather gloves, took a folded handkerchief from his suit pocket, and leaned into the driver's seat of the Studebaker. He wiped the steering wheel, the gearshift, the radio knobs, and the window roller; on his way out, he removed the keys from the ignition, then wiped the door handle. Sliding the keys into his pocket, he stood up straight and put a hand on Charlie's shoulder.

"Let's burn rubber," he said.

Charlie let himself be guided briskly up to the road and the Dodge, where he collapsed with relief in the passenger seat as La-Montagne shut the door firmly.

Halfway around the front of the car, the man suddenly stopped. Through the windshield, Charlie saw him looking down at the narrow shoulder of the road.

13

"Charlie," LaMontagne said, a seriousness in his baritone Charlie had never heard before. "You need to see this."

Charlie exited and joined LaMontagne, who was staring at what at first appeared to be a bundle of discarded clothes in a narrow drainage ditch but upon closer examination proved to be a young woman lying on her right side, facing away from the road, her left arm twisted awkwardly behind her. Blood had soaked through the back of her low-cut dress.

Charlie's heart thudding into his lungs, he slowly knelt on the grass and gently rolled the woman toward him; she fell onto her back. She had red hair and couldn't have been more than twenty-two. Charlie had vague memories of her from the night before. *Is she a cocktail waitress, maybe?*

He looked up at LaMontagne in disbelief, but the man's gaze was elsewhere, back toward the spot where he'd found Charlie. "I didn't think anything of it before, but the passenger door of that Studebaker is open. Jesus. Do you think she fell out of your car?"

Fighting his rising anxiety, Charlie gingerly placed two fingers on the side of the woman's neck. She was porcelain pale and still. Her eyes were closed, sealed by thick fake lashes. Her body was cool to the touch.

He could feel no pulse.

He looked at LaMontagne and shook his head slowly.

"Christ," said LaMontagne. He squatted and put two fingers on the woman's neck to see for himself. Then on her wrist. He hung his head briefly, then seemed to collect himself. He stood, moved behind the young woman's lifeless body, bent down, and threaded his arms beneath her shoulders.

Charlie was numb, motionless.

LaMontagne looked at him with gravity and impatience.

"Congressman," he said sharply. "Grab her feet."

CHAPTER TWO:
THURSDAY, JANUARY 14, 1954

Arena Stage, Washington, DC

The self-satisfaction was almost like a physical presence in the theater lobby, a distinct mélange of aromas exclusive to the halls of power — high-priced perfume and expensive hors d'oeuvres, top-shelf liquor and freshly minted cash. It all billowed into a rich toxic cloud that made Charlie Marder's throat constrict.

Charlie generally prided himself on his ease in social settings, but tonight he was on edge, feeling oddly exposed while he waited for Margaret to return from the powder room. As a professor at Columbia, he'd given countless lectures, attended dozens of professional functions, and even made a few TV appearances when *Sons of Liberty,* his book on the Founding Fathers, hit the bestseller list four years before. Tall and broad-shouldered with piercing blue eyes, Charlie had found it easy to navigate the worlds of academia and literary celebrity. But he felt out of his element here, surrounded by political and press powerhouses drinking and smoking and chortling among themselves.

He rubbed the back of his neck, scanning the room for any sign of Margaret. The crowd, of course, couldn't have cared less about his anxiety, busy as they were with their own competing agendas. He ambled around the auditorium to pass the time; bits of conversations flew by his ears:

Let's just say my respect for the congressman knows bounds.

If the court rules to desegregate, it's going to get ugly.

No, I don't hate musicals. I just don't understand them. Why would people break out in song? And even suspending disbelief, the songs are seldom any good.

No kids. She's a work nun.

Has anyone actually gotten a look at the naval records of PT-109?

I'll say it: If Ike was as weak against the Krauts as he is against McCarthy, we'd all be speaking German right now.

Did you see it? First issue came out last month. Naked Marilyn Monroe.

17

No, when I said they were bums, I meant
    the baseball team the Senators, not
    actual senators.
We still have troops in Korea, darling. We'll
    have them there forever.

Miserably self-conscious, Charlie gulped
his martini, swallowed wrong, and coughed
loudly just as Senator Jack Kennedy made
his entrance. Heads turned as the handsome
senator glided past Charlie, glamorous new
wife in tow. Charlie caught a strong whiff of
bandages and ointment. He wondered
which of them had recently sustained an
injury. From his earliest days, Charlie had
possessed an abnormally keen sense of
smell. He did not consider it a gift.

He gave his empty glass to a passing waiter
and watched the celebrity couple as they
made their way across the plush maroon
carpet to join the senator's brother Robert.
The younger Kennedy was deep in conversation with Senator Joseph McCarthy, the
Republican from Wisconsin currently about
to start the fifth consecutive year of a reckless smear campaign designed to drive the
threat of Communism, real and imagined,
from every corner of American society.
Charlie knew that Robert Kennedy and
McCarthy worked together on the commit-

18

tee McCarthy chaired, and from all appearances, they were pals as well.

Charlie's pondering of their seemingly odd friendship ended when Margaret reappeared. Even after nine years of marriage, Charlie still felt his heart jump when he saw her. Her blond hair was swept off her forehead; a simply cut emerald-green dress made the most of her athletic frame, its color highlighting her kelly-green eyes. Eyes that betrayed no sign of the frayed nerves Charlie felt, he noticed, although she was just as new to this scene as he was; they had arrived in Washington, DC, only three weeks earlier, after Charlie was appointed to fill a congressional seat that had suddenly become vacant.

"This with-child business is murder," Margaret said, rubbing her still-flat stomach. "It feels like our little one has rented a one-bedroom on top of my bladder." She was roughly six weeks pregnant, they'd learned a few days ago. "Has Senator Kefauver shown up yet?"

"Nope," said Charlie. "But the Kennedy boys have. My mom would melt like a Popsicle."

Charlie's mother somewhat secretly worshipped the Kennedy brood. His father, Winston, a powerful Republican lawyer in

Manhattan, had a more skeptical view of Ambassador Joseph Kennedy and, through the transitive property, his scions. He faulted the Kennedy patriarch for wanting to appease Hitler. For fun, he'd also bad-mouth him for having made his fortune in bootlegging during Prohibition.

Margaret glanced sideways, where a very old Herbert Hoover was hobbling through the crowd. She grimaced sympathetically as the former president gripped the golden banister and, with an expression of great pain, made his way slowly up the red-carpeted stairs.

"Mothballs," Charlie said of Hoover after he was out of earshot.

"Poor Charlie," Margaret said. "That nose of yours."

"The world is not primarily peppermint." Charlie turned his attention to the colorful lobby poster for the show preview they were about to see, *The Pajama Game,* which was set to debut on Broadway in the spring. "What's it about, anyway? I mean, besides being about ninety minutes too long." Charlie was not a fan of musicals.

"It's about strikes," said Margaret.

"Baseball? Bowling?" He enjoyed playing clueless sidekick to Margaret's straight man.

"Unions, dear."

"Of course," said Charlie. "Who wouldn't look at sweaty longshoremen in Hoboken, New Jersey, and think, *You know what? I'd love to see them sing and dance!*"

"This isn't *On the Waterfront,* sweetheart, this strike is at a pajama factory." Margaret straightened his tie. "Remember that book I read last summer? *Seven and a Half Cents?*"

"Honey, I can't keep track," Charlie said. "You go through more bestsellers than a McCarthy bonfire."

Margaret tsked and rolled her eyes. "Anyway, this is based on the book I read. The head of the grievance committee, a lady, falls in love with the supervisor who's rejecting her pleas for a seven-and-a-half-cent wage increase."

"In bed with the opposition," Charlie said. "This crowd will love it."

Margaret gestured toward the Kennedys. "That's right, I'd read that McCarthy and the Kennedys were very close. And isn't 'Tail Gunner Joe' godfather to one of Bobby's kids?"

"Dad says no one who knows him calls him Bobby — it's Bob," Charlie said. "I think the godfather thing is just a rumor. It's odd, though, these Democratic princes befriending my party's fire-breathing dragon. We're going to need a flowchart to keep track of all the alliances."

"I guess Irishmen can be pretty tribal," Margaret observed. She watched the Kennedy brothers, a blur of hair and teeth, as they greeted well-wishers. She leaned closer to her husband and lowered her voice when she said, "Speaking of rumors, I heard quite a few about Jack from the nurses."

"Such as?"

"All the stuff you'd expect. That the Boston crowd rounds up girls to join them in private parties. Coeds from GW and Catholic U."

"From Catholic?" Charlie said. "Not with all those nuns around. Even Jack would be scared."

"Charlie," Margaret said incredulously, "you think our courageous Lieutenant Kennedy, who survived the Japs taking out his PT boat, braved sharks and riptides, and beat back dengue fever and cannibals, will be deterred by a couple of bearded nuns?"

"I don't recall that story having cannibals before." Charlie smiled. "Ambassador Kennedy ought to put you on the payroll along with the rest of the press corps; that's a nice touch."

Margaret grinned, then swallowed half the smile. "It's disappointing to hear," she said. "About Jack. I thought he was presidential timber."

"Oh, you shouldn't be surprised, Margaret. If he's really presidential material, one expects a certain sangfroid."

Margaret looked askance at her husband. "You're actually making the argument that presidential timber requires a willingness to commit adultery? As if it's an *asset*?"

"Not an asset per se." Charlie smiled, lighting a cigarette. "How would Aristotle put it? All men who cheat are bastards. All presidents need to be able to be bastards. Therefore, all presidents should cheat!"

"That's not what I meant by *presidential timber*, Charlie," Margaret said. She laughed and took a drag from his cigarette before returning it to him.

"There's Carlin." Charlie gave a friendly wave to a tall and wiry man with slicked-back gray hair: Congressman Franklin Harris Carlin, the GOP chairman of the all-powerful House Appropriations Committee, which disbursed almost fifty billion dollars each year. The Republicans had recaptured control of the House in 1952 in the Eisenhower landslide. With discretion over the distribution of such largesse, Carlin was one of the most popular men in town. Even in a city built on the swampy foundation of transaction, Carlin was notorious for always seeking out ways he could gain even more advantage.

Carlin saw Charlie's wave and responded with a cold look of disdain before he turned his head.

"Goodness!" Margaret gave a short laugh of surprise. "Did you kill his puppy or something, Charlie?"

Although reeling a bit from the snub, Charlie had a feeling he knew its source. "My first Appropriations Committee meeting was today," Charlie said. "I said one thing. One thing! There was a company I didn't think deserved taxpayer dollars."

"What company?"

"Goodstone," Charlie said. "They made the gas masks. The ones that didn't work."

"Oh dear," said Margaret.

As an army captain in Europe during World War II, Charlie had led a platoon in battle for almost a year. In France there had been a tragedy caused by defective gas masks; Margaret knew little about the catastrophe other than the fact that Charlie remained haunted by it. Only twice in the nine years since the war had ended had Charlie tried to describe any of the horrors he'd witnessed, and both times he'd become so shaken by emotion, he had to leave the room. This was the first time she'd heard the masks were made by the famous Goodstone Rubber and Tire Company.

A waiter with a tray of martinis was passing. Charlie snagged two glasses and handed one to his wife. He gulped down his as if it were water from a canteen.

"One of the Democrats on the committee said, 'That was a decade ago.' " Charlie shook his head. "I reminded him that Truman as a senator raked a bunch of companies over the coals for profiteering and shoddy workmanship."

"That's right," Margaret said. "Carnegie sent steel that caused the hull of that ship to crack."

"Right," said Charlie, "and there were cruddy plane engines, dud grenades. Those companies were punished. Of course, Democrats don't much like talking about Truman these days."

"How come I never read anything about Goodstone?" Margaret asked, sipping her drink.

"I guess journalists don't know about it. And I don't know if there were any other incidents. I tried to get information after the war but I hit a wall. Maybe I should try again; maybe the calls of a congressman will get returned."

Margaret peered into the crowd. "Isn't

that Joe Alsop?" She tilted her chin toward a dark-haired man in his forties gracelessly gesturing as he explained something to a small group. Alsop and his brother wrote an influential syndicated newspaper column.

"Yep," said Charlie. "Navy man. POW."

"Well, tell him about Goodstone!" she said. "Now's your chance!"

"Oh no, Margaret," he said. "This isn't the time or place." He paused, thoughtful. "It was probably naive of me to think I could get my way so soon; I don't have enough capital here yet to push anything. I just said I wasn't going to vote to give Goodstone any money after their masks failed me and my men."

"What happened after you told them that?"

"The discussion kind of just stopped, and they all started talking among themselves, pretty much ignoring me. Lots of murmuring. Then Chairman Carlin said we would reconvene at a later date. When I approached him after to try to smooth matters over, he gave me the brush-off."

"Hmm," Margaret said. She sipped her drink and met Charlie's gaze.

"Actually, come to think of it, some of the other vets — Strongfellow and MacLachlan and a few others — were the most, um,

26

murmury. Is that a word?"

"It most certainly is not."

"Look over there," said Charlie, discreetly pointing through the crowd to a plain-looking man with a wide smile who was leaning on metal crutches. "There's Strongfellow by the bar."

"The war hero, right?"

"Every veteran in politics claims to be a war hero," Charlie said. "But Strongfellow really is one."

"Well, you're all heroes as far as I'm concerned," Margaret said. "Either way, you should convince him and all the other veterans in Congress to block this nonsense. We don't need the next generation of American soldiers dying in Indochina or Hungary because of war profit —"

Margaret was interrupted by a clamor at the door; Vice President Richard Nixon and his wife, Patricia, had arrived. A coterie of photographers and reporters began peppering the Second Couple with questions and requests for posed pictures. The Nixons obliged, after which the vice president made a beeline for the Kennedys. Jack shook Nixon's hand while Bob Kennedy patted him on the back.

Margaret placed her empty martini glass on the windowsill and pulled a cigarette from the pack in her purse; Charlie deftly lit it for her with an aluminum trench lighter he pulled from his pocket. It was a souvenir he'd taken from a dead German soldier in France, though he was the only one who knew its provenance.

"It's both reassuring and disconcerting to see them all friendly-like," Margaret said, waving her cigarette toward the circle of the Kennedys, the Nixons, and McCarthy.

The lobby lights flickered on and off, signaling the start of the show. The audience began filtering into the theater, clearing the lobby. Charlie grabbed one more martini from a passing waiter. Margaret raised an eyebrow. "Slow down, tiger, the night is young."

Charlie shrugged unapologetically. "We're about to watch a musical. About a union strike. I need all the fortification I can get." Margaret jutted out her lower lip, mocking a sulk. "And more important, I want to take this occasion to toast you!" Charlie quickly added. "To have you here with me, breathing on me — I count that something of a miracle," he said, paraphrasing Henry Miller.

He scanned the room again. "Where the devil is Kefauver, anyway?"

"Isn't that him?" Margaret nodded at a

bookish, big-boned man with a broad smile and thick spectacles moving toward them at a rapid pace. He greeted Charlie with an enthusiastic handshake.

"Charlie, what a great pleasure to meet you at last. I'm Estes Kefauver," he said softly, emphasizing the first syllable of his last name: "*Key*-fawv-er." "And you must be Margaret," he said, enveloping her hand in his while he leaned closer with a genial wink. "You'd better be careful; you're not allowed to be too beautiful in this town. You're going to make a lot of enemies."

Margaret smiled insincerely. She didn't mind compliments, or tried not to, but she had already been wary of moving south, where she feared she might be viewed as nothing more than a decoration for Charlie's arm, even more so than she was in New York City. She had her own career — as a zoologist — and it was irritating to be admired for only her exterior.

"You look so familiar," Kefauver told Charlie. "And not just because you resemble your father."

People routinely greeted Charlie with a vague sense of recognition. His road to semi-notoriety had begun some years earlier when he'd purchased a heavy wooden trunk for his father's birthday at a Brooklyn junk shop. He'd brought it home, picked the lock, and found it contained a dozen books from the eighteenth and nineteenth centuries, among them the diaries of a former page at the Continental Congress. Nicholas Mezedes had recorded his intimate impressions of the Founding Fathers, some of whom were involved in rather scandalous behavior at the time. With Margaret's organizational help and editing, Charlie had smoothed Mezedes's prose into more colloquial dialogue and a compelling narrative. The resulting book — *Sons of Liberty* — had become a runaway bestseller. Charlie had thrived. Columbia University offered him a path to a full professorship. At the time, the public was infatuated with intellectual celebrities, and Charlie appeared on popular shows such as *What's My Line?* and *Art Linkletter's House Party.*

"You may have seen me on television a few years ago when my book on the Founding Fathers came out," Charlie said now.

"Maybe that's it," Kefauver said. "I was on *What's My Line?* too, you know!" He smiled.

Ushers began circling the lobby with chimes, alerting the crowd that the show was just minutes from starting. "We'd better head in," Kefauver said, leading them into the theater.

"Maybe the senator can give you some advice on blocking the Goodstone funds," Margaret said quietly to Charlie. "You need to rally folks."

Charlie nodded.

"Jack Kennedy might help too," she said. "He would be a great ally."

"Great idea," said Charlie. "And I'll just join Ike on the links tomorrow and get him on board as well."

She smacked him playfully on the shoulder.

The lights in the theater dimmed except for those closest to the stage. The crowd, well versed in protocol, applauded for the vice president and his wife, sitting in a prestigious box near stage left. The Nixons at first seemed uncertain the applause was for them, then stood hesitantly. The vice president offered a stiff bow and then a wide grin that couldn't have looked less sincere.

"Oh dear," Margaret whispered.

Kefauver nodded toward the vice president.

"Earlier this month, I met a guy who knew Dick during the war. They were stationed at Bougainville Island."

"Where?" asked Charlie.

"It's in Papua New Guinea," Margaret

told her husband. "Forgive Charlie," she said to Kefauver, "they didn't get much news about the Pacific campaign in the foxholes of France."

"They don't have newspapers in France?" Kefauver joked.

"Charlie was too busy trying to keep his platoon alive while they breathed in poison gas because of junky American gas masks," Margaret said tartly.

"I didn't get much news about anything when I was in Europe," Charlie said, lightly squeezing Margaret's hand. "It left some odd holes in my knowledge."

"Anyway, Dick basically ran a burger joint for pilots there," Kefauver said. "Beer, coffee, toast. But the most interesting thing this gentleman told me was that Dick was a cardsharp. He cleaned up. 'Best poker face you've ever seen,' he said. He bluffed just enough to guarantee that everyone stayed in when he actually had the cards."

He leaned over as if confiding some great wisdom. "Watch out for the poker faces in this town," Kefauver whispered.

Margaret intertwined her fingers with Charlie's as the lights went out and the opening number of the musical began.

Charlie hated it.

CHAPTER THREE:
FRIDAY, JANUARY 15, 1954 — MORNING

Georgetown, Washington, DC

Margaret paused to roll her eyes and suppress a smile while her husband, on his knees, gently kissed her stomach. She was standing at the bathroom mirror in her camisole, carefully applying her eyeliner, just recovered from another bout of morning sickness. So she wasn't strictly in the mood to be touched, but she also didn't want to push Charlie away.

"Bye-bye, little Alger," Charlie sang to the baby in her womb. He made it a daily habit to come up with the worst possible names to bestow upon their impending arrival. "Good-bye, sweet little Hirohito Marder."

Margaret laughed, then spat into the sink, wiped her mouth, and reached for her favorite pair of khakis. "I can't believe these pants still fit," she said, stepping into them. "I feel so bloated, like the boa digesting the elephant in *The Little Prince.*"

"And yet you still look *très belle,*" Charlie said in the grunty French accent he and his troops would use mockingly to lighten the mood. He eyed her valise while he knotted his tie. "Excited about the trip?" he asked, trying his best to hide his concern and, yes, disapproval of Margaret's participation in the zoological study of the mysterious ponies out on Nanticoke and Susquehannock Islands in Maryland. Prior to their move to Washington, DC, she had discussed writing a book about the ponies for a university publishing house, but the editors there — in addition to being dismissive of a woman zoologist — felt the book would need firsthand accounts from a full team in the field. Margaret had planned to spend her first year in Washington, DC, trying to secure funding and partnerships for such an excursion. Then, almost like magic, an older zoologist she knew — one who shared her minor obsession with the ponies — had called her in December and offered her a job as a researcher on his own trip to the very same islands. She could join his study and they could co-author a paper.

Charlie had supported her desire to keep working in her field. In theory. In fact, the opportunity for her to join the Maryland study was partly how he'd convinced her to abandon their lives in New York City and move to the nation's capital for his new job. But ever since the baby news the week before, he'd deeply regretted their agreement. He kept imagining Margaret in a field getting kicked in the abdomen by a wild pony.

"So someone from the research team is picking you up?" he asked. "How long is the drive?"

"Two and a half hours, I think," she said. "Wait, let me show you."

She retrieved a map from her purse and showed him the route they'd be taking. They would drive from the city through rural Maryland and to the tip of an isthmus, then proceed by boat to the far island, Nanticoke. He followed her finger absently, picturing her out there in the middle of nowhere surrounded by wild animals and sleeping on the ground in a tent. He fretted but out loud said only, "Just don't work too hard."

Margaret chuckled to herself; Charlie was as easy to read as the top line of an eye chart. Did he think she couldn't take care of herself? "I'll be back a week from tomorrow at the very latest," she said, yielding at the sight of his worried face. "*We'll* be fine, I promise." She patted her belly and gave him what she hoped was a reassuring smile.

The ponies had been a fascination of Margaret's since she was a child, when her mother had taken her and her sister on a long camping vacation after their father had been killed in an airship disaster. A few hundred wild ponies roamed the beaches and marshes of Susquehannock Island every spring and summer, then inexplicably crossed the bay every autumn to return to Nanticoke Island a few hundred yards south. No one knew where the ponies had originally come from or why they behaved the way they did or even how they made the trek. Margaret would be part of a small group of similarly fascinated zoologists, a loosely affiliated research team headed by Dr. Louis Gwinnett, whom she had met at an annual conference; they were going to try to figure out how and why the animals made the seasonal crossings.

Charlie raised his hands in surrender. "Just find a way to call me if you can. Miss Leopold can always track me down. She's like a bloodhound."

Catherine Leopold, a Southern former beauty queen in her forties with a helmet of thick brown hair and penetrating pale blue eyes, served as Charlie's office manager. He'd inherited her from his predecessor,

Congressman Martin Van Waganan, and in their three weeks together, he'd come to rely on her. Her ruthless efficiency was candy-coated, charming, and deft; Charlie depended on her wholly.

Margaret buttoned her blouse. "I'm not sure how many phone booths we'll find out there in the fields, but if I need to reach you, I promise I will. And I'll try to find a way to call you at work on Monday. Just try to be in your office as much as possible so I don't miss you; I'm not sure when I'll be able to get away."

Charlie reached his arms around her and gently pulled her close. "I'll miss you two," he said.

"Us too, darling," she said. "While we're gone, you stay focused. You enlist some fellow veterans and kill that Goodstone funding. And don't drink too much! You were comatose last night after just a few martinis. I couldn't wake you at all when you started your three a.m. snore-a-bration."

"Yes, ma'am." Charlie grinned, but with a slight wince. Political life seemed to require new levels of drinking, and lately liquor had become a slow-motion "Goodnight Irene" punch to the face, knocking him out for the night. Which, to be honest, he sometimes preferred to sober insomnia and nightmares about France, the hangover notwithstanding.

He kissed her good-bye and went downstairs to the foyer, where he bundled up in his heavy coat, put on his fedora, and descended the town-house stairs. As he stood outside on Dent Place, the cruel January chill felt like pins pricking his cheeks. Days-old snow and ice had turned the cobblestoned streets grimy, like mashed coal. Dodging ice puddles and frozen slush banks, he made his way around the corner to his new car, a silver Oldsmobile Super 88. Margaret had protested mildly when he chose it upon arriving in Washington — for a day or so she'd called him Hot Rod — but Charlie still had book royalties to spend. He felt a boyish thrill every time he saw its gleaming wraparound windshield, the chrome streak on each side creating the illusion of speed even when the car was standing still. It was his first car — as a New Yorker, he'd had no need for one — and despite his left-leaning wife's occasional anti-consumerist gibes, he felt no guilt about his joy in the smell of the car's interior leather and the satisfying hum of its 185-horsepower Rocket V-8 engine.

Even though it was chilly, he rolled down the windows and kept them open as he maneuvered through Georgetown. For Charlie, it was an aromatic tour as much as a visual one: garbage, brown sugar, cat urine, freshly baked bread. As he entered Rock Creek Parkway, he flipped on the radio. Playing defense against McCarthy, President Eisenhower was proposing to strip U.S. citizenship from Communists convicted of treason, but the broadcasters devoted much more time to the marriage of Yankee great Joe DiMaggio to Marilyn Monroe.

Charlie passed the Washington Monument on his left and the Jefferson Memorial, across the Tidal Basin, on his right. By nine a.m., he'd parked and begun his journey on foot to the very worst quarters in the House Office Building.

Three weeks after he'd first moved in, Charlie wondered if the novelty of walking into his office at the U.S. House of Representatives would ever wear off. This time last year, he'd been a rising academic star at Columbia, settling into the life he'd plotted for himself since he was a boy. But that all changed in December when Representative Martin Van Waganan, Democrat from New York's Thirteenth Congressional District, was indicted for corruption and racketeering. Hours after the grand jury handed down its decision, Van Waganan's dead body was found in a cheap motel in a blighted ghetto of Northeast Washington, DC. Police had no suspects; the crime scene was messy and inconclusive. The FBI had taken over, and the status of the investigation was uncertain. It was a grim business that had triggered Manhattan power broker Winston Marder's quick phone call to Republican governor Tom Dewey to arrange for Charlie to fill the vacant seat for the remainder of the term.

The stated reasons for Charlie's selection, the ones soon whispered to newspaper reporters by "the governor's top aides," were Charlie's war record, his respected bestseller, his and his wife's telegenic looks, and his GOP affiliation (important for Dewey at a time when his party controlled the House and White House). The subtext of Winston Marder's pitch to Dewey went unstated: Dewey owed him. Charlie knew that his selection had been unusual, to put it mildly, and that there were plenty of congressmen and journalists who were waiting for him to fall flat on his face on Congress's marble floors.

Charlie navigated the dim halls to find Catherine Leopold stationed in her usual position next to his congressional office's open door, clipboard in hand, wearing the slightly disapproving expression she'd probably had since birth. "Good morning, Congressman," she said crisply. "Today might be a good day to start emptying out those boxes in your office. The ones that you insisted you didn't want me to unpack. The new intern will fetch you some coffee at the House Restaurant. Black, I presume?"

For all her attention to detail, Catherine Leopold seemed possessed by a peculiar determination to ignore Charlie's stated preference; every day she asked him if he'd like his coffee black, and every day he said no. Black was how he'd had to take it in the trenches, black and like a mud puddle — if his platoon was lucky. Sometimes he had not been entirely certain the java wasn't just sewage.

"I'd love cream and sugar," he said, as he did every day.

He could have sworn he heard Leopold give a mild harrumph of disapproval. He wasn't sure if this was a rebuke of his dietary habits or a comment on his lack of manliness, though he didn't care. The notion of what any particular civilian might think about his masculinity meant little to Charlie after he had experienced and borne witness in the war to all its various and

41

grisly manifestations.

In his personal office, he hung up his coat and hat and turned to face the boxes full of books and pictures he'd been avoiding, all of them neatly stacked along one side of the small room. He knew he should just buckle down and unpack, but he also took some small delight in aggravating the über-efficient Leopold with his procrastination, and he was enjoying this rare moment of calm before his day swung into gear.

After carrying one box of books to the mahogany desk that dwarfed the room, Charlie eased himself into the leather swivel chair whose headrest had been smoothed and darkened by countless predecessors and emitted a small sigh of satisfaction. He tipped the chair back tentatively and peeked outside to see if Leopold was nearby, then he propped his feet on the desk's broad surface and reclined, surveying his tiny kingdom.

The sound of Leopold's voice outside his door brought him clattering to his feet; he knocked open the desk's central drawer as he stood. He slid a pile of new pens and pencils that had been left for him on top of the desk into the drawer, and as he did, he felt something brush his fingertips. He pulled the drawer further open, looked down, and extricated a folded scrap of white memo paper. *U Chicago, 2,4-D 2,4,5-T cereal grains broadleaf crops,* it read. An inscrutable relic, perhaps from the previous occupant. Leopold knocked from the open doorway and Charlie absentmindedly tucked the scrap into his pocket, not wanting to be seen wasting his time on such nonsense. He began removing books from the box on his desk just as Leopold entered. *Why does she make me feel like an errant schoolboy?* he wondered as he looked at her expectantly.

"There's a regular poker game among some of the veterans," she said. "Congressman Strongfellow holds it in his office. His secretary just called to ask if you'd like to join them. Are you free Monday? It will be a good chance for you to meet some of your colleagues."

It made sense that other veterans would be flocking to Strongfellow, a former POW who'd escaped from behind enemy lines; his war heroism was legendary. "Yes, I'd love to go," Charlie said, thinking he'd make a few friends and maybe even recruit some allies against Goodstone. Which reminded him: "Miss Leopold, if you have a minute, I've been meaning to tell you about this thing that happened at Appropriations yesterday."

"Oh, I heard all about it." She closed the office door behind her and stood almost at attention across from Charlie. "Quite a declaration of independence."

"What have you heard?"

She frowned. "Mixed reviews, I would say."

"I'm not giving a dime to that company," Charlie said.

"Well, now, Congressman —" she said, then hesitated.

"Go ahead."

"Sir," she said, "do you want me to help you, the way I helped Congressman Van Waganan? Or would you prefer a yes-woman to just tell you your teeth are white and your shoes are shiny? Because I can do that, and it will be a lot easier. For me. Not for you. The opposite for you."

Charlie smiled. "Okay," he said, "you're right. Tell me. What else are you hearing?"

"Nothing you wouldn't expect," she said in her charming Southern lilt. She was from Durham, North Carolina, and her voice conveyed warmth and a debutante's coy wisdom. "You haven't paid any dues and you weren't even elected, so how dare you mouth off; you're only here because of your father's connections; and, of course, why on earth did you get Van Waganan's seat on Appropriations?"

"Right," said Charlie. "I would probably think that about me too. But that's not really relevant to the point I was making, which seems more important than how I got here."

He returned to the business of unpacking, and Leopold put down her clipboard to help. The next box contained books from his work library; Leopold handed him volumes to line his mahogany bookshelves. *The Oxford English Dictionary*, Richard Hofstadter's *The American Political Tradition*, *The New Yorker Twenty-Fifth Anniversary Album* . . .

After a few minutes of companionable silence, Charlie asked Leopold: "Did you work for Congressman Van Waganan long?"

"I did," she said. "He was here for fifteen years and I was by his side for all of them. I started as his secretary and worked my way up to office manager."

"Impressive." Charlie stacked and then strained to lift all six volumes of Winston Churchill's series on the Second World War. Leopold stepped forward, took the top two volumes, and placed them alongside the others on the shelf.

Charlie cleared his throat. "Miss Leopold . . . I'm sorry about what happened with Van Waganan." She looked up, and their sudden proximity seemed to make her uncomfortable; she took a couple of steps back.

"He was a good man," she said. "And then he wasn't." She blinked and briefly looked away.

Awkwardly, Charlie busied himself straightening the Churchill volumes.

"Oh, well," she said, immediately regaining her composure. "Do what thou wilt, I suppose."

Charlie was about to ask what she meant by that cryptic remark when there was a knock at the door and a young woman peeked in. She was in her early twenties and attractively wholesome, with brown hair, a dusting of freckles, and a sweet smile. Handing a cup of coffee to Leopold to give to the congressman, she seemed to have trouble meeting Charlie's direct gaze. He suspected it was shyness; he'd seen it before with some of his students at the beginning of a new semester. His bestselling book gave him a kind of celebrity that Charlie didn't feel was particularly deserved.

"There's a phone call," the woman said to Leopold. "Senator Kefauver's office. The senator would like the congressman to swing by today. After lunch."

"Did he say what it was about?" Leopold asked.

The young woman's face flushed. "I didn't know I could ask!"

Leopold turned to Charlie. "Congressman, this is Sheryl Ann Bernstein, a senior at Georgetown, majoring in American history. She's our new intern this semester, and as luck would have it, an admirer of your book."

"It's nice to meet you, Miss Bernstein."

Bernstein cleared her throat. "I have to tell you how much *Sons of Liberty* meant to me," she said. "It made me love history in a way I never had before; to be honest, it set me on my current path. I'm going to pursue a PhD."

"Thanks," said Charlie, "it's kind of you to say that. What are you going to focus on?"

"Colonial history, I think. I'm doing my senior thesis on the propaganda techniques of Sam Adams."

"What a scoundrel," Charlie said. "Him, not you."

"Thank you, Sheryl Ann," Leopold interjected, dismissing her. "Congressman, I'll set up your meeting with Senator Kefauver, and I'll let Congressman Strongfellow know you'll be in attendance Monday evening."

The two women turned to leave. Leopold slowed her pace until the intern was out of earshot, and then she turned again to face Charlie. She drew back her shoulders and smoothed her sensible tweed skirt.

"Congressman, I say this in the spirit of what we discussed earlier, about my helping you," she said. "I wouldn't push the Goodstone approp issue. And if you want me to alert the chairman's office that you'll be backing off, I'm happy to do so in a discreet way."

Charlie's jaw clenched slightly. His voice was firm: "No."

"This is a man who will kick you off the committee just for spitting on the sidewalk."

"I'll be polite," Charlie said. "But I'm not going to back down."

Chapter Four:
Friday, January 15, 1954 —
Afternoon

U.S. Capitol

Sheryl Ann Bernstein's eyes were bright and she seemed to be trying hard not to bounce in excitement as she followed Charlie into the wicker coach. "Thanks for inviting me to tag along," she said as they boarded the monorail from the Capitol to the Senate Office Building. "This contraption is amazing!"

"Don't get used to it, Bernstein," Charlie teased as they sat down. "We can only use this train when I have an actual appointment with a senator."

"Why don't members of the House have an underground train to reach the Capitol? Why do you guys have to walk?"

"You need to ask?" he said. "We're serfs. Lucky the senators deign to even acknowledge us."

"Well, you have to admit," she said,

"members of the House can be rather unsavory."

"Malodorous?"

"Opprobrious."

Charlie smiled, but he felt he should steer the conversation to something more educational. "Pop quiz: What do you know about Kefauver?"

"Let me see," Bernstein said, her eyes darting skyward as if that's where the information was stored. "He ran those organized-crime hearings a few years ago. He's incredibly popular with Democrats. He was on TV shows like *What's My Line?* and such. He ran for president in 1952 and won the New Hampshire primary."

"Correct," said Charlie. "Beating President Truman and essentially chasing him away from the idea of running for reelection."

"Really? I thought ol' Harry was already planning not to run."

"Revisionism. Truman would have run, but Kefauver cleaned his clock," said Charlie, which prompted a loud chuckle from the tall senator in the cart in front of them. Charlie looked and realized they were seated behind Senate minority leader Lyndon Johnson, Democrat of Texas, who looked back at Charlie, smiled, and winked, then returned his attention to the *Washington Star.*

"Kefauver then went on to run the table in the primaries," Charlie said in a more hushed tone. "So why wasn't he the Democratic presidential nominee?"

"Party bosses thought Stevenson a better candidate?" Bernstein guessed.

Johnson folded his newspaper and twisted his body to face Charlie and his intern. "There's a few reasons for that, young lady," LBJ said in his thick South Texas drawl, taking off his glasses and rubbing his eyes. "Some of the party bosses liked Truman, who sure didn't like Estes. Some of the bosses are big-city Democrats who didn't much care for Senator Kefauver looking into organized crime in the big cities. For reasons you might expect." He chuckled.

Charlie stole a glance at Bernstein, who was quite obviously stunned to be getting a history lesson from the Senate Democratic leader.

"I never thought that old egghead Adlai would win," Johnson said. "I bet on a different horse, Dick Russell, in the primaries. But the thing about Estes is, he's a lone wolf. He's not on a team. You can't win without allies, not in Congress, and not if you're tryin' to get to the White House."

Johnson turned around and reopened his newspaper.

Bernstein took a Camel cigarette from her petite clutch bag, prompting Charlie to reach into his pocket for his German lighter. A paper scrap was sticking to it: the note he'd found in the desk that morning. Once again, he thought of the late congressman Martin Van Waganan and wondered what had happened to him, how a man so admired could throw it all away for petty corruption, meeting such a sordid and grotesque end.

"What's that?" Bernstein asked him.

"Nothing," Charlie said, tucking the note into his inside jacket pocket and lighting Bernstein's cigarette for her.

The monorail was slowing down. "This is our stop," Senator Johnson drawled over his shoulder to them.

"Thank you, Mr. Leader," Charlie said as the three of them exited onto the marble floor.

"You're Winston's boy, aren't you?" Johnson said, extending his hand. "You can call me Lyndon." Charlie shook his hand, an act that Johnson made seem oddly warm and intimate. Johnson caught sight of an aide waiting for him and smiled good-bye to Charlie, then threw a wink to Bernstein

52

before he strode down the hall.

"Geez," said Bernstein. "My senior-thesis adviser isn't going to believe this." She paused, then nodded toward Charlie's pocket. "What's with the little scraps of paper? Should I be taking notes for you so you don't have to keep notes in your pocket? Miss Leopold gave me a stenographer's pad." She lifted the corner of it from her purse to show him.

Charlie pulled the folded note from his inner pocket and handed it to her. "I found it in my new desk. I think it was Van Waganan's."

She looked at the cryptic note — *U Chicago, 2,4-D 2,4,5-T cereal grains broadleaf crops* — and said, "What does it mean?"

"Beats me," said Charlie. "If you figure it out, let me know."

"Great!" she said with a note of sarcasm, tucking the note into her purse. "More homework!"

"Actually, I do have some homework for you, Bernstein," Charlie said. "And don't feel compelled to keep Miss Leopold completely up to date on all aspects of this research. We can make this our little project."

The walls of the reception area of suite 410

in the Senate Office Building were festooned with photographs of the fourteen-city, fifteen-month Kefauver Committee hearings on organized crime. In a central place of honor was a framed copy of the March 12, 1951, *Time* magazine cover illustration of Kefauver next to an octopus, which was meant to represent the Mafia. Displayed in three different spots were coonskin caps, souvenirs from Kefauver's 1948 Senate campaign, during which his nemesis, Tennessee political boss Ed Crump, had claimed he was "working for the Communists with the stealth of a raccoon"; Kefauver had laughed it off by donning a coonskin cap and embracing it as a trademark.

The young receptionist was expecting Charlie. "Welcome," she said with an expansive smile. "May I take your coat? Your aide can wait out here."

Charlie removed his overcoat and handed it to her, silently noting her perfume as she reached for it: Gourielli Moonlight Mist, a scent he recalled from a recent shopping trip with Margaret. Bernstein took a seat in the reception area while Charlie was led into a conference room down the hall. Inside, Kefauver was chain-smoking and flipping through a stack of reports. He stubbed out his cigarette, then took off his glasses and began polishing them with his pocket square. The room smelled like an ashtray.

"Senator Kefauver," Charlie said, reaching out for a handshake. "Thanks again for inviting my wife and me to see the show; Margaret loved it."

"It was my pleasure," Kefauver said with a smile. He brought a new cigarette to his lips.

"I know you're aware that Dad was a big admirer of yours in '52 during the primaries. From across the aisle and behind the scenes, obviously, since we're Republicans. Confidentially, I myself would have gone for you over Ike had you not been cheated out of the nomination."

"But alas," said Kefauver.

"Alas," Charlie said, sitting down.

"Well, thank you, Charlie," Kefauver said. "That means a great deal to me. Have faith. Another presidential election's coming up."

Charlie shifted in his chair uncomfortably. He would never have voted for Kefauver over Ike! And he'd never told a lie like that to ingratiate himself before. Why had he said that?

"There's someone I want you to meet, Charlie," Kefauver said. "He'll be here in a minute. While we wait, can I offer you a drink?"

Charlie's eyes quickly darted to the clock on the wall; it was shortly after two p.m. Charlie had already discerned that this was hardly Kefauver's first cocktail of the day.

"Sure," said Charlie.

The senator nodded to an aide whom Charlie hadn't even realized was there, sitting in the corner near the door; the aide rose and reached for a square glass decanter from a bookcase, poured two glasses of bourbon, neat, and placed them, along with the decanter, on Kefauver's desk. Kefauver nodded again and the aide left the room.

"Normally a scotch man, but I just got this bottle as a gift from a constituent. As Mark Twain once said" — Kefauver raised his glass — " 'Too much of anything is bad, but too much good whiskey is barely enough.' "

Charlie smiled and lifted his glass in return. For a second he remembered his first bourbon experiment in high school; it had started with a meek sip and ended with him praying to a giant rock in Central Park. By now, however, it went down fast.

Charlie raised his glass again. "Churchill: 'The water was not fit to drink. To make it palatable, we had to add whiskey. By diligent effort, I learned to like it.' "

"Now, son." Kefauver lifted a finger from his glass to wag it in Charlie's direction. "Some of my House colleagues told me about your stunt at the Appropriations markup."

"With respect, sir, it wasn't a stunt," Charlie said. "Houdini did stunts. The Wallendas do stunts. I took a stand."

Kefauver narrowed his eyes, and when he spoke again his voice had lost a degree of its earlier warmth, though he was still making an effort to sound casual. "Well, now, that's a matter of interpretation, I suppose." He smiled, but there was no humor in his eyes. "Imagine that you're a committee chairman who's been here for decades, and some little pissant" — he saw Charlie about to object, so he amended his statement — "some *freshly appointed* congressman whom you *perceive* to be a *nuisance* comes along and objects to millions of dollars you've procured for an American company that provides thousands of jobs in congressional districts all around the nation," Kefauver said.

"Right, I get that," Charlie said.

"Those jobs belong to voters who are, of course, the ones who send us here," Kefauver said. "They're our bosses."

"And surely our bosses would object to giving money to war profiteers who provided shoddy goods, risking and even costing the lives of our men," Charlie said. "This is a fight I didn't seek, sir, but to be frank, I'm stunned that any of my colleagues in Congress would challenge me on it."

"Well, Charlie, I'm talking about the chairman of the committee and some others in leadership, and I'm quite certain they don't think of you as a colleague. But of course you should fight for what you think is right. That's an admirable trait, and too few of us possess it. Just know that this town isn't built to reward it."

"I'm starting to get that impression," Charlie said.

Kefauver looked down at his glass. Charlie felt obliged to fill the slightly prickly silence.

"W. C. Fields," Charlie said. " 'Always carry a flagon of whiskey in case of snakebite, and furthermore always carry a small snake.' "

Kefauver smiled. "What else shall we drink to?"

"To a real leader at the top of your party's ticket two years from now," Charlie said. *Clink, clink.* Kefauver downed the entire glass in one easy gulp.

The door to the conference room opened without warning and an older man walked in. His jowls sagged like a mastiff's. Behind him stood one of the senator's aides, who apparently had been trying to politely prevent the man from bursting in unannounced. Kefauver waved the aide off.

"Why, hello, Doctor," Kefauver said, standing and extending a hand. "Congressman Marder, may I present Dr. Fredric Wertham."

"It's very nice to meet you, sir," Charlie said, following Kefauver's lead and standing to shake the doctor's hand.

"This is the young congressman I told you about, Fredric," Kefauver said. "His father and I are old friends." He motioned for both men to sit down. "Charlie, I assume you're acquainted with the groundbreaking psychiatric work Dr. Wertham has done at Bellevue and his philanthropic work with the colored people of your home city. The Lafargue Clinic — did I pronounce the name correctly, Doctor?"

"We're in Harlem," Wertham said, ignoring the question. "I set up the clinic just after the war, a project with Richard Wright and some others. You know Wright, I assume?"

"The writer?" asked Charlie.

"Of course," snapped Wertham, as if it had been glaringly obvious that the only Richard Wright he might know would be the author of the acclaimed *Native Son.*

"Well, it's not an uncommon name," Charlie couldn't help observing. "Anyway, I don't personally know him, but the book was haunting. Could have done without the stage adaptation."

"On that we are in agreement." Wertham softened a bit. "In any case, Richard and I established a mental-hygiene clinic for the good people of Harlem who are unable to afford psychiatric care, not only because of the unjust capitalist system that keeps them impoverished but also because most psychiatric institutions do not admit Negroes."

Wertham's face had turned pink and his voice was rising. "How are we to solve the problem of crime in New York City without addressing the psychiatric needs of the very underclass committing the crimes!" He was only about three feet away from Charlie, close enough for Charlie to identify the smell on the gust of bad breath he exhaled. Tuna fish.

There was an uncomfortable silence, one Charlie filled when he suddenly remembered the first time he'd heard Wertham's name.

"Correct me if I'm wrong," Charlie said, "but weren't you part of the defense in Albert Fish's trial?"

Albert Fish was a child molester, a murderer, and a cannibal. He had been executed in 1936, when Charlie was sixteen.

"Yes, I testified in that trial," Wertham said to Charlie. "What a travesty. The jury did not care in the slightest that Mr. Fish had no control over himself. His illness was just as real as if he'd had a tumor rotting his brain. And yet they punished him for his disease. The twelve boors on that jury had bloodlust just as bad as Mr. Fish's — but their taste for flesh was the kind that society deems socially acceptable."

"My father was on the defense team," Charlie said. "Winston Marder?" Wertham looked at him blankly. "Anyway, admirable work for the people of New York," Charlie said. "How can I help? What can I do?"

"I'm glad you asked," said Kefauver. "We're holding hearings on juvenile delinquency this spring. Maybe April. Wertham is our key witness. The hearings will be in New York, in your congressional district, and we'd like you to help host and arrange a venue. We'd also like you to participate." He glanced at Wertham.

"Estes here feels we need some *youth* on

the panel," Wertham said.

"I'm thirty-three," said Charlie. "Hardly young."

"For Congress, you're an infant," said Wertham. "This place is practically a museum exhibit of sarcophagi."

"These are going to be big, Charlie," said Kefauver. "We're going to tear the lid off one of the most pernicious influences in our culture today. There will be a lot of press coverage; it will be a stellar opportunity to establish yourself. When folks hear you're part of my next project, my guess is they'll be more inclined to treat you with the respect you clearly feel you deserve."

"And what are we going after?" Charlie asked, ignoring the gibe. "What exactly is the pernicious influence?"

Wertham smiled; it was the moment he'd been waiting for.

"Comic books," he said.

CHAPTER FIVE:
MONDAY, JANUARY 18, 1954

Maryland Rural Route 32/U.S. Capitol
"Comic books?" Asked Margaret. "So did you laugh in his face?"

Margaret was using the desk phone at Polly's Lodging, a motel about five miles from the Nanticoke Island campsite where she'd been conducting her research for the last two days. She'd volunteered to drive back to the mainland to buy some batteries and bread for the group, and she'd seized the opportunity to phone Charlie at work. She'd asked the long-distance operator to call back after their conversation was done and tell her the charges so she could give that amount to the motel owner, a dour older woman, presumably Polly.

"You should have seen their faces," said Charlie. He was sitting behind the desk in his congressional office staring at a framed photograph of Margaret from their wedding day, one that captured her laughing uproariously, her head thrown back. He reached for a cigarette. "It was as if they were revealing that milk causes cancer. But it was about goddamn Batman."

Charlie looked out his office window. Being the most junior member of the Eighty-Third Congress, he had a view of the air-conditioning unit of the second-most-junior member.

"Right after the meeting, Kefauver couriered over a package. Wertham has a book coming out in a few months . . . what's it called —" He leafed through the manila folder. *"Seduction of the Innocent."*

"Sounds very dangerous," she said. "Innocent people shouldn't be seduced!"

"This is no joke, Margaret!" Charlie protested in mock horror. "Kefauver sent me an issue of *Ladies' Home Journal* from last November. On the front of the magazine: 'What Parents Don't Know About Comic Books.' " He paused to read dramatically: " 'Here is the startling truth about the ninety million comic books America's children read each month.' He argues that comic books are literally instruction manuals for children to become hardened criminals."

"It sounds . . . kind of silly," Margaret said.

"Yes, and Kefauver wants to hold god-damn hearings on this in Manhattan in April!"

Margaret paused and Charlie had a feeling he knew why. She probably didn't care to hear him discuss doing something he didn't want to do, something he thought was an idiotic distraction. Their lives until now had been refreshingly free of any need for compromise. They were academics, idealists who'd participated in fund-raisers to fight polio and to foster better education for poor children. For the first time, they were facing choices they didn't like.

"More important," she finally said, "how's the Goodstone fight?"

"Nothing since we last spoke, really. Kefauver cautioned me to be careful; Miss Leopold is against my doing it. I'm going to a poker game for veterans in Congress tonight. I'll see if I can get them on board."

"Sounds like a plan," she said.

"So how are the ponies?"

"They're grand," said Margaret. "About an hour after we arrived on Nanticoke, we saw some of the ponies literally frolicking in the surf."

"So one research team's on Nanticoke and the other is on Susquehannock?"

"Yes, I'm with Louis and one of his

research assistants from Wisconsin."

"And," he said, hesitating, "when will I get to see you again?"

"Probably Saturday. It's so nice being back in the field, and if this is my last project for a while because of the baby, I don't want to leave too soon."

"Sounds like wild horses couldn't drag you away," he muttered.

"Ugh, awful," she chided him. "You know, you shouldn't make bad dad puns until you actually become a dad."

"But you won't really need to return to the field *after* the baby," Charlie said. "If you want to make this book project a reality, you can work from home, right?"

"Sure," said Margaret. "And I suppose we could set up a situation where I just squeeze out baby after baby between edits? Maybe one per project?"

He was rapidly coming to understand that there was nothing that he could say on this topic that didn't sound selfish or, alternatively, insincere. So, not for the first time, Charlie didn't say anything in response. He chuckled and tried to change the subject, and the momentum of their phone call quickly petered out.

Just after seven that evening, Charlie

knocked on Strongfellow's congressional office door. No one answered, but the door was unlocked, so he went in. Through the smog of cigar smoke, he saw a glorious view of the Capitol out the window. Twenty members of Congress were standing around and sitting at tables in Strongfellow's reception area and conference room.

Strongfellow swung around on his crutches, greeted Charlie, and shook his hand. "Thanks for coming, Charlie," he said, his boyishness offset by the gravity of his war wounds.

"Thanks for the invitation," Charlie answered, looking around the room.

"We started this during freshman orientation, back in November '52. We called it Dogface Poker because it was just me and three infantry guys. Just a way to blow off a little steam. But then it kept going and cav and then navy and air force and others joined, and they didn't care for the name —"

"Because we don't have hideous dogfaces like you goddamn blister-feet!" This from a handsome dark-haired man seated nearby; Charlie recognized him as Congressman Pat Sutton from Tennessee, a navy man and a Democrat. Strongfellow laughed.

"Anyway, it took on a life of its own.

Bipartisan. Just vets. Everyone here fought in the war, so we know how doggone meaningless most of this Capitol Hill 'Ta-ra-ra boom-de-ay' is. It's a good place to unwind. The only rule is that nothing leaves here unless it's supposed to."

"And just so you know," Sutton said, "this is only for real fighters. No JAGs, no cushy office jobs in personnel. If you were in the air force and you're here, you weren't a fucking penguin — you flew. Guns in hand, mud on boots."

Charlie wondered if the remark had been a veiled reference to Senator McCarthy's supposedly exaggerated war record. Sutton shifted around in his seat to shake Charlie's hand. "Offer him some bourbon, you Mormon bastard," he said to Strongfellow before turning back to the game and examining his cards.

"I hear Kefauver's taken you under his wing," Sutton said to Charlie. "I raise fifty cents."

"He's been very kind," Charlie said.

"Pat's taking him on in the primary," said Strongfellow.

"Looks like Estes is going to get beat anyhow, so I might as well be the man to do it," Sutton said.

Charlie looked at Strongfellow, who

68

seemed happy and in his element, surrounded by fellow veterans.

He recalled reading Strongfellow's widely publicized story. Part of the clandestine military intelligence Office of Strategic Services, or OSS, Strongfellow, a former Mormon missionary, had parachuted into Germany during the war to rescue an atomic physicist and bring him to Allied territory so he could be whisked to Los Alamos, New Mexico, to work with the team building the first atomic bomb. But one of his contacts was a double agent, and after a furious gun battle in which Strongfellow was gravely wounded, he was taken to the Belsen prison at Bergen-Belsen concentration camp.

One night during his imprisonment, Strongfellow experienced a religious epiphany. God was with him and would guide him out of the prison. Amazingly, whether through divine providence or dumb luck, Strongfellow did manage to escape and make it to safety. After he recuperated and returned to Utah, members of the Church of Jesus Christ of Latter-Day Saints found his tale so compelling they took him around the state to preach the power of faith. His congressional election victory in 1952 followed easily soon after.

"I don't drink, Charlie, but Sutton brought a bottle of what I'm told is some stellar Tennessee whiskey," Strongfellow said, gesturing toward a half-full jug sitting on his receptionist's desk. "We're starting a new game over here," he added, pointing at the couch, where another congressman was shuffling cards.

Charlie poured himself a drink and took a seat on the couch as Strongfellow grabbed a chair. The other congressman introduced himself as Chris "Mac" MacLachlan of Indiana. In his fifties, steely-eyed, balding, with bushy eyebrows and an expanding waist, MacLachlan was a Lutheran minister.

"Army?" MacLachlan asked Charlie.

"First Battalion, Hundred and Seventy-Fifth infantry," Charlie said.

"Mac was also in D-Day," Strongfellow said. "Hundred and First Airborne."

"Second Battalion, Five Hundred and Sixth Parachute Infantry, under Colonel Sink," MacLachlan said as he unpinned his cuff links and rolled up his sleeves. "Drop Zone C. Between Hiesville and Sainte-Marie-du-Mont."

"We landed at Omaha," said Charlie, loosening his tie. "I was in K Company — we secured the bridge over the Vire River and protected the right flank."

MacLachlan raised his glass and waited for Charlie's to greet it.

"To those still there," MacLachlan said.

Clink.

MacLachlan dealt. Charlie waited until all five cards hit the coffee table before he picked up his hand. The cards were unusually thick. He studied the queen of spades.

"Is this a Map Deck?" Charlie asked. MacLachlan and Strongfellow both beamed. During the war, American and British intelligence agencies had worked with a playing-card company to manufacture a special deck of cards that hid within them maps of escape routes on German territory near POW camps. Cards could be peeled apart to produce the maps, so they were ever so slightly thicker than average.

"You bet," said MacLachlan.

"I got one from the OSS before I dropped into Germany," said Strongfellow.

Charlie held a card up to the light, then examined its ridge.

"One of the cards has been opened if you want to see." Strongfellow reached into the deck box and slid out a joker. He handed it to Charlie, who peeled it open to reveal an escape route through the German village of Dallgow-Döberitz. "Mac loves puzzles and hidden clues and such."

Charlie whistled. "Amazing."

"I had to soak it first," said Strongfellow.

"Ante up," said MacLachlan. "Nickels in."

Charlie reached into his pocket, withdrew a dozen or so coins, and dropped them on the table. He steered a nickel into the pot.

"Speaking of anteing up, that was quite a move you made in Appropriations," MacLachlan said. "Not sitting out any hands, I see." He smiled.

As much as he hated to relive the event that had led him to speak up at the previous week's meeting, Charlie knew this was his moment. Looking at his cards, he began: "Ten days after we landed on Omaha Beach, on June seventeenth, our orders were to seize Isigny, the bridge over the Vire River, then recapture Saint-Lô, La Madeleine, Pont Renard, La Heresneserie, on and on. Basically nonstop combat until we met up with the Soviets at the Elbe."

The two men were listening intently as Charlie paused to sip his drink.

"Cards?" MacLachlan asked.

Charlie looked at his hand and threw down the two he didn't want. MacLachlan tossed replacements in front of him. An eight of hearts and a nine of spades. A straight, almost a straight flush.

MacLachlan gave Strongfellow three cards

and gave one to himself. They assessed their hands as Charlie continued.

"So we were in the midst of recapturing Le Meaune. We had Easy Company with us too. There were Jerries everywhere, and Vichy French. It was a mess. You could hardly tell who was on whose side."

"Open with a dime," said MacLachlan. Charlie moved a dime from his pile to the center of the table.

"I see you," he said.

"See you and raise," Strongfellow said, putting fifteen cents into the pot. He slid a cigar from his inside suit-jacket pocket and began lighting it, swirling the cigar, sucking in, and waving the lighter beneath it. Charlie was momentarily confused, since he'd thought Mormons didn't smoke, but he let it pass. None of his business.

"We were in a farmhouse outside of town, me and my platoon," Charlie continued. "Mortars were going off in the distance but nothing near us. This French family was being friendly. Mom, dad, four kids, a grandma. We were just talking, trying to communicate — none of us spoke French — trying to figure out which Germans were around. And suddenly, the older son, maybe sixteen, took out a knife and tried to stab me. He was scared sloppy, and the blade hit

73

my helmet, which I was holding."

Strongfellow leaned back on the couch. MacLachlan took a sip from his glass.

"So we restrained the kid and got concerned that something was going on, you know? We looked around the house, found nothing, then told the dad to show us the barn. He was nervous. He insisted on taking two of his kids with him, a boy and girl. Young. Under ten. I guess his thinking was that if they were with him, we'd be less inclined to kill him.

"It was me, Rodriguez, Hillman . . ." Charlie could name all his men in his sleep, but he realized it didn't much matter to the other congressmen. "Anyway, most of my platoon went with me, and a couple stayed back in the house." He vividly recalled the faces of the men in his platoon, a motley gang of teenagers and guys in their thirties, some educated and others street-smart.

"So we're in the barn," Charlie went on, "and Rodriguez, this skinny private first class from Spanish Harlem, he notices some crates in a stall. They don't look like they belong there, so he goes to check it out, and right at that moment a mortar explodes outside. Parts of the barn are blown away, a support beam falls right on top of the French family, and some sort of gas starts

74

seeping out of one of the crates."

"Gas?" said Strongfellow. "Krauts didn't use gas."

"Not on soldiers, they didn't," Mac-Lachlan corrected. "Jews were another story."

"I don't know that it was German gas. It might have been left over from the First World War. Who knows where it came from. Anyway, Hillman, our platoon sergeant, shouted for us to put on our gas masks, so we all fastened these cheap rubber things around our heads. Mortars are still going off outside the barn so no one runs out, but we all sprint to the other end of the barn. Except the family. And Rodriguez. Rodriguez's pinned down under the beam too. And he can't even reach his mask.

"Hillman had always thought the masks were pieces of garbage, so when he looked at me through the cheap plastic, I knew what he was thinking. I was the captain, though, and we had a man in trouble. I grabbed Corporal Miller's mask, told the platoon sergeant to follow me, and we ran to Rodriguez. I put the mask over Rodriguez's face while Hillman tried to move the beam off Rodriguez and the French family. More of my guys came over, with their masks on, and they all tried to move the beam. But then they started choking. With the masks on. Rodriguez, too, was choking. With his mask on. The French kids and the dad were choking without masks."

"What about you?" MacLachlan asked.

"Mine worked," Charlie said, wincing slightly. He took a sip from his glass and looked down, as if there were answers in the ice cubes.

"And then?" Strongfellow asked after the pause grew uncomfortable.

Charlie exhaled dramatically, as if he were exhausted. "The platoon sergeant and the other guys ran outside, vomiting. Their masks were worthless. If they'd stayed to save Rodriguez and the family, they would have died. The mortars started moving north. Somehow I managed to push the beam enough to wedge Rodriguez out and get him outside in the fresh air. But he was in bad shape. Foaming at the mouth. Eyes crossed. Skin turning green."

"What was it?" Strongfellow asked. "Mustard?"

"Don't know," Charlie said. "We left the barn at once. Rodriguez was messed up. We had a few of the guys take him to an aid station a couple miles back. Toward the beach. He died before he got there, we later were told. My other two men also got wounded in the process. Shot. They survived, but we never saw them again either. Haber, Scully. Shipped back home. Whole thing was FUBAR."

There was a pause as Strongfellow and MacLachlan collected their thoughts.

"The French family?" MacLachlan finally asked. "The dad and his two kids?"

Charlie shook his head.

"So this is why you want to block Goodstone?" MacLachlan continued. "They made the gas masks?"

"They did, sir," Charlie said.

"Did you report it?" MacLachlan asked.

"Yes, sir," Charlie said. "To my CO. And then later, with paperwork related to Rodriguez's death."

"Did they ever own up to it?" asked MacLachlan. "Issue any sort of report explaining what happened and why it will never happen again? Compensate the Rodriguez family?"

"You know, I wondered that as well," Charlie said. "After the markup, I had an aide look into it. Best I can tell, Goodstone did nothing. Though the army did tell me they notified the company."

"Good Lord," MacLachlan said, shaking his head. "Wish I could say I was surprised."

"You going to keep pushing it?" Strongfellow asked. "Carlin seemed pretty PO'ed."

Before they could continue the conversation, there was a knock at the door and a black man in his thirties wearing a gray flannel suit poked his head into the room.

"Is this the card game?" he asked.

There was an uncomfortable silence as the roomful of white veterans decided what to do. Washington, DC, like much of the nation, remained segregated in almost every way.

"You sure you're in the right place?" one of the congressmen in the back of the room asked.

"This is the card game for veterans, unless I am mistaken," the man said. He thrust a hand into his baggy trouser pocket, then slowly began to extricate it. He raised his hand; between his fingers dangled a blue-and-white-striped ribbon with one strip of red in the middle. Attached to the ribbon swung a small bronze replica of a propeller laid upon a cross pattée.

A Distinguished Flying Cross.

Charlie realized the man with the medal was Isaiah Street, a former Tuskegee Airman, one of the elite flying aces in segregated units of the U.S. Army Air Forces and a particularly decorated one at that. He and Representative Adam Clayton Powell Jr. of

New York were the only black men in Congress.

"I got a Purple Heart, too, in my other jacket," Street said. "But all I did to earn that one was not die."

"We need a fourth over here, Congressman," Charlie said, glancing at Strongfellow and MacLachlan, who nodded to affirm the invitation. The rest of the room turned back to their card games.

"Thank you, gentlemen," Street said, taking off his jacket as the other three finished up their hand. MacLachlan won with a full house.

"My deal," said Strongfellow. "Texas hold 'em okay?"

"Only if we stick with cash," Charlie said. "I can't call if Street throws down his Distinguished Flying Cross."

Street laughed. "I like to get in the door on the first try," he said.

Strongfellow dealt each man two cards and placed three other shared cards faceup on the table. The men fell into a brief silence, each contemplating his pair.

"Check," said MacLachlan, and then he glanced at Charlie with one bushy eyebrow raised. "I hear you've been shanghaied by Kefauver to sign up for his latest publicity tour."

"What's he up to now?" asked Street. "Check."

"Check," said Charlie.

"Check," said Strongfellow. He threw down a fourth shared card in the middle of the table.

"Nickel in," said MacLachlan, throwing a coin into the pot. "Oh, he's cooked up a bullshit hearing about comic books being the reason for urban crime waves," MacLachlan said. "Kefauver's latest attempt to cast himself as a white knight in preparation for '56."

After Street anted up, Charlie came to terms with the fact that he was holding a garbage hand.

"I'm out," he said.

"Raise," said Strongfellow, tossing a dime into the pot. He slid the fifth and final shared card faceup, prompting a harrumph from MacLachlan.

"Fold," he said.

"Sounds like the old okey-doke to me," Street said. "Raise." He put down a quarter, and Strongfellow groaned mildly and tossed his cards on the table. Street reassembled the deck and began shuffling.

"Okey-doke?" asked Strongfellow.

"You'll forgive him, Street, he's from Utah," Charlie joked.

"A distraction," explained Street. "Omaha Hi-Lo, gentlemen," he announced as he dealt the cards. "Okey-doke's a scam. The guy on the street who holds up his hat with one hand and says, 'Look at my hat, nothing in my hat,' and with the other hand he's pinching your wallet."

"I don't think it's a distraction," said Charlie. "I think they mean it. And I'm in no position to say no."

"Course not," said MacLachlan.

As Street finished dealing each man four cards facedown, Charlie wondered how much he could press his case with his new friends. He inspected his cards: the ace of hearts, the ace of spades, the two of clubs, the seven of diamonds. Two aces before even one flop card had been dealt; a great start, but he couldn't seem too eager. He threw down a nickel.

"I need Kefauver on my side because of the cruddy gas masks I told you about," Charlie said as everyone else anted up. "I don't think Goodstone should get another nickel from the taxpayers. And I can use any support. Whether it's from Kefauver, someone else on the Subcommittee on Juvenile Delinquency, or any of you fine gentlemen."

Charlie turned to a confused-looking

Street to offer a brief synopsis of the saga of the gas masks and Private First Class Rodriguez. Strongfellow chimed in with the more pressing issue of Chairman Carlin's anger at Charlie for trying to block federal funds from Goodstone.

"I know the answer before I ask," said Street, "but I assume Goodstone never reached out to the private's family?"

Charlie shook his head. His two priorities upon returning to Manhattan after the war had been marrying Margaret and sitting down with the Rodriguezes to tell them what had happened. He saw them every June at St. Cecilia's in Manhattan, where they all lit candles. "Near as I can tell, Goodstone's done everything they can to pretend it didn't happen."

"Pretty crummy," Street said. "Brother Powell's on Appropriations; I can talk to him, see what he thinks."

"I'd keep it quiet for now, boys," Strongfellow cautioned. "Carlin is a mercenary."

"But don't you think if we can get a sizable group of veterans in the House to oppose this, Carlin will see the writing on the wall?" Charlie asked. "Why would this be worth making a stink about? I doubt Goodstone would want the publicity."

"This isn't some Andy Hardy movie,

Charlie," MacLachlan said. "Folks don't band together when the chips are down and put on a show."

"Mac is right," Street said. "We need to learn a lot more before we do anything. We don't know if Goodstone has connections or a loose wallet or powerful friends or what."

"You don't want to get in over your head," Strongfellow warned.

"They had to have paid someone off to have gotten away with it," said Street.

"Or someones," agreed MacLachlan.

"I get it, I get it," said Charlie, now a bit embarrassed.

"One just needs to be a bit more stealthy on this battlefield, Charlie," MacLachlan said. "And we need to do a lot more recon."

"Carlin is mean," said Strongfellow. "You can't just take him on willy-nilly."

"But you're actually ahead of the game, here, in one way," said MacLachlan. "It makes more sense for you to try to get Kefauver to remove the Goodstone money when the bill gets to the Senate."

"Here's the flop," said Street, throwing down the first shared card for the table: the ace of clubs.

Charlie didn't believe in omens, but having two aces in the hole and a third on the table improved his mood a touch. Still, he felt naive and dejected and couldn't help reflecting that principles had been a lot easier to fight for before he entered a world where there were actual consequences.

CHAPTER SIX:
SUNDAY, DECEMBER 7, 1941

New York City, New York

Charles Everett Marder had been born prematurely in Manhattan on December 7, 1920, a date of little consequence in any way until the day he turned twenty-one. A birthday-celebration lunch was planned around his schedule, and at two o'clock he met his parents at P. J. Clarke's on Fifty-Fifth and Third. It was their favorite restaurant, unassuming and lively, and Mary Marder pretended not to know that its chief attraction for her husband and son was the barroom radio, always tuned to whatever game was being played that day.

As the Marders walked in, the Brooklyn Dodgers football team, which outer-borough-born Winston rooted for, had won the coin toss in its game against Manhattan's New York Giants, a favorite of Charlie's, at the Polo Grounds. The family eased into a back booth as a waiter materialized, pen poised.

"Hamburger, please, medium rare, with extra fries and a black-and-white shake," Charlie said. "Starving," he explained to his mother when she looked shocked at his abrupt order.

"I was about to ask how it could be possible that my baby is officially an adult, but you still order like a nine-year-old," Mary Marder teased.

"Martini for me, dry as a desert," put in Winston. "I want to see tumbleweeds skimming across the meniscus. Oh, and get one for my boy too. Eighty-six his milk shake unless you plan on bringing it in a bottle with a nipple."

Mary did her best to ignore her husband's crudities, as did Charlie, who began to tell his parents about his upcoming exams while he and his father pretended they weren't also listening to the football game blaring on the radio behind the bar. Mary had just asked Charlie about his plans, or lack thereof, after graduation in June when Winston shushed them so he could hear more of the important bulletin interrupting the game.

"Flash: Washington," barked the broadcaster. *"The White House announces Japanese attack on Pearl Harbor."*

As the waiter delivered the martinis, the restaurant fell into silence except for a man's tinny, scratchy voice on the radio.

"Hello, NBC. Hello, NBC. This is KTU in Honolulu, Hawaii. I am speaking from the roof of the Advertiser Publishing Company Building. We have witnessed this morning the distant view of a brief full battle of Pearl Harbor and the severe bombing of Pearl Harbor by enemy planes, undoubtedly Japanese. The city of Honolulu has also been attacked and considerable damage done."

Gasps throughout the restaurant. Waiters stood frozen in place; diners stared at one another in disbelief.

"This battle has been going on for nearly three hours," the man continued. *"One of the bombs dropped within fifty feet of KTU tower. It is no joke. It is a real war."*

Mary Marder looked at her husband gravely and then at her son. Her eyes welled up and she reached across the table to grasp Charlie's hand tightly. Winston pulled out his wallet and threw bills blindly on the table, then he pulled Mary to her feet and shepherded his reeling family outside.

In their brownstone on the Upper East Side, Winston, Mary, and Charlie spent the rest of that Sunday the same way millions of Americans did, huddled around their radio, terrified that Japanese planes would soon be attacking the U.S. mainland.

Charlie became filled with an emotion other than fear. He was furious. A sneak attack on Honolulu by the Japanese — he could think of nothing more cowardly.

The moment had been inevitable. Anyone with basic cognitive skills had been able to see for months that sooner or later the United States was going to have to make a choice about whether it was going to enter the war or allow the Fascists to seize Europe.

Charlie had long ago concluded that the United States needed to do the former. He had listened to all of Edward R. Murrow's broadcasts about the Nazi bombing of London the previous year, in September 1940. Since then, the Germans had started attacking American ships in the Atlantic Ocean; a U-boat had torpedoed the USS *Kearny* in October, killing eleven navy men. President Roosevelt had begun painting a dire picture of what the Western Hemisphere would look like under Nazi control; in a speech just a few weeks before Charlie's birthday, the president had claimed that he'd obtained a secret map made by the Nazis showing how after they seized Europe, they intended to carve up Central and

South America into five vassal states. Message: they're headed to our hemisphere next.

Neither Charlie nor his parents were fans of FDR, but that speech had affected him. The president had acknowledged how difficult it was for Americans to grasp what the Nazis were doing, "to adjust ourselves to the shocking realities of a world in which the principles of common humanity and common decency are being mowed down by the firing squads of the Gestapo." FDR added that some critics thought perhaps the American people had grown so "fat, and flabby, and lazy" they would be "now no match for the regimented masses who have been trained in the Spartan ways of ruthless brutality." But nothing could be further from the truth, he'd said, as if anticipating the Pearl Harbor attack: "We Americans have cleared our decks and taken our battle stations. We stand ready in the defense of our nation and the faith of our fathers to do what God has given us the power to see as our full duty."

Our duty, Charlie recalled. *And our homeland is now directly under attack.*

His father was studying his face. "Don't get any ideas, Charlie," Winston said.

The news got worse throughout the day. Wave after wave of Japanese aircraft had killed at least four hundred Americans, though accurate numbers were difficult to come by; it was possible that thousands had been killed. The governor of Hawaii revealed that it hadn't just been sailors killed; civilians in Honolulu had been slaughtered as well. Unconfirmed reports suggested that the U.S. battleships *Oklahoma* and *West Virginia* had been sunk, along with up to seven U.S. destroyers. More than three hundred American airplanes were believed to have been obliterated.

Later that night, after Mary had fallen asleep on the couch, Winston turned off the radio and guided his son into his study, where he poured eighteen-year-old scotch into two glasses. A single lamp illuminated the wood-paneled room, which was packed with books of law and history and held one small locked file cabinet where he kept papers too important to leave at his downtown office.

Winston eased his bulky frame into his favorite leather chair and motioned Charlie to the sofa. They sat silently for a few minutes, the only sound a muted tick from the nearby desk clock. Charlie looked at his dad, a big bear of a man whose hair was beginning to thin up top. Winston looked at his son, his only child, the person he knew best in the world.

"You have to graduate in May," his father said.

"Tomorrow, I'm going to register with Selective Service," Charlie responded. "It's the law. I'm twenty-one."

"I know that," said Winston. The lamp sat to his left, silhouetting his face. "We anticipated this day. Your mother will push you to go to divinity school to escape the draft."

"Divinity school?" Charlie laughed.

"Yes, divinity students get deferments," Winston said. "Of course, she already asked me to look into getting you a job at the draft board. Another way to avoid shipping out."

Charlie was about to protest, but he decided to hold back and hear what else his father had to say. His mother was always after him for rushing-rushing-rushing in speech and not allowing conversation to breathe, not letting decisions and realizations happen naturally.

"I'm not going to do that," Winston finally said.

"I'm not going to shirk this. I have a duty. I'm enlisting."

"I know," said his dad. "But let's . . . let's do this wisely."

"I don't want a desk job at the Pentagon," Charlie said. "I want to do my part, just like everyone else has to, just like all the kids in the Brooklyn neighborhood where you grew up. My life is worth no more than theirs."

His father looked at him gravely. Charlie didn't know much about his dad's time overseas after being drafted to fight the Germans in 1918, just that he had been there and he didn't talk about it.

"The Battle of the Argonne Forest . . ." His voice trailed off and he stared at the floor. He scratched his cheek with his right forefinger. Charlie held his breath. "This was before the Battle of Montfaucon, before Corporal York caught all those Krauts. It was a bad time. The Thirty-Fifth Division got shredded." He took a sip of his drink. "I can't even begin to describe how awful it was," he said. "I would never wish it on you. If someone tried to draft you into it, I would do everything I could to prevent it."

"I know, Dad. But I don't think I have a choice here. They attacked us."

His father stood and walked over to the small fireplace. The housekeeper had already prepared the kindling, so all Winston needed to do was light a match, but the box, perched near a small stack of wood, was empty. "Damn," he said. Charlie got up and handed his father his Zippo lighter. Winston struck the spark wheel six times before a flame appeared.

"Should have got you a new lighter for your twenty-first," he said with a small smile. "Birthdays seem sort of stupid right now, don't they?" He ignited the rolled-up newspapers tucked under the stack of wood in the fireplace. The kindling began to crackle.

Charlie leaned his elbows on his knees and stared absently at the flames as they grew higher until at last his father broke the silence.

"Charlie," his father said, "you need to finish school. Graduate. After that, I know you might enlist. I'll pull whatever strings you want for you to fight the Axis scum in whatever way you think best."

Charlie shook his head. "I don't want special treatment."

"You're not just any guy off the street in Brooklyn," his father said. "You're smarter. And you're softer. We've been protecting you."

"Softer?" Charlie asked. "Dad, I'm not —"

"Please, Charlie, I know exactly who you are," Winston Marder said. "Maybe *softer* isn't the right word, but you're good. And

even more than that, you believe in goodness."

"You don't?"

"No, I don't," Winston said bluntly. And
then he gave his son a tender smile. "It's
funny. You and I are motivated by dia-
metrically opposed views of human nature.
But we agree on the need to kill as many
Nazis and Japs as possible."

They sat in silence, the fire warming but
not comforting them.

"You may prove to be a great soldier,"
Winston Marder said. "Not because you're
tough. Because you're smart. But sacrifices
are made in the field of battle, Charlie.
Sacrifices will have to be made."

It was just about three weeks later, on
December 27 — the day after Prime Minister Winston Churchill's address to a joint
session of Congress — that Charlie met
Margaret.

Seeking refuge from all the war news, he
was spelunking deep in the stacks of Columbia University's Butler Library on West
114th Street in Manhattan. What had
started as an effort to research a term paper
had become, characteristically, a form of
free-association scholarship wherein the
hunt for one book became the discovery of

another, leading to a fascinating trove of rare manuscripts and oddities having nothing to do with the original project.

Margaret Elizabeth Anne McDowell was a freshman at Barnard, routinely referred to by her roommate as a grind in the body of a cover girl. That night, in addition to preparing for calculus and biology exams, she was looking for a container of maps and notebooks from the estate of Benjamin Carroll, a Revolutionary War–era member of the Maryland elite whose family had claimed the isthmus near Susquehannock and Nanticoke Islands. She hoped they might mention the ponies on the islands, Margaret's lifelong obsession and the topic of a term paper she was writing for zoology.

It was the Saturday night before New Year's Eve. Most Columbia and Barnard students had fled campus for the winter break, and the library was exactly as Margaret preferred it: empty and hushed. Balancing four heavy textbooks, she staggered into her favorite spot, a quiet nook tucked under the staircase from the fourth to the fifth floors that nobody else seemed to have discovered. Tonight, however, she was unhappy to turn the corner and see her usual desk occupied: a young man wearing white cotton gloves was peering closely at a book so old and fragile it looked as though a sneeze might cause it to explode into dust. Her shoe squeaked on the floor and he looked up sharply.

Caught in mutual surprise, Margaret and the interloper considered each other. He was broad-shouldered and bookish — not an uncommon breed on campus. The window rattled as the wind outside the library howled. The heater next to Charlie's table began to clank and hum.

"Hello," she said finally.

He seemed to shake himself out of a mild stupor and smiled.

"Hello yourself." He motioned, somewhat possessively, she thought, toward the official sign on the wall. "What brings you here to 'Colonial Manuscripts and Letters Archives — Recent Acquisitions'?"

Margaret shifted her arms to alleviate the strain of the books she was carrying. "I imagine the same thing as you — research? Homework?" She was accustomed to the men she met on campus assuming her studies were a token effort in her pursuit of an Mrs. degree.

But Charlie actually blushed, something she was less accustomed to seeing. "Sorry, I meant *what* are you studying?"

Margaret relaxed and deposited her books

on the unoccupied corner of the desk with a small sigh of relief. She shook out her arms and began to unwind her heavy scarf. Charlie pulled out the other chair for her and she resisted informing him that he was playing host in a place she considered her own.

"These books are for exams, but I'm also here looking for some 'Recent Acquisitions' having to do with these wild ponies in Maryland. No one knows where they came from," she explained.

"You're a history major?"

"Zoology," she said. "There are these new journals the library obtained from the Colonial era from rural Maryland, from the estate of the Carroll family. Kind of a crapshoot, but I wanted to see if there was any mention of the ponies from around that time."

"Fascinating," Charlie said.

"Yes, they're an amazing string," she said.

"String?"

"That's what you call a group of ponies," she said. "Like a pride of lions or a flock of geese."

"Or a murder of crows."

"Precisely," she said. "Or a congregation of alligators. Or . . . an obstinacy of buffalo. A crash of rhinoceroses. A gaze of raccoons." She was showing off, but she enjoyed it.

"I think you've got me beat." He smiled. "But wait — something you were saying about your research. I think . . ."

He paused and she looked at him expectantly.

"I think I remember reading a diary of a doctor who'd been visiting that family — the Carrolls? — around that time. This was a few months ago. Let me check. Don't go anywhere! I'll be right back!"

"Okay," Margaret said. "But only because I have to study, and this is where I always do that."

Margaret watched him retreat into the darkness of the stacks and smiled. His eagerness to please was hard to resist. She turned to the shelves and began her hunt for items from the estate of Maryland delegate Benjamin Carroll, which had yet to be categorized and labeled.

When she returned to the table, roughly forty-five minutes later, Charlie was back in his seat reading an old journal — one, he explained, that was kept by a physician, Dr. Solomon McClintock, who had been called to the Carroll estate during the Maryland smallpox epidemic of 1750. He was there to infect the Carrolls, Charlie explained. Margaret took a seat and wondered what this had to do with her research, but soon she was swept up in his enthusiastic account of the doctor's discovery.

"It was groundbreaking medicine at the time," said Charlie, "the concept of inoculation. Infecting those who didn't have smallpox with a small dose of the disease. Cotton Mather popularized it, after learning about it from —"

"Mather from the Salem witch trials?" Margaret interrupted.

Charlie nodded. "One and the same. Mather's slave taught him about the concept of inoculation, and then Mather shared it with the rest of the colonies. McClintock learned about it from Mather, and he was summoned to the Carroll estate to save them after a cousin contracted smallpox in Baltimore and returned to rural Maryland and infected them all."

"And you just happened to have been reading this a few months ago? Is this your field of study? Are you premed?"

"No, history. But this wasn't part of that either. I was doing a favor for my dad, actually, during that smallpox outbreak in Queens earlier this year. He was working with the mayor and the commissioner of health on a mass inoculation."

"Oh, interesting," said Margaret. "I lost money on a bet after the smallpox inoculation in April."

"Because Bevens got sick?" Charlie asked. The Yankee pitcher's inoculation had temporarily put him on the disabled list.

"It threw off the whole rotation," Margaret said. "When he returned to the mound against the Sox, he was shaky."

"Great season, though," Charlie said.

"Can't argue with the World Series."

"Anyway, he asked me to look into the history of public sentiment and vaccinations," Charlie said. "I took a couple detours down some rabbit holes, and one of them was Cotton Mather."

"But what does that have to do with my ponies?" she finally asked.

Charlie beamed with the satisfaction of someone about to deliver good news and raised a gloved finger. "I'll show you." Using tweezers, he carefully opened McClintock's journal. He turned to Margaret. "When were the ponies first mentioned?"

"The first reference to them anyone has been able to find was in 1752," she recalled. "On Susquehannock Island, which is closest to the mainland."

Charlie nodded thoughtfully. "I have a vague memory of McClintock mentioning an island."

He turned the fragile journal pages. The doctor's messy script and the eighteenth-century language made for slow going.

"Here it is," he finally said.

"May I look?" Margaret asked. He glanced up and she smiled.

"Sure, of course." He stood, removed the white gloves, and handed them to her. She took his seat, put them on, and began delicately perusing the diary. Charlie lingered for a few seconds before he decided to resume his work at the next desk.

The library was dead silent for several minutes until Margaret gasped. "I can't believe this," she said.

"What?" said Charlie, rising and walking over to her. *"What?"*

"So almost as an afterthought, the doctor writes of all these events that took place in the area before he arrived. One of them is a Spanish galleon that wrecked off the coast of Maryland earlier that year. After a hurricane. The wreck of *La Galga.*"

" 'The Greyhound.' "

"Indeed. And look right here," she said, pointing at one passage. "The doctor notes that *La Galga* was believed to have been carrying ponies, because after the storm, a number of them were seen on both the

101

mainland and Susquehannock."

"Let me see that." He leaned in. "Incredible!"

"This is going to be huge news among the, oh, at least ten people who care," she said, but the excitement on her face was genuine.

"By the way, a ship from that same fleet inspired Stevenson to write *Treasure Island,*" Charlie added. "Everything is connected."

Margaret looked at him and grinned.

The wind outside the library whistled, and the radiator clanked, and that was that.

CHAPTER SEVEN:
WEDNESDAY, JANUARY 20,
1954

Nanticoke Island, Maryland

Margaret huddled in her coat as she lay on the damp grass, silently watching a string of five ponies wading into a marsh. The beasts bent their necks toward the saltwater cordgrass that grew thick on the west side of Nanticoke Island. The sun rising behind them began to brighten the silhouetted scene, the beach and water emerging like a pale blue and gray canvas behind the dark outlines of the animals. A ray of light landed on the forehead of one of the larger ponies, revealing a white teardrop-shaped spot. He repeatedly snorted and bared his teeth.

"What's he doing?" Margaret whispered to Dr. Louis Gwinnett, the head of the research team, who lay on his stomach next to her, binoculars in hand and a notepad by his side.

He leaned in closer and put his mouth next to her ear: "Don't know," he whispered.

She raised an eyebrow at him and he smiled. The grazing ponies remained oblivious to their presence.

"Notice how distended their stomachs are," Gwinnett whispered. "They all look pregnant, even the two males."

Margaret blanched at his mention of pregnancy. She knew she didn't show yet, but she was concerned that news of her condition would prompt some paternalistic impulse on Gwinnett's part. Men seemed to treat pregnant women like invalids, she'd observed, and she had seven and a half months to go and a lot of work to do before this baby arrived; she was determined to make the most of her time while it was still her own.

"Do you think that's because of all the cordgrass they eat?" Margaret asked, focusing on the matter at hand. "Its salt content is quite high. So they would have to drink more."

"That's likely it," Gwinnett agreed. Margaret stole a look at him. With his shock of thick, prematurely white hair, deep-set, sky-blue eyes, and a jawline so sharp it could cut wood, he looked more an international captain of industry or a New England governor than a zoologist.

Teardrop, as they'd decided to call him,

casually sidled up to one of the mares and began sniffing her front legs, then proceeded down to her ribs, her rear legs, and her tail. The mare looked unbothered by this attention, until, without warning, Teardrop pushed his head forward and bit the mare's rear end, prompting her to emit a guttural shriek. She backed quickly away and took refuge between the other two mares.

The other stallion in the string, pitch-black and slightly larger than Teardrop, snorted, whinnied, then reared onto his hind legs, briefly almost standing. Roaring, he landed angrily, stomping onto the sand a hair's distance from Teardrop, who backed up a few steps. The two stallions locked eyes. Teardrop had a decision to make.

The three mares stood frozen in rapt attention. Margaret and Gwinnett lay still on the sand, similarly enthralled. If birds were chirping, Margaret couldn't hear them.

Teardrop gave a snort, then quickly turned tail and trotted away from the other four ponies. As quickly as the conflict had started, it came to an unremarkable end. The remaining ponies in the string continued grazing on the cordgrass.

Margaret exhaled. Adrenaline was coursing through her veins, pounding into her stomach. The raw confrontation — sex, violence, status — terrified and thrilled her.

"That was intense!" she finally said. "I could use a drink."

Gwinnett looked at his watch. "It's six fifteen in the morning, Mags." He smiled. "And more important, my flask is back at the campsite."

Half an hour later, after the ponies had galloped off, Margaret and Gwinnett walked back to their camp, where another researcher — a cheery blond graduate student named Annabelle Lane — was lighting a match from a small fire over which a pot of hot water was just starting to boil. The match blazed and she lit her cigarette. Gwinnett ducked into his tent, and Lane continued to heat water for their coffee.

"Tell me everything!" Annabelle said, and Margaret described how Teardrop had challenged the alpha in the string and been chased away.

"So where does he go now?"

"After the colts run off they all tend to find one another and then they form these roving bands of bachelor stallions."

Annabelle rolled her eyes. "Sounds like commons on a Saturday night." She opened a collapsible metal cup and shook in some instant coffee from a tin. She handed it to Margaret, then carefully poured hot water from the pot into the cup. "Hold on, I'll get you a spoon," Annabelle said.

"And some sugar, if you have it?"

Gwinnett emerged from his tent with a small flask. With Margaret's assent, he poured a couple of sips of bourbon into her coffee.

"How'd you sleep?" Annabelle asked, handing Margaret a spoon and two sugar cubes.

"Like a baby," Margaret said. "I woke up every hour and cried."

Annabelle and Gwinnett smiled indulgently.

"You should get a vinyl airbed," Annabelle suggested.

Margaret settled herself on the ground next to Annabelle. "When I was a kid, my mom and sister and I moved right near here, on the mainland, to stay with my uncle, and the three of us would sleep in a tent throughout the whole summer and into the fall. Slept soundly every night." Margaret recalled the comfort and security she'd felt in those moments, ensconced between her older sister and mother in two sleeping bags her mom had ripped apart and sewn together, a cocoon for the three of them.

"Where was your father?" Gwinnett asked,

taking a seat on a large rock.

"You ever hear of the USS *Shenandoah*?" she asked.

"Of course," Gwinnett said. "I'm navy myself." He paused, clearly aware of what her question implied. "Horrible thing."

"What was it?" Annabelle said.

"Dirigible crash in Ohio," Margaret said. "My dad was killed, along with thirteen other men." She hadn't spoken of her father's accident since the first time she told Charlie about it, more than a decade before. She wasn't sure why she had just decided to break her long silence — maybe being back on Nanticoke justified a moment to indulge that pain. She felt anew that sinking feeling in her chest, the fresh grief always there no matter how skilled she'd become at ignoring it.

"Oh, I'm so sorry," Annabelle said, looking down into her coffee.

"What Mags isn't saying is that her father was a true hero," Gwinnett said. "The military at the time was convinced rigid airships like the *Shenandoah* were the future of warfare because they could fly so high. And this was the navy's first one, so it was akin to on-the-job training for its crew. Margaret's father and the other men were truly on the front lines."

Margaret walked to the fire to pour herself another cup of coffee. "It was a real mess," she said. "We found out later the commander had tinkered with the design. The navy had ordered everyone to fly despite the bad weather. No one wanted to. But there was this mad race to come up with a vessel that would be the world's best. We weren't even in a war!"

"Kind of like the way the U.S. is treating the atomic race today," Gwinnett said.

Margaret stirred the instant coffee in her cup. Annabelle and Gwinnett were silent; the only sound came from a distant chorus of gulls, egrets, and red-winged blackbirds.

"There were forty-three men in the crew," Margaret said. "Twenty-nine survived. My father was not among them." She lowered herself to sit cross-legged on the ground.

"There were four zeppelins in the U.S. around that time," Gwinnett recalled. "Three were made by the Americans. They all crashed. One was made by the Germans. It didn't." He took a swig from his flask. "Our great infallible capitalist system at work."

Margaret didn't know how to take his remarks. She looked at Annabelle, who was nodding in agreement.

"I'll be right back," Annabelle said, suddenly standing. She went to her tent, reached in, grabbed a roll of toilet paper, and headed to a nearby grove.

"So, Margaret," Gwinnett said, moving so close to her that their knees were nearly touching. She looked at him expectantly. "I noticed you threw up this morning. Twice."

Margaret grimaced. She knew what was coming.

"When were you going to tell me you're pregnant?" he asked.

Damn it, Margaret thought. She'd really counted on more time to keep the news to herself. "Well, I figured I could keep participating in the fieldwork until I had to stop," she said. "I was going to tell you, I just didn't know exactly how. And — honestly? I was hoping to get away with not being treated differently for as long as I could."

"It's fine," Gwinnett said. "I'm sure neither Annabelle nor any of the others picked up on it. I would have noticed sooner or later — I'm a connoisseur of the female form. Especially yours." He held up the flask as a toast and took another swig.

She had been ignoring men's inappropriate comments since she was twelve, but Margaret felt differently about Gwinnett's come-on. In some small corner of her mind, she wanted him to find her appealing. Her heart began beating more quickly; she thought of a hummingbird.

"Well, to be perfectly candid, Charlie and I didn't plan this," she said, motioning vaguely toward her womb.

Gwinnett smiled. "You know how it happens though, right?"

Margaret laughed. "Yes, I understand the basic cause and effect."

He turned away and muttered something — the cadence made her think it was "I'll bet you do" — but she tried to ignore it. She liked Gwinnett; they worked well together, and he was a respected figure in their field. She hoped this baby, and this conversation, wouldn't change things between them.

They'd first met at the 1943 Zoological Association of America annual summer conference at the University of Wisconsin at Madison, where Gwinnett, a renowned Equus expert, taught. Margaret, then about to begin her junior year at Barnard, ate lunch every day with the other women in attendance — there were six of them, at a conference with eighty-four participants. Most of the men ignored them, but Gwinnett pulled up a chair and talked to all of them about what areas of the field they were most interested in as well as his concerns about the difficulties the London Zoo was having during the war. Learning that she was hoping to write her senior thesis focused on the mysterious wild ponies of Nanticoke and Susquehannock Islands, he invited her to keep in touch. Margaret suspected it was a casual remark but she was still thrilled to be noticed by a scholar she'd long admired. And, she had to admit, by someone so undeniably handsome.

She had missed the conference in 1945, when Charlie finally returned from war and he and Margaret were engaged and married in haste. At the 1946 conference Margaret attended at Cornell University in Ithaca, New York, Gwinnett shook her right hand hello and simultaneously grabbed her left hand, admiring the wedding band, and making a regretful *tsk* sound. Over the course of the weekend, they shared an obvious chemistry, as well as a few meals together, but Gwinnett was careful not to openly flirt, and Margaret, very much a blissful newlywed in all other respects, worked hard to tamp down the attraction she felt toward him, going so far as to look in the hotel mirror one morning and say sternly and dramatically to herself, as if she were in a Cary Grant screwball comedy, "You are a married woman, Mrs. Marder!"

She and Gwinnett attended panels and lectures together, and she diligently kept every conversation completely appropriate, as if Charlie were there with them. Gwinnett followed her lead; to end one particularly loaded silence after her hand accidentally grazed his, he clumsily launched into the details of an article he'd read about the recent discovery of echolocation by bats. She was relieved when the conference was over and they shared a friendly, brief farewell with vague promises to keep in touch, just like every other casual academic acquaintance.

And then . . . that was it. Margaret had wondered if their friendship would blossom (carefully, chastely) with each successive encounter — twenty years her senior, he was full of experience and brilliance — but Gwinnett didn't show up at the 1947 or 1948 conference. He was there in 1949 but he kept a respectful distance, and their relationship continued that way until just a few months ago, two days after Charlie had accepted Governor Dewey's offer to serve out the remainder of Congressman Van Waganan's term. Out of the blue on a December day, a letter had arrived special delivery from Gwinnett, informing Margaret that he had received a grant to study the ponies that had been their shared interest. He was putting together a small team to conduct field research throughout the year, starting in January, and there was a role and a tent for her if she so desired. Suddenly, moving to Washington, DC, a mere two or so hours away from the islands, offered her more than just the opportunity to be a congressional spouse.

And now, here they were.

"May I ask you a personal question, Mags?" he said. "And I'm sorry for flirting, I'll calm it down. I'm just tired, and the whiskey isn't helping."

"Sure."

"Have you been trying to have a baby all this time and it's only now happening?"

"Because I'm a bit old, you mean?"

"You're a perfectly healthy specimen, it's just that I'm used to observing an earlier breeding process." He smiled.

"Well, we just kept putting it off," she confessed. "Charlie and I were working on his book, and —"

"You worked on *Sons of Liberty*?"

"Yes, as an editor. And I helped organize his research. And we both just got caught up in the world of academia and scholarship — for a time I was working with the City Parks Department to catalog every wild animal in Manhattan."

"Including the alligators in the sewer?"

She grinned. "No alligators, sadly. I had to debunk that myth in the summer of 1950. No, no alligators, but quite a few sewer rats and even some sad colonies of people under there."

"Well, I'm crushed," Gwinnett said. "You're very special. We'll miss you when you have to leave."

Margaret was irritated. She was having a baby, not retiring, and she was certainly not ready to mourn for her career. She started to assure him of this when something in the distance caught her eye.

"Look," she said, pointing toward the western horizon. Gwinnett turned to see a pony. Margaret picked herself up off the ground and slowly, quietly, deliberately began heading toward the pony, slogging through the wet marsh, the weeds squishing beneath her feet. In her hurry she accidentally dropped her binoculars into the swamp, but she was too preoccupied to stop to retrieve them.

Gwinnett followed her. Margaret was twenty feet away when the pony turned and, it seemed to Margaret, looked directly into her eyes. It was Teardrop.

"Hi there, beauty," Margaret said, approaching prudently.

The pony snorted and looked down, splashing his forelegs in the marshy shallows. Margaret took another cautious step forward, one hand outstretched, barely able to breathe. Very few people ever got this close to one of these ponies — for all she knew, she was the first human he'd ever encountered. She was desperate to touch him, to pat the soft side of his stocky neck. Again he looked at her and she felt a shudder of connection.

Gwinnett stood behind her, silent, as she slowly moved toward Teardrop, murmuring in low tones she hoped would reassure him, never taking her gaze from his. Her heart was pounding; her mouth was dry. She reached the beast and slowly put her hand on his forehead, then softly patted him down to his muzzle. He leaned into her and closed his eyes. And then, abruptly, Teardrop tossed his head and pawed the water before turning and galloping into the distance.

Margaret stood watching him, trying to understand what had just happened. Gwinnett's voice broke the spell.

"Wow," said Gwinnett, coming up to stand next to her. "That was incredible."

Margaret nodded mutely.

"We should go back to camp and write up

our notes. Annabelle will be jealous when she hears how close you got."

Margaret felt a sharp pang of loneliness. The person she most wanted to tell was Charlie, who was a hundred miles away. She missed him deeply. She looked one last time at the spot where Teardrop had just stood, then turned and followed Gwinnett back to see if she could find her binoculars in the swamp.

CHAPTER EIGHT:
SATURDAY, JANUARY 23, 1954

Georgetown, Washington, DC

Margaret had been home from Nanticoke Island for only an hour when, still unshowered and exhausted, she answered the townhouse doorbell and was greeted by a pretty, college-age woman holding Charlie's drycleaned tuxedo.

"Hello, Mrs. Marder! I'm Sheryl Ann Bernstein, the congressman's intern. Miss Leopold asked me to deliver this — I hope I'm not intruding." She handed over the garment and smiled so brightly Margaret almost wanted to shield her eyes. "Thank you!" she said. "I hope you and the congressman have a good weekend."

The intern was halfway down the townhouse steps when she turned around. "Oh! Mrs. Marder!" she cried. "Please tell the congressman I made some progress on my homework assignment!" She smiled yet again and then bounced away, a vision of

118

perky youth that made Margaret feel ancient.

Charlie was tucked away in his first-floor study, surrounded by tall stacks of thick reference books.

"Some Debbie Reynolds look-alike just dropped this off," she said, hanging the tuxedo on the doorknob.

"Oh, crud," Charlie said. "I forgot to tell you, I have to go to a dinner this evening. The Alfalfa Club."

"Alfalfa like from the Little Rascals?"

"No, Alfalfa like the plant," he said distractedly. "The roots of which will apparently do anything to find a drink. That's the conceit of the name, at any rate. Har-har."

"Yes, I get it, Charlie," Margaret said drily. "You're spending too much time educating infatuated interns, perhaps. Assigning them homework."

Preoccupied by the book in his hand, Charlie raised an eyebrow. "What?"

"Nothing. Anyway, I'm filthy and I need to shower." She headed upstairs, and Charlie decided to let her comment dissolve in the ether, returning his attention to the *Funk and Wagnalls New World Encyclopedia*. He'd been looking for more information about Chairman Carlin when he'd stumbled on the entry for the University of Chicago;

recalling the odd note he'd found in his desk, he read more in hopes of learning what the school might have had to do with cereal grains or broadleaf crops. Messrs. Funk and Wagnalls offered no help. No matter. Charlie turned instead to entries on Kefauver and others whom he thought he might encounter that evening.

The Alfalfa Club was among the most elite social organizations in Washington, DC, its membership consisting of two hundred business leaders, politicians, sometimes even presidents. Charlie's invitation was obviously an afterthought, but that didn't diminish his anticipation. Yesterday he had been having lunch in the private Senate Dining Room with Senator Margaret Chase Smith, Republican of Maine, when Kefauver stopped by their table.

"I see you've met the conscience of the Republican Party," Kefauver said playfully, tilting his head in Smith's direction. It had been four years since Joe McCarthy saw Margaret Smith on the Senate subway and told her she looked very serious. "Are you going to make a speech?" he asked. "Yes," she responded, "and you will not like it." Smith's "Declaration of Conscience," delivered on the Senate floor, derided McCarthy's "Four Horsemen of Calumny — Fear,

Ignorance, Bigotry, and Smear." She and Kefauver were thus allies against McCarthy, whose demagogic mudslinging campaign against anyone to the left of Generalissimo Francisco Franco had been roiling the republic for too long. McCarthy's opponents were beginning to gain ground, but Tail Gunner Joe, as he'd been nicknamed by someone, perhaps McCarthy himself, was winning the war of attrition; his adversaries were exhausted. He remained popular with a strong segment of the public, whose support of him seemed impervious to obvious moments of indecency and prevarication. Those who feared McCarthy might never actually go away and that the fever of McCarthyism might never break were growing despondent.

Kefauver handed Charlie a folded-over *New York Times* and tapped a finger on a page 9 story: "Rival for Senate Assails Kefauver: Sutton, House Member, Runs in the Tennessee Primary, as 'Ultra-Conservative.' "

Charlie had read the story about Congressman Pat Sutton, one of his new poker buddies. Sutton was quoted saying he liked Kefauver personally, that they had visited each other's homes, but he didn't like the senior senator's record, that he "has consistently voted as a left winger against the loyalty oath in the Government, and he has voted against wire-tapping to catch the Reds."

"Do you know this jackanapes, Charlie?" Kefauver asked. "It's not enough that the Republicans in Knoxville have all but issued a hit on me this year, not enough that the newspapers are all controlled by Boss Crump's corrupt machine — now this little blunderbuss with whom I've broken bread is accusing me of being a Commie symp."

Charlie shifted in his seat. Sutton was a former navy lieutenant whose many medals included the Distinguished Service Cross and the Silver Star with oak leaf clusters. A demolitions expert, he was a bona fide war hero and a fair poker player whose tell was boasting about his hand; that meant his cards were garbage. Charlie liked him.

"I don't know him well, sir," Charlie said. "He's in my poker group, along with all the other veterans." He held his tongue and stole a look at Smith, whose lips were pursed and whose eyes were distant; she seemed to be used to other senators talking as if she weren't there.

"They'll come at me as a Negro lover, for one, same way Russell did in Florida back in '52," Kefauver said. "Sutton is already pursuing the Dixiecrats. And goddamn Earl Warren's Supreme Court is going to vote to desegregate schools any minute, which the good people of Tennessee are decidedly not prepared for. And as if that weren't enough, a guy with a chestful of medals is coming into the Democratic primary and is damn sure going to ask why I didn't fight in the war. Though a businessman I know told me that a guy with that many medals is either reckless or foolish."

"Do you want me to say something to him about tempering his rhetoric, sir?" Charlie asked. "And if I may, I don't know that I would repeat that 'reckless or foolish' line on the stump."

"No, no, of course not," Kefauver said. He looked at his young protégé. "Say, Charlie, what are you doing tomorrow night? I have an extra ticket to the Alfalfa Club dinner." Charlie hesitated — Margaret was due home tomorrow, and he was longing to see her. Kefauver pressed him: "It will be a roomful of people you need to know better, Charlie."

Charlie knew this would be an opportunity to lobby against Goodstone, and he also had to admit that he'd long been curious about the club. "I'd be glad to join you, sir. Thank you."

"Get some rest," the senator said. "It can be a wild night. Wives — and girlfriends — are not invited."

As Kefauver walked away, Charlie glanced sympathetically at the fourteen-year congressional veteran in the pearls and cashmere sweater across the table who had sat silently, with a bemused smile, throughout the exchange.

"Don't you worry about it any, Congressman," Smith said, dipping her spoon into a bowl of New England clam chowder. "I'm used to it."

The next night, as Charlie entered the lobby of the Mayflower Hotel to attend the dinner, he felt as dashing as the main character in the spy novel he'd read on summer vacation, an agent who played high-stakes baccarat in northern France, posing as a rich Jamaican playboy. Ushered into the Grand Ballroom, where multiple bartenders were stationed like sentries, Charlie immediately ran into Kefauver as he was delivering what appeared to be a successful punch line to Robert Hendrickson, the Republican from New Jersey with whom Kefauver was working on the comic-book hearings.

Charlie waited politely for their laughter to fade. Kefauver turned to him with a jovial grin. "Charlie, great to see you," he said, switching his scotch rocks into his left hand and extending his right.

"Thank you so much for having me," Charlie said. "I must confess, I know nothing about the Alfalfas except why you call yourselves that."

"Not much to tell," Kefauver assured him. "Just another one of these ridiculous clubs. DC is full of them, and some are more nefarious than others. This dinner is pretty much the club's raison d'être. It all started as a way to honor the birthday of Robert E. Lee."

"We Yankees always find it curious how much love is continually bestowed upon the losers of that conflict," said Hendrickson, whom Kefauver then proceeded to jokingly elbow.

"Washington seems to have a lot of these clubs," Charlie added. "Alfalfa, Gridiron . . ."

"Oh, these aren't the ones that matter," Kefauver said. "These are just excuses for frivolity. The clubs to keep an eye on are the ones whose memberships are secret. The ones we only hear whispers about. The John Birch Society. The Southern Heritage Alliance. The Sons of Gettysburg. Something called Hellfire."

Charlie looked at Kefauver curiously. "There was a Hellfire Club in England in the 1700s."

"Is that right?" the senator responded flatly, seemingly uninterested.

"Oh, Estes, those are just Beltway rumors," Hendrickson said. "Just like the Loch Ness Monster or the Jersey Devil. We hear about them, but no one has ever really seen them."

An athletic older man with a strong jaw and a full head of gray hair walked by.

"Is that —" Charlie asked.

"Yes, that's Gene Tunney," Kefauver said. "Gene!" the senator called to the former heavyweight champion, who turned his head, smiled, and held up his fists as if posing for a promotional boxing photo.

"Pavlovian," observed Charlie.

"Gene's one of our inductees this evening," Hendrickson said. He pointed out others in the crowd as he named them. "In addition to Gene, we're honoring Arthur Krock from the *Times,* the House majority leader, plus General Bradley, and . . . who is it? Oh, yes, General Doolittle."

"Not necessarily in that order, I hope," Charlie joked. He was a great admirer of Bradley, who'd commanded U.S. forces in Europe during World War II. And of course the entire nation was proud of Medal of Honor recipient Jimmy Doolittle, who had personally led a dangerous mission into Japan.

Kefauver suddenly looked serious. He glanced at Hendrickson, who took the hint and announced that he needed to go find a refill. "Charlie," he said, "I got an earful from Chairman Carlin at the members' meeting earlier tonight. He's heard that you're organizing your fellow veterans against this Goodstone appropriation, and he is not happy."

"Not really organizing, per se," Charlie said. "Just some conversations over poker. This is getting blown out of proportion."

"Welcome to Washington," Kefauver said. "Listen: You need to fix this. You're about to get gelded, son."

Charlie was briefly spared by a baritone shout. "Estes!" Barreling toward them was an older man smoking a cigar and holding a martini glass. He looked like an editorial cartoon of a robber baron: deeply tanned bald pate, V-shaped scowl, enormous belly.

"Good to see you, Connie!" Kefauver said. "Charlie, you know Conrad Hilton."

"I know of him, of course," said Charlie. "Pleasure to meet you, sir."

"And this is Davis LaMontagne," Hilton

said, introducing the younger man to his right. "He's my guest — a rising star at Janus Electronics. Do you know of them? Very exciting young company specializing in electronics and technology for the Cold War era."

"Oh, I just handle legal and lobbying in a little office here," LaMontagne said, shrugging off the compliment with the assurance of someone accustomed to being reminded of his own accomplishments. "How do you do?" LaMontagne was movie-star handsome, maybe forty, with slicked-back dark hair; he held a scotch on the rocks and was wearing a smoky cologne. Charlie thought he recognized the scent: Cuir de Russie, the same pricey cologne worn by one of his more annoying trust-fund students at Columbia, a boy who'd asked a Russian history professor if the scent truly captured the rich aromas of Russian leather.

LaMontagne extended a hand toward Charlie without waiting for an introduction.

"Congressman Charlie Marder from New York," he said. "You're my congressman, in fact. Manhattan is my official residence."

"Mine too," said Hilton. Hilton had a type of handshake favored by a particular sort of domineering male: he clasped Charlie's hand in a viselike grip and tried to jerk him

128

forward. There had been a guy in basic training who'd pulled this same "America's number-one he-man" nonsense, so Charlie knew to immediately freeze his arm and hold his ground. Hilton gave him a brief, appraising glance in return.

"Nice to meet you," Charlie said, feeling a bit like a teenager being introduced to his father's friends, Hilton so full of wealthy bluster and LaMontagne so polished and smooth.

"Gentlemen, I'm going to need your help with something," Hilton said. "Especially yours, Senator."

"Of course," said Kefauver. "What is it?"

There was a pause, during which Charlie realized that, again like a teenager, his company was not required. He tilted an imaginary glass toward his mouth, to the evident relief of his companions, and started wandering through the crowd, searching for a destination.

Fat men in tuxedos stood in a circle. Black waiters hustled out of the kitchen holding trays of Swedish meatballs, shrimp boats, anchovies soaked in wine. Charlie caught snatches of conversations:

So why is it exactly that McCarthy isn't married?

Thank God we have Nasser. He just locked up three hundred of those fanatics.

Wife is fine. Mistress better.

A Frenchman. Cousteau, I think. Exploring a sunken ship off Marseille. Great television.

Still talking about the goddamn war. It was almost a decade ago.

Well, she's a nuclear sub, so she can stay out there forever.

Is he smart? Smart enough to be dangerous.

Yeah, yeah, we're the problem. Us and Wall Street. Everyone's to blame but the voters.

Standing with Lyndon Johnson against a wall, Bob Kennedy swiped his hair off his forehead and looked around the room, seemingly searching for an escape. Chairman Carlin was horsing around with Gene Tunney, pretending to box with him while a photographer captured the moment for posterity.

"Choose your poison," said a bartender after Charlie finally settled on a bar, the one farthest from the masses.

"Have any hemlock?" Charlie asked.

The bartender smiled and shook his head.

"Two vodkas, one glass, then," Charlie said.

"Rough day?" Congressman Chris Mac-Lachlan appeared at his side.

"Just thirsty." Charlie held up his glass. "Good to see you, Mac, even if you did clean my clock at poker."

MacLachlan smiled and raised his glass. "May ye be in heaven half an hour afore the devil knows you're dead." He took a healthy swallow from a gin and tonic.

"Did you see Carlin?" Charlie asked.

"The old ham can't resist a chance to pose for the cameras."

"Well, that old ham knows about my suggestion that the veterans stick together and kill the Goodstone earmark," Charlie said. "Kefauver told me he's furious."

MacLachlan sipped his drink, then exhaled. "Sweet baby Moses, we didn't even decide to carry out that play."

"People in this town can't keep their mouths shut."

"Keep fighting the good fight," Mac-Lachlan said. "You're following the trail Van Waganan blazed."

"If I'm doing that, it's not on purpose," Charlie said. "I don't know much about him. Just that he was an aide on the Truman Committee and helped him take on Wright

131

Aeronautical."

"Yeah, the bastards. Shit engines, faked inspections, dead American pilots." He paused and motioned to the bartender for a refill. "That's what started him on his mission."

"Yeah, I remember headlines about Van Waganan challenging various corporations. Malfeasance and such."

"When he got going, he was like a dog with a goddamn bone," MacLachlan said.

The din of the all-male crowd — deep, baritone, crescendos of laughter and shouts — highlighted the silence between Charlie and MacLachlan.

"He made a lot of enemies," MacLachlan noted.

MacLachlan turned to get a better view of the crowd and those around him, then leaned closer to Charlie. "This postwar economic boom, the Long Boom, they're calling it . . . it's wonderful for our standing in the world and for our constituents' standard of living, but there's an accompanying madness. A recklessness. So much money being made — like nothing this country has ever seen before. And here in Washington, there are a lot of people working to stop anyone even asking questions about what is sometimes a clear . . . disregard . . . for our own people. Van Waganan may have been a victim —"

MacLachlan stopped himself as Chairman Carlin suddenly stepped into his line of sight, perhaps thirty feet away. "Oh, boy," Charlie said as the chairman started walking toward him with the determination of a crocodile moving in on an oblivious gazelle.

"Don't forget your oath," MacLachlan said under his breath. "Protecting America from enemies foreign *and* domestic. Goodstone counts." He patted Charlie's shoulder and vanished into the crowd.

Charlie steeled himself, remembering that he had been through tougher stuff than the ire of a powerful congressman. He leaned into the encounter, throwing his handshake at the chairman like a Robin Roberts fastball and deploying every available ounce of charisma he had as aggressively as he could.

"Chairman Carlin, I owe you an apology," Charlie said, looking into Carlin's rheumy eyes, his irises the color of swamp algae. "I should never have spoken up at the committee markup, nor should I have engaged in any small talk about Goodstone with my fellow veterans. Of the former, I can only tell you that I am young and inexperienced — in other words, dumb. Of the latter, well, sir, you served in the Great War, and I'm

133

certain you know what it's like when veterans get around drink."

Charlie had read that morning that Carlin had served as a U.S. Army officer from 1917 to 1919, though he had never left the continental United States, having worked in the Pentagon procurement office. Still, service was service.

"Why, Charlie," said Carlin, clearly taken aback after arriving loaded for bear. "That's mighty white of you."

"With your permission, sir, I would beg a moment of your time to try to explain myself."

Carlin smiled. Charlie's military deference seemed familiar to him, perhaps a nostalgic echo from his service at the Pentagon. "Permission granted."

So Charlie told a short version of the recapture of the town of Le Meaune: the French family, the stash of poison gas hidden in the barn, the errant mortar, the shoddy Goodstone gas masks, the deaths of Private First Class Rodriguez and the French father and his two small children.

Carlin listened impassively.

"So I got emotional, I suppose," Charlie said. "I'm sorry about how I handled this and the last thing I want to do is be disrespectful. I have great admiration for you."

Carlin paused, then said, "Well, thank you, Charlie. We will figure this out." He put a paternal arm around Charlie's shoulders; he reeked of Aqua Velva and anchovies. "A lot of things can happen in this town when people work together. I'm glad we had this talk."

Relieved to see Carlin walk away but also slightly disgusted by his own obsequiousness, even though it was in the service of a larger goal, Charlie took a deep breath.

"Gentlemen, gentlemen, please take your seats!" shouted Senator Harry Byrd, Democrat of Virginia, into the microphone.

Across the room, Kefauver was waving him toward their long table, and soon Charlie found himself seated between the senator and LaMontagne and across from Conrad Hilton.

"What are we to expect tonight?" LaMontagne asked Charlie. "I'm a virgin here."

"I am too," Charlie said. "I believe it's a mock political convention. They nominate a faux presidential candidate, and he gives a silly speech."

From the right side of the stage, the Marine Corps band began playing "Hail to the Chief," and the five hundred or so attendees — Alfalfa Club members and guests

135

— stood and applauded as President Eisenhower appeared onstage, beaming and waving. Some of the generals and admirals, wearing their dress uniforms, saluted as he approached the microphone.

"At ease, dogfaces," he said, prompting laughter from the crowd, along with the clinking of glass and ice cubes. Eisenhower took his seat at one of the long tables, and Byrd resumed speaking, working through a number of self-congratulatory references to the club and the attendees. Charlie was lost in thoughts of his conversations with MacLachlan and Carlin. Was the Goodstone money going to be killed? He wasn't sure what Carlin had meant when he said they would figure it all out.

"This is exactly what I hate about coming down here to DC for these rubber-chicken affairs," LaMontagne whispered, his breath warm and minty. "A bunch of old guys balling each other off and a room of brown-nosers laughing like their next performance review depended on it."

Charlie noted the contrast between LaMontagne's smooth, polished demeanor when they'd met earlier and his one-of-the-boys crudeness now that he was in different company. Social chameleons were a source of fascination to him; he envied their ability to fit into any situation, a talent he lacked. He'd felt its absence acutely since arriving in the capital.

Onstage, Byrd was "nominating" for president Henry Cabot Lodge Jr., the Eisenhower administration's ambassador to the United Nations. Lodge, a Republican, had been the U.S. senator from Massachusetts until Jack Kennedy defeated him two years before.

"Did you know Kennedy's grandfather lost a race to Lodge's father for the same Senate seat?" Charlie whispered to LaMontagne. "The very same one! In 1916."

"Jack's around here somewhere, I saw him hobble in earlier," LaMontagne said. "I'm hearing a lot of chatter about him making a play for VP in '56."

"Good thing we fought that war against royalty."

"My overprivileged friends," Lodge began, prompting disproportionate howls of laughter.

"What's the ratio going to be tonight of laughter to quality of joke?" LaMontagne quietly asked.

"Twenty to one, I'd wager," Charlie said. He was enjoying LaMontagne's company as well as the liberal supply of cocktails.

Kefauver, sitting to Charlie's left, shot

Charlie a look that seemed to suggest that he and his new friend needed to pipe down.

"Once I am elected," Lodge said grandly, "I can guarantee you one thing: It will always look as though big things are happening. Maybe they won't be happening, but it will *look* that way!"

Riotous laughter.

"I may be doing nothing to stop the war in Korea, or nothing to balance the budget, or nothing to solve anything, but there'll be a lot of name-calling, there'll be all sorts of headlines!" Lodge pledged. "The trivial will reach a new place in American politics and believe me: when you consider the place it has had in previous administrations, that is no idle boast!"

Hysterics in the crowd. Kefauver actually wiped tears from his eyes. LaMontagne slipped Charlie a business card.

"I can only take so much of this," he whispered. "Give me a call, let's tell war stories." He got up and then leaned in one more time. "Enjoy yourself if you can." He swiftly exited the ballroom, as graceful and stealthy as a leopard. Charlie felt woozy from the booze and the bullshit and the conversational whiplash. He wanted desperately to talk to Margaret, but he'd never felt further away from her.

CHAPTER NINE:
THURSDAY, FEBRUARY 18, 1954

Georgetown, Washington, DC

"You're up early," said Margaret, not looking up from her book as Charlie walked into the kitchen.

"I have meetings and an early committee vote," he replied. He yawned and removed the Maxwell House percolator from the cupboard. "The defense spending bill — thankfully without any money going to Goodstone this time."

In the three weeks since the Alfalfa Club dinner, Chairman Carlin had told Charlie that he would remove the earmark for Goodstone if Charlie would just drop the matter and entrust it to him. Sensing no other option and disarmed by Carlin's responsiveness, he agreed and told his fellow veterans that all was well.

"You've no doubt been up for hours already?" he asked, reaching for the tin of coffee grounds in the cabinet.

She shrugged. The early pregnancy had meant not just morning sickness but also insomnia. She'd been awake since before dawn, vaguely troubled and uneasy.

A silence hung in the air, but it wasn't the normal one born of comfort. Since Margaret's return from Nanticoke Island and Charlie's official baptism in the DC swamp by the Alfalfas, she felt that they'd drifted apart a bit. She suspected the pregnancy was a likely culprit, or at least an accomplice; every evening when Charlie returned home from work or from one of the various fund-raisers and social functions he had to attend, she was often sound asleep. But there were grievances too, growing stronger and healthier.

She felt exasperated and stretched thin, trying to work with the research team's notes and conclusions from their first outing to the Maryland island. Plus she was finishing up a paper for the *Journal of Zoology* comparing the health of giraffes at the Bronx Zoo with those at the Philadelphia Zoo, based on research she'd completed the previous November, plus unpacking their moving boxes and decorating their new town house, plus keeping a home for Charlie — who meanwhile was consumed with his new job. They were on completely different tracks and traveling in opposite directions.

Margaret watched Charlie pour himself a cup of coffee from the percolator, surely their most useful wedding present, and she thought about the space that had grown between them. It didn't seem unbridgeable. She imagined Charlie as being like a beach ball in the surf that a sudden breeze had carried away from shore — retrievable, but it would require effort. They had been married for almost nine years now, so the notion that marriage was work was hardly revelatory, but she felt further away from him than she had in years, perhaps even since those early days when the war was too much with him.

She thought about their life in New York. Conversations had been lively and frequent, and they shared a genuine interest in each other's lives and careers. She had loved to hear his stories about the ridiculous, vicious battles within the Columbia University faculty; his odd brush with intellectual celebrity visiting *What's My Line?* and other shows to promote *Sons of Liberty;* the few memories that he was willing to share of his time in the army. And he was as good a listener as he was a storyteller; she could lay out a knotty research problem or writing challenge and he was eager to talk it through with her until she arrived at possible solutions. He was her sounding board for her frustrations with her mother and sister, and though Charlie never spoke an ill word about his parents, he laughed when she did.

But somehow, all that had changed a few weeks after their move. Beyond her unavailability after seven p.m., she knew some blame lay with her and her growing impatience with the political world he seemed to find increasingly seductive. Or, if not seductive, irresistible. Its rituals and caste systems were abhorrent to her, and sometimes she couldn't help reacting to Charlie's stories with eye-rolls and crossed arms.

She'd been bitterly disappointed in him when he told her he had backed off his behind-the-scenes campaign against Goodstone because the chairman had made a noncommittal remark about taking care of matters. And the comic-book hearing seemed like the height of nonsense to her; she'd given up pretending to understand why he was taking part.

Margaret held her tongue as often as she could, but he made that difficult by confiding in her and telling her everything — about his moments of unctuousness with Kefauver and Carlin, about each of his compromises. Each instance of confessed deference became a presence in the house, an ugly piece of furniture they had to walk around. Charlie eventually stopped telling her about his day in anything but the broadest and most positive outlines, and she in turn felt less inclined to tell him about hers. She was sure that he resented her refusal to join him in his new world, but she just couldn't make herself comfortable in a place where compromise and obsequiousness were as much a part of the landscape as traffic circles and monuments to long-dead generals.

Charlie sat down at the table with his coffee, picked up the *Washington Times-Herald,* and folded it lengthwise, as all New York subway commuters learned to do, no matter that he'd be leaving it behind to drive to work shortly. She felt a burst of affection for him suddenly, for his predictable habits; now he was adding milk to his coffee and as he reached for the small sugar bowl, she counted down silently — *Three, two, one* — until his daily utterance "I forgot to get a spoon." He got up to retrieve one.

He sat back down and looked over at her. "What's that you're reading?"

Being reminded of the book she was holding extinguished the tiny spark of fondness she'd been so happy to welcome just now. She found her bookmark — a faded National Park Service ribbon given to her by a park ranger that summer she spent in Maryland as a girl — and flipped back to an earlier page. "A load of manure," Margaret said. "See if you recognize it: A six-year-old boy, an ardent comic-book reader, fashioned for himself a cape and — quote — jumped off the cliff to fly as his comic-book heroes did. Seriously injured, he told his mother, 'Mama, I almost did fly!' A few days later he died from the injuries he had received."

She held up the book: Fredric Wertham's *Seduction of the Innocent,* which was to be published next month and which was the basis for the special investigative hearing that Kefauver and Hendrickson hoped to hold in Charlie's district in April.

"Have you actually read this, Charlie?" she asked. "No footnotes. No endnotes. No citations. Nothing."

As academics, Charlie and Margaret had both developed healthy skepticism about anecdotes that proved too perfect. A rival of Charlie's on the Columbia University faculty had been ignominiously terminated when it became clear that he'd massaged details in his book about Joseph Stalin. It had caused something of a stir, since the details that the professor had tweaked — and, in at least two cases, that he seemed to have created out of whole cloth — depicted Stalin's actions during the Great Purge in an even more horrific light. The professor, a conservative, claimed that the faculty was compromised and was treasonously trying to cover up for their comrade. Charlie agreed that the faculty was jam-packed with Communists and socialists and liberals who didn't take the evils of Communism seriously, but he happened to side with his pinko colleagues in this case when it came to academic standards.

"I've read it," Charlie said. "And I agree with you."

The book was filled with shoddy scholarship and twisted interpretations, a conclusion in search of evidence. Batman and Robin were "like a wish dream of two homosexuals living together." Superman was a fascist, Wonder Woman a lesbian dominatrix.

"And yet you're still actually participating in this hearing?" she asked. "Are you really helping them book the Foley Square Courthouse?" She shook her head in disbelief. "I don't understand how you can be a part of any of this."

He mumbled something about needing to work with Congress in order to be able to do some larger good. But it didn't sound any more convincing than all the previous times he'd said it, and the look on his face told her the disappointment on her own devastated him.

Charlie walked into his congressional office just before eight thirty and was surprised to find LaMontagne standing there, smoking a cigarette and examining the various pictures and framed political memorabilia on the wall. Leopold, who had followed Charlie into the office with her ubiquitous clipboard in hand, emitted a sharp gasp of surprise.

"How did you get in here?" she asked. "What the —"

"It's okay, Miss Leopold," Charlie said. "Davis LaMontagne, this is Miss Leopold, who runs my office."

They exchanged terse pleasantries before Leopold, still clearly unhappy about the intrusion, left the two men alone. Since their first encounter at the Alfalfa Club, they'd run into each other several times, never making plans to get together but often ending up in the same corner of a social event, swapping war stories and mocking the various displays before them. LaMontagne had advised Charlie to go along to get along, do what Kefauver and Carlin and others asked him to do. And it seemed to be working, with Kefauver singing his praises in an interview with the *New York Herald Tribune* and promising to give him a showy role during the comic-book hearings.

Charlie took off his suit jacket and loosened his Brooks Brothers tie while LaMontagne moved to the couch and held out his pack of cigarettes, offering one. Charlie nodded and LaMontagne tossed him the pack of Chesterfields. Charlie used his German lighter.

LaMontagne gestured toward the lighter. "Looks familiar," he said. "I got one too, plucked it off a dead Jerry. So, listen, I'm here because I know something, and I thought you could maybe bring this information to the right people. But I need your discretion, of course."

"Of course." Charlie sat down behind his desk. "How can I help you?"

"A guy who used to work for us . . ."

"At Janus Electronics."

LaMontagne nodded. "A few years ago we were told that he was a Communist."

"In what way? Actively?"

"Exactly — what way," LaMontagne said. "I don't really care if someone believes in

147

some pie-in-the-sky notion of equality in theory — we fought alongside Stalin's army in the war, after all. But no, this was more than watercooler talk. He went to meetings. He distributed literature."

"How'd you find out?"

"Jackass handed a brochure to one of our clients, who recognized him from a pitch meeting."

"Pitch meeting?" asked Charlie.

"Yes," said LaMontagne. "This wasn't the guy who pushed the pastry cart. This was one of our main guys in R and D."

"Working on what, if you don't mind my asking?"

"I really need you to keep this between us, Charlie."

"Of course."

"Surveillance technology," LaMontagne confided. "It has commercial applications but the research is much more for the Pentagon and Central Intelligence."

"Commercial applications?"

"They're called baby monitors," LaMontagne said. "Zenith invented them after the Lindbergh baby's kidnapping. A few years ago they introduced the Radio Nurse. When your baby is born, you and the missus will be able to sit in the living room while the sounds of your baby are piped in from his bedroom."

"One-way, so the baby doesn't hear you?" Charlie said.

"Right. A good idea, but the ones in the stores right now are clunky and the reception is awful. The signal is sent through your own electrical wiring in your home, so signals get crossed and you might all of a sudden pick up the latest Senators game. Plus, they're pricey, like twenty bucks each, so they're not exactly flying off the shelves. But we have a good model that's about to hit the stores. I'll get you one."

"No need, but forget the commercial application — you want Central Intelligence to buy this baby-monitor technology for what? Listening devices at the Soviet embassy?" He'd meant it as a joke, but as soon as he said it, he realized it actually made sense.

"Bingo," said LaMontagne, and he landed an elegant forefinger on his nose in approval. "But we didn't trust that the Communist-leaflet guy, Boschwitz — that's his name, Ira Boschwitz — wasn't going to tip off his ideological brethren at the embassy. Or, even worse, give them the blueprints. So we fired him."

"And how can I help?"

"Well, believe it or not," LaMontagne

said, stubbing out his cigarette, "Zenith hired him."

"And McCarthy's holding hearings right now on the Army Signal Corps."

"That's why I'm in town, they're going after Leo Kantrowitz today. Zenith fired him as soon as he got subpoenaed." Charlie had read in the morning paper — indubitably leaked by McCarthy's chief counsel, Roy Cohn — that prior to Zenith, Kantrowitz had done classified work for the Army Signal Corps while he was a member of the Communist Party. "But Kantrowitz is small potatoes," LaMontagne said. "They're missing the real problem."

"Boschwitz?"

"Boschwitz."

"Why haven't you just gone right to the committee? I'm sure they'd be interested in hearing this."

LaMontagne lit another Chesterfield. "Our in-house counsel advised us against direct coordination. We've attempted other avenues, but so far members of the committee have thought we were just bad-mouthing a competitor. Also we didn't have any evidence other than anecdotal."

He withdrew a manila folder from his briefcase and tossed it onto the coffee table in front of Charlie, who picked it up but didn't open it.

"*Are* you just bad-mouthing a competitor? Is the fact that he went to Zenith a big part of this?"

LaMontagne stood. "Just open the folder. Anything you could do to pass it on to Cohn or Bob Kennedy would be very deeply appreciated." He looked at his watch. "But I gotta run, have a thing with Dulles in an hour."

"John Foster or Allen?" Charlie asked, as he had to wonder why a midlevel electronics executive would be meeting with either the secretary of state or the director of Central Intelligence, both of whom quietly wove their tentacles around anything and everything that could be construed as being in the national security interests of the United States.

"Does it matter?" LaMontagne asked. He grabbed his hat and jacket from the coatrack and nearly bumped into Sheryl Ann Bernstein on his way out the door. She smiled at him brightly — Charlie sometimes wondered if there was any encounter that wouldn't prompt that cheerful Midwestern smile — and stood aside to let him pass.

Bernstein reminded Charlie of many of the Barnard students he'd taught: bright, eager, wide-eyed. And, though he'd be loath to make such an observation aloud, a touch flirtatious — very mildly, like a teenager permitted to apply only some modest lipstick, her coy glances almost like a risqué outfit she was trying on in the store just to see how it felt. Not that there was anything particularly sensual about the bond they were forming, which was rooted in intellectual pursuits more than anything else. But he would be lying if he pretended that being around a woman who seemed delighted to be talking to him wasn't a welcome change. He knew this was the emotional equivalent of a Hershey Bar, but that didn't make it taste any less sweet.

She held a folder aloft like a trophy she'd just won. "Do you remember that scrap of paper you told me to look into, Congressman? It's taken me a few weeks, but I have some possible leads."

Charlie motioned her to a seat and silently mourned the loss of the productive early morning he'd planned. He would have been inclined to forget about those cryptic scribbles: *U Chicago, 2,4-D 2,4,5-T cereal grains broadleaf crops.*

She provided her update. After he'd handed her the weird note while they were getting off the Senate subway, she'd cold-called the University of Chicago's Department of Botany, and the department librarian had said she'd look into it.

"She was so helpful when we first spoke, and she even said she had a good idea about where to look for more information. But since then —" Bernstein paused dramatically and Charlie stifled a small sigh of impatience while he glanced at his watch. "I've been calling and calling and she has not taken my call. For almost a month now!"

"Odd," said Charlie, though he couldn't help wondering if a departmental librarian had more pressing duties to attend to than chasing down a stranger's out-of-left-field requests.

"I know!" Bernstein enthused, her excitement suddenly bubbling over. "But then I had *another* idea. My brother goes to Northwestern, so I asked him to stop by the department and see what he could find out." She paused again. "He's pretty handsome, and the librarian was very friendly to him until he revealed why he was there. He said she got really cold, really fast. Said the study he was asking about was subject to wartime secrecy laws and that there was nothing that could be shared with the public in any way. And she had campus security escort him out."

Charlie sat up a little straighter now. Maybe this wild-goose chase wasn't so wild after all. "Were you able to get any information about the study? The name of the professors?"

"Yes," Bernstein said, leafing through her steno pad. "Kraus. And Mitchell."

"Okay," Charlie said, writing down their names. "I guess the next step would be for me to ask about it at the Pentagon. Or to get someone on the Armed Services Committee to do so."

"What about Strongfellow?"

"Perfect."

Leopold poked her head into the office. "Sheryl Ann, you need to finish up that typing I gave you. And Congressman, you have just enough time to stop in and see Senator Kefauver before the morning vote if you leave right now."

Charlie didn't feel like taking the monorail to get to the Senate Office Building — the SOB, as everyone on the Hill called it — he wanted to stretch his legs. After making his way up to the second floor of the U.S. Capitol, he spotted Congressman Isaiah Street standing in National Statuary Hall, a semicircular room right off the House Chamber featuring statues of notable Americans. Each of the forty-eight states had contributed two of the immense likenesses, with thirty-six standing in the room like soldiers in formation, curving along the wall of the Statuary Hall chamber. Dozens of others were scattered throughout nearby rooms and halls.

Charlie had seen Street every poker night but seldom ran into him anywhere else. They had developed an easy rapport during the weekly games. Street stood glowering at one of the statues contributed by Georgia, the figure of former governor Alexander Stephens.

"Charlie," he said, a smile stretching across his face. "I have good news. Congressman Powell is going to vote however you want today, depending on whether the Goodstone provision has been removed." Representative Adam Clayton Powell Jr., Democrat of New York, was a member of the House Appropriations Committee. Street had offered to lobby Powell on Charlie's behalf to get his support on Goodstone.

"Thank you, but I'm not sure I need it. I'm told it's gone."

Street looked confused. "Really? I thought I just read that General Kinetics was making a play to buy Goodstone. Blacklisting them will be bad for both companies. And for the deal."

"I hadn't heard that," Charlie said, stunned by the news. Learning that General Kinetics was attempting to purchase Goodstone was like finding out the Chinese were sending troops in to defend North Korea.

Charlie pointed to a statue of Supreme Court chief justice Morrison "Mott" Waite, the image of regality, leaning on a cane. "See how his forefingers are crossed on the handle of the cane? That's a sign he was a member of the Yale secret society Skull and Bones."

Street shook his head. "Folks at home . . . voters would be amazed if they ever found out how many decisions are actually made by these secret societies and clubs."

"Who else is there besides Skull and Bones?" Charlie asked. "The Masons? The Illuminati?"

"The Klan," Street said. He motioned back toward the statue of Governor Stephens. "Quote: 'Our new government's cornerstone rests upon the great truth that the Negro is not equal to the white man,' " he recited, " 'that slavery, subordination to the superior race is his natural and normal condition.' Unquote."

Charlie looked down at the statue's foundation, where the engraving read: *I am afraid of nothing on the earth, above the earth, beneath the earth, except to do wrong.*

Street shrugged. "He said what I said too. Vice president of the Confederacy. That's all you need to know."

"To be fair, how many white men in Georgia opposed slavery in the 1860s?" Charlie said. In his teaching days, he had always asked his students to consider the context of the era they studied.

"The British outlawed slavery in 1833," Street countered.

"George Washington had slaves. Do you want to change the name of this city?"

Street pointed to a majestic bronze caped figure from Mississippi, Jefferson Davis. "President of the Confederacy," Street said. "Why is it that almost a hundred years later, society still hasn't labeled these men traitors?"

"I don't know," Charlie said. He was done playing devil's advocate on an issue where he actually did think of the clients as devils.

"The good guys won. So to speak. So why are there statues of the bad guys? It's not as though the French have statues of their traitors from the war, the Vichy French."

"That's not entirely true," Charlie said. "Marshal Pétain died just a few years ago and they have a bunch of streets named after him in France."

"But that's not *because* he collaborated with the Nazis, it's *despite* the fact that he did," Street said. "You know damn well it's because he was a hero in the Great War."

"I'm just saying, it's all more complicated than you're making it seem," Charlie said. "De Gaulle led the Free French but he placed a wreath on Pétain's tomb."

Street shoved his hands in his pockets and looked at the ceiling. He wasn't concealing his disgust; he was making it clear that refraining from voicing it was a struggle.

"Forgive me," Charlie said. "You know I'm an academic. Sometimes we get caught up in the abstract rather than the reality. These men contained multitudes. They did heinous, unforgivable things. Don't misunderstand me. But they're more than their misdeeds, right? FDR sent the Japanese to camps. Lincoln suspended habeas corpus. Twelve U.S. presidents were slave owners, including the one who'd been the top general of the Union Army!"

Street shook his head. "I don't know, Charlie. John Adams knew better. John Quincy Adams knew better. Lincoln knew better. Right is right and wrong is wrong. You fought for your country, you married a good woman, you work hard to protect troops from future shitty gas masks. You're not betraying your principles. You don't contain multitudes." He paused. "Do you, Charlie?"

"Charlie, how are you?" Senator Kefauver greeted him with his attention focused more on the Zenith television. Senator McCarthy was interrogating a witness.

"I'm fine, sir. I need some advice," Charlie said. He had brought two things to the meeting: the Boschwitz dossier LaMontagne had given him and Wertham's *Seduction of the Innocent*. He set both on the coffee table and sat in the chair in front of the senator's desk. "I've got —"

Kefauver held up a hand to hush Charlie and pointed toward the television console in the corner. Using a Lazy Bones remote control hooked up to the television by a wire, he turned up the volume.

"Look, mister, I am not going to waste all afternoon with you," Senator Joseph McCarthy bellowed at a witness. *"I have asked you a very simple question. You will answer it, unless you want to take the Fifth Amendment. If you think it will incriminate you, you can take the Fifth Amendment."*

"Restate the question," said the witness.

The hearing's reporter read back from her notes. " *'When you got this job working on Army ordnance, do you know whether or not the man who hired you knew that you had been accused of Communist activities prior to that time,'* " she said. The witness and his lawyers huddled in consultation.

"I see you're reading *Seduction of the Innocent*," Kefauver noted. "It is amazing the twisted things children are learning about murder and rape and torture. This is going to be a big hearing, Charlie."

On television, Senator McCarthy had now turned over the hearings to his chief counsel, Roy Cohn, who appeared to be eviscerating a new witness.

"While you were attending Cornell, did you know a man named Alfred Sarant?"

Cohn, a pit bull of a man, was clearly already in possession of the answer.

"I refuse to answer that question on the grounds of the Fifth Amendment," said the witness.

"Did Sarant recruit you into the Rosenberg spy ring?"

"I refuse to answer that question on the grounds of the Fifth Amendment."

"Did you engage in a conspiracy to commit espionage with certain persons working for the Army Signal Corps?"

160

"I refuse to answer that question on the grounds of the Fifth Amendment."

"Jesus," said Kefauver, standing. "The Rosenbergs!"

"Did you ever visit Julius Rosenberg at the Emerson Electric Company and obtain from him material which you transmitted to a Soviet spy ring?"

"I refuse to answer that question on the grounds of the Fifth Amendment."

"I mean, good Christ, Charlie."

Kefauver exhaled loudly, sank his bulky frame back down into his chair, and grabbed a cigar stub from his desk that he commenced chewing. His dull blue eyes ping-ponged between Charlie and the television.

"So, speaking of McCarthy and the Army Signal Corps," Charlie said, "an acquaintance of mine handed me a file on one of Zenith's guys. Asked me to pass it on to Bob Kennedy or Cohn."

Kefauver looked as though he had just detected an unpleasant odor.

"Yeah, that was my reaction, too," said Charlie. "Making matters worse, he's with a direct competitor of Zenith."

"Oh, Lordy," said Kefauver.

"But what happens if I don't hand the information over and it's real?"

"Or even if it's not real but McCarthy

leaks to his stooges in the press that you refused to inform the committee about a Commie," Kefauver said. "You've got to worry about those things now. We all do. McCarthyism is a cancer. And it won't just be an election you don't win." Kefauver warmed to his topic with alarming speed. "You'll be ruined. Columbia won't let you back; you'll end up teaching at Barnyard High in East Turtle-Turd, Kentucky."

Charlie suddenly realized that until just now, he had regarded his new life in Washington almost as if it were a summer camp in the Catskills or the home of a college buddy he was visiting for a long weekend — someplace he could parachute into and soon leave with no impact on his real life. But he knew Kefauver was right: Columbia would invoke the standard clause about bringing shame and embarrassment to the university community. His publishing house would stop returning his phone calls. Charlie had seen how even the liberal Manhattan elite dealt with publicly ostracized Communists in their midst, and it wasn't pretty: sociology lecturer Bernhard Stern saw his name dragged through the mud not only by the McCarthy Committee but by the university; anthropology lecturer Gene Weltfish had been dismissed altogether. And these weren't individuals accused of espionage; their transgressions had been in thought and belief. There was no escaping the stink of the Red Scare.

Kefauver eyed Charlie's *Seduction of the Innocent* on the coffee table.

"With regards to the juvenile delinquency hearing," he said, "have you lined up the courthouse for us?"

"Not yet. Working on it."

"Dr. Wertham is a good man. I had lunch with him last week in New York."

"Sir, have you read this book?"

"Read it?" asked Kefauver. "I helped pay for it. Steered federal funding so he could diagnose this scourge. My God, Charlie, when Hendrickson and I started the Subcommittee on Juvenile Delinquency last year, we had Dr. Wertham in mind the whole time. Something has got to be done about this epidemic, even if we just shine a spotlight on it, like I did with organized crime."

Charlie was silent. The muscle that kept him from expressing his thoughts and principles was getting quite a workout. Kefauver pointed at a framed magazine article hanging on the wall to Charlie's right.

"Read that," Kefauver ordered. "It's from *Life*."

Charlie obediently stood and examined it.

The week of March 12, 1951, will occupy a special place in history, the article read. *The U.S. and the world had never experienced anything like it . . . Never before had the attention of the nation been so completely riveted on a single matter. The Senate investigation into interstate crime was almost the sole subject of national conversation.*

"Impressive, sir," Charlie said, "but —"

"Charlie, do you know how many people watched Frank Costello testify before my committee?" Kefauver asked. "Thirty million. That's even more than watched your Yankees win the World Series." He smiled, a big, goofy cornball grin, so wide and uninhibited that his molars were almost visible. "Now, you're no Mickey Mantle, Charlie, but you might have a chance at becoming the next best thing!"

Chapter Ten:
Saturday, February 27, 1954

Georgetown, Washington, DC

For the first time in weeks, Charlie found himself facing a Saturday and Sunday with no work plans — no receptions or cocktail parties, no hearing preparation or research — so he was determined to make the weekend enjoyable for him and Margaret. On Saturday morning he surprised her with breakfast in bed — toast, eggs, bacon, coffee — though her lingering morning sickness meant most of her bites and sips were in the name of love, not hunger. He settled next to her on the bed and opened up Friday's *Washington Star.* "Should we see a movie?" In New York they saw films so often, it didn't matter which one they picked on any given night since odds were they'd see another within the week. But since moving to Washington, they hadn't been to the cinema once.

Margaret nodded but patted her still-small

belly and said, "I'm asserting my right to pregnancy-veto."

Charlie rolled his eyes playfully and checked the listings.

"How to Marry a Millionaire," Charlie read.

"That's with" — Margaret paused and then whispered breathlessly — "Marilyn Monroe?" She put her finger on her lips, widened her eyes: *Baby girl so confused!*

"All right, all right," Charlie said, smiling, well aware of Margaret's aversion to Miss Cheesecake 1951 — an aversion he didn't share, but now was not the time to press the issue. He glanced at the next ad. *"Hondo,* starring John Wayne."

"Ugh," she said. Two years before, Wayne's *Big Jim McLain* depicted him as a heroic agent of the House Un-American Activities Committee, with cameos by actual HUAC members; ever since, Margaret had considered him a propaganda puppet of the more jingoistic drum majors in the U.S. Congress.

"The Wild One with Brando, that's a no," he announced. Charlie found Brando, and indeed the whole belly-scratching, teeth-picking Method-acting school, mumbly and contrived. "What's *A Lion Is in the Streets* about? Cagney's in it."

"I think it's about a crooked politician."

"No politics, thank you," Charlie said.

"*The Robe* with Richard Burton?"

Margaret leaned closer to Charlie and looked at the ad. "Looks religious," she said. "Let's see something fun; we can do piety and suffering some other time."

That left *Roman Holiday,* a romantic comedy with Gregory Peck and a newcomer named Audrey Hepburn.

Margaret was not only excited to get out of the house but touched by Charlie's effort. Both on their best behavior, later that evening, after a lazy, comfy day at home, they walked hand in hand to the nearby cinema. They'd opted for the Calvert Theater, a classic movie house with luxurious and spacious seating. He put his arm around her as soon as the Paramount Pictures mountain logo appeared on the screen, and she accepted it, nestling into his chest.

He patted her tummy.

"I'm glad the rabbit died," he whispered.

"That's such a strange saying," she whispered back. "The rabbit dies no matter what. They inject my urine into the bunny; a few days later they open the bunny to inspect her ovaries."

"Bunny dies either way?"

"Bunny dies either way."

They enjoyed the film, though they agreed

that the what-might-have-been ending was unsatisfying. Charlie didn't mention to Margaret that he'd grown a bit uncomfortable at the moral dilemma presented to the Gregory Peck character, who opts to do the noble thing; was Charlie choosing the same path? But he'd shaken off the discomfort and lost himself in the charm of the film. Afterward they retreated to Martin's Tavern, a small Italian bistro on Wisconsin Avenue, where they ordered veal piccata and a carafe of Chianti.

They were trying to remind themselves of what they enjoyed about each other outside of the newly hectic tenor of their DC life. Ten days before, Charlie rushed home after the defense appropriations bill markup, excited to show his skeptical wife that his strategy had worked, that the money for Goodstone had been deleted in the latest draft. But even though he raced red lights and arrived home by six thirty, Margaret had already fallen into a deep sleep on the couch. The next morning, still eager to share his news, Charlie headed into the kitchen, only to find Margaret furious. The day before, she'd learned that Gwinnett's research team had returned to Nanticoke and Susquehannock Islands without her. Her encounter with Teardrop the pony was the most noteworthy event in all their research. "But of course, my being a woman — and one with child, no less — all but erases that," she fumed. "Can't wait to see what gender pronouns are used to describe the researcher's encounter with the pony in the final published work!" Charlie tried to be sympathetic, and he realized that this wouldn't be the moment to share his own professional triumph. He left for work feeling vaguely disgruntled, and it wasn't until a day later that she asked him about Goodstone. By then, he'd built up a head of righteous petulance and didn't answer, even though he knew it was childish, and the simmering tensions between them continued.

Tonight, however, they were both trying to put aside the resentments they'd let fester. And as soon as they had their first sips of wine, she brought up the appropriations bill. She reached across the table to hold his hand. "Proud of you," she said. He would have proposed again right there if he'd had a ring.

"It was great," Charlie said. "I was trying to keep a low profile, but during the markup, Chairman Carlin took a moment to thank all the veterans for our service and for sharing our experiences with them. The other guys on the committee applauded; it was really nice."

"And the appropriation money for Goodstone is gone?"

"Gone with the wind," Charlie said. "The provision was literally x-ed out, a line struck through the whole paragraph. And on the floor of the House later, a bunch of the vets — Strongfellow, MacLachlan, Sutton, Street — all patted me on the back. Highlight of the year." He caught himself — Margaret had told him she was pregnant in January. "In terms of Congress, I mean," he added.

The tavern was full of revelers — Georgetown University students, professionals whose postwork happy hours had morphed into sloppy dinners, married couples trying to catch up after busy weeks. It was dark, the restaurant's maroon ceiling and oak floors providing little reflection from the hanging chandeliers and candles on each table. Waiters bustled in and out of the kitchen, ferrying hamburgers, oyster stew, and hot browns to customers, while the saloon seemed almost like an assembly line for martinis.

Margaret rested her elbows on the table and ticked off the names on her fingers.

"Strongfellow is the OSS guy on crutches; MacLachlan, or 'Mac,' is the minister from Indiana; Sutton is the conservative Democrat who's challenging Kefauver. Who's Street?"

"The Tuskegee Airman," Charlie said. "Distinguished Flying Cross."

"Oh, right," she said. "We should have him over for dinner. Is he married?"

"Yes," Charlie said. "With twins. Just born last year."

Margaret shuddered a bit. "Twins! I can't imagine. Let's hope we don't get that lucky," she said with a smile.

"Good God, no. Can't imagine two; I'm terrified of one."

"I wonder if people having twins say, 'The rabbits died.' Or if they think there were three dead rabbits for triplets."

"Good Lord," said Charlie. "If it's triplets, I'll have what the rabbits are having."

She chuckled. "I've been meaning to ask you — does your office manager have children?"

"Miss Leopold? I don't believe she's even married. She's never discussed any family. She wears rings, but none on her left ring finger. I can't imagine she doesn't have suitors — she's a knockout for her age — but none that I know of. Why do you ask?"

"I want to visit your office more," Margaret said. "If this is our life now, I need to get to know the people you're working with."

"Any time. It would be great to show you around the Capitol now that I know it better. I'm close to not getting lost on my way to the bathroom."

"Knockout, huh?" Margaret asked.

"For a woman in her forties," Charlie said. "If you like that Southern-beauty-queen type. Which I don't. Not that you're not a beauty queen."

"Uh-huh," said Margaret, smiling.

"You know what I mean, sweetie. I'm going to go to the bathroom." Charlie excused himself from the table.

"Good idea." Margaret laughed.

On his way back, Charlie spotted the Kennedys — Jack and Jackie and Bob and Ethel — seated at a more private corner table near the back. Jack and Jackie lived across the street and a few doors down from the Marders, on Dent Place, in another Federal-style town house — a much larger one, of course. After they finished dessert and Charlie paid the check, he suggested to Margaret that they go say hi.

"Oh, that seems silly," Margaret said.

"Why? We're neighbors. People do say hi, Margaret."

She rolled her eyes but relented, as he'd

known she would. Even Margaret was not immune to a certain type of luminary.

They approached the Kennedys' table; Bob Kennedy looked up and motioned them closer, his grin deployed instantly and convincingly. Charlie couldn't help wondering if he himself would ever possess the same natural ease; it was definitely an asset in this town.

"You're Winston Marder's boy," Bob Kennedy said, shaking his hand.

"That's right," Charlie said. "My wife, Margaret."

"So nice to meet you," Jackie said in her high, almost childlike voice as she delicately reached out to take Margaret's hand. She was twenty-five but looked eighteen. "You must be the zoologist I've heard so much about!"

"Yes," said Margaret bashfully, unsure of what Jackie had heard and knowing how odd it was for a congressman's wife to have an actual career. Jackie herself had been the "Inquiring Camera Girl" for the *Washington Times-Herald,* though her career seemed to have ended with her marriage to the senator, as was standard. It made Margaret feel self-conscious and she wondered if other wives thought her selfish or a freak.

"Jack," Bob said, "this is the congressman

that's taking on Goodstone. Father told us about it."

His older brother nodded and looked appraisingly at Charlie. "I see," he said non-committally.

"That was a risky venture, what with General Kinetics making a move on them," Bob said. "Lot of money and jobs at stake."

"Lot of lives at stake if they keep making cruddy products," Margaret said. "Charlie lost a soldier because of one of their gas masks." Charlie suddenly realized that she'd helped him finish that large carafe of Chianti over dinner.

Bob and Jack seemed taken aback at her boldness, but then Jack decided to smile, and Jackie and Ethel and Charlie exhaled.

"Quite a firecracker," Jack said to his brother, as if the Marders weren't standing right there.

"She's my lodestar," said Charlie somewhat dramatically, and then, having had his own fair share of Chianti, he found himself reciting a poem he'd read over and over in his tent in France:

A star, but no cold, heavenly star —
A warm red star of welcome in the night.
Far off it burned upon the black hillside,
Sole star of earth in all that waste so

174

wide —
A little human lantern in the night,
Yet more to me than all the bright
Unfriendly stars of heaven, so cold and
    white.

He finished, slightly abashed at this impromptu tableside recital.

"Who is that?" asked Bob. "Gibson?"

"Yes, sir," Charlie said. "And forgive me. The wine."

Bob waved his hand to dismiss any self-consciousness.

"I'm not acquainted with Gibson," said Jackie.

"Wilfrid Gibson," said Jack. "British poet, served in the infantry on the western front in World War One. An admiral gave me a book of his poems after I got back from the island."

"Well, it was just lovely," said Jackie.

"Thank you," said Charlie. "Got me through a few long nights, reading Gibson and thinking of this lady here."

Margaret smiled indulgently and squeezed his arm lightly: a signal. "Anyway, we've taken up enough of your time."

"Do you know Alan Seeger?" Jackie asked.

"Is he in Congress?" Margaret replied.

"No, he was in the French Foreign Legion

during the Great War," Jackie said. "He was killed in Belloy-en-Santerre." She put her hand on her husband's shoulder. "He wrote one of Jack's favorite poems. He asks me to recite it sometimes."

"Harvard man," said Jack. "He joined the Foreign Legion because we hadn't entered the war yet and he wanted to fight. Give us a sample, Jackie."

His wife smiled and began.

I have a rendezvous with Death
At some disputed barricade
When Spring comes back with rustling
    shade
And apple-blossoms fill the air —
I have a rendezvous with Death
When Spring brings back blue days and
    fair.

She stopped and shrugged and Bob began to clap.

"Well done, girl," he said.

Chapter Eleven:
Monday, March 1, 1954 —
Morning

Georgetown, Washington, DC

Margaret sprang from her bed Monday morning at 5:30 as if answering a fire alarm. This was how mornings were for her in this early pregnant state; she snapped from a near-coma into high-adrenaline alertness. She made her way downstairs and started the percolator for Charlie, turning the nearby wall calendar to March while it brewed. The elm that stood in front of their town house was starting to sprout sawtooth leaves. The rising sun presented a clear sky. Was spring here?

The milk truck veered around the corner onto Dent Place; it belched exhaust, jerked forward, and came to an abrupt stop in the middle of the street. The milkman hopped out of his truck. He emptied a milk churn into six bottles and filled his metal carrier. A minute later, he walked up the steps of the Marders' town house and shouted out to Margaret.

"Package on the stoop here," he bellowed. Her previous encounters with the milkman had taught her that he spoke only at top volume.

Charlie appeared in the doorway between the stairwell and the kitchen. "I'll get it, honey." Margaret turned on the radio.

"—dent Eisenhower has asked the Republican Senate leadership to put an end to Senator Joseph McCarthy's one-man prosecutorial hearings," the newsman intoned. "Reliable sources tell this reporter that the president has beseeched McCarthy's GOP colleagues on the subcommittee, including Senator Everett Dirksen of Illinois, to be present any time McCarthy is presiding over a hearing. Eisenhower's secretary of the army, Robert Stevens, last week accused McCarthy of browbeating and humiliating army off—"

Charlie turned off the radio and placed a large box on the kitchen counter. On the side was emblazoned the Janus Electronics logo. Charlie retrieved a steak knife from its drawer.

"What is it?" Margaret asked.

"It's . . ." said Charlie, uncertain. He cut open the box, reached into it, and handed her two electronic contraptions. "Um . . ." He took the instruction manual out of the box. "It's a baby monitor!"

"A what?"

"A baby monitor," Charlie said.

"What's that?" Margaret asked.

"Do you remember a few years ago Zenith had the Radio Nurse? Basically a radio from the kid's room to the living room so parents could hear the baby?"

Margaret thought about it for a second. "I don't think so," she said.

"Apparently it was designed after the Lindbergh baby kidnapping. The original product wasn't very good; it kept picking up other radio signals. Anyway, this is the new technology."

"Who's it from?"

"I think it's from my father," Charlie lied. He thought of LaMontagne's file on Boschwitz, sitting on his office desk, and how whatever he did with it might be wrong.

He was holding that dossier roughly an hour later as he made his way from his congressional office to the House Chamber, where he and his fellow members had been called for a vote on a bill allowing more Mexican migrant workers into the country. Stopping for a cup of coffee at the House Restaurant, Charlie ran into one of his poker buddies, Congressman Chris MacLachlan. The Indiana Republican was devouring a cruller while waiting in line for the cashier in the take-out section of the eatery. In his left hand, he held yet another pastry, this one with some sort of red and purple preserves.

"Hungry?" Charlie asked.

MacLachlan chewed until it was safe to speak. "A tad."

The cashier rang them up and Mac-Lachlan nodded his thanks as he patted his belly, which to Charlie's eye had expanded in the previous month or so. He now looked like someone who had eaten the version of himself depicted in his most recent congressional portrait. MacLachlan seemed to be reading Charlie's thoughts and a sheepish expression crept across his face. "I've got to stop," he acknowledged. He indicated his half-eaten pastry to Charlie. "Want it?"

Charlie shook his head. "I've already had breakfast."

They walked out of the restaurant. Members of Congress and their aides, journalists, and lobbyists filled the hallways. The two congressmen took a left and proceeded up a narrow staircase to the second floor. MacLachlan gestured to a step beneath their feet. "See those stains?" he asked, pointing out clusters of a dozen dark brown splotches on the seventh and eighth marble steps. "Congressman William Taulbee's blood."

"What?"

"A reporter killed Taulbee in 1890, shot him dead right here. Long and seedy story, but bottom line: The reporter wrote about an affair Taulbee had. Taulbee beat him up. And then one day the reporter brought a pistol to the Capitol and shot him."

They began walking up the stairs again, MacLachlan breathing heavily, removing his pocket square to blot beads of perspiration starting to form on his upper lip.

"I definitely do not recall hearing about Taulbee being murdered right here during my high-school tour of the Capitol," Charlie said. "But then again, they didn't talk much about the ugly bits."

"Ha, no, the tour guides don't talk about it. I've been visiting the members-only collection at the Library of Congress. Fascinating stuff in there — as a scholar, you should really check it out. An incredible collection of history nobody seems to know about."

"And there's a section on Taulbee?"

"On him and others whose ghosts haunt these halls. Civil War soldiers and the like." He lowered his voice dramatically. "Some people claim to have seen Taulbee's ghost right on the stairway."

"I never understood the whole ghost phenomenon," Charlie mused. "People only claim to see historic figures or those killed under horrific conditions. But what about all the old people who died? If there's a world with ghosts, shouldn't we be constantly walking through hundreds of apparitions of just regular old people?"

"You raise a decent point," said MacLachlan. "And it cannot be mere injustice that provokes a haunting — why, there have been people killed for unjust reasons all over this city; we'd all be haunted day and night. Perhaps it's the *specialness* of the death that creates the need for a ghost to haunt. And this was odd, a journalist killing a congressman at the Capitol!"

"And we think today's reporters are rough," Charlie joked.

MacLachlan raised an eyebrow. "We do? I don't. You've gotten some tough coverage?"

Charlie thought about it. There had been a few vicious jabs at him in tabloid political columns — mostly about his father's role in his appointment and his privileged background — but as a married academic and war veteran with a shiny clean reputation, he had largely avoided bad ink. The same could not be said for his predecessor, Congressman Van Waganan, whose reputation was still being dragged through the grimiest mud imaginable, with no lurid rumor spared repetition.

"I suppose not, not me personally," Charlie admitted as they continued their journey toward the second floor.

"Truth is, most of our so-called Fourth Estate is focused on nonsense. Even the ones fixated on McCarthy's daily theater. Same so-called journalists he's attacking as Commies today were only too happy to give McCarthy's character-assassination campaign front-page attention a few years ago with nary a scintilla of editorial discretion or judgment that what he was peddling was pure balderdash. As if there does not exist such a thing as empirical fact!"

"You don't think there are Reds in the government, Mac?" Charlie was surprised to hear MacLachlan's skepticism about McCarthy, given his deep conservatism and loathing of the Godless Communists. He'd made a few comments over poker one night about how happy he was that Alger Hiss was in Lewisburg Federal Prison; he'd been imprisoned for perjury, since the statute of limitations had run out on his acts of espionage. "I don't care if they get him for jaywalking as long as they get him," he'd said.

"*Of course* there are Reds in the government," MacLachlan replied. "They're infesting it like termites. But McCarthy isn't finding them. *Hoover* is. McCarthy hasn't produced the name of one proven, clear, actual Communist agent. Not one! And that's not even the point. It's a distraction, or — what did Isaiah call it? — the old okey-doke. Look over here! Look over here! And meanwhile your pocket's being picked."

"Yeah, he said that about the comic-book hearings," Charlie said, wincing a bit internally at the thought of an event he dreaded.

MacLachlan patted his shoulder and grinned. "Better you than me, my friend." Charlie grimaced and followed MacLachlan down two hallways of the second floor to the door of the Speaker's Lobby. "Talking about ghosts, Charlie, John Quincy Adams is said to haunt this room," he said, opening one of the doors; Charlie peered inside. "In the middle of a debate over some fairly innocuous issue, he had a stroke on the House floor," MacLachlan said, pointing at a sturdy couch with light green cushions. "The Adams box sofa, where he died. Awful way to go."

"Can't think of many good ones," Charlie replied. "Hey, where are the Senate bathtubs, the place where Vice President Wilson fell asleep, nearly froze to death, and then died of a stroke?"

"In the basement somewhere," Mac-Lachlan said. "The basements here are confusing and they go on forever, like ancient caves."

"I've heard that sometimes late at night, right outside the room where Vice President Wilson died, folks can catch a whiff of the soap they once used."

"Yes, I've heard those tales as well," said MacLachlan. "And some people claim they hear Wilson coughing. All very silly. Like the wails of agony from the ghost of the Union soldier who died in the Capitol Rotunda. The tales are nonsense. But the deaths are very real. And those are just the ones we know about. Think of all the . . . *inconvenient* people over the years who must have met their ends in this building or nearby and then vanished forever."

Charlie was too startled to ask what in the hell MacLachlan was talking about, and anyway they were now walking onto the House floor, where hundreds of members of Congress were convening. They joined a small circle of friendly faces. No one seemed to be paying much attention to the debate at the front of the room about whether or not to allow more Mexican migrant workers into the country. Democratic congressman Ray Madden was railing against the bill, which he claimed would allow Mexicans to "take over jobs that millions of unemployed Americans are entitled to."

On the floor, House Speaker Joe Martin, a Republican from Massachusetts with a boyish face and a mass of hair he always had to brush away from his eyes, was diligently trying to buttress his narrow seven-seat Republican majority by enlisting the support of Southern Democrats eager to help the farmers and big businesses who relied upon cheap Mexican labor.

Strongfellow swung himself over to Charlie on his crutches.

"Ted Williams broke his collarbone today," Strongfellow said.

"How?" asked Congressman Ben Jensen. He was a mousy Midwest Republican who had served in World War One and loved talking about Iowa.

"Shoestring catch," said Strongfellow. "Line drive."

"He's about twenty pounds overweight," noted Charlie.

"Ike is dropping another H-bomb on the Marshall Islands today," said Democratic congressman George Hyde Fallon, a machine politician from Baltimore. "And you

186

fools are talking about Ted Williams's collarbone."

They tried and failed to look contrite. The debate over the migrant-worker bill continued, with various House deputy whips dispatched to corral votes.

Charlie leaned closer to Strongfellow and said in a low voice, "Phil, I need a favor."

"Anything," he said.

"I'm trying to find out about a Pentagon-backed study done at the University of Chicago," Charlie said, reaching into his inside suit pocket to retrieve the notes Bernstein had handed him earlier that day. "Something to do with cereal grains and broadleaf crops. It's blocked by wartime secrecy laws. I thought maybe your Armed Services Committee connections could help me get it unblocked."

"Done," said Strongfellow, seemingly unsurprised by the request and uninterested in its origins. Charlie imagined he was used to doling out random favors and just as used to calling them in when he needed to. Strongfellow took the paper Charlie handed him and slipped it into his inside suit pocket, nodded, and shuffled away to talk to someone presumably more important. Charlie took a seat and listened to the conversations fluttering around his head like a flock of startled pigeons:

I'm not going to do it if you're not.
I said at least buy me dinner first if you're
    going to fuck me, Mr. Chairman.
What do we care about cheap Mexican
    labor in Maine?
Technically he's a socialist, not a Com-
    munist, but that's an argument for him to
    make, not me.
My constituents couldn't give a shit about
    Syria.
Doris Day, I think.
That hairdo might be the worst cover-up in
    political history.

MacLachlan eased himself into the chair next to Charlie's; it creaked under the sudden weight. "How are you going to vote?" he asked.

"Not too many crops on the Upper West Side," Charlie said.

"That's fine if you don't have national ambitions," MacLachlan said. "Jack Kennedy's going to get screwed in the Midwest in '56 because of his hostility to my people."

"Your people?"

"Farmers," MacLachlan said. "Though I suppose this is all going to get wrapped into the farm bill anyway."

188

"When you say these issues are all a distraction, the juvenile delinquency hearings, McCarthy naming names, this migrant debate," Charlie asked, stealing a glance at the file folder on his lap, "you're leaving out a key part of the puzzle."

"And what's that?"

"Distraction from what? You think this is all being done to keep our eyes off the ball. What's the ball?"

Before MacLachlan could answer, Charlie heard a tumult above him. He followed the sound to the visitors' gallery, where four tourists were brandishing a Puerto Rican flag.

"*¡Viva Puerto Rico libre!*" they shouted. "*¡Viva Puerto Rico libre!*"

Then came sounds — *Pop! Pop! Pop! Pop!* — echoing throughout the House Chamber.

Charlie heard a colleague mutter something about firecrackers. But Charlie knew the sounds, as did MacLachlan. It was a gun. More specifically, a German pistol, probably a .38. Members of Congress and their aides were shouting, some running for the exit doors, others hitting the ground or seeking shelter behind chairs or tables.

Snapping back to wartime training, Charlie took cover, leaping behind a small oak desk used by House Republican leaders, and assessed the situation. One, then two bullets whizzed past his head.

The shots seemed to be coming from the visitors' gallery, and they were clearly being aimed at members of Congress standing on the floor of the House Chamber. Were they targeting anyone in particular? He couldn't tell.

He heard a grunt and turned around to see blood spreading across the chest of Alvin Bentley, a strapping Michigan Republican with a crew cut and glasses; he fell back on the floor, a confused look on his face.

Ben Jensen, whom Charlie had exchanged pleasantries with minutes earlier, fell forward abruptly, blood spurting from his right shoulder.

Shot after shot after shot streamed across the floor. It was all happening in just seconds but it felt endless. *Where the hell are the Capitol Police?* Charlie wondered.

The scene was chaos. Charlie watched in horror as George Hyde Fallon fell to the ground. Seconds later, Cliff Davis, the old Tennessee Democrat who was a former judge and Klansman, was shot in the leg and went down.

Charlie, crouched behind the desk, was getting his bearings and trying to figure out how to respond. He locked eyes with Congressman James Van Zandt, a Pennsylvania Republican and navy captain who had served in both world wars. Van Zandt pointed to the stairwell that led to the visitors' gallery.

Charlie tapped his chest, then pointed up and swirled his finger to suggest motion; he would stand and distract the shooters.

Van Zandt nodded. They had a plan.

Three . . . two . . . one . . .

Charlie stood and looked up to the gallery.

All four of the Puerto Rican activists — three men and one woman, in their twenties and thirties — were brandishing firearms. An elderly tourist was frantically trying to grab one of the guns; he was weak but determined. One of the shooters hit him in the head with the butt of his rifle, sending him falling into the aisle. Two of the shooters spotted Charlie and took aim at him. Charlie faked left, then moved right. Van Zandt suddenly appeared in the visitors' gallery and tackled one of them, and before the shooters could respond, a half a dozen Capitol Police officers entered the balcony and descended on them.

Charlie ran to Jensen; Isaiah Street was already checking his neck for a pulse.

"Medic!" Charlie yelled, as if he were back in France. "Medic!" But no medic appeared.

Somewhere in the distance, a bit bizarrely, Speaker Martin declared the House to be in recess.

All Charlie could see was a blur of panicked faces of politicians and pages. The gunfire had ceased. Street, crouched over Jensen, was attempting to plug the bleeding hole in Jensen's shoulder as if he were a sinking ship.

A burly redheaded page, maybe eighteen, approached Charlie and asked if he was all right. It was only then that Charlie looked down and saw that his white oxford shirt was soaked with blood. He patted himself down, found no obvious wounds, and continued trying to tend to Jensen with Street. He suddenly wondered what had happened to MacLachlan and turned his head to the spot where the two had been sitting. There he saw MacLachlan on the floor, a dark stain expanding at the small of his back, prone and as still as a stone.

CHAPTER TWELVE:
MONDAY, MARCH 1, 1954 —
AFTERNOON

Eastern Dispensary Casualty Hospital,
Southeast Washington, DC

Charlie sat in the emergency room examination area, separated from other patients by maroon curtains. A nurse's brief inspection had ended when she concluded that the blood on his shirt wasn't his; she told Charlie to relax and wait for a doctor to discharge him. The surrounding cubicles were full of congressmen who were actually wounded; she scurried off to join the other nurses and doctors tending to them. Charlie lay back on the examination table, listening to the conversations swirling around the busy room, sounding as if they were far away.

Where's the trauma patient?
MacLachlan. OR.
Bad?
One bullet lodged in his spine, between L two and three. Another one shredded

his spleen.

How many congressmen were shot?

Six total. Four here. Jensen and Davis at Bethesda.

Let me see. Bentley took one to the chest. He looked dead when he got here.

He's critical in the OR. I'd say it's fifty-fifty. Bullet perforated the right lung, went through the diaphragm, liver, stomach.

Marder is over there; he's fine. Fallon — bullet through his right thigh. He's stable. Over there, Roberts, shot in his left leg, bullet entered thigh above knee and went downward. Also stable.

The squeaky wheels of a gurney ripped Charlie out of his dream state; he focused his attention on the examination cubicle to his left, where he could hear Fallon offering faint responses to a doctor's questions. The hospital intercom blared periodic bulletins: a certain doctor was needed in the OR, a different one was needed in the ER. Background beeps from machines were randomly scattered through the area, like the sounds of birds and bugs around a campsite.

They just caught a fourth Puerto Rican at the bus station.

Suction, please.

I don't understand. This is about independence?

Something like that.

Doesn't American Sugar own half the island?

I'm not saying they don't have a grievance
or two. Hemostat. Hold that there. Just
like that, right. Good.

They tried to assassinate Truman.

When was that, '50?

Something like that. Blair House.

Killed a cop.

Yes, I remember because that was the
year I got married and we were going to
honeymoon in Puerto Rico but we had
to cancel because of riots.

Well, you know what they say: One man's
terrorist is another man's freedom fighter.

Dr. Klein!

He can't hear us.

Obviously these are murderous zealots.

I'm just saying they see themselves as
minutemen.

Dr. Klein!

Harriet, I didn't say I see them that way.

Didn't the Puerto Ricans vote not long ago
to remain an American commonwealth?
Did I dream that?

There are people around —

Charlie's eavesdropping was interrupted by a sharp voice he recognized: "Can you please just tell me where my husband is?"

"Margaret!" He stood and poked his head through the curtains. She ran to him and buried herself in his embrace. She pulled away to look at him and then burst into tears.

"Margaret, Margaret, I'm okay," he said. "This isn't my blood."

She wiped her eyes and took a deep breath.

"I've never even heard of this hospital," she said.

"It's closest to the Capitol."

She crossed her arms and looked at him sternly. "I was told about your 'heroics' today." And then she punched him with both fists, not hard, but not jokingly either. He grasped her wrists and held them gently, lowered his forehead to meet hers. They stayed there silently, the buzz and hum of the hospital noises surrounding them.

Both Bentley and MacLachlan were still in surgery when Charlie was discharged that evening. In the waiting room he ran into

Strongfellow.

"What are you hearing?" he asked Charlie.

"I overheard a doctor saying Bentley is fifty-fifty," Charlie said. "They're even less optimistic about Mac." Margaret tugged him toward the door. He shook Strongfellow's hand in parting. "I'll come back in the morning."

A Capitol Police officer hailed a cab for the two of them. The car radio was broadcasting news about the shooting.

"Could you turn that off, please?" Margaret asked the cabbie, who complied.

They sat in silence for fifteen blocks.

Finally, Margaret said, "I was talking with my sister on the phone when all of a sudden there was someone at the door. It was Jackie Kennedy; she'd heard what happened and ran over to make sure I knew. So I turned on the radio."

Her bottom lip was quivering; having been tested at such a young age by her father's death, Margaret was not one for whom tears came quickly. She looked out the window as Charlie reached to hold her hand. She took it, intertwined her fingers with his.

"The reporter on the radio knew nothing. Shooting in the House, at least half a dozen members rushed to area emergency rooms,

197

blah-blah-blah. He seemed far more interested in the assailants than the victims. Puerto Rican extremists, one a woman. A note in her purse said something about her blood, the independence of Puerto Rico, the subjugation of her people . . . The reporter read every word of the note, as if it explained this, as if it justified it. I turned off the radio. It was making me sick."

Charlie noticed her absentmindedly place her left hand over her abdomen, underlining why this had shaken her so badly.

"I tried to call your office, the Speaker's office, House leadership, the cloakroom, all those numbers you gave me, but all the lines were busy," she went on. "Couldn't get through to police, couldn't get through to any emergency rooms."

"How'd you find me?"

"Sheryl Ann Bernstein called me and told me where you were. While I was waiting for the cab, Miss Leopold called to tell me too. They said they'd been trying to call but the switchboard was jammed."

He gripped her hand more tightly. "I'm so sorry, Margaret. I had blood on me, so they whisked me away. There was no phone for me to call you from; the hospital said they had to keep their lines open. It was total chaos."

But she was looking out the window again, distracted and still angry. "Sheryl Ann told me what you did. To draw fire. You didn't have to be a goddamn hero. Good headlines aren't going to be of any use to a baby without a father. *My* father got plenty of headlines after the crash. Worthless."

She let go of his hand and continued staring out the window as evening fell upon Washington. He looked out his.

It was almost disconcerting, after the violent chaos of the day, to find their tree-lined street and stately town house quiet and unaltered under the street lamps. Life had changed forever a few miles away; here, it was just the same. They got out of the cab and walked silently up the stairs and inside, both too numb to speak more than necessary.

While he took a shower, she made soup, and he came down and ate it hungrily. Before long he had passed out on the living-room sofa in front of the gray haze of the television, immune to the comedic charms of Sid Caesar. Margaret woke him and gently guided him up the two flights to their bedroom. Hours later, though it felt like seconds, he was jolted awake by Margaret's hand on his shoulder. He had been dreaming of Private Rodriguez. "Charlie, Congressman Street is at the door."

Charlie sat up and rubbed his eyes. His muscles ached. "What time is it?"

"It's morning."

"What does he want?"

"He wants to bring you to the hospital. Mac is out of surgery and it doesn't look good."

Charlie dressed quickly and headed downstairs to find Street and Margaret at the kitchen table drinking coffee, their faces somber. Street's eyes met Charlie's and he gave a small shake of his head, then he stood up and reached for his fedora.

The Capitol Police officer standing guard outside MacLachlan's room at Casualty Hospital balked when he saw Street. Other than orderlies and the custodial staff, few nonwhites were seen here. Most of the city's black population went to Freedmen's Hospital for medical treatment.

"He's a member of Congress, as am I, and we're here to see our friend," Charlie said, and he walked past the guard. Street looked at the police officer, who nodded sullenly in acknowledgment.

Inside the dimly lit room, MacLachlan lay still, an oxygen mask over his face, his chest slowly rising and falling with each struggling breath. MacLachlan's wife sat by his side, her eyes puffy from hours of weeping. She wore pearls and a pink suit — more Beltway than Terre Haute; she looked as if she'd been at a Daughters of the American Revolution luncheon when she got word of the shooting the day before.

Jesus, thought Charlie, *was that only just yesterday?* It felt like a month had passed; this was a whole new Washington, DC, reality to which he hadn't yet adjusted, one where death wasn't something that happened just to our boys in Korea.

The tiny room was crowded: House Speaker Joe Martin was standing off to the side talking to majority leader Charles Halleck from MacLachlan's home state of Indiana and Democratic leader Sam Rayburn of Texas. Near them stood the vice president, Richard Nixon, with a complexion almost as wan as the patient's.

Charlie and Street introduced themselves to MacLachlan's wife, Henrietta, who struggled to maintain her composure. She raised her hands helplessly. "The idea that he could survive the Nazis in France but not the Puerto Ricans in Washington . . ." Her eyes darted toward Street, presumably to see if he might have taken offense. But Street's face revealed only sympathy.

"I've known him for only a short while," Charlie told her, "but he is one of the most principled men I've ever met. And he's strong. If anyone can fight this and survive, it will be him." The words rang hollow as he said them. In France, he had seen the mightiest fighters perish in pathetic accidents and the weakest cowards make it through the grisliest of conflicts. None of it meant anything.

"Oh, Congressman Marder, he has such nice things to say about you," she replied.

The room settled into silence for a few moments until two staff members poked their heads in the doorway to retrieve Vice President Nixon, followed not long afterward by aides collecting the Speaker of the House. Charlie and Street engaged in some small talk with Halleck and Rayburn.

"How are the others?" Street asked.

"They're okay," Rayburn said. "Better 'n Mac."

"We just saw Davis and Jensen at Bethesda," said Halleck. "They're sharing a room. Doctors say they're going to be fine."

"Sumbitches were arguing." Rayburn chortled softly, casting a cautious glance toward Mrs. MacLachlan before he lowered his voice. "Davis wanted to listen to *The Lone Ranger* on the radio. Jensen wanted music, said he'd had all the shooting he could take for one day."

Charlie smiled politely, too aware of the gravity of MacLachlan's situation to feel comfortable joking at his bedside about survivors. He and Street sat down on two metal folding chairs and stared at the patient as he labored to breathe. They didn't know what to say or where to look.

"Mrs. MacLachlan, Sam and I need to stop by and visit some of the other wounded members of Congress," Halleck said, "but we'll be back soon. If there is anything at all we can do for you, please don't hesitate to call."

She accepted his farewell absently, with a small nod. The congressmen made their way out of the room and Charlie turned his attention to the bed. In addition to the oxygen mask, MacLachlan had two IVs that were dripping clear fluids into his forearms. Charlie was following the trail of a blue tube from MacLachlan's arm through a mess of cords and wires when Street nudged him.

MacLachlan's eyes were open.

His wife jumped to her feet. "Christian?" Mrs. MacLachlan asked "Christian?"

MacLachlan didn't move his head or neck. He blinked rapidly, a look of incomprehension on his face. His gaze shifted from right to left, taking in Charlie and Street, and then to his wife. His right hand slowly rose from the bed, and she clasped it with both of hers; tears began to stream down her cheeks.

MacLachlan struggled to speak; he laboriously yanked the oxygen mask from his face. His wife gasped and looked at Charlie and Street, alarmed. MacLachlan, grimacing with pain, turned his eyes to Charlie and sent him a piercing glare.

"Jen . . . Jennifer," MacLachlan said. "Under Jennifer."

He looked depleted by the effort; his eyes closed as the oxygen machine suddenly emitted alarmed, loud beeps. Two nurses and a doctor raced into the room. A nurse replaced the oxygen mask, then looked over her shoulder at Street and Charlie. "Gentlemen, we're going to have to ask you to leave," she said firmly. Charlie and Street barely had time to grab their coats before the door slammed behind them.

"Jesus," Street said.

Charlie was shaking his head, trying to make sense of what they'd just heard.

" 'Under Jennifer'?"

CHAPTER THIRTEEN:
THURSDAY, MARCH 4, 1954 —
MORNING

Capitol Hill

Charlie felt as spent as a wrung dishrag. He pushed himself up from his chair and dragged himself out of his office to walk to the Capitol. A joint session of Congress awaited him, where he would be treated to a bipartisan welcoming of the governor-general of Canada. Part of Charlie couldn't believe — indeed, was appalled — that so many folks proceeded as if there hadn't been a mass shooting in the House Chamber just three days ago. It felt as though they were behaving as if the shooting was a normal, if unfortunate, event — a fender bender, a coffee spill, though all six wounded members of Congress remained in the hospital, MacLachlan in a coma. Charlie tried to continue his day-to-day activities in a barely awake zombielike state he hadn't experienced since France.

From the end of the hallway, he heard a

familiar voice. "You okay?" He turned around to see Davis LaMontagne and was instantly reminded of the lobbyist's request and the damning folder about Boschwitz, the one Charlie had last seen right before the Puerto Ricans started shooting. In the previous three weeks, Charlie had studiously avoided saying anything other than a brief hello to LaMontagne, and here he was to finally force the matter.

"Davis," Charlie said. "Damn."

"You didn't give it to anyone?" LaMontagne said.

"I lost it on the House floor during the shooting," Charlie conceded.

LaMontagne's face was hard to read. "I gave you that folder three weeks ago. You were still carrying it around Monday?"

"Yes," said Charlie. "Sorry."

"And you don't know where it is, I presume?"

"I don't."

LaMontagne's eyes narrowed.

"You do know six congressmen got shot?" Charlie asked, an edge in his voice. "And that MacLachlan's probably going to die?"

LaMontagne turned around without answering and walked away down the hall. Charlie shook his head in disbelief.

"What was all that about?"

Charlie turned; Isaiah Street emerged from around a corner of the hallway, where apparently he'd heard the exchange.

"You know how once you get this job, everybody wants something from you?" Charlie asked as the two proceeded down the four flights of stairs.

"You bet," said Street. "Everybody from the Speaker to my aunt Estelle. So?" Street prompted as they both stopped on the second floor to light cigarettes. "What's LaMontagne after you for?"

"He wanted me to provide the McCarthy Committee with some pretty damning information about one of his business competitors."

"And is the competitor a Red?"

Charlie shrugged as he put away his German lighter. "Dunno. Maybe. I was supposed to give it to Bob Kennedy. Three weeks ago."

"Just taking your time."

"I don't know why I was waiting so long."

"Yes, you do."

"Yes, I do."

Cigarettes in hand, they proceeded down the stairs.

"Listen, speaking of requests, I was just about to make one of you," Street said. "I want you to use your Manhattan connections to block permitting on a General Kinetics factory they're trying to build in Harlem. Civil rights activists in New York are making this a national cause, so I'm getting heat back home too."

"They want to stop it? They don't want the jobs? I can't imagine Congressman Powell trying to stop any employment opportunities in Harlem."

"No, you're right. Powell isn't on board with me here."

"So why are you and the civil rights activists opposed?"

"It's a chemical plant, Charlie. Vinyl chloride."

Charlie looked at him blankly.

"Have you ever heard of Mossville, Louisiana?"

"Where?"

The two exited the House Office Building, where tourists were gathering, many living up to their stereotype in gaudy and inappropriately casual dress, Pentax cameras hanging like albatrosses around the necks of the dads. In an apparent show of force in the wake of the shooting, two Capitol Police officers stood at the corner; they nodded at Charlie and ignored Street. A chill remained in the air, for which the coatless congressmen braced themselves, but the sun was blinding, and spring had unmistakably arrived.

They stopped at the crosswalk of Independence Avenue, where the driver of a red convertible Mustang honked at them. It took them a second to realize it was Strongfellow; he stopped his car even though he had a green light. "Hey, boys!" he shouted. "You coming tonight?" Other cars began steering around him on the four-lane road, some honking angrily. The Capitol Police ignored the transgression.

"How on earth can you afford those wheels?" Street asked him.

"Rights to my life story paid for it," Strongfellow said. "What do you think of James Dean for the movie?"

"As the car?" Charlie quipped.

"Har-de-har-har," Strongfellow said. A dairy-truck driver shook a fist out his window as he leaned on his horn, while more cars backed up behind him. Strongfellow maneuvered his way closer to the curb, making it only slightly easier for anyone to pass him. "I was going to call you, Charlie, to make sure you're coming tonight."

"To what?" Charlie asked.

"Party in Connie Hilton's suite at the Mayflower. Invitation only. Black tie."

"Hilton's throwing a party?" asked Charlie. "What for?"

"Let me guess," said Street, knowing that he wasn't invited for obvious reasons. "For reauthorizing the Mexican migrant workers. So he can keep paying pennies to his hotel maids and kitchen staff."

"Winner!" shouted Strongfellow, cheerfully oblivious to the traffic chaos he was still causing. A moving-van driver blared his horn, leaning out his window and cursing at Strongfellow. It was tough to make out every word of the explosive monologue but certain terms were loud and clear. Charlie wondered how long Strongfellow might sit there tying up traffic, since law enforcement seemed uninterested in the matter. Strongfellow ignored it all completely.

"Bill got through the Senate and is now on its way to Ike," he said. "I'm not exactly sure who's throwing the party. Some club that Carlin is a member of? Hey — did you hear Senator Lehman claimed that a hundred Commies cross the Mexican border every day?"

"A hundred a day?" asked Charlie as another car honked at Strongfellow; Charlie felt slightly embarrassed to be part of this spectacle of entitlement. "Where does a claim like that even come from?"

"One's nether regions, I suppose," said

Strongfellow.

"And Humphrey backed him," said Street. "He said the Reds have one of their strongest infiltration programs out of Mexico."

"Mexico?" asked Charlie incredulously.

"Kennedy voted against the braceros bill," Street said. "Kefauver too. Big labor flexing some muscle."

A heavy-duty Mack truck pulled up behind Strongfellow, and its driver started pounding on the horn.

Strongfellow sighed as if to say, *Impatient drivers will be the death of us all,* and eased his car into first gear. "So nine p.m. at the Mayflower?" Strongfellow asked as he pulled away. "See you there, Charlie."

"Wait, Phil —" Charlie began, but it was too late; Strongfellow was already a full city block away, driving as if he were in the Grand Prix.

The light turned green and Charlie and Street crossed the street, resuming their walk toward the Capitol. The white and pink flowers of the cherry blossom trees were beginning to bud. Groundskeepers unfurled rolls of sod to cover the acres of barren, frozen dirt surrounding the Capitol grounds; turf harvesting was a postwar agricultural development that significantly enhanced the appearance of the capital's tourist spots.

"What did you want to ask him?"

"It's dumb. This note I found in my desk maybe belonged to Van Waganan," Charlie said. "Scribbles about broadleaf crops and the University of Chicago. My intern called and wasn't able to get any information about it because of wartime secrecy laws. Phil said he'd look into it for me."

"Sounds pretty random."

"It is. I don't know much about Van Waganan. It's probably nothing."

"All I know about him is that his body was found in a cheap hotel room next to a dead hooker. That might be as much as I need to know, to be honest."

Charlie stopped walking and looked at Street, stunned. "Really? A hooker? Everything I've heard made it sound like it was suicide."

"Nope," said Street. "They kept it out of the papers, a friend of mine with connections told me. To spare his family, they put the hooker's dead body in a different room."

"And what do they think happened?"

"They have no idea," said Street. "It remains an open case."

"Amazing. A dead congressman is an open case."

"In company towns, like this one or

Hollywood or Detroit or Nashville, police are often encouraged to let some crimes go unsolved. People in power don't want them solved."

"What?"

"Someday, for kicks, go to the homicide division here in DC and see how many dead young women are in the cold-case files. Attractive ones. You'll be stunned."

"Right, but Van Waganan and a dead prostitute — that has to be some form of murder-suicide, no?"

"All I know is what my guy told me. They think he didn't kill her and she didn't kill him. No cause of death. No evidence of sexual contact. There was no evidence of any relationship at all, actually — no phone records, no witnesses. Nothing tying the two together."

"Other than their corpses being found in the same room," Charlie said.

"Right." Street laughed. "Except that."

"It's hard to believe the local police wouldn't care about such a case," Charlie said.

"They care," said Street. "But when there's a VIP involved, the FBI bursts in and claims jurisdiction and that's it. We don't hear about it after that. Hoover's own private police force."

They continued into the Capitol Building and walked up the stairs to the House Chamber. By now Charlie knew better than to ask Street if he was offended at not having been invited to the party that evening. With the exception of the veterans' poker night, Street shunned most social functions, presumably to avoid the blatant racism so prevalent in Washington. Which wasn't to say he was a shrinking violet; Street ate daily at the purportedly whites-only House Dining Room, and he didn't give an inch when bigotry reared its head in his presence, routinely challenging the offhand remarks and "funny stories" that exposed his colleagues' often unwitting, careless prejudices. Did Street care that he wasn't invited to the bacchanal tonight? He'd already made it clear to Charlie that he far preferred to spend his evenings with his wife and twin baby boys than with most members of Congress. "Honestly, Charlie, most of them are just imbeciles," he said once.

They reached the second floor of the Capitol Building, and Charlie paused to look at the immense oil painting of the Founding Fathers that hung on the wall of the landing. As imagined by artist Howard Chandler Christy, George Washington stood on a dais in Philadelphia's Independence

Hall in 1787, lit and posed as if God had just handed down to him the U.S. Constitution. James Madison sat in the front row, a worried expression on his face, while front and center sat Alexander Hamilton, whispering into the ear of a lounging Benjamin Franklin. It was a complicated portrayal, half class photo of almost forty Founding Fathers, half patriotic rah-rah. Since it had been painted, fourteen years earlier, *Scene at the Signing of the Constitution of the United States* had become one of the most famous works of art in the country.

So much had changed since the last time he'd stopped to look at the portrait, a few weeks before. He'd been with MacLachlan and Street, all of them on their way from the House Chamber to their offices after a vote, Bernstein in tow with a sheaf of phone messages for Charlie's attention.

"Hold up," MacLachlan had called out from the second floor as the others headed downstairs. They turned and rejoined him. MacLachlan was staring up at the painting as he reached into his jacket pocket and pulled out a leaflet. "I've been meaning to get a better look at this. Christy spent years chasing down portraits of all these men, it says here." He waved the leaflet toward the painting, then turned with a grin to the others. "Can you name them all?"

"This a pop quiz, Mac?" Street asked.

"Thirty-nine people signed the Constitution; you want me to ID all of them?" Charlie protested. But he accepted the challenge and proceeded to rattle off names with ease, aware that he was showing off but unable to resist.

"Okay, that's John Dickinson," Charlie said, walking up a couple of stairs and pointing to the right of Washington's table. The painting was so enormous, the figures were almost life-size. "But that's not accurate, he signed the Constitution by proxy. He wasn't there that day; he was sick."

"Not bad," said MacLachlan.

"As far as I know, there aren't any portraits anywhere of two of the signers, Jacob Broom and Thomas FitzSimons," Charlie continued. "We — history — have no idea what they look like. So on this, one of them must be that guy whose face is blocked by Charles Cotesworth Pinckney's arm, and the other is next to Dickinson, with just the top of his wig showing? Is that right?"

"Very nice," Street said, looking over Mac-Lachlan's shoulder at the key.

Charlie had continued to name the signers, frankly enjoying the chance to flex his academic muscles, unused since December exams and, until then, of no interest to his congressional colleagues. He'd been grateful to MacLachlan for allowing the lowliest freshman in Congress a brief moment in the sun.

And now, standing in the same spot just a few weeks later, looking up at the immense painting that filled the entire wall, he felt both small and acutely aware of MacLachlan's absence. He had tried to project strength to Henrietta MacLachlan, but he felt as though they both knew she would soon be a widow. Street lightly tapped Charlie's shoulder, seeming to know the reason behind the moment of melancholy, and they resumed their journey.

Street led the way and they found two seats in the House Chamber. Charlie sat right behind Congressman Adam Clayton Powell Jr. Charlie thought about the two men and their wildly different approaches to dealing with the ubiquitous racism Charlie had only really started to notice since becoming Street's friend. Street had told him that after Powell was elected to Congress in 1944, Speaker Rayburn had cautioned him not to push matters too quickly. "Adam, everybody thinks you're coming down here with a bomb in each hand. Maybe you are. But don't throw them. Feel your way around. You have a great future." That had lasted all of eight weeks, until Powell stood on the House floor and called for the impeachment of a Mississippi Democrat who said *nigger* and *kike* almost as often as he said *hello* and *good-bye*.

Beyond their race and job, Street and Powell had not much in common. For one, no one would ever mistake Street for a white man, as happened with Powell. In that, Street's election by the good people of Chicago's North Side — academics and liberal Jews in addition to a sizable black population — was a radical act for an era when Lena Horne was considered exotic. At Colgate, Powell had been able to "pass" and join a white fraternity. Street, who attended Morehouse, couldn't and wouldn't."

In a way, Charlie thought as he tuned out the Canadian governor-general, Street conducted himself according to the stark black-and-white limitations of newspaper photographs. Powell thrived in his world of ethical and moral grays; he was on his second marriage, to a Trinidadian singer, and was rumored to live in a Long Island estate far from his Harlem district, enjoying a chauffeur-driven limousine of mysterious provenance. But beyond his fondness for drink, which was common to most of the veterans Charlie knew, Street was the picture of moral rectitude. When poker nights devolved into bawdy tales of grateful or desperate French or Filipino women, Street would shake his head and focus on the game. Unlike many of the other young veterans, including Charlie, Street had not added any postwar padding.

Charlie couldn't imagine what it was like for Isaiah to have risked everything for his nation in war and then return home and be treated not just as a lower caste but a potential menace. They had known each other for only two months, but Charlie's glances at the world through his friend's eyes had been revelatory. He was shocked by the disregard and hostility shown to Street by their fellow congressmen. Congressman Howard Smith of Virginia was one of the worst offenders, a man who would proudly proclaim his bigoted views from his perch on the Rules Committee. He automatically blocked any legislation that might help blacks and often pompously declared that the good folk of the Commonwealth of Virginia had "never accepted the colored race as a race of people who had equal intelligence to the white people of the South." He said this within yards of Powell and Street and was applauded by his fellow

Southern Democrats for doing so. After a particularly egregious display in which Judge Smith said that Truman's move to desegregate the army meant the United States would never again win a war, Charlie had tried to stand and register a protest, but Street, seated nearby, caught Charlie's eye and shook his head slightly, motioning for him to stay seated.

"That kind of thinking isn't going to be defeated by you taking on Judge Smith," Street said at the time as they walked from the House floor. "Remember what Branch Rickey said to Jackie Robinson: 'I'm looking for a ballplayer with guts enough *not* to fight back!' " Street and Charlie rarely talked about race, but it was the subtext of many policy debates, not to mention the culture. Charlie suspected that Street's stoicism came at a price. Just as Jackie Robinson did not naturally possess the patience of Job, just as Second Lieutenant Jackie Robinson had nearly been court-martialed in 1944 for refusing to move to the back of a military bus, Street seemed to struggle with the notion that a black man had to tolerate abuse to be seen by whites as noble. India had gained its independence from the British, Street noted, but Gandhi had had to take three bullets to the chest.

And an "uppity" Jackie Robinson would never have been voted Rookie of the Year, Street assured Charlie drily.

Charlie had come to conclude that Street was less visible but more radical than Powell. Congressman Powell embraced the employment opportunities offered by the new plant that General Kinetics wanted to build north of 125th Street. Perhaps he was truly a believer that any job was a good job; perhaps he was beholden to General Kinetics in one way or another — graft and corruption were certainly not new terrain for members of Congress of any race. Street seemed to be fighting more stealthily than Powell while giving his enemies no ammunition.

"Who knows what Powell's reasoning is," Street suddenly whispered to Charlie after making sure no one could overhear them, randomly picking up the conversation fifteen minutes into the Canadian leader's droning speech. "It's like trying to figure out why a lion takes a left. And it's irrelevant. I need you to see if there's some way you can quietly block permitting for the plant."

"What did you say about Mosstown —"

"Moss*ville.* Louisiana."

"Yes. That."

"I'll explain if this guy ever stops talking," Street whispered back.

At last the Canadian governor-general finished his speech, to polite and sustained applause. After a few minutes, as Street and Charlie walked back to the House Office Building, Street elaborated. His wife had been raised in Mossville, and her family still lived in and around the town, in Calcasieu Parish, Louisiana. General Kinetics all but ran the parish, since it owned a number of plants there — oil and gas refineries, factories that produced synthetic rubber, ammonia, magnesium, salt cake.

"Sounds like it would be booming."

"It is," Street agreed. "A lucrative express train to the cemetery."

After the plants had been operating for a few years, the scent of the air changed. No one who lived there noticed; the change came gradually. But those who visited from outside the parish would note the vinegary scent in their nostrils and the odd flavor in the backs of their throats. Tap water soon took on a smoky aftertaste.

"First to die were the mud lizards Renee and her brothers used to catch as children," Street said. "The kids would find piles of their dead bodies on the shores of the bayou. Then came the herons and gulls and pelicans. Bloated corpses just floating by the dozens. Then the livestock followed: chickens and cattle and horses. Then Renee's grandparents got sick.

"These plants are booming now, Charlie," Street said as they reached the top of the stairs. "But that sound you hear isn't just the engine of capitalism. It's also a ticking time bomb. Might not go off for twenty, thirty, even forty years. But it's going to go off."

On the fourth floor, they prepared to go their separate ways. "I'll do whatever I can to help block the plant, Isaiah," Charlie said. "I don't know that I can do much, but I will try."

The rest of his day was spent catching up with work he'd let fall by the wayside, returning calls and going over memos with Leopold. "Senators Kefauver and Hendrickson's offices both called this morning to see if we've arranged for a venue in Manhattan for the juvenile delinquency hearing," she said. She made no secret of her irritation; for weeks, he'd declined to give her the go-ahead to do so.

From behind his desk, Charlie bit his lower lip; Leopold stood before him, refusing to indulge his ambivalence.

"Congressman, if you don't mind my saying so, you're going to end up doing this, so you might as well do it now and get the credit for it," she observed. "I'm going to exit this room and call the Foley Square Courthouse. Unless you physically block my path, this is what's going to happen."

She left his office. Charlie remained in his seat, staring glumly at the closed door.

The sun had already set by the time Charlie drove himself from Capitol Hill to Dent Place in Georgetown, parked, and walked up the steps of his brownstone. Turning the key and entering quietly so as not to wake Margaret, he was surprised to see the lights on in the foyer, the living room, and upstairs in the kitchen, where he found Margaret drinking tea at the kitchen table. He looked at his watch; it was after eight p.m.

"You're up late," he said with a smile, bending over to kiss her on the back of her head as he reached for the day's stack of letters.

Margaret put her hand on top of his. "I have two things to tell you."

"Okay," he said.

"Strongfellow just called from the hospital." Charlie sensed what was coming. "I'm really sorry, Charlie, but Mac didn't make it."

He stood frozen for a second.

"I'm so sorry, honey," Margaret said, now gripping his hand tightly.

He gave her hand a slight squeeze, then let it go. Suddenly he was a world away. Private Rodriguez had ripped off his gas mask, which was of no help. His nose was streaming mucus; his eyes were red, and tears ran down his cheeks. His body, pinned beneath the beam, began bouncing off the floor in convulsive spasms. Death was seizing Rodriguez and dragging him away, and there was nothing Charlie could do.

The wall clock in the Marders' Georgetown kitchen delivered its tinny half-hour chime and returned Charlie to the present. He looked bleakly at Margaret, shaking his head in disbelief.

Through the window, which was cracked open, came the sound of a swallow chirping. It was interrupted by the vroom of a car, its radio blasting one of the latest from Frank Sinatra.

A foggy day in London town . . . had me low and it had me down.

They sat in silence for one minute. Two minutes.

"How's the baby?" Charlie finally asked.

"She's good," Margaret said.

"She?"

"He. It. Whatever." She rubbed her stom-

225

ach. "He-she-it is great."

Charlie smiled sadly.

"Good," he said, his gaze drifting out the darkened window.

"Honey?"

"I'm okay. I knew he wasn't going to make it."

"It's horrible. Just awful." She stood and embraced him. But he patted her absently on the back and broke away.

"I have to go to a meeting," he told her.

"A meeting? At eight thirty at night?"

"A reception. At the Mayflower."

"Really?" she asked incredulously.

"Believe me, it's the last thing I want to do."

She stared at him as if she didn't recognize him.

"Thanks for waiting up to tell me about Mac," he said.

They were maybe five feet away from each other, but it felt like a mile.

"What's the second thing?" he asked her.

Through the fog of his grief, Charlie could sense Margaret wanting to say more; her disappointment in him had lingered between them for weeks now. It was a conversation he would not be able to face tonight.

"Nothing," she said.

"Okay," Charlie said. He went upstairs,

changed into his tux, came back down, and grabbed his car keys from the counter.

And without another word to his pregnant wife, he walked out of the room, down the stairs, and back onto their chilly Georgetown street.

The Mayflower was a popular venue for DC events, and Charlie had already been there half a dozen times. Its first-floor bar, the Mayflower Lounge, was nicknamed the Snake Pit; on Friday nights, it became a rogues' gallery of politicians, lobbyists, captains of industry, and local women eager to make their acquaintance. Until tonight Charlie hadn't known the hotel had a penthouse, and what he encountered when the elevator deposited him there made the Snake Pit look like a Boy Scout meeting.

Standing in the foyer, facing two immense oak doors, Charlie could hear the muted blare of a trumpet and the deep roar of a party in full swing. A young curly-haired woman dressed like a chorus dancer at a burlesque show greeted him with a smile and asked him to remove his shoes.

"My shoes?" he asked

"Yes, please, sir," she said. "Connie feels it helps everyone relax."

Charlie reluctantly surrendered his shoes

and, feeling surprisingly disarmed by their loss, squared his shoulders as she opened the door, flashed a bright and possibly flirtatious smile at him, and ushered him inside.

CHAPTER FOURTEEN:
THURSDAY, MARCH 4, 1954 — EVENING

Mayflower Hotel, Washington, DC

The immense room was dark and rich with a bouquet of sinful aromas — cigars and cigarettes and grain alcohol and fruity cocktails being enjoyed by a roomful of older men and younger women. Thanks to DC's restrictive 1899 Height of Buildings Act, the Mayflower stood as the tallest building in the neighborhood, so the ceiling-high windows offered revelers a clear panoramic view of the city at night — the floodlit Capitol Building on the far left, the glorious White House straight ahead, the Washington Monument and Lincoln Memorial farther toward the horion. A dozen or so beautiful waitresses — *nubile* was the word that sprang to Charlie's mind — glided around, tending to the men's drink and food and conversational needs. Charlie accepted a martini and made his way into the room.

Je cherche un millionnaire, avec des grands Cadillac car, sang Eartha Kitt through the hi-fi speakers.

"I wish I knew French," said an unusually gregarious Chairman Carlin, sidling up to Charlie. "That Eartha Kitt is something else."

"She's singing, um, 'I'm looking for a millionaire with big Cadillacs,' " Charlie translated. He paused, took in more of the lyrics. " 'Mink coats, jewels up to the neck, you know?' I think that's the gist."

"Sounds better when she says it," Carlin said, lighting a cigarette and flagging down a waitress. "Darling, can I trouble you for another Glenfiddich single-malt?" She smiled and touched his cheek affectionately. "Man, I do love Connie's parties," Carlin said, more to himself than to Charlie.

"All this just to thank us for helping him get cheap Mexican labor?"

Carlin shrugged. "He likes his braceros. I prefer to think of it as a demonstration of appreciation from a constituent. And with hotels all over the country, he's basically everyone's constituent."

Abruptly, Carlin looked at Charlie with an expression close to a sneer, then walked away. Charlie looked around to see if someone other than himself had been the focus of that disdain. Nope. *Such an odd man,* Charlie thought.

He stepped deeper into the throng. Members of the House and Senate mingled with business leaders and young women who were cocktail waitresses or guests. There was a slight undercurrent of carelessness, an atmosphere even freer than the Snake Pit twelve floors below them. They were safe — no journalists, no gossips, no wives, no one uninvited.

"I didn't know they let dogfaces in here!" Congressman Pat Sutton, the navy man and Kefauver challenger, slapped Charlie on the back with more aggression than seemed necessary. Half of Charlie's martini spilled onto his pants and the thick Oriental carpet.

"Hello, Pat," Charlie said, annoyed, surveying the damp damage below.

"Charlie, you tell your friend Kefauver that I am going to whip his ass!" Reeking of gin, Sutton wrapped the crook of his elbow around Charlie's neck and pulled him closer, then kissed the top of his head. Charlie concentrated on preserving what was left of his martini.

"Good luck to ya," Charlie said. "Unseating an incumbent is tough for anyone, let alone in a primary. But what do I know, I'm new here."

"Oh, you know stuff, Charlie," Sutton said earnestly, mistaking Charlie's false modesty for legitimate humility. "Your book was a great read!"

"Thanks." Charlie seriously doubted that Sutton knew the book's title, much less that he had cracked its spine. "Listen, have you really thought this through? Kefauver has a national following. Why not wait for a better moment? Why risk ending your trajectory so soon?"

Sutton snorted. "Charlie, Kefauver isn't going to know what hit him. I'm getting tons of support from folks who want to send that pansy packing." He pointed vaguely toward the crowd. "You see that man with the waxed mustache? Made a killing when General Kinetics bought those defense contractors after the war. He told me I could travel the state using his helicopter! They're lining up to back me. And believe me, a lot of cash is going to come my way from Chicago. Estes made a lot of enemies there during his last crusade!" He held up his tumbler in a salute, then poured the remaining whiskey down his throat and stumbled off.

Information was ammunition in Washington, Charlie thought, and Sutton had just given him some that could be used against him. It was amazing how foolish, how reckless, people in this town could be. The copious amounts of booze with which politicians regularly pickled themselves played a significant role in this, of course.

He looked around the room, surveying the other guests. A leather-faced politician from out west, bearing more than a slight resemblance to the desert tortoises indigenous to his congressional district, sat on a cushiony sofa, his enormous gut protruding over his crotch. Charlie watched as he grabbed a passing waitress and pulled her onto what little lap could be found. She tried to laugh it off, but her eyes revealed her revulsion.

I've got the world on a string, sittin' on a rainbow, Sinatra sang over the suite's hi-fi system.

Charlie walked to one of the immense windows and stood staring out at the White House, five blocks away. Should he tell Kefauver what Sutton told him? Saying cash would flow in from Chicago was essentially a confession that Sutton would find his campaign coffers filled by mobsters still angry with Kefauver for his hearings against organized crime. Charlie was trying to ingratiate himself in this world and Sutton had just sloppily handed him the coin of the realm.

He had to consider his own motives. Why would he run to tell Kefauver about Sutton but blanch when asked to share the Boschwitz dossier with Bob Kennedy? Just because Kefauver had been nice to him? What kind of principle was that?

"You seem like the kind of guy who thinks too much," came a flat voice with a Bronx accent. Charlie turned around to see Roy Cohn, McCarthy's chief counsel on his committee. With dark and deep eye bags that belied his twenty-seven years and a crooked nose that made him look like he'd been punched in the face a few times, Cohn exuded a confidence that perplexed Charlie.

"Roy Cohn," the attorney said, putting out his hand to shake Charlie's. Charlie greeted him, trying to keep a neutral expression that wouldn't betray what he thought of Cohn and McCarthy.

"Nice to meet you," he said reflexively. He could almost see Margaret's disapproving face hovering in the background. "Charlie Marder."

"I know your dad," Cohn said. "A good man. He gets it. He gets it."

In '46, as a favor to a Wisconsin power broker, Winston Marder had hosted a fundraiser for McCarthy's first Senate race.

When McCarthy was up for reelection in '52, two years after he launched his crusade against Communists real and imagined, Winston continued his support for him out of inertia more than anything else. Or so he had rationalized it to Charlie.

Over Cohn's shoulder, Charlie noticed Senator Kennedy and Ambassador Lodge, opponents in a fierce U.S. Senate race two years before. They were smiling and warmly toasting each other with martini glasses. Bygones, Charlie supposed. A third man came up to Kennedy and Lodge.

"That's Joe Alsop," Cohn told Charlie, following his line of sight. "The columnist. You know him?"

"I know *of* him," said Charlie.

A waitress approached them. Charlie and Cohn swapped their empty glasses for fresh and ice-cold dirty martinis.

"You might recall that Senator McCarthy called Alsop a queer in that letter to the *Saturday Evening Post,*" Cohn remarked.

"I do," Charlie said, still focused on Kennedy, Lodge, and Alsop, who were now joined by a tall man with a mustache and round glasses: Central Intelligence director Allen Dulles.

"Part of our campaign to remove perverts from the government," Cohn said. "Alsop *is* a queer, you know."

Charlie nodded and finished his martini, so cold it barely even had a flavor. He was supremely uninterested in Alsop's sexuality, and he couldn't help finding it odd that Cohn was pressing the issue, given the rumors he'd heard about the lawyer's own private life.

"They look like they're up to something," Charlie noted.

"Maybe another assignment?" Cohn hypothesized. "Alsop went to Laos a couple years ago to do some work for Central Intelligence, then last year same thing in the Philippines."

"Alsop did work for Central Intelligence?" Charlie asked, stunned that a journalist would be secretly working for the government. Having first made his name covering the trial of the Lindbergh baby kidnapper and murderer, Bruno Hauptmann, Alsop was one of the most highly regarded newsmen of the day. He'd written a bestseller about FDR's attempts to pack the Supreme Court, and three times a week he and his brother Stewart wrote a widely read column for the *New York Herald Tribune*.

"Proudly," Cohn said, spitting as he talked. "If I may quote Mr. Alsop, 'The notion that a newspaperman doesn't have a duty to his country is perfect balls.' He's a patriot. And a pervert. A patriotic pervert." Cohn laughed at his own remark.

Charlie did not know what to say. Homosexuality was not something he gave much thought to, other than when he heard rumors about J. Edgar Hoover or Cohn himself. The two men stood at the hub of the national security apparatus, so powerful that they thrived despite Eisenhower's executive order from April 1953 that essentially banned homosexuals from the federal workforce, since they were regarded as susceptible to blackmail and were thus obvious security risks.

"You see, Charlie, there are the domestic political fights we Americans have with one another, and then there is the common struggle against the Reds," Cohn continued as if a microphone had been placed before him. "The Communist Party is not a political party, it's a criminal conspiracy. Its object is the overthrow of the government of the United States by force and violence when the right time arises. The Communist Party's most important work until then is espionage on behalf of the Soviet Union."

"Don't tell me, let me guess," Charlie said, attempting to lighten the mood, "you hold in your hand a list of a hundred and twenty-three individuals in this room known to be members of the Communist Party?"

Cohn's face twisted into something that seemed half smile, half snarl. "Cute," he said.

Charlie was done trying to be polite to a man who made his skin crawl. He looked away from Cohn. Nearby, four guests — two slick business types and two young women in tight sweaters — laughed uproariously. Senator Kennedy was on his way to the door. The old desert tortoise was helped up from his seat by the young woman whom he had snared earlier. Les Paul and Mary Ford's "Vaya Con Dios" filled the air.

Now the hacienda's dark, the town is sleeping, they sang. *Now the time has come to part, the time for weeping.*

"*Vaya con Dios,* my darling," Carlin bellowed from across the room, where he was sitting on a plush leather chair fit for a king and surrounded by hangers-on, his own personal court. "*Vaya con Dios,* my love."

One of the young women began mimicking a Mexican dance, raising her dress above her knees dramatically. Carlin's toadies began shouting, "*¡Olé, olé!*"

"Look at them, celebrating how they're letting more spics come into the country," Cohn said. "No doubt with some Reds among them. Disgusting."

Charlie didn't disagree with Cohn's estimation of Carlin and his court, but the ethnic slur shot a bolt of adrenaline and anxiety into his stomach. He hadn't known many Mexican-Americans in his life except for Private First Class Rodriguez.

"I wish my old army buddy Manny Rodriguez were here so you could say that to him," he finally said.

"Why isn't he?"

"He's dead."

"Under your command, was he?" Cohn said smoothly. He signaled a waitress for another drink. "Look at the headlights on this one," he said a little too enthusiastically as the young woman approached. The Rubenesque waitress, barely staying within the confines of her outfit, handed highballs to Cohn and Charlie. Someone bumped into her and she jostled Charlie; her long red hair swept across his neck and cheek but she kept the drink tray steady.

"Arpège," Charlie said. "By Lanvin."

"Huh?" said Cohn.

"Very impressive," said the redhead, a slight Southern lilt in her voice. Charlie smiled.

"What are you talking about?" asked Cohn. "Ar-pej?"

"It's my perfume," she said. "I didn't even put any on today."

"I have an unusually keen sense of smell," Charlie said.

"Wow, like a superhero," said the waitress. "That must be quite a gift."

"If this were a world where there were more of you than of him," Charlie said, motioning to Cohn, "it might be."

"Evening, Roy," Bob Kennedy said, approaching them. Recognizing Charlie, he nodded. "Congressman," he said.

"Charlie Marder," Charlie said, not sure if Kennedy remembered his name. In Washington, Charlie had noticed, people tended to avoid names in case they got them wrong; they tended to say "Nice to see you" instead of "Nice to meet you," in case they had met you before. New social rules for an egoistic town where every monument and street was named for their predecessors.

"Right, of course," said Kennedy. "We met you and your lovely wife at Martin's Tavern. I just heard you're working with Estes on the upcoming juvenile delinquency hearings."

Cohn choked on his drink. It turned out he was laughing.

"You're part of those bullshit comic-book hearings?" He guffawed dramatically.

Kennedy grinned and looked at Charlie apologetically. Charlie was not particularly amused. He'd had enough of Cohn's abrasive company by now.

"You were asking me about the Commie symps in this room, Congressman," Cohn said. "Well, they worry me more than Wonder Woman does." He took another swig of his drink and stared out the window. "But none of them concern me as much as the Commie symps over there in that big white building," Cohn said, motioning with his chin toward the White House. "What must the world look like from that address? Must look upside down. Goddamn Ike protects the Commies and fucks with Senator McCarthy." Cohn looked at Kennedy. "He's terrified Joe will run for president, you know. Joe could beat him too."

"Joe McCarthy could beat President Eisenhower?" asked Charlie incredulously. "Beat the smartest general we've had since Sherman?"

"*Smart?* MacArthur called Ike the best clerk he ever had!"

"And Ike said he studied drama under General MacArthur for four years."

Kennedy chuckled. "Now, gentlemen."

"MacArthur . . . MacArthur . . ." said Charlie sarcastically, pretending to search the skies for a reminder of the general so ignominiously fired by Truman three years earlier. "The name rings a bell."

"MacArthur is a great man, a patriot," said Cohn. "I'm sure you have a Medal of Honor under your shirt there."

"No," said Charlie. "Just some shrapnel." He finished the rest of his drink. "Nothing like your paper cuts from the Battle of Torts 101."

An awkward silence hung like a noose. Charlie had surprised even himself with that one. Liquid courage, he supposed.

Kennedy tried to break the tension. "Why do you think Joe would be a good president, Roy?"

"If Joe were president, the first thing he would do would be to end the Cold War," Cohn said. "He'd pick up the phone and call Joe Stalin and say, 'This is Joe McCarthy, I'm coming over tomorrow to talk about things, meet me at the Moscow airport at one o'clock.' When he arrived in Moscow, he would sit down with Stalin in a closed room. First he'd tell a couple dirty jokes. Then he'd look Stalin right in the eye and say, 'Joe, what do you want?' And Stalin would tell him. They would talk man to man, not like pansy diplomats. They'd find out what each of them wanted and settle their differences. But when Joe left, he'd tell Stalin, 'The first time I catch you breaking this agreement, I'll blow you and your whole goddamn country off the map.' "

Charlie turned to Kennedy. "He can't honestly believe this rubbish, can he?"

"You little establishment punk," spat Cohn, "you think you know anything about defending this nation?" He looked at Kennedy. "Isn't this the same little shit whose daddy got him his seat? Who was trying to fuck with the General Kinetics acquisition of Goodstone?"

Charlie and Kennedy were both taken aback at Cohn's outburst; it was delivered with the virulence of a cobra strike, drawing attention from nearby guests.

"Er, uh, that's not quite how I would put it, Roy," Kennedy said, patting him on the back, trying to calm him. "But, yeah. Charlie tried to stop the funding for Goodstone. It had something to do with bad gas masks they made in the war that cost the life of one of your men, right, Charlie?"

"That's right," said Charlie. "Company made a cruddy product. Clear case of war profiteering."

Cohn waved his arms as if he were washing a car with two sponges. "Forest," he said. Then he started pointing at imaginary items in the air. "Trees," he said.

"Pretty glib talk about the death of an American soldier," Charlie said. "Though, Bob, I guess that kind of sacrifice is not a subject Mr. Cohn here could understand. Especially these days, when he's busy maligning the army."

"You just don't get it," Cohn said, shaking his head and taking another swig of his drink. "Alexander Charleston, the CEO of Goodstone, is a patriot. Duncan Whitney, the CEO of General Kinetics, is a patriot. These are men who support Senator McCarthy's work and the work of his committee. *They* can see the forest for the trees. The Reds are about more than the loss of one Mexican private."

"He wasn't Mexican," said Charlie. "He was born in New York."

"The Reds don't care about the loss of one soldier," Cohn continued. "One soldier? They slaughter millions. Are you defending that? I mean, you need to have a little respect for Senator McCarthy."

Charlie squinted, as if looking at Cohn through an adjusted lens would make sense of him. "I do have little respect for Senator McCarthy," he said.

Cohn's eyes seemed to redden, turning bloodshot with his internal fury. Kennedy put his arm around Charlie. "I think this conversation has come to its logical conclusion," he said. "Charlie, why don't you go mingle, socialize for a while."

"I can't wait to see this little snot's face when McCarthy accepts the nomination in two years," Cohn said. "We'll make sure to put the New York delegation up front so the cameras don't miss you all crying."

Charlie polished off the rest of his drink and locked eyes with Cohn. He handed his empty glass to Kennedy and slowly walked away.

"Adios, amigo," Cohn said.

Charlie paused but then decided to let it go; he made his way, stumbling somewhat, to the bar. He'd lost count of how many drinks he'd had by now. He wished Margaret were with him. Or Street. Even Strongfellow — a friendly face. Someone had dimmed the lights of the room even lower. A toxic cloud of cigar and cigarette smoke hovered over the crowd.

Oh, my papa, to me he was so wonderful, sang Eddie Fisher over the speakers. *Oh, my papa, to me he was so good . . .*

Charlie wobbled around the periphery of the room, taking in the scene as the guests marinated in free booze. An overweight senator from the Midwest had all but hijacked a waitress and was voraciously wolfing down canapés from her hors d'oeuvres tray as if it were his kitchen table. A powerful House member so old and shriveled he resembled a baked apple slow-danced with one of the cocktail waitresses, hands like talons edging their way down her hips. When the couple turned around, Charlie was surprised to see that her expression was nonchalant. Indeed, many of the women here seemed remarkably at ease among the powerful, drooling old men. At the far side of the room, four U.S. senators began singing "Let Me Call You Sweetheart" a cappella.

"Charlie, I wasn't sure if you were going to come! Pregnant wife and all."

Charlie turned around. It was Strongfellow, looking more urbane than ever, wearing a blue blazer over a turtleneck. He pivoted on his crutches, swung toward Charlie, and grabbed his hand in an enthusiastic hello.

"Strong!" said Charlie, delighted to have some friendly company at last. "What is this place, anyway?"

"Some sort of club. It's kind of mysterious," Strongfellow said. "Don't know much about it other than you find out more when they want you to find out more."

Charlie looked around the room. "Pretty august company. Bipartisan leaders of, well, everything. Vanderbilts and Rockefellers. Powerful, impressive men. Plus you and me," he joked.

"Carlin told me to find you and bring you to the library," Strongfellow said. "It's this way."

Charlie followed Strongfellow along the outskirts of the room to two thick mahogany doors, which swung open to reveal a cocktail waitress — the same redhead from before. She smiled demurely at Charlie and held the door open for them. A hallway presented them with choices: a kitchen to the left, a library to the right, and who-knew-what straight ahead.

"This way," Strongfellow said, veering toward the library doorway, which was flanked by two small stone statues, a man and a woman, both holding fingers to their lips: ssshh! Between them, a man in a dark suit with sharp cheekbones and a high-and-tight haircut stood, blocking their path.

"Do what thou wilt," Strongfellow said to him, and the man stepped to the side, letting them through. Charlie trailed behind his friend, wondering what the hell he had just said — was it a password? — and where he had heard it before.

The library was smoky, the lighting low. One wall was occupied by floor-to-ceiling shelves packed with leather-bound books. The wall to Charlie's left was dominated by an enormous fireplace with an ornate marble mantelpiece on which had been carved the words *Hospes negare, si potes, quod offerat.* " 'Stranger, refuse, if you can, what we have to offer,' " Charlie translated to himself. Around the fireplace hung twelve stained-glass images of various politicians and CEO types, each in an obscene pose with a naked woman. Given the medium, their identities were difficult to discern with precision, though they seemed to be depictions of specific individuals. One resembled Carlin. Another Ambassador Joseph Kennedy. The one on the far end appeared to be FBI director Hoover. The wall to the right was covered with portraits of U.S. presidents and women whom Charlie did not recognize, women wearing plunging necklines and sultry expressions.

In the center of the room, a half a dozen men played cards around a green-baize-covered table, while others in various corners spoke in low tones over cigars and highballs. In his haze, before he knew what he was doing, Charlie was suddenly standing in the far left corner of the room by

Senator McCarthy and Duncan Whitney, the CEO of General Kinetics, whom Cohn had just extolled as a great patriot. The two men were sinking into immense red armchairs facing the center of the room on opposite sides of a small round accent table on which burned a thick white candle.

"Speak of the devil," McCarthy said dramatically to Whitney. "Duncan, *this* is the congressman who made the stink about Goodstone." He smiled at his friend, then at Charlie, who was disarmed by McCarthy's almost palpable charisma. He recalled his father warning him that he would like the Wisconsin senator if he ever met him. Charlie had rolled his eyes at that, but now, in his presence, he could see what his dad had been talking about.

"Another scotch and another bicarbonate of soda," McCarthy said to a waitress fluttering by. "And bring me a stick of butter, if you can. With a fork." Charlie shot him a confused look at that, and the senator explained: "It's helpful on a night like this. You should try it."

"You're the young man whose platoon had a gas mask a soldier couldn't operate properly," said Whitney, who bore a strong resemblance to affable everyman actor Fred MacMurray: genial face, twinkling eyes.

"It wasn't the soldier that was the problem, but yes, sir."

"I'm sorry to hear about that. The folks at Goodstone said they fixed the problem, but after this acquisition goes through we're going to make doubly sure that never happens again."

"You're Winston's boy!" said McCarthy, as if it were just dawning on him. He held out his big meaty catcher's mitt of a hand to shake Charlie's. "So good to have you in Washington. I haven't spoken to your father in some time; tell him I said hello." The waitress brought him a glass of scotch and he downed it like a thirsty man at an oasis, emptying the tumbler in seconds. The waitress handed him the glass of bicarbonate of soda; he took a sip and handed it back to her.

"Anyway, where were we?" he asked Whitney, pounding on his armrest. "Oh! Murrow! Anyway, I don't care what he does. If you want to be against McCarthy, you gotta be a Communist or a cocksucker!" He guffawed loudly, a deep, boisterous belly laugh that drew the attention of everyone in the room. "Boy," he said to Charlie, "we're on the most important skunk hunt ever. And look, I know my methods aren't refined. But you don't go skunk-hunting in striped trousers and a tall hat while waving a lace handkerchief!" He laughed hard at his own joke; Whitney tittered.

Charlie observed McCarthy — the charm, the menace, the glint in his eyes that seemed to suggest that you were in on it with him, and wasn't this fun? There was something about McCarthy that instantly conveyed to people that he liked and cared about them, Charlie could see — and something inside Charlie, he recognized, sought McCarthy's approval. It was a kind of twisted magic.

McCarthy smiled as the waitress came back with a stick of butter on a plate, a fork, and a napkin, and he motioned for her to put it on the table next to him.

"Charlie!" said Chairman Carlin from the corner of the room where he was sitting with Davis LaMontagne and Strongfellow. "Come join us!" McCarthy and Whitney had resumed their conversation as if Charlie were no longer standing there, so he walked over, greeted the men, and assumed a space being made for him on the couch, next to Carlin. LaMontagne's smile was friendlier than Charlie would have expected.

"Nice to see you in the club," he said.

Charlie gave what he hoped was a noncommittal expression, still reeling from the bizarreness of meeting McCarthy and Whitney and wondering again what he had unwittingly joined tonight. He gave a slight nod of his head toward two gentlemen seated in deep leather armchairs. One was Allen Dulles, director of Central Intelligence, the other a wrinkled old man with thick glasses and a face like a fist.

"Who's the guy with Dulles?"

Strongfellow peered at the man over his whiskey glass and shrugged. "Got me."

"You two sure are freshmen, aren't you?" LaMontagne said teasingly.

"Strongfellow and Marder, you are embarrassing me!" exclaimed Carlin with mock outrage. "That's Sam the Banana Man!"

Charlie and Strongfellow looked at each other blankly.

"C'mon, guys, Sam Zemurray!" LaMontagne said. "The president of United Fruit Company?"

"He's only one of the most influential people in the world," Carlin said. "United Fruit has banana plantations all over the Caribbean and Latin America. They helped fund our big push against the Commies in Guatemala last year."

"Yeah, the Dulles brothers have worked with the Banana Man for decades," added LaMontagne. "They were on the payroll for years. They still work for them, essentially.

The company's top lobbyist is married to Ike's personal secretary. Ambassador Lodge is a stockholder. It's all one giant fucking banana split."

"Do what thou wilt," muttered Carlin and the group laughed, even Charlie, whose fascination with the ways of Washington often edged out his disgust. He felt a bit woozy and realized he was heading well past bombed. He hadn't been much of a drinker until they moved here, when he'd quickly adopted the habit, more out of circumstance than desire; there were always free drinks being offered to him in rooms packed with outwardly respectable elected officials slowly getting embarrassingly soused.

It wasn't that his previous life in academia was teetotaling; indeed, the Columbia faculty had more than its share of drinkers. Rather, it was a matter of discretion. Boozing professors tended to keep their pre-sundown imbibing private, an occasional nip from a flask, wine during office hours. On and near Capitol Hill, however, fully stocked bars in professional workspaces were as common as any other pieces of furniture — they were right off the House Chamber, in the conference rooms of law firms, next to the teletype machines in the offices of newspaper editors.

"What the hell is this place?" Charlie asked. "Pornographic stained glass? And is that Senator MacKeever in that one over there?"

"Just some harmless fun," LaMontagne said with a shrug.

"Hey, Charlie." Carlin put a beefy arm around Charlie's shoulder and leaned close to whisper in a boozy drawl, "Do you want to know a secret?"

"Sure." Although at the moment what Charlie wanted most was to get upwind of Carlin's 90-proof breath.

Carlin pulled Charlie even closer. "I screwed you on Goodstone," he said, a big beaming smile exploding on his face, a fat finger landing on Charlie's lapel for emphasis.

Charlie blinked.

LaMontagne and Strongfellow chuckled, though it wasn't clear if they were laughing at the news or the shocking way it had been delivered.

"But . . . I saw the bill," Charlie said. "You struck out the provision."

"That is true," Carlin said, now wagging his finger in the air, granting the point. "But what you didn't see was a provision we added in a separate part of the bill allocating the same amount for any subsidiaries of

General Kinetics."

"Which, as you may know, Charlie, Goodstone is about to become," said LaMontagne, a smug look on his face.

Charlie rocked back slightly in his seat. He felt as if he'd just been punched in the stomach.

"Now, son," said Carlin, giving him a patronizing pat on the back. "Don't take it so hard. You're not the first pretty young thing I've screwed this week, and you won't be the last."

Charlie felt a hand on his shoulder. Strongfellow was trying to console him.

"The larger point, Charlie, is you're right — Goodstone fucked up," added LaMontagne. "But these companies were rushing product for the war effort. No one was trying to kill anyone."

"And the fight goes on, Charlie," said Carlin.

"And the fight goes on," Strongfellow repeated.

Charlie felt deflated. An expert in the deal making, debauchery, and duplicity of the Founding Fathers, he wasn't naive about politics: it could be vicious. And it was ever thus. Charlie had written a well-received article about how the ferocious and cruel attacks by John Quincy Adams's friends against Andrew Jackson's wife, Rachel, accusing her of bigamy, had all but certainly led to her death after the election of 1828. In a historical context, Carlin's maneuver wouldn't even be a footnote in an encyclopedia of chicanery. But no one had ever lied to Charlie's face like that before, much less relished the revelation of the deception. It enraged and humiliated him.

The redheaded waitress appeared with her ubiquitous silver tray, this time bearing bottles and implements as if she were about to assist in a surgical procedure.

"Ah, Suzannah," said Carlin. "Thank you."

"Absinthe?" asked LaMontagne. "What's the occasion?"

"It's almost Friday," joked Carlin.

Suzannah deposited the tray on a table and began an elaborate preparation. First she held up a silver slotted spoon, then, with some pageantry, she displayed a sugar cube as if it were a chunk of gold panned from a river. Then she delicately put the sugar cube on the spoon. She was joined by a second, waifish waitress who produced a delicate dark bottle and poured a green liquid into a glass, then put it in front of Charlie. Suzannah placed the spoon with its sugar cube on top of the glass and then used a syringe to slowly drip ice water onto the cube.

"What ratio are you going with?" Carlin asked her.

"One to four, I think," she said.

"Better make it one to five," Carlin said. "This is probably Charlie's first absinthe. Right, Charlie?"

Charlie nodded. It was something that hadn't interested him — or been readily available — during his time in France.

Clouds billowed in the glass as the drink took on a milky look, and Charlie began to smell its pungent licorice scent. He looked anxiously at Suzannah.

"This is how the French do it," Carlin said, and Suzannah nodded.

"Carlin and I normally go for the Bohemian way of preparing it," said LaMontagne.

Carlin reached into Suzannah's pouch, snatched a sugar cube, and popped it in his mouth.

"The cubes are soaked in alcohol for Bohemian, then set on fire. It's stronger that way."

"But you don't need it stronger for this first venture," said LaMontagne.

Charlie raised his glass to them, wondering why he was toasting the man who had betrayed him. "May you be in heaven half an hour before the devil knows you're dead," he said.

It was all stumbles and swirls after that.

Singing and dancing. Something about abbots and friars, about the men in the stained glass being apostles.

Slices of succulent pork slid onto plates.

Much wine.

More singing.

More young women. Inebriated, willing.

A moment to himself. Thoughts about MacLachlan. Guilt about MacLachlan. Confusion about "under Jennifer."

Then someone shook him out of it. Back to the revelry. *You're the top / You're the breasts on Venus / You're the top / You're King Kong's penis.*

Dulles and Dulles and Sam the Banana Man and Cohn and Strongfellow and La-Montagne, and that redheaded waitress, Su-zannah, on his lap, and . . . a whirlpool of images, blurry, hard to understand, as if he were underwater.

Stumbling onto the street.

Falling.

Laughing.

Getting up.

Then blackness.

Charlie awoke hours later, his head

pounding, his face in the mud. Next to him lay a shiny black 1953 Studebaker Commander Starliner partly submerged in Rock Creek.

CHAPTER FIFTEEN:
FRIDAY, MARCH 5, 1954

Georgetown, Washington, DC

Margaret slept restlessly that night, tossing fitfully until the sound of a car door slamming brought her fully awake. She turned on the lamp on her night table, reached for the clock by her bed, and drew it to her heavy-lidded eyes: 5:33 a.m.

In a state of sorrow, she'd gone to bed as soon as Charlie left last night. She couldn't imagine what the night was like for Henrietta MacLachlan and her four children, the oldest only fourteen years old. And she was sorely disappointed in Charlie; how could he just head back into the night on the heels of such awful news? She realized that things got done in DC only because of who you knew and whose back you scratched, and she'd tried to be understanding about Charlie's frequent nights out, but if this was going to be their new way of life, she wasn't sure how long she would last. These troubled thoughts kept deep sleep at bay, and she had hovered unsatisfyingly between awareness and oblivion. It had been almost worse than if she had stayed up all night.

Echoes of the turning tumblers of the lock on the front door bounced up two flights of stairs to the bedroom, the deliberate movements of someone trying to be quiet and the sudden sharp sounds of that same someone having difficulty doing it.

She heard the creaks from the floorboards as Charlie crept carefully upstairs and then slowly opened the door to their bedroom. Margaret lay on her side, facing the door, her eyes narrow slits. In his left hand, Charlie held his shoes, and Margaret felt a surge of exasperation at his faux consideration at five thirty in the morning.

He tiptoed into their bathroom and re-emerged in pajamas, then eased himself into bed as quickly as he could. One didn't need Charlie's superhuman sense of smell to detect the excess alcohol oozing from every pore, a sudden punch of stink that was not unlike approaching the Socony-Mobil oil refinery on the brand-new New Jersey Turnpike.

He sighed dramatically, an expression of weariness or worry, Margaret couldn't tell. Then he cleared his throat, seemingly testing to see if she was awake. She stayed still.

"Margaret?" he whispered.

She didn't know how to react. She was angry and he reeked and she didn't want to deal with him and whatever piffle was troubling him. She lay there silently, wondering what was happening to him and to them.

Beyond how let down she felt about Charlie's behavior last night and the mess he was this morning, Margaret had something to tell him, and she knew it wasn't going to help matters. For whatever reason, perhaps the folly of holding on to a shred of power by maintaining control of this information, she had decided not to tell him the night before. Louis Gwinnett had telephoned the previous afternoon, before Charlie came home from work. He and his team were out at Nanticoke and Susquehannock Islands again, and a researcher had dropped out at the last minute because of a death in the family.

"We really could use you. If you're willing," he had said.

Margaret hadn't responded.

"Think of the ponies, Margaret. This is the time when they swim from Nanticoke to Susquehannock. Now. Any minute now!"

"It's tempting."

"You are actually going to make me beg," Gwinnett said, and Margaret could practically hear his smile.

She was surprised that her heart had begun beating a little faster at the sound of his voice. They had not spoken in two months, since January. He had written her a glowing letter about her work on the previous expedition — one that walked right up to the line of inappropriate but did not cross it. They had communicated in letters about how to write up the research from their days in the field, but she kept everything professional.

But all the while she and Charlie were drifting, with forces pushing Charlie out to sea while she remained alone on the beach, each watching the other recede into the distance and neither doing much about it. And then: Dr. Louis Gwinnett had reared his head once again.

Margaret was secure enough in her emotional stability and her self-control, particularly in her current pregnant state, to trust that she would not say yes just because of her attraction to him. What pulled her most was the memory of how alive she felt in the field. It wasn't that she was unhappy in her Georgetown home or even more generally in stuffy Washington, DC — though that surely played a part. But the sudden transition from their old life in New York to one here in which Charlie pursued a new career while she waited for their baby to arrive had made her feel as though she'd gone from being a scientist to being a laboratory.

She'd let a moment pass before she'd answered Gwinnett.

"I'd love to be there," Margaret had finally told him. "I just need to check on a few things."

Those few things were all contained in one drunken husband who was now lightly snoring beside her. It wasn't a hard decision. Margaret got up and prepared to phone the research assistant who Gwinnett had said would give her a ride. As soon as the clock struck seven, she would call him and arrange to leave for the Maryland islands as soon as possible.

The phone woke Charlie at ten a.m. He was used to Margaret answering when someone called, but by the seventh ring he realized she wasn't going to do so. His head was throbbing and the inside of his mouth tasted even worse than when he'd woken up with it full of mud just hours before. His tongue felt as if it were coated with a paste made of absinthe and bile and cheap perfume. The phone ringing exacerbated the pounding in his skull, so he mustered the strength to roll over and reach for the phone on the night table on Margaret's side of the bed.

"Hello?" he croaked.

"Congressman, it's Catherine Leopold. Where are you? You have a very busy day today."

Gripping his forehead as if pressure would make the pain go away, Charlie apologized and promised he'd be in as soon as possible. He hung up and then everything from the night before hit him like a wave: MacLachlan's death, the drunken party at the club, Rock Creek, the dead girl.

Good Lord. The dead girl.

That gorgeous young redhead. What was her name?

Oh Christ, what have I done?

He sat frozen for one minute, then five. The phone rang again and he ignored all eight rings. Finally, as if on autopilot, he stood unsteadily and began to fumble his way to the bathroom. He tripped over the box containing the baby monitor, the gift from LaMontagne a lifetime ago. Charlie shaved and brushed his teeth. In a fog of sleep deprivation, booze, and trauma, he stepped into the steam of the shower.

The memories of the night before came

back to him in glimpses, puzzle pieces he was in no condition to assemble. He didn't remember leaving the Mayflower; all was black until he awoke facedown in the muck of Rock Creek. LaMontagne had arrived and attempted to whisk him away until he'd found the dead girl. Charlie had scurried to her side to try and find any signs of life. La-Montagne had then barked at him to help him carry her to the crashed Studebaker.

"No," Charlie said.

"What?"

"I said no. I'm not going to carry her to the car."

LaMontagne had bent down and grabbed Charlie by the shoulders. "Listen to me, you little shit. If you don't do exactly as I say, your child will never see you anywhere other than inside a cell. Margaret will leave you and marry another man. You are throwing everything away for what? For fucking what?"

"It's wrong," Charlie had said.

Off in the distance they could hear another car. LaMontagne let go of Charlie, bent down, scooped up the young woman, and carried her to the Studebaker on his own. He wedged her into the driver's seat.

"Come over here and help me set the Studebaker on fire, Charlie."

"No," Charlie said.

"Help me set the fucking Studebaker on fire!"

"Go to hell, Davis."

"You fucking idiot," LaMontagne said. He unscrewed the gas cap, took some papers from his pocket, and ignited the ends with a lighter. Then he delicately inserted the roll into the gas-tank opening and ran up the bank to Charlie on the road. "Get in the car!" he ordered, and this time Charlie obeyed. LaMontagne turned the key of his Dodge Firearrow and floored the pedal and they sped off.

Charlie replayed this as he stood in the shower, groaning and rubbing his face. He slowly toweled himself off and dressed, every movement requiring extra effort. Adjusting his thin blue Brooks Brothers tie, Charlie made his way downstairs, preparing an answer for the questions Margaret would surely have about his late night.

The kitchen was empty.

"Margaret?" No response. He moved through the house, looping in his cuff links, and peered into the living room — also empty. Had she had something to do this morning that she'd told him about and he'd forgotten? He looked on the kitchen table for a note and found none. The seed of a new anxiety began to take root in his stomach.

Looking outside, wondering where his wife was, he saw dark clouds gathering, and as he made a mental note to bring an umbrella, he realized he wasn't sure where his car was. The last place he remembered seeing it was with the valet at the Mayflower Hotel. One more loose end, but a trifle, comparatively.

Charlie called for a taxi, then sat down heavily at the kitchen table, head in hands. Outside, a growl of thunder sounded ominously close. Inside, the house felt unnaturally quiet without Margaret there. He still could not believe his memories of the night before.

Initially, he thought the flashes of heat he felt had something to do with the approaching thunderstorm. Beads of sweat began collecting on Charlie's forehead, the nape of his neck, the small of his back. He shivered, then stood and raced to the sink, where his abdominal muscles and diaphragm contracted, emptying everything out of his stomach, splashing the coffee cup Margaret had used at breakfast. Hyperventilating, he steeled himself for a second spasm and retched again. He fell to his knees, continuing to hold the rim of the sink. He hung there for a minute, two minutes, three minutes, as he slowed his breathing.

Okay. Focus.

He stared at the yellow linoleum and tried to steady himself.

Sheets of rain began hitting the street outside, sounding like an enthusiastic round of applause. Individual drops plinked hard on the windowpanes like snipers' bullets.

Charlie stood up slowly and reached for the kitchen telephone on the wall. He asked the operator to connect him to Winston Marder on Seventy-Second Street in Manhattan and gave her the number.

"Connecting."

A minute or so later, Charlie heard Winston's booming baritone, loud enough to make him wince a bit and pull the receiver away from his ear.

"Charles, how are you, my son?"

"Not . . . not well, Dad."

"Is Margaret all right? The baby?"

"They're both fine. It's not that."

"What is it?"

"Are you alone?" Charlie asked.

"I am — as far as I know," Winston said drily. "One can never be certain."

Charlie was tempted to tell his father this was no time for philosophical cutesiness but he stopped when he recalled that in a recent letter, his father had speculated that J. Edgar Hoover was tapping phones all over Manhattan and Washington without bothering with the nuisance of lawfully obtained warrants.

"I was just reading a fascinating story about J. Edgar Hoover and the magnificent job the FBI is doing these days to root out the Communist menace," his father said, confirming Charlie's suspicions. "I would love to talk to you about it, and your mother would love to see you and Margaret this weekend. And if not this weekend, then sometime soon. Congress is breaking for recess next week, isn't it?"

"I'll talk about it with her," Charlie said. "It would be great to see you and catch up."

"That sounds like a plan," Winston replied.

Charlie hung up. With his father wary of speaking on the phone and Margaret AWOL, he had no one to talk to, no way to unburden himself. Not that he was sure he'd be able to divulge every detail about the previous night to his wife or father either.

Washing his face at the kitchen sink, he heard the honk of a car horn. The cab. He ran through the rain and had the driver take him to the Mayflower.

270

After Margaret left her town house that morning, she visited the Birder Emporium, a shop tucked into Waters Alley off the very busy Wisconsin Avenue. A large tabby cat curled up near a heating vent meowed, then returned to its nap. The store sold anything a bird-watcher would ever need: bookshelves of field guides organized by state, country, and continent; warm clothing and hiking shoes; insect repellent, chairs, blankets, thermoses, pocketknives, camping equipment, backpacks, and lanterns. The walls were lined with photographs of a couple on various excursions through the decades, interspersed with posters of John James Audubon's paintings of rare birds: Attwater's greater prairie chicken, Kirtland's warbler, the San Clemente loggerhead shrike.

The owners, Sidney and Bernice Greenstein, emerged from the back of the store to welcome Margaret as warmly as if she were a guest they'd been expecting for lunch. They'd aged considerably since the last photograph had been taken, Margaret could see, but they were lively and cheerful. She told them the purpose of her visit and about her upcoming trip to research the ponies, her need for a new pair of binoculars to replace the ones she'd dropped into the marsh on Nanticoke Island.

Sidney Greenstein led Margaret to a file cabinet in the corner of the store and, with painstaking precision, showed her the many options available. Margaret early on decided that a pair of Ross binoculars would suffice, but the old man seemed to be enjoying the opportunity to show off his expertise, so she patiently sat through the entire presentation. After its merciful conclusion, Bernice Greenstein reminded her husband that there was one box in the bottom drawer he hadn't brought out. "Why don't you show her that one as well, Sidney?" And so it was that Margaret emerged from the store with not only a new pair of Ross binoculars but also a short-lived product from RCA, night-vision binoculars, built using guided-missile technology but discontinued after consumers found them too expensive and too heavy. Eager to unload them, the Greensteins had offered Margaret a substantial discount, and Margaret was excited to show off the new toy to Gwinnett and the other researchers.

Under darkening, cloud-heavy skies, she made her way home through the rain, happily burdened by her new acquisitions, less happily by thoughts of Charlie; she knew he would not be pleased about this sudden trip. She would tell him as soon as possible, either in person, if he was still at the house nursing his hangover, or on the phone. As she walked, she prepared some rational counter-arguments to any objections he might make.

But Charlie wasn't home. Margaret phoned and found he was not yet at work. So she dashed off a quick note, collected her suitcase and coat, and called her ride to tell him that she was ready. As she waited, she fretted about Charlie. She didn't know what was motivating him anymore. At first he'd seemed focused on stopping Goodstone, but now he seemed entirely preoccupied with other goals, ones he didn't seem eager to share with her — likely because he knew she would disapprove. Who knew what backroom deals he was now part of?

The human soul isn't sold once but rather slowly and methodically and piece by piece, she thought. They hadn't even been in Washington for three months; how had things changed so quickly?

Margaret looked sternly at herself in the hallway mirror. She could almost hear her mother's voice admonishing her to stiffen her spine and get on with things. Well, then, that's what she was going to do. She heard the honking of a car horn, and she left the house, locking the door behind her.

Battling his raging hangover and the pouring rain, Charlie retrieved his car from the Mayflower and drove to Capitol Hill. Staring grimly out at the wet gray city, he fought the impulse to think about last night while also being unable to think of anything else. He'd felt remorse after Rodriguez was killed in France, but there were too many other villains — the Krauts, the Vichy French, Goodstone — for him to hold himself responsible in any real way. There were no alternative bad guys in the tale of his having killed a girl while driving in a drunken stupor. He chased away the remorse as best he could, focusing on all the unknowns and his inability to remember any of it, as if an alcoholic blackout provided some sort of cloak, a protection from sin.

For once, the alarming news on the radio served as a welcome distraction; more drama between the Eisenhower administration and McCarthy as the defense secretary called McCarthy's charges that the U.S. Army was coddling Communists "just damn tommyrot." But the administration

had also just given McCarthy more ammunition; the latest tabulation of government employees who'd been fired or resigned after being deemed a "security risk"
had just been updated, and the number now
stood at 2,429, with 422 directly or indi-
rectly tied to subversive activities. Moreover,
in Caracas, Venezuela, Secretary of State
Dulles warned his fellow foreign ministers
that there wasn't "a single country in this
hemisphere which has not been penetrated
by the apparatus of international communism acting under orders from Moscow."

Charlie parked; an attendant with an
umbrella walked him across the street. He
felt outside of his own body, as if he were
watching himself in a documentary about
himself, he and the attendant in grainy
black-and-white, filmed in secret from a
third-floor window, the voice of Ed Murrow
intoning, *Watch the guilty man, fresh from
his act of vehicular manslaughter, walking to
work just hours later as if nothing had trans-
pired at all . . .*

Leopold was waiting for Charlie outside
the door to his House office, an anxious
look on her face and a to-do list in her hand.

"Miss Leopold, could you call Congressman Street? I'd like to get together —"

"Sir." She cut him off firmly. "Mr. La-

Montagne asked —"

"Davis called?" Charlie said, taking off his damp overcoat and handing it to Bernstein, who exchanged it for a cup of coffee, light and sweet; Miss Leopold had finally conceded that battle. He took the mug and walked into his personal office.

"No need for me to call," said LaMontagne, who was draped comfortably on the couch, smoking a Chesterfield.

Charlie was distressed to see LaMontagne; his presence immediately destroyed whatever emotional wall Charlie had managed to build to protect himself.

"As always, Mr. LaMontagne made his way into your office without seeking permission first," Leopold said.

"He's like a cat burglar," Bernstein said under her breath from the receptionist's desk.

Charlie turned to Leopold. "Okay, thank you." He shut the door.

"You look surprised to see me," LaMontagne said.

"Not as surprised as I was earlier this morning," Charlie said. He took a swig of his coffee and sat down behind his desk.

"You're fortunate I was up so early. And driving by."

"Am I going to consider myself fortunate

that you're here right now?" Charlie asked. His mouth was parched, his throat so dry it felt like cacti would sprout up. Images of the Rosenbergs heading to the electric chair sprang into his mind. He told himself he was being melodramatic, but he also knew LaMontagne held his future in his hands.

LaMontagne said nothing, just stretched out on the couch with a faint smile on his face. They looked at each other, the dead cocktail waitress an unspoken presence.

"It was the only option, Charlie," La-Montagne finally said.

Charlie didn't want to address it. He didn't know if anyone was listening in and he didn't want to think about her. He noticed a manila folder on his desk — a new copy of the Boschwitz file, Charlie presumed, to replace the version he'd lost during the House shootings.

"The latest version of the dossier," La-Montagne said. "Just as well you lost the old one, since we now have some photos. So it's all ready for you to turn over to Bob. Or Roy. Though it sounds like you and Roy didn't exactly get along swimmingly last night."

"No, we drowned," Charlie agreed. He looked down at the Boschwitz dossier and opened it, finding inside various incriminating papers, photographs, and memos. He surprised himself by saying aloud what he was thinking: "What I still don't get is why you haven't just given this to them yourself. Why do you need me?"

LaMontagne's grin conveyed annoyance more than humor. "There are so many responses I'm tempted to give," he said. He stubbed out his cigarette in the ashtray on the coffee table.

"Shoot."

"The first and obvious one. What I don't get is why you think after last night, you can respond with anything other than a mad dash to Bob Kennedy's office, dossier in hand."

Charlie nodded. "Fair," he said. "What else you got?"

"You're awfully flippant."

"I don't mean to be," Charlie said, smiling. "Possibly still a little drunk." He tried to ease into a steadier pose; his anxiety and terror were manifesting themselves as anger, and that wasn't doing him any good. He thought of the mental exercises he'd performed back in France, willing himself to be the tough guy he felt nothing like.

LaMontagne put another cigarette between his lips and flicked his lighter; it failed him once, then twice, then a third time.

Charlie reached into his suit pocket, withdrew his aluminum trench lighter, and tossed it to LaMontagne, who caught it effortlessly with one hand and lit up another Chesterfield.

"I know I told you that the firm doesn't want to be tied to this in any way, but the honest answer is that I don't want any paper trail from this leading back to me. If there are any questions, Bob or Roy will say they got it from a New York lawmaker who got it from a constituent, and it ends there. But from a lobbyist who represents a Zenith competitor? Can't have that."

"Why would there be any sort of inquiry?"

LaMontagne took a deep drag, then shrugged. "Winds blow, daddy-o. Things seem good for McCarthy right now, but Ike is setting traps behind the scenes and I have no idea if or when Tail Gunner Joe will get strafed. He's getting drunker by the day, and Cohn is blinded by . . . other matters."

Charlie gamed it out in his head. "So if McCarthy crashes and the Democrats retake the Senate and start looking into everything that went wrong and how McCarthyism took hold, you want to make sure nothing leads back to you."

"Decidedly so."

"McCarthy's thriving. Almost no Republicans and barely any Democrats are even willing to take him on in public."

LaMontagne shrugged and blew two smoke rings, which connected midair. "A good soldier always has a plan B. Didn't you learn that in the army?"

"What's my plan B?" Charlie asked, only half joking.

LaMontagne rose and buttoned his suit jacket, preparing to leave. "After last night, you, my friend, aren't in a position to be making any plans. You just carry them out."

The underground subway between the Capitol Dome and the SOB had been built in 1909, so the technology sometimes failed. On his way to deliver the Boschwitz dossier, Charlie, already in a fervor of self-pity, suffered the further indignity of a subway breakdown; the lights dimmed and then returned at half strength, and the monorail, at capacity thanks to the torrential downpour outside, came to a shuddering halt.

"I'm not sure what's happening, but it's probably best if you all go from here on foot," the conductor announced after a few minutes of false starts.

The wicker coaches began to empty. Charlie, in the last cart, noticed a few VIPs, including Kefauver and minority leader

Lyndon Johnson and, in front of them, Bob and Jack Kennedy, along with a coterie of the Massachusetts senator's aides and wingmen.

Johnson and Kefauver quickly outpaced the Boston boys. Senator Kennedy, in apparent agony from back pain, crept along the path slowly and deliberately, with his brother and entourage shuffling along at his speed. Charlie quickly caught up with them and handed Robert Kennedy the Boschwitz dossier. Kennedy nodded as if he knew what it was, as if he'd been handed hundreds of packets like that before.

"You gentlemen doing all right?" Charlie said. Senator Kennedy shook his head as if to say, *Don't ask.*

"Better than we look, Congressman," said one member of Kennedy's entourage, patting Charlie on the back as if he were joining them at the pub.

"I swear, Kenny, we need to look into whether we can get one of those offices just off the Senate floor," Kennedy said, hobbling along. "This constant back-and-forth is murder. I might as well just sit at my desk in the Chamber and do my work there."

An attractive college-age woman, likely an intern, walked by them on her way to the Capitol, prompting the senator to murmur something under his breath that Charlie couldn't quite make out. One of the senator's aides turned and followed the young woman as if he had been given an assignment.

Charlie felt oafish walking slowly to keep pace with the Kennedy gang, a clique to which he didn't belong, so he sped up and soon found himself with Johnson and Kefauver. They were discussing a draft letter Southern members of the House and Senate were circulating — a Southern manifesto accusing the Supreme Court of abusing its judicial power if it ruled school segregation unconstitutional. Neither Johnson nor Kefauver wanted to sign any such letter, but neither did they want to be the only Southerners in Congress who didn't sign it.

"Hello there, Charlie," Kefauver said warmly.

"Why, it's Winston Marder's boy!" Johnson said. "You cozying up to the Kennedys back there? Poor Jack hobbles around like an old nun with rickets."

"Now, Lyndon," Kefauver tut-tutted.

"It's different from what the cameras catch, isn't it?" Johnson said to Charlie, wrapping his arm around his shoulders as they reached the end of the tunnel. "You gotta play to the cameras, but don't you believe what they show you."

"Speaking of cameras," Charlie said, turning to Kefauver as they walked up the stairs to the first floor, "I've secured the Foley Square Courthouse for the hearing, Senator. I'm told there will be ample space and power for them to be televised."

"Good work," Kefauver said. "Appreciate it." He patted Charlie's arm.

"And one more thing," Charlie said, looking around to make sure no one could overhear what he was about to tell Kefauver and Johnson. "You didn't get this from me, but you might want to have your folks look into who is funding Sutton's race against you. He told me about a helicopter some businessman was lending him, and there was a fishy reference to Chicago cash."

"Oh, really?" said Kefauver, beaming as if this were the best possible news. "That sounds quite interesting, Charlie. Thank you!"

"You got yourself a regular *Casino Royale* secret agent!" Johnson remarked to Kefauver. "Sign me up for your services as well, young man!"

The senators bade Charlie farewell and then rushed off, leaving him standing there, his task accomplished. He felt sullied; he needed to talk to Margaret. The list of his failures was only growing. He had been rolled on his crusade to stop Goodstone; he had failed to protect his friend from the Puerto Rican terrorists, and now he was an errand boy for the devil. And the worst of it, of course, chilled his soul throughout the day, whenever he contemplated that he had killed a girl in a drunken car accident and conspired to cover it up. Nothing was right and he didn't know what to do or to whom he could turn.

Chapter Sixteen:
Saturday, March 6, 1954

Capitol Hill / Nanticoke Island, Maryland

Charlie sat on Isaiah Street's living-room sofa staring at a painting of a voodoo priest, his brown face smeared with reds and blues, spitting fire into a jubilant crowd.

The picture hung above a fireplace. Congressman Street handed Charlie a brandy and sat down on a chair next to him. Renee Street's family hailed from deep in a Louisiana bayou, and before that from Haiti, and the art in the Streets' modest Capitol Hill apartment displayed her roots. Isaiah Street had been quick to correct Charlie when he'd praised the painting of the "witch doctor"; the correct term was *houngan,* and this one was Renee's great-uncle, and Charlie wasn't to use the other term anywhere near her unless he had an hour to listen to a lecture about Yankee arrogance and American imperialism.

Not that Renee had heard Charlie's gaffe;

she'd been occupied with the twins, nursing and soothing. When one was being fed, the other was protesting, and vice versa.

In need of a friend, Charlie had called Street earlier that day. Street's schedule was jam-packed with committee hearings and meetings with civil rights groups — the pending *Brown v. Board of Education* Supreme Court decision had everyone nervous and preparing for all possible outcomes — so he suggested Charlie come over for dinner. Isaiah had hinted that Renee was not particularly happy to hear of her husband's generous offer, given that she would obviously end up doing all the work, but she'd believed her husband when he told her Charlie had sounded a bit distraught, so she'd made her standby dish for new guests, jambalaya, and divided her time at dinner between tending to the meal and tending to the twins.

Charlie tried to act convivial, but the events of the past few days made it hard to think of anything beyond the morass into which he had fallen. Finally, after the twins had taken Renee away, the two men went into the living room, where Charlie had sunk into the couch with a sigh and then reached a bit too eagerly for the glass of brandy Isaiah had handed him. It took little more than Isaiah's raised eyebrow for Charlie to begin unspooling his troubles.

Charlie told him everything. Street winced when he heard about Charlie handing the Boschwitz dossier to Robert Kennedy. He was unsurprised to hear that Chairman Carlin had lied to them all about funding Goodstone, but he didn't understand why Carlin bothered telling Charlie about it.

"We were all drinking quite a bit," Charlie explained. "Absinthe. It got wild. Everyone was clobbered. Truly out of control. In a bad way."

Street gave Charlie an impatient look, as if to say, *Go ahead, spill it.* "*How* out of control?" he asked, leaning forward in his chair.

"I blacked out and woke up in Rock Creek. I'd crashed in the water." Each sentence was a confession, and a struggle. "I don't even know whose car it was." He stared at a floral pattern on the carpet, avoiding Street's face. "There was . . . there was a body. Someone who'd apparently been in the car I was driving."

Street leaned back. "A dead body?"

Charlie nodded.

"Good Christ."

Charlie nodded at that too. Then he added: "It was this girl who'd been at the party. A cocktail waitress."

"Holy hell," said Street.

"Yeah."

"So did you go to the police?"

"No. LaMontagne was there. He's the one who found the girl. He showed up after I woke up. He told me to help him carry her to the Studebaker."

"Why?"

Charlie downed the rest of the brandy. "So he could put her in it and then set it all on fire. Destroy all evidence. As if it had never happened. LaMontagne was trying to help me. I know that what we did was wrong. God, what have I done?" He put his head in his hands then looked imploringly up at Street.

Street sat back in his chair. "Did it even *occur* to you to go to the police?"

Charlie slid a finger around his collar and shifted in his seat. The gravity of the situation and the choices he faced seemed to come into focus under the fierce beam of Street's glare. "Yeah, maybe," Charlie said. "But Davis seemed to know what he was doing . . ." His voice trailed off as he heard how weak and spineless he sounded. He was disgusted with himself.

"Did you help him carry her to the car?" Street's voice was cold, calm. They'd both seen men do bad things; each had faced down evil in his own way, but that was in Europe, in the war, which felt almost like another planet.

"No," Charlie said. "I didn't do it."

"You told him no?"

"Correct."

"And then?"

"Then he got mad. Furious. But I wouldn't move. He cursed but he wasn't going to take the time to fight, I guess. He carried her to the car and wedged her into the driver's seat."

"And then?"

"Then he lit some papers on fire and put them in the gas tank, and we sped off before it blew."

"Jesus Christ," Street said.

Charlie's time in Washington was teaching him that trusting anyone was a risky bet, but he'd decided he could trust Street. It wasn't as if the history department at Columbia University had been Plato's Republic, but Charlie had enjoyed friendships and alliances, and for the most part, everyone just tried to keep his head down and pursue scholarship. Washington, by contrast, seemed populated by pickpockets, grifters, and con artists. There were exceptions, however, and Street was one of them.

Or so Charlie hoped.

He was, truth be told, grateful to have him as a friend. Yesterday, after he'd battled his hangover to survive the day, he had arrived home to find the house empty and a note from Margaret on the kitchen counter — he wasn't sure if it had been there before and he'd missed it — explaining that she was heading back to Nanticoke Island to try to solve the mystery of the Maryland ponies' island-hopping. *Remember* La Galga *that night back in the stacks?* she wrote. *Now I need to solve the puzzle for once and for all.* To Charlie it seemed a halfhearted attempt to make nice in the midst of an abrupt departure. Though to be fair to her, he realized that she knew nothing of his troubles, only that he had staggered into their bedroom drunk hours after she'd expected him.

Street, however, was proving almost as tough a customer as Margaret would have been.

"You realize, of course, that this was like the psychology test they give officers," Street said. "You have a moral quandary, and you are picking the answer that ends up with you not getting a promotion."

"A test on paper is different from one in real life," Charlie protested. "I get you on the should-haves. Of course. No argument.

But let us abandon your world of the theoretical for one second. First of all, instead of being primed and ready for your officer's test with six cups of joe in your gullet, imagine you've swigged a bottle of absinthe. Then here's your choice: One path means you throw career, marriage, and any future with your children into the trash. You get defined by your worst moment ever for the rest of your life." He paused. "My obit would read 'Charles Marder, Fifty, Single, Unemployed, Disowned, Life Ruined by Fatal Car Crash.' Do you have any more brandy?"

Street stood and refilled his friend's glass, concern radiating from his stern and silent face.

From the bedroom, one baby stopped crying and the other one started.

"Your babies," Charlie said. "You would risk leaving them and Renee in the lurch for something you don't remember doing, something almost no one else knows about?"

Street stared at him.

"I'm not talking about an answer on an officer's test," Charlie said. "This isn't about the moral stance you can defend in Philosophy 101 at Morehouse. I mean right here, right now. In reality. You can walk away or you can risk it all. And not just your life — Renee's and the twins' and everyone who depends upon you. Anyone back in Chicago you want to help. Anyone in Mossville, Louisiana. *Poof,* gone. Forget your time as a Tuskegee Airman, forget your Distinguished Flying Cross. You'll just be the sum total of your worst moment. You know how Washington works."

"I see your point," Street said after a long silence.

Charlie was surprised by the relief he felt at this grudging acknowledgment, as if Street had the power to absolve him.

"Thank you," he said.

"So what now?" Street asked. "LaMontagne would seem to have you over a barrel."

"I don't know what to do," Charlie said. "But you're right; I'm under his thumb."

Street looked up at the painting of the voodoo priest and rubbed his chin.

"Speaking of 'under', we still haven't figured out who Jennifer is, much less what Mac was trying to say with 'under Jennifer.' All due respect to the dead, what the hell does that mean?"

Charlie dropped his head in his hands. "Jesus. Mac. What a narcissistic bastard I've become." He gulped down more brandy. "I don't even know when the funeral is. That feels like a hundred years ago."

"We visited Mac in the hospital on Monday," Street reminded him. "Five days ago."

At that very moment, Margaret, Louis Gwinnett, and two other researchers were sitting cross-legged around a campfire, drinking soup from thermos mugs. They had set up camp between the surf and a string of ponies, which had been within sight until sundown. The researchers on Susquehannock Island reported via walkie-talkie that no ponies had yet made the journey from Nanticoke to their location; Gwinnett's team was determined to be awake and watching when they did.

Nursing a flask of whiskey, Gwinnett talked campus politics with the two researchers from the University of Wisconsin, graduate students named Isaac Kessler and Matthew Cornelius. Margaret kept silent, fermenting in her marital angst. The moon was waxing crescent with only 3 percent visibility — Gwinnett hoped the cloak of darkness would help their mission in observing the ponies — so the stars shone particularly bright. Kessler, gazing at the constellations in the stars, misidentified Lupus, the eleven-starred wolf, as Lepus, the eight-starred hare. It was impossible for Margaret not to correct him.

"I learned about the constellations from my uncle," she explained after rectifying his astronomical error. "He was a park ranger, and he loved to take my sister and me outside late at night — he said he was 'teaching us the sky,' " she said. "For Lupus, he told us a very dark story about a wolf."

"Children's stories are always macabre," Gwinnett observed. "I suppose it's to prepare them for real life."

"Seriously," said Cornelius. "I was traumatized by *Bambi* and *Dumbo.* What's Walt Disney's obsession with killing off moms?"

"Dumbo's mom wasn't killed, she was just imprisoned," corrected Kessler.

"There does seem to be a common theme of losing a parent, or both parents," said Margaret. "Snow White and Cinderella lost their moms, hence the wicked stepmothers. And wasn't Peter Pan an orphan?"

"What was the wolf story your uncle told you?" asked Gwinnett, nudging her and handing her his flask.

"It's a weird one," she said, declining his offer. "Golden apples are being stolen from a tree and the king sends his three sons — the youngest is Ivan — to figure out who's doing it. They set out on horseback and come upon a sign and three paths. One path will lead to cold and hunger. On the second, your horse will die. On the third, your horse will live but you will die —"

"Oh, I know this story!" said Gwinnett. "It's Ivan and the Gray Wolf! Does it end with the brothers chopping up Ivan but the Gray Wolf brings him back to life?"

"Yes! So awful for a child to hear!"

"That's an old Soviet folktale," Gwinnett said.

"Huh," said Margaret.

"Watch out, Doc," said Kessler. "Her husband's a congressman. Talk too much about the Gray Wolf and next thing you know, you'll be sitting before the House Un-American Activities Committee!"

"What does your husband think of McCarthy, Margaret?" Gwinnett asked.

"He hates McCarthy," she said. "But he hates the Communists too."

"Is he Democrat or Republican?" asked Cornelius.

"Registered Republican, but he kind of inherited that from his father, an admirer of TR. Truly not a particularly partisan man. He's only been there a few months." She paused and was surprised to find her eyes tearing up a bit while she thought about him. "He's just Charlie." She shook her head, glad the dim light made it hard for anyone to see her clearly.

"But surely Charlie has an opinion on the madness that has infected Washington," Gwinnett said. "Seeing Reds under every park bench, thinking people who merely want a more just and equitable society are trying to undermine America. People are fighting for a better world. They see the United States inflicting pain and suffering on places such as Cuba and Puerto Rico and Korea. They see our ideals falling by the wayside as the big corporations take over our politics and wrest control of our foreign policy. Americans who want racial justice and harmony aren't to be ostracized. We're to be listened to."

Margaret had met plenty of Communists at Columbia; they had once been common throughout the academic world. For many, joining the party had been dilettantism, a passing fad, a trendy and vaguely rebellious form of socializing. Some saw it as just the natural extension of idealistic, progressive activism — a way to support racial equality and labor unions and to oppose fascism. By the late 1940s, however, the barbarism of Stalin's USSR was evident to all — even those who had previously tried to explain away his Great Purge as a mere internal matter. Upon Stalin's death in 1953, even progressive editorialists who had heralded his efforts alongside FDR during World War II had to mention the millions of dead bodies upon which his kingdom had been built.

The Cold War and the presence of Soviet spies in the United States made it Columbia University's particular shame, however, that the Ivy League college counted a number of Soviet agents among its alumni, including one who'd ultimately been sent to the Gulag and executed by Stalin, another who'd worked his way to a senior position in the FDR and Truman administrations, and, most infamously, Whittaker Chambers, who'd ultimately switched sides and been the key witness against accused Soviet agent Alger Hiss. The university's leaders had become, a bit too late for Charlie and Margaret's tastes, sensitive to their campus hosting so many fifth columnists; one outspoken history professor had been fired two weeks before he appeared in front of McCarthy's committee.

Margaret had been at parties and faculty mixers with the academics fired for Communist ties. They were tiresome; whatever bold truths they told about the United States were undermined by their blindness to the crimes of Stalin. Neither she nor Charlie cared for them. But she'd come to know how they talked and the terms in which they couched their beliefs, and right now Gwinnett sounded like one of them.

"Margaret?" Gwinnett said, having received no response to his question about Charlie.

"Hmm? Oh." She'd been lost in thought. "Charlie isn't a fan of either McCarthy or the Communists."

"With respect," said Kessler, "how does that make any sense? It's a battle between the two. One has to pick a side."

Shrouded by darkness, Margaret rolled her eyes at the graduate student and his insistence on seeing the world in stark simplicities.

"I'm afraid I'm with the grad students here, Margaret," Gwinnett said. "An ideology based on the equality of mankind positing an end to fascism and an end to war is being challenged by a drunk demagogue. If you don't stand for —"

An echo from the beach on the other side of the brush stopped Gwinnett midsentence, and all four turned toward the noise; above the low din of the tides came the distinct sound of splashing. Margaret, first to her feet, grabbed her flashlight and jogged to the beach, Kessler and Cornelius at her heels, their flashlights providing a jumping set of lights on either side of her. She looked back and saw that Gwinnett was well behind them, presumably having stopped by his tent to grab equipment of some sort.

Margaret hadn't run in years, and she almost surprised herself at how quickly she moved, even with child, racing through the brush of the forest and dunes. The strength of her desire to see the ponies making their curious journey — if that's indeed what the splashing was — could not be measured. The mystery could never truly be solved, she knew, beyond the concept of instinct, but the possibility that she might be able to learn how the trek was made each year and prompt some scientific discussion about it made her heart pump faster.

Switching from running on dirt to the soft sand slowed her, as did the incline of the dune, allowing Kessler and Cornelius to pass her. After cresting the top of the dune, she descended to the beach, but without any moonlight, the sound of the splashing was all they had to guide them. Their flashlights showed them where sand met surf, but that was it.

"Shit," said Kessler.

"Can you tell at all where the sound is coming from?" Margaret asked, cupping her hand around her right ear.

"Not really," said Cornelius.

Panting, Gwinnett appeared, holding his flashlight and something else. Margaret aimed her flashlight at him.

"What is that?" she asked.

"Your night-vision binoculars," he said.

"God bless you, Mr. and Mrs. Greenstein," she said as Gwinnett handed her the heavy instrument. Margaret turned on the power switch and brought the eyepieces to her face. She squinted and tried to make sense of the images she was seeing — a black ocean, a dark green sky.

Margaret scanned the horizon. She squinted and focused the device. "I see two . . . no, three. Three shapes, triangles." She adjusted the lenses again. "They're heads. They're moving. Bobbing. They're walking through the waves. They're out deeper than I would have thought."

"Are they headed right for Susquehannock?" asked Kessler.

"Directly," she said. "Did anyone bring the walkie-talkie? We should let Quadrani and Hinman know." Salvatore Quadrani and Ken Hinman were the researchers on Susquehannock Island, based there until

Gwinnett moved his camp to Susquehan-nock in a couple of weeks.

Keeping the lenses focused and aimed in the right direction, she invited Gwinnett to have a look.

"Amazing," he said. "Do you think they're swimming? They're out so far!"

"I don't know; one of them might be a foal," she said. "Maybe there's a sandbar."

Kessler and Cornelius soon got their turns as well. "Three ponies. Huh," said Kessler.

"Three colts? Three stallions? A mare and two foals? A family?" Cornelius asked.

"That's sure the question," she replied.

Margaret and Gwinnett took a few steps back and sat down on the dune. Gwinnett whipped out his flask, unscrewed it, took a swig, and passed it to her.

"I'm so glad that you brought those glasses," Gwinnett said.

"It was kind of dumb luck that the shop owners wanted to unload them," Margaret said.

"I'll take dumb luck over smart grad students any day of the week," Gwinnett said.

"Gaah," she said, grimacing after taking a swig. "Usually you buy finer stuff."

"Cheaper is better than none," he said. She smiled and wondered if that was true.

■ ■ ■ ■

After several brandies, Charlie opted to call a cab to take him the six miles from Street's house on Capitol Hill to his own in Georgetown. It took several tries before one would agree to pick him up in Street's segregated neighborhood, and even then Charlie had to agree to walk three blocks to a more commercial thoroughfare.

He was halfway up the steps to his town house when he heard someone say, "Congressman Charlie Marder." The gruff and famous voice stated his name matter-of-factly, as if narrating a live broadcast of individuals walking down the street. Charlie turned to see, across the street, a black Lincoln Continental with a driver and a passenger in the back. He walked to the car, and as he did, the driver jumped out and escorted Charlie to the other side of the car, adjacent to the sidewalk. He opened the door and Charlie climbed in the backseat.

"Senator McCarthy," Charlie said as he eased himself in and closed the door behind him. "Were you sitting here waiting for me?" The car smelled like Old Spice, Lucky Strikes, and whiskey.

"How are preparations going for your

comic-book hearing?" McCarthy asked, ignoring Charlie's question. "You and Kefauver and Hendrickson all ready to fricassee Scrooge McDuck?"

Charlie sighed. "Yes, it all looks good. Though I'm sure your hearings won't lose any viewers to ours."

"Oh, I'm not concerned." McCarthy chortled. They were sitting in the darkness, Charlie twisted at an angle to better see McCarthy, who was sprawled out and facing forward, though he occasionally turned his head to make eye contact with his guest and smile at him warmly. Once again Charlie was taken aback by how charming and avuncular McCarthy was. When he was being warm to you, the last thing you wanted to do was disappoint him. McCarthy reached into his inside jacket pocket and withdrew a pint bottle, from which he took three gulps. He offered it to Charlie, who had learned in the army never to reject a swig.

"That Fred Werthman . . . Werth . . . what's his name?" McCarthy asked. "The headshrinker who's your main witness?"

"Fredric Wertham."

"Him. He consorts with some shady characters, like the Negro author Richard Wright, various other Communists. I'm not

303

saying much about it because I have bigger fish to fry right now, but I wouldn't associate with him outside of the hearings if I were you."

"I've only met him on official business relating to the juvenile delinquency hearings, sir."

McCarthy grunted, then took another drink, after which he wiped his mouth with his sleeve. "You ever hear of a guy named Clinton Brewer? He was a convict. Wertham got him out of prison."

"No, never heard of him," Charlie said, wondering where all this was headed.

"So your boy Wertham wrote a book a few years ago, *Dark Legend.* It was about some dago, maybe seventeen, whose mom gets widowed and whores around a bunch, and then the dago kills her. Matricide. So Wertham's book comes out, it offers the bleeding-heart sob story about why this greaser did what he did, how he was compelled to, blah-blah-blah, and Richard Wright gets all excited. He knows someone else who is guilty but not really guilty. A fellow murderer — and again it was society's fault. Just like with the greaser."

"Someone else?"

A noisy jalopy clanged by, distracting McCarthy. A street lamp revealed his face as he turned to the window to focus on the ruckus. By late morning, McCarthy had a five o'clock shadow, Charlie had noticed. Now, after midnight, he resembled Lon Chaney Jr. in *The Wolf Man*.

"Yes, someone else," McCarthy said. "Clinton Brewer. Colored boy, killed a woman for refusing to marry him. She had two kids, the victim. Brewer was sentenced to life. In prison in New Jersey, he developed musical skills — he had real talent, if you like that jungle music. Some musical folks hear about him, get Wright involved, a bunch of liberals and Commies get together and petition for Brewer to get out. And they succeed. In 1941, he gets paroled. Nineteen years of a life sentence under his belt, Wright hooks him up with Count Basie."

"That's a nice story, I suppose," Charlie said. "Redemption."

"That's not the whole story," McCarthy said. "Three months later Clinton Brewer kills another woman for refusing to marry him. And that's the case Richard Wright is phoning Wertham about. The kid is headed to the chair; Wright wants Wertham to testify that Brewer's a psychopath, doesn't know right from wrong, can't be guilty of murder. Wertham agrees, he testifies, and that's what happened. Brewer's doing life. Again."

"That's awful," Charlie said.

"Those are your allies, Charlie," McCarthy said, furrowing his thick caterpillar eyebrows. "This is your Commie star witness in your idiotic comic-book hearing. Bad company in a dubious cause. Whereas there are others in this town, with other affiliations, who spend their time trying to defend this nation, rather than freeing murderers because they can carry a tune. We fight for America, Charlie. We don't undermine it. We fight for it."

He sat back in his seat and stared straight ahead. The street was silent.

"There's something I need you to do for us, Charlie," McCarthy finally said. "For *us*. For *your team*."

"Sir?"

"Your father does work for NBC," McCarthy said.

"My father?"

"Yes, Winston. You know he raised money for me for both Senate runs, right? Great American. I've been to your house, Charlie."

"Right. I know."

"So he does work for NBC."

"If you say so."

"People at NBC have told me that."

"People?"

"I have a lot of friends." McCarthy grinned. "Friends who share information with me. About Communists and all sorts of other indecent types."

"Okay."

The senator took a swig from his pint bottle and grimaced.

"You know the show *This Is Your Life,* I assume?" he asked.

"Of course. My friend Strongfellow is going to be on it."

"Exactly. So the show does a lot of research on the folks they celebrate. In the course of their preparation for Strongfellow's episode, they found some unsavory information. Your dad is in possession of this research."

"Okay," said Charlie, not liking where this was heading or the alarming extent of McCarthy's insider knowledge.

"I need you to get it for me. For us. For our team. Give Cohn a call when you have it. Need this *tout de suite.*" He patted Charlie on the knee twice, then gave his thigh a little squeeze.

"Wait a sec, you're asking me to steal something from my *father*? Your *friend*?"

"I didn't say anything about anyone stealing anything," McCarthy said. "I don't care how you get it. You can ask for it, you can obtain it any way you see fit. I just need the file. *We* need the file, Charlie. We do. Your father won't miss that folder; he was just asked to hold on to it by NBC so they could claim plausible deniability."

"What is it? What's in this file?"

"You can read it if you want," McCarthy said.

And before Charlie knew what was happening, the driver had opened his car door, extricated him from the vehicle, returned to the driver's seat, and zoomed off. Charlie was left standing in the pale light of the street lamp wondering if these demands on him would ever end.

CHAPTER SEVENTEEN:
MONDAY, MARCH 8, 1954 —
MORNING

Washington, DC
Charlie hadn't left the house on Sunday, hoping that Margaret might call. She didn't. He was in a pit and had no way to reach her.

Not long after dawn on Monday morning, Charlie frantically read both the *Washington Times-Herald* and the *Washington Post* and found nothing in either paper about the car crash. The accident had been before dawn Friday, so it would have been discovered that day and been in the papers as soon as that afternoon. But there hadn't been anything all weekend. He couldn't believe only three days had passed since he'd woken up in Rock Creek.

He then met Street for breakfast at a greasy spoon on Constitution Avenue, where they engaged in small talk over coffee and toast and more casually perused their newspapers: McCarthy was demanding equal television time to respond to a Saturday-night address by Adlai Stevenson in which the Democrat claimed that the GOP was becoming the party of deceit and demagoguery; Secretary of State Dulles was having a tough time rallying votes at the Inter-American Conference in Venezuela for the United States' anti-Communist resolution; in a post-shooting crackdown, six Communists had been arrested in Puerto Rico with an estimated three hundred on the loose on the island.

The *New York Times* business pages reported that an executive from Zenith named Ira Boschwitz had been fired amid rumors he would be called to testify before McCarthy's committee. *That was fast,* Charlie thought. He'd only given the Boschwitz file to Kennedy on Friday. He showed the story to Street, who shook his head.

"How much do you think the U.S. is actually under threat of Communist takeover?" Charlie asked as he soaked his white toast in the yolk of his sunny-side-up egg.

"Not at all," Street said. "The papers sure do a good job of scaring the crap out of everyone about it, though."

Charlie barely heard his answer; his initial relief that there was no mention of the car crash in the papers gave way to a sudden anxiety that the police were holding back information from the press as they gleaned more clues and investigated the matter.

"Gentlemen!" came a friendly voice.

Charlie looked up to see Congressman Pat Sutton approaching their table accompanied by Abner Lance, one of Chairman Carlin's top aides. Lance had just returned from the Korean War, but he didn't like talking about it. He didn't much like talking about anything, as far as Charlie could tell. With hair so blond it almost looked white, a ruddy complexion, steely black eyes, and a catlike gift for the silent approach, Lance cut an imposing figure when he showed up at Republican conference meetings.

"Y'all coming to poker tonight?" Sutton asked. "Should be a good time. At ten, we're going to take a break to watch Strongfellow on *This Is Your Life!*"

"That's airing already?" asked Street. "I thought he just taped it a few weeks ago."

"It's tonight," Sutton said. "You gotta come. Strongfellow deserves to be honored! And razzed too, of course." He grinned. Veterans often had mixed emotions when one of their own was recognized, Charlie had observed over the years, an odd combination of envy and pride leading to hazing and resentment.

Street raised an eyebrow at Sutton, then turned to Charlie. "Shall we?"

"I'll try to be there," said Charlie. "Sounds fun."

"Sutton's an odd bird," Street said as they walked from the diner to the U.S. Capitol for a morning vote. "And why the hell is he challenging Kefauver in a primary? Fool's errand."

"Kefauver's a little effete for Tennessee, maybe," Charlie said.

"Oh, bull," said Street. "He plays good ol' boy with the best of 'em."

"You don't have to tell me," Charlie said. "He's not even my party."

They often compared notes on their colleagues, those they feared, those they respected, those they disdained. Sometimes they invented their own superlative awards. Charlie had privately identified the stupidest member of the U.S. House of Representatives; he had watched him walk into a broom closet during a hearing, then bashfully walk out, in full view of the packed room. Street was convinced that a certain committee chairman from the Northeast was the most corrupt; he had actually seen several hundred-dollar bills sticking out of the silver rim of his briefcase. There were the members of Congress who were not only old and infirm but also in the throes of dementia whose staff members and wives paraded them around from event to event, riding the train of their stature until the very end of the line, confident that constituents would never know and journalists would never tell. The incomprehensible mumblings these members made on the House floor would be "translated" by staffers for the official *Congressional Record* and for press releases to be read by the folks back home.

"You know what they say," Street said. "You spend your first six months in Congress wondering just how the hell you got here and the next six months wondering how the hell everyone else did."

Charlie chuckled, smiling for the first time in a while. "One of the best I've met was MacLachlan," he said.

"Agreed. He was a damn fine card player, he served honorably, and he seemed an eminently decent man." He paused. "We never —"

"Hello there, Congressmen!" Sheryl Ann Bernstein materialized by Charlie's side as he and Street made their way up the stairs of the Capitol.

"Bernstein!" said Charlie. "My best student! Were you just outside pounding the erasers for me?"

"No, but you should feel free to go pound sand," she said with a grin.

"That's quite a student you have there," Street said. "I'd hire a taster before partaking of any apples she brings you."

"She's great," said Charlie. "Don't let the Lauren Bacall sass fool you; she's brilliant."

"He just says that because I love his book," Bernstein said as they began walking up the stairwell to the second floor of the Capitol.

"Ah, you've cracked the Charlie code." Street laughed. "Your brilliance is proven in your appreciation of his."

"You know, I'm right here," Charlie reminded them mildly.

"By the way, speaking of brilliance, or our lack thereof, we never did figure out who the hell Jennifer is," Street said.

"Jennifer?" asked Bernstein.

"It was MacLachlan's last words to us. He mentioned someone named Jennifer," said Charlie. "Only we don't know who he was talking about."

"Maybe he meant him?" Bernstein said, looking up at the wall.

"What?" Charlie asked. "Him? Who?"

Bernstein pointed at the painting of the signing of the U.S. Constitution that hung in the stairwell.

Charlie stopped in his tracks and stared up at the painting of the forty attendees of the Philadelphia Constitutional convention. Fifth from the right, with his back to the viewer, stood an obscure Maryland delegate.

"Who is it?" asked Street.

"Daniel of St. Thomas Jenifer," Bernstein said. "Jenifer, one *n*."

"Jenifer," said Charlie. "Holy cow, you're brilliant."

"Do you think that's what he meant?" Street asked.

Charlie, staring up at the painting, shrugged thoughtfully. "I don't know. But Mac and I did discuss this painting, and obscure Founding Fathers, and it's the first Jennifer I've encountered since he said it."

"He said '*under* Jenifer,' " Street reminded him. They all peered more closely to see what was under Daniel of St. Thomas Jenifer in the painting. The delegate stood with his hands held behind him adjacent to a chair cloaked by someone's coat.

"The chair?" asked Bernstein.

Charlie's gaze dropped below the frame, to a marble ledge maybe three feet above their heads. "What if by 'under Jenifer,' he meant under the painting?"

Street walked up the stairs so his line of

315

sight was parallel to the ledge. "There's a vent there."

They looked around. At that moment, no one else appeared to be in the vicinity. The three of them looked at one another, then at the ledge. Charlie and Street were approximately the same height, but Street was much broader and more muscular. "Want to give me a boost?" Charlie asked.

Street interlaced his fingers and bent over; Charlie used the step to pull himself up to the ledge and the vent. Through the slits he could see dust and steam pipes — and nothing else.

"Anything?" Street said.

"Nope."

Street lowered Charlie to the floor and let out a grunt.

"I'm lighter." Bernstein shrugged.

Charlie rolled his eyes at her; obviously, he wasn't going to hoist her up, particularly in such a setting, and Street certainly wouldn't. She rolled her eyes back at Charlie exaggeratedly.

"Don't be silly, Bernstein," he said.

Two other members of Congress started walking up the stairs; the three of them continued walking and talking discreetly.

"So what does 'under Jenifer' mean, then?" Street asked.

"I don't know," said Charlie. "Maybe Miss Bernstein here can learn more about Daniel of St. Thomas Jenifer."

"Or maybe," said Street, "Mac was just a grievously wounded man experiencing death's delirium."

"Sometimes it's stunning that a man as brave as Ike was fighting Hitler can be so weak when confronted with a drunk demagogue like McCarthy," Kefauver told Charlie over lunch later that day.

They'd been seated at the same table in the Senate Dining Room where a few weeks before — though it seemed like years — Charlie had lunched with Margaret Chase Smith.

Kefauver poured more sugar into his iced tea. "Just last year, ol' Ike was up at Dartmouth telling the students not to join the book-burners, that we all needed to understand the Communists in order to defeat them on the battleground of ideas. And now this: a bill to outlaw the Communist Party."

"But surely Ike wouldn't enforce such a thing," Charlie said as a waiter silently placed their lunches before them. "Just last night, at the White House Correspondents' Dinner, I hear he called for the army secretary to stand so everyone could applaud him. That seems like a clear rebuke."

"Really, Charlie? In the larger scheme of things, when you look at what McCarthy is doing to this country and how Ike could be responding, you think that one tepid gesture in a roomful of reporters is the red badge of courage?" The Tennessee senator began to slice his veal piccata with an angry zeal.

Kefauver's office had called Leopold to set up the lunch. As they were being shown to their table, Kefauver had leaned toward Charlie and said, "Winston's worried about you, you know. I told him he had no reason to be." Charlie tried to disguise his wince — everybody could use a helping hand but nobody wanted to have it quite so openly acknowledged. Kefauver didn't inquire about the specifics and Charlie didn't volunteer anything.

"Afternoon, Charlie," said Congressman Strongfellow, hobbling over on his crutches. "What a treat to see you with your eyes open!" He slugged Charlie playfully on the shoulder. "You were completely knocked out last time I saw you, on a couch!"

Charlie coughed into his napkin and tried to calm his nerves as he stood to greet Strongfellow and introduce him to Kefauver. His throat was dry and his heart was racing at the memory of Conrad Hilton's party; he hadn't seen his colleague since that night and he had no memory of how he'd behaved in front of him after the absinthe made its appearance and no idea what Strongfellow might know of what had happened later. He scanned his colleague's face to see if he could discern any trace of disapproval or judgment; he saw nothing.

Strongfellow gave him a grin. "Now, what's this I hear about you scrapping with Roy Cohn?"

"Excuse me?" asked Kefauver.

"Nothing," said Charlie. "Cohn and I had a few words the other night. I was defending General Eisenhower. *President* Eisenhower, rather."

"They're going after the generals now," Kefauver said. "First McCarthy smeared General Marshall and now they're going after the whole goddamned army."

"It's madness," said Charlie. "His whole tail-gunner mythos is a load. He couldn't shine General Marshall's army boots. And *Cohn* —"

"Cohn's a nasty cuss, Charlie," the senator said. "You come at him, he'll come back ten times harder. His boss has a framed quote in his office: 'Oh, God, don't let me weaken. And when I go down, let me go down like an oak tree felled by a woodsman's ax.' "

"In an ideal world, sure," Charlie said.

"But who's going to wield the ax?" Kefauver asked. "I thought the army secretary's acquiescence to McCarthy the other day was shameful. You two are the army men, not me. But McCarthy was in the Senate cloakroom joking about how Secretary Stevens got on his knees for him like a 'double-dime Milwaukee whore.' Just pathetic."

"The army's going to fight back," Strongfellow said. "I was just at the Pentagon. Expect details about all the ways Cohn has tried to get special privileges for his 'friend' on their staff, Private Schine."

"You boys weren't here when McCarthy was literally defending Nazis," Kefauver said. "Do you remember that?"

Charlie and Strongfellow looked at him blankly.

"I swear to God, nobody remembers anything that happened ten minutes ago," Kefauver said. "Do you recall the massacre at Malmedy?"

"Of course," said Charlie. During Hitler's last desperate push at the beginning of the Battle of the Bulge in 1944, the First SS Panzer Division captured and slaughtered eighty-four U.S. troops near Malmedy, Belgium.

"Did you later hear about the allegations that after the war, the U.S. abused the storm troopers who were part of that massacre?"

"Vaguely," said Strongfellow.

"That was Tail Gunner Joe, who just happens to have a lot of German-American constituents who might have been feeling a little guilty, postwar. McCarthy heard the charges that the interrogators had abused the Nazis, and he pushed and pushed and pushed. It all ended up before me and the Senate Armed Services Committee in '49. I would note that it all took on a very anti-Semitic subtext, except there was nothing *sub* about it. All sorts of characters alleged that the U.S. interrogators were Jews out for vengeance. McCarthy was among them. And it was all fake. None of it was real. There was no systematic abuse of the Nazis. Just a smear campaign against Jews and against Americans trying to rebuild Germany postwar. Led by you-know-who."

"So he was defending Nazis?" Charlie asked. "This great defender of our republic?"

"Holy smokes," said Strongfellow. "You'd think Nazis would be one thing we can all agree on."

"No one remembers anything," said Kefauver. "And now he's taking on the Pentagon. And they're scared."

"Charlie, before I forget, I've been meaning to tell you," Strongfellow said, "the Pentagon knows nothing about that University of Chicago study."

"Really?"

"My Pentagon guy says they have no idea who — what were their names?"

"Mitchell and Kraus."

"Right, no idea who Mitchell and Kraus are or what study you're talking about," Strongfellow said. He glanced toward a table where Carlin's aide Abner Lance was shooting a cuff to look pointedly at his watch. "Anyway, see you on the floor. Last vote before Easter recess."

Charlie stood on the floor of the House while his fellow members of Congress buzzed around him. Just a week before, the Puerto Rican terrorists had fired on them, killing MacLachlan and wounding five others. And here they all were, debating a military aid bill for the United Kingdom as if nothing had happened. In the real world, Charlie noted, people took time to grieve; institutions were shuttered for days in the wake of horrific events that involved friends, family, and colleagues. But in Washington, the cogs in the machines kept turning regardless of damage to other wheels. This wasn't an oddity of the federal bureaucracy, he had come to realize; this was one of its purposes.

Charlie took it all in. He could still see bloodstains on the carpet where Mac-Lachlan had fallen, not unlike the spots on the marble stairs MacLachlan had shown him just minutes before he was shot. Meanwhile, the House Foreign Affairs Committee chairman was yielding the floor to his Democratic counterpart to debate how much the United States should cooperate with UK efforts to suppress a guerrilla rebellion in a Southeast Asia British colony most Americans had never heard of, the Malayan Union.

Then again, Charlie thought to himself, was the House's ability to move on any different than his own? He considered the accident, the dead young woman, the Studebaker that LaMontagne had set on fire. He was a mess inside but strong enough to fake it in front of hundreds of members of Congress, journalists, the public.

"Bet you didn't think you'd be focused on the Malayan emergency when you first got the call from Governor Dewey to join us here," said Carlin, wrapping an arm around Charlie's shoulders. Charlie's heart rate suddenly increased. He wondered what Carlin knew. LaMontagne had to have told him everything.

"Malaya? Ha. No, not really," Charlie confessed, struggling to act normally, as if they were just two members of Congress chitchatting about world affairs, no subtext, scandals, or corpses. He willed himself back into the conversation. *Malaya. Yes, Malaya.* "I know after the Japs pulled out of the peninsula after the war, the economy tanked and the Commies jumped," he said.

"It's the same old story," Carlin said with a casual shrug. He seemed in a friendlier mood than usual. "Communists prey upon the peasants, feed them a load of crap about worker exploitation. Next thing you know, the workers are killing their bosses."

Carlin looked at Charlie, seeming to size him up.

"Malaya's a big source of rubber, you know," Carlin said, his eyes locking briefly with Charlie's, purposefully reminding him of Goodstone. Charlie said nothing. He was trying to determine what Carlin knew. Likely everything. Last time Charlie saw him, he was with LaMontagne. But maybe LaMontagne wanted to wield this power on his own. And it wasn't as if LaMontagne weren't complicit as well.

Carlin gave his shoulder a hearty pat before withdrawing his arm. "Come sit with me, Charlie," he said.

Charlie, not eager for more of Carlin's companionship but not seeing an easy exit, dutifully followed him to seats at the far end of the front row. He felt light-headed.

"One of my friends on the Agriculture Committee came up with a good idea for our farm bill," Carlin said. "We always have a hard time getting Yankees to support it. But what if *you* become an original co-sponsor of our bill?"

Charlie knew better than to fall for Carlin's casual come-on. The farm bill was a notorious gift of subsidies from Washington politicians to heartland voters. FDR had started the program in 1933 as part of the New Deal, paying farmers not to grow anything on portions of their land to prevent any surpluses; the government wanted to keep prices artificially high. It didn't really work. Charlie and other urban congressmen thought the program corrupt and essentially graft.

"Now, why would I do that?" Charlie tried to soften his response with what he hoped was a winning smile. "Aside from your ask-

325

ing so nicely, of course. I mean, how would I explain to the good people of Manhattan why they have to live according to the capitalist system but their cousins in Alabama get paid by the government not to grow things?"

"Well," Carlin said, his voice smooth and confident, "I just thought you and I could maybe start over here and try to get onto more solid footing. Our mutual friend Davis LaMontagne has been trying to convince me that I have you all wrong, that you want to be doing good here, that you just need some . . . guidance on how this town operates."

His mouth spread into an expression that almost resembled a smile but was more akin, Charlie thought, to the look of a fox that had picked up a scent. "Working together, compromises; that's how things get done here." He landed two patronizing taps on Charlie's knee.

Abner Lance, Carlin's aide, appeared at his boss's side and handed him a manila folder bulging with the farm bill. Carlin took it without looking at his assistant and gave it to Charlie. "Read it over when you can." Again he offered something that might have been his version of a smile. "Now. Is there anything I can help *you* with?"

Charlie decided to treat this as a sincere question, though he had his doubts. Seeing Street across the House Chamber, he had an idea.

"I could use your help on something, yes," Charlie said. "There's a chemical plant for which General Kinetics is trying to get a permit in Harlem. A lot of local civil rights activists are after me to block it. Total headache. If you could kill it and handle Congressman Powell, that would be extremely helpful. I could try, but it would be nasty for me to get involved in any way, since Powell supports it."

"Why don't you want it?" Carlin asked. "Actually, never mind, that's your business. Let me see what I can do." Carlin lifted himself up off the chair, nodded to Charlie, and walked away.

The Pennsylvania Railroad's *Afternoon Congressional* train departed DC's Union Station at 4:30 p.m. sharp each weekday and made the 227-mile journey north to New York City's Penn Station in three hours and thirty-five minutes.

Following the vote to provide military aid to the UK for its crackdown against Malayan guerrillas, Charlie walked the mile from the Capitol to Union Station and bought a ticket, and he still had time for a shoeshine before he boarded the train to Manhattan.

He had no overnight bag, hadn't told his office where he was going, and had no way to leave a note for Margaret in case she came home and wondered where he was. In fact, he thought grimly as he sat waiting for his shoeshine, there was part of him that hoped that would happen, that wanted her to worry about him and even mildly panic. *Why should I be the only one uneasy?* he thought, disgusted with his marching orders from McCarthy and even more sickened by the fact that he was going to carry them out.

He felt ill. His stomach churned, and the anxiety and loneliness he'd been trying to keep at bay began falling upon him like a dark cloak. *Get it together,* he said to himself. *Take control.* He stood and walked to his gate, showed his ticket, boarded, walked through the stainless-steel cars — coach, dining, observation car. He found a seat in the parlor car just as the locomotive jerked forward and the train began slowly chugging north on its journey, through the ghettos of Northeast Washington, past the Columbia Institution for the Instruction of the Deaf and Dumb on the right and the

Basilica of the National Shrine of the Immaculate Conception, and Catholic University on the left.

He picked up the afternoon *Star* from the empty seat beside him. The U.S. government had rounded up ninety-one Puerto Ricans in New York City and brought them to the Foley Square Courthouse, part of the investigation into the Capitol Hill shooting the previous week. The RNC had decided that Vice President Nixon would be better suited to respond to Adlai Stevenson than Senator McCarthy would. Once again, he could find nothing about the car crash.

As the train crossed the border into Maryland, Charlie caught himself feeling as if he'd managed to escape from behind enemy lines. Though he knew, of course, he had freed himself from precisely nothing.

CHAPTER EIGHTEEN:
MONDAY, MARCH 8, 1954 —
AFTERNOON

On the Train from Washington, DC, to New York City

"You look lost in thought" came a maternal voice as Charlie sat down in the club car of the train. Charlie turned around to see Senator Margaret Chase Smith standing at the tiny bar, holding a glass of ginger ale.

He smiled.

"Hello, Senator. Wasn't expecting to see you here."

"Oh, I love the train. I take it all the way up to Boston, then drive to Portland." She raised her glass and took a sip.

Charlie was too distracted to come up with any suitable small talk. Smith, the practiced politician, filled the silence easily as he made room for her to join him in the seat next to his.

"You know, I have been meaning to tell you, after we had lunch, I read your book. It was marvelous. I found the section on

Benjamin Franklin at the Hellfire Club especially fascinating. I wanted to know more!"

Charlie caught the bartender's eye and ordered a beer. "I did too, but that's all I could find," Charlie said. "And even that was pretty controversial. I received letters from a number of DAR and historical societies in Pennsylvania who were not happy to hear about ol' Ben's secret life."

"Why, if they knew anything at all about him, they must have known he was a libertine."

"One would think," Charlie said.

"You know what I wondered about Franklin's time at the Hellfire Club?"

Charlie raised an encouraging eyebrow.

"Well, he seemed to think it quite useful — all these powerful men in one wanton association where they could do business and engage in revelry and whatnot."

"Especially the whatnot." Charlie smiled. "But yes, they did a lot of business there, as you know."

"Indeed." She grinned. "So — did he attempt to re-create anything like it upon returning to the colonies?"

Charlie rubbed his chin. "There was nothing about that in the diaries and nothing in the Franklin papers at Yale."

The train gave a bit of a jump, causing both Smith and Charlie to lurch forward. Smith spilled some of her ginger ale on the floor.

"Oh dear," she said.

"You okay?"

"Fine, dear boy. Fine." She looked around the car, seeming to make sure nobody was listening to their conversation. "Do you know about the members-only collection at the Library of Congress?"

"I heard about it from, um, the late Congressman MacLachlan," he said. "Should I pay it a visit?"

"Oh, I think you'd find it of great interest." She gave Charlie a look that he found hard to read. "A collection of papers and books only accessible to members of the House and Senate. It's in a special room in the Adams Building of the library. You should check it out, see if there's more on Franklin there. I myself would love a sequel to your book, as I suspect would many of your fans." She patted his arm — encouragingly or condescendingly? Charlie again couldn't quite tell.

"The Hellfire Club," she remarked, almost to herself. "Seems like a secret society like that one, replicated in modern times, could be very influential. Theoretically."

Charlie looked at her, but trying to read her face was like trying to read Esperanto.

"I'm sure you're more than aware that there are any number of secret societies throughout Washington," she added. "Skull and Bones, Sons of Liberty, the Patriotic Order, the Elks, the Klan. One hears whispers about them, but of course nothing concrete. Washington makes much more sense once you realize that there are factions that people like you and me know nothing about."

"People like you and me?"

"Moral people," she said. "Good people. And people who are outsiders, to a degree."

"Well, I don't know that I belong in your esteemed company," Charlie said. "That was a brave thing you did, coming out against McCarthy back in — when was it, 1950? And it's been pretty dispiriting to see so many of our fellow Republicans sit back and let this . . . indecency . . . continue."

She blushed. "Why, thank you, Charlie."

"No, I mean it," he said. "I don't think I understood until recently how tough it is to stand up for what's right in politics. It all looks so easy from the outside. But inside, the imperatives, the forces, the motivations almost always push one toward complicity or silence. If not worse. The system seems designed to grind away our better natures."

Smith took a second, apparently to contemplate what Charlie was saying and decide how to properly respond. "It has been incredibly disappointing, yes, to see otherwise good and decent men think they can straddle the worlds of decent and indecent," she finally said. "Senator Taft thought he could do that. He could not. One cannot. One must make a choice. Taft thought he could avoid having to condemn that which he knew was wrong. And then he died. And his cowardice is now regrettably part of his legacy. McCarthy isn't just a demagogue and a serial prevaricator — he's a phony. He won his first election, against La Follette, by winking toward the Communists of Wisconsin, saying nice things about Stalin. None of it means anything to him; it's all just about power and ego. I mean, it often is, that's not unique to Senator McCarthy. But he's a fraud. I feel bad for those whom he is so sadistically fooling."

Charlie's eyes flickered with a memory. "Kefauver told me something about McCarthy siding with Nazis once? Against U.S. interrogators?"

"Oh, yes," said Smith. "This was before he took up the cause of demonizing the

State Department; he was still, I believe, looking for an issue to make him famous. He took over a committee hearing he wasn't even a member of, vilifying the U.S. interrogators as anti-German. Didn't get much press here, but in occupied Germany it was huge. I think McCarthy was even getting information for his smears from Communists in Germany at the time. He left an envelope from a Red behind in committee, once, as I recall. Just unbelievable. And none of it was true. Ray Baldwin was the chairman of the committee and McCarthy attacked him too, accused him of trying to whitewash U.S. war crimes. Baldwin resigned, he was so exhausted and demoralized. He was a good man. Served in the navy in World War One. A judge. Good Republican. But our leaders just sat back and watched it all happen."

"Good Lord," Charlie said.

"There's a lesson there, of course," Smith said. "When a rat pokes his head up from the sewer, he needs to be hit on the head with a shovel immediately. You cannot just sit back and think, *Well, it's just one rat* or *That's somebody else's problem.* Because it's never just one rat, and it eventually becomes *your* problem." And with that, she patted Charlie on the arm again. "Well, I'll go back to my seat now. Lovely to run into you, Charlie."

With a wave of her hand, the senator nodded good-bye to Charlie and he watched as she slowly, steadily made her way to the rear of the train.

A train delay in Wilmington, Delaware, and a midtown Manhattan traffic jam prevented Charlie from ringing his parents' doorbell until just after ten p.m. Standing at the top of the front stoop, he could hear his father stumbling down the brownstone stairs before the door swung open to reveal the man himself. He met his son with a scowl and a powerful aromatic punch of scotch.

"Your mother's asleep," he snarled by way of greeting. Charlie knew well this side of his father — three sheets to the wind, obviously had a bad day at work but wouldn't want to talk about it, tired, surly. "You could have called first."

Winston Marder's paternal instincts were strong enough for him to reach for Charlie's briefcase and carry it up to the living room on the second floor, where a television set provided the only illumination. "Murrow's going after McCarthy," his father said. Charlie sat on the couch, and together the two watched as Murrow, in his calm and careful way, eviscerated the Wisconsin Republican, destroying his lies one by one, from the relatively inconsequential ones to a blatantly misleading claim McCarthy had made about Adlai Stevenson toward the end of the 1952 presidential campaign.

"This is no time for men who oppose Senator McCarthy's methods to keep silent, or for those who approve," Murrow intoned at the end of the broadcast. "The actions of the junior senator from Wisconsin have caused alarm and dismay amongst our allies abroad, and given considerable comfort to our enemies. And whose fault is that? Not really his. He didn't create this situation of fear; he merely exploited it — and rather successfully. Cassius was right. 'The fault, dear Brutus, is not in our stars, but in ourselves.' "

Murrow ended the broadcast with his signature "Good night and good luck."

Winston Marder emitted a sound that was something between a snore and a scoff. Charlie looked at him, surprised, having been impressed by Murrow's monologue, though he did wonder what had taken the journalist so long. Plenty of his peers had been going after McCarthy for years. Muckraking columnist Drew Pearson had been such a persistent critic, rumor had it, that

McCarthy had once punched him so hard he'd flown into the air. Journalist Jack Anderson had written a scathing investigative biography of McCarthy in 1952, and one year later cartoonist Walt Kelly started mocking the Wisconsin senator in his popular *Pogo* comic strip, depicting him as a menacing, shotgun-toting bobcat with disdain for social mores and the U.S. Constitution. Still, Charlie knew Murrow's taking such a stand was significant. These words were coming from a dignified journalist on the giant platform he enjoyed, the cautious, highly rated CBS. Everyone has his own timeline for heroism, Charlie supposed.

"So?" Charlie asked.

"McCarthy's a drunk but he's not wrong about everything," said Winston. "Alger Hiss was a spy. The Rosenbergs were spies. There are Soviet spies throughout the government. In the schools, in universities. Yeah, McCarthy's a blowhard and a liar, but isn't the Communist menace a bigger deal than whatever nonsense he says at rallies? I guess I just don't see why everyone is giving McCarthy much attention. Just ignore him."

"He's impossible to ignore. He's become this . . . planet . . . blocking the sun. And whatever points he makes that have validity are blotted out by his indecency and his lies and his predilection to smear. On the Hill, he's all they talk about. Kefauver, Margaret Chase Smith."

"Of course, he's embarrassing. But even when Smith gave her big fancy speech attacking McCarthy, she noted the Truman administration had been sitting on their asses and doing nothing while Commies began swarming the U.S. like locusts." He paused and looked more carefully at Charlie. "Did you not even pack a bag? Just the briefcase?"

"Yeah, this trip is a little spur-of-the-moment." He didn't mention Margaret's current whereabouts, since he knew his folks wouldn't approve.

Winston lifted himself out of his chair with a groan and began shuffling toward his study. His earlier irritation at Charlie's surprise late arrival had apparently subsided.

"Come on in for a nightcap if you want."

Winston's study was where he kept his most important documents, as well as a giant floor globe and his collection of nineteenth-century books, most of them focused on the presidency and assassination of Abraham Lincoln and on the life of Teddy

Roosevelt. As his dad occupied himself at the side table where decanters held his scotch and bourbon, Charlie took in the comforting scent of the room: cigar smoke and ancient texts and his dad's musky cologne. When he was a boy, this room had seemed to hold all the secrets of adulthood: serious men in serious trouble and whispered agreements and handshakes like vise grips and the lingering menace of debts owed.

"Estes tells me you seem to be getting along better now," Winston Marder said, handing Charlie a tumbler containing two fingers of bourbon and one ice cube. He sank into his chair, a walnut Victorian parlor armchair with intricately carved designs resembling tassels. The nineteenth-century antique creaked beneath his weight, which was increasing around his middle as he approached sixty.

"I suppose," said Charlie, "that depends on how one defines *getting along better.* Doing things other people want me to that I'm not particularly proud of — yes, I'm doing more of that. Passing on files to the McCarthy Committee and participating in the great comic-book hearing."

Winston Marder chuckled and Charlie suppressed a sigh of irritation. "Yes, I suppose that's how I would define it at this stage of your nascent political career. You're not getting anything for yourself?"

"I asked Chairman Carlin if he would block a permit for a chemical plant in Harlem. Negro friend of mine asked me to help him with that."

Winston's eyes lit up. "That was you? I heard about that. Adam Powell is furious. General Kinetics too. No matter. Now Harley Staggers and Bob Mollohan are fighting over which pocket of Appalachia the plant should move to." Staggers and Mollohan were West Virginia Democrats, aggressive seekers of the federal dole and anything else that might improve the plight of their impoverished constituents. Charlie would have liked to bask in his father's approval, but he could only stare grimly into the glass in his hands.

"What's eating you?"

Charlie paused before admitting, "I hadn't really thought about the fact that whatever ill effects come from this chemical plant will now be inflicted on other people."

Winston's smile was part amusement, part acknowledgment of the injustice of the world. "Yep. That's how it works, Charlie." He yawned, looking like a lion growling. Charlie wished he could be comforted by his father's benevolent world-weariness; instead, he found himself fighting a mounting sense of frustrated indignation. He needed direction, not aphorisms.

"Chairman Carlin wants me to co-sponsor the farm bill with him. He's trying to use me to co-opt the other veterans and any other skeptical Yankees."

"That's good. Nothing wrong with having a record farmers can like. Costs you nothing and could pay off later. How about Estes's latest project, these Nuremberg Trials for Bugs Bunny? You set that up for him?"

"Yep, next month at the Foley Square Courthouse."

"Ever the good soldier."

"Yes, sir."

Winston stood and stretched his arms as high as they could go and then spread them out, as if he were on a crucifix. "Pooped," he said. "Let's have lunch tomorrow at the club. Noon?"

He patted Charlie's shoulder as he left the room, leaving his son sitting in the dim glow of the lamp that stood next to the wooden file cabinet where the most sensitive files were kept. It was the only cabinet that his father took the time to lock.

Atop the cabinet was a small clay sculpture of Teddy Roosevelt on horseback from the

Rough Riders era. A gifted artist, Charlie's mother had made it for Winston years before, and the best parts of the intricate rendering were the detachable pieces fashioned from other media — the aluminum canteen that hung from a strap slung over his shoulder, the wooden replica of a Krag-Jørgensen M1896 carbine, and the cloth wide-brimmed slouch hat.

Charlie carefully lifted the hat; the key still sat tucked inside the liner where he had discovered it years earlier. He plucked it out and unlocked the wooden cabinet.

Winston Marder was a man for whom the need for order and the demands upon him were constantly at war, and the messy but alphabetized files bore witness to this struggle. Charlie soon found the NBC section with the red folder containing the *This Is Your Life* investigation into Strongfellow. He took what he needed, locked the cabinet, returned the key to Teddy's hat, and left his father's study, his heart pounding.

In his dreams, he was being shaken, up and down, left and right, taken across bumps and troughs, reminiscent of his ride on a Higgins boat from his battleship through the chop to Normandy Beach. His mother came into his room shortly after eight a.m.

343

carrying a tray with buttered wheat toast, scrambled eggs, and coffee. She set the tray on his nightstand and folded her arms with a pointed glance at her wristwatch. There was nothing like a night spent in one's childhood bed to make one feel young again, and not necessarily in a good way. Charlie flung an arm across his eyes and peered out at her from beneath it.

"Your father is expecting you at the club at noon," she said. "He asked me to let you know he's very interested in discussing the farm bill."

"Okay, Mom, thanks."

"He read the bill earlier. Took it from your briefcase." Charlie couldn't tell if she was irritated or proud. "I told him not to, I said that those papers belonged to a United States congressman and he couldn't just open up your valise as if you were still a child, but he said you wanted to discuss it with him." She shook her head in a gesture that was both familiar and familiarly inscrutable and then left, closing the door firmly behind her.

Charlie put his arm back down. His bedroom had remained untouched since he left for college in 1938, complete with 1927, 1929, 1932, 1936, 1937, and 1938 World Series Champions New York Yankees banners and a cache of photographs of Hollywood starlets in a folder buried in his bottom desk drawer. His mother would have frozen the room in amber — and Charlie with it — if she could have; she clearly preferred him as a boy, cuddly and curious. He felt a pang of nostalgia, not exactly for his youth but for a time when Babe Ruth's salary demands were his most pressing concern. He swung his feet to the floor, reached beneath the mattress, and groped with mild panic for the *This Is Your Life* folder on Strongfellow before he found it, extracted it, and prepared to face his day.

The Harvard Club of New York was one of Winston Marder's favorite places on earth and one of Charlie's least favorite; the power broker made a point of visiting the club on West Forty-Fourth Street frequently so as to circulate among other powerful men on the squash court or at the bar or while sipping brandy from a snifter in front of a fireplace. He was frequently leaned on by fellow members for favors and deals; he had helped raise money for the recently added ladies' annex and World War II memorial at the club and was currently lobbying for the New York Community Trust to recognize their building as an honorary landmark, though it had been around for only sixty years or so.

That Charlie hadn't even applied to Harvard disappointed Winston, though he never admitted it to even his wife; if Charlie wanted to blaze his own path, that was fine, he said, but he knew that also might have meant that Charlie didn't want to end up like him.

In the dark, mahogany-paneled room where a violinist walked table to table performing Vivaldi, Winston was two sips into his ice-cold martini and one bite into his shrimp cocktail when Charlie appeared and sat down. The waiters knew what Winston Marder expected to have prepared for him when he arrived, always exactly on time. Charlie sat and ordered coffee while he perused the menu. Winston looked up to see his son wearing a shirt and tie he'd taken from his father's closet.

"Nice duds," he said.

"You're the one who picked a place with a dress code."

His father chose to ignore this, and, dispensing with conversational niceties, he went straight to the point.

"I perused the farm bill in your briefcase and I thought I might help you decode some of the legislative-ese."

346

"I think I can read a bill, Pop."

"You missed the fine print when it came to the Goodstone earmark, did you not?" Winston asked, biting into a shrimp. He licked a dollop of cocktail sauce off his thumb. "Bottom line," Winston continued, "amid the normal subsidies the federal government gives out, the price supports and whatnot, this bill also gives hundreds of millions of dollars to General Kinetics to build new pesticide plants all over the country, essentially however they see fit, with no government supervision."

Charlie's dad squeezed a lemon slice onto his three remaining shrimp, then wolfed down two of them in rapid succession. He gulped the rest of his martini and looked sternly over the tops of his glasses at Charlie. Charlie thought about his father's crude eating habits, which he had always believed betrayed his outer-borough roots. In front of more refined company, he displayed more elegant manners, but if it was just family around — even at a restaurant — he returned to the practices of his youth in a modest tenement house, where, as the youngest of seven children, he had to grab food and scarf it down or he would go to bed hungry.

Winston peered at his son through his

glasses. "I would cosponsor it, were I you," he said.

"That wasn't where I thought you were going with this," Charlie said.

"No, because I gave you the BLUF, the 'bottom line up front,' the stuff you're going to worry about. Two reasons why you should co-sponsor: politics and policy. Which do you want first?"

"Politics is fine."

"Jack Kennedy has been making enemies by voting against farm interests. It might stand in the way of his getting the veep slot in '56. Why not make friends instead? It's not as though anyone in your district gives a crap one way or the other."

"All right," Charlie said. "And policy?"

Winston drained the last of his martini. "Pesticides are not only a huge part of how we feed our own people, they're vital to how we and our allies fight Communism. Right now, in Malaya, the Brits are using defoliation to destroy where the Communists hide."

"We just voted on a bill to send aid to the Brits for that," he said.

The waiter approached the table and asked Charlie's father if he was going to have his usual; Winston nodded. Charlie requested the soup and sandwich of the day.

"What's the downside?" Winston asked his son. "You make a friend in Chairman Carlin, you get some fund-raising from the heartland, you help farmers, you help defeat the Red Menace abroad."

"You're asking me, an army captain who lost a soldier to nerve gas, what can go wrong with chemicals? This is why I pushed to block permitting on the General Kinetics plant in Harlem."

"Things can go wrong with any factory. Out in Queens today, a forklift operator will drop a box of Slinkys on his co-worker's head. In Iowa, a farmhand will trip and drown in a feed silo. At a Texas slaughterhouse, a meat cleaver will land in the wrong place. They're all the casualties of progress."

"Was Private Rodriguez a casualty of progress?"

Winston waved his hand at his son's question as if he were swatting away a gnat. A waiter deftly placed a filet mignon in front of him while a cocktail waitress replaced his martini. Winston took up his fork and steak knife and tucked into his meal.

"Charlie," he said while chewing, "did you ever hear of Martin Couney?"

"I don't think so," Charlie said, looking around for his soup and sandwich.

"He died a few years ago. Considered the

349

father of neonatology."

"Okay."

"You were born a few weeks premature, I think you know that."

Charlie nodded; his parents had never been comfortable talking about his birth, and he knew few details.

"You were tiny and sickly and your mother was worried about you. The doctors assured us you'd be fine, but a nurse told me about Couney. He had set up an incubator ward out in Brooklyn. Dozens of premature babies being cared for and watched round the clock. The newest state-of-the-art incubators imported from Europe."

"Why from Europe?"

The waiter placed Charlie's soup and sandwich before him. He started with the chicken noodle.

"Europe was decades ahead of the U.S. on premature babies. Believe it or not, here in this country, premature babies were regarded as weaklings, deficient — like miscarriages, an act of God."

"Darwinism."

"Exactly. Survival of the fittest. But Couney didn't see it that way. Not only that, he wanted to help babies of all colors and races and religions and stations in life. Poor babies, rich babies. At no charge. I was truly amazed when I went out to see him on Coney Island."

"Coney Island?"

"Twenty-five cents a head, step right up to see the teeny-tiny babies in the incubators! A big sign outside said 'All the World Loves a Baby.' In the summer, crowds would line up to gawk at the baby-incubator show."

Charlie blinked. "Seriously?"

"Yes. Right next to the bearded lady and Jo-Jo the Dog-Faced Boy. About twenty or so premature babies, fighting for their lives. Shrunken. Shriveled. Pink. Tragic."

"I'm not sure of the point of the story," Charlie said. "I guess it's 'Thanks for not leaving me at the freak show'?"

Winston chewed a bite of his steak, then washed it down with a gulp of martini. "Actually, we did. Leave you there."

Charlie was shocked. "Excuse me?"

"You stayed there for nine days," Winston said, slicing off another bite of filet, "after which Couney and the staff thought you were fine to go home."

"Jesus, Dad, you left me at a freak show?"

"Charlie. I would have volunteered to stay at the freak show myself, swallowing swords or covering my body with tattoos, if I'd thought it would keep you alive. Shame

351

doesn't enter the picture when your baby's life is at stake!"

"No, I just mean —"

"Good Christ, you are still in a goddamn incubator. You don't see the world as it is, Charlie. So safely ensconced —"

"You think when I was slogging —"

"Oh, spare me your war stories," his dad said, stunning him into silence. "I know you were a goddamn patriot, but for some reason you failed to connect the evil you saw there and what the Allies had to do to stamp it out with the same imperatives here. Let me tell you something. When I was working on that trial of that goddamn cannibal? Fish? I saw the kind of evil that exists out there. And what you might not get is that the threat from the Communists is just as evil and just as real, and those fighting them need ammunition — and you keep standing in the goddamn way!" He banged on the table, prompting nearby club members to shoot Charlie concerned looks.

Charlie looked down at his briefcase, where he'd stowed the stolen NBC Strongfellow investigation. He was doing what he had to do, even to his own father's detriment; he was no longer standing in the way. But he knew he could hardly present this line he'd crossed as proof of his understanding.

"Ever since you got back from France, you've been in a goddamn academic ivory tower thinking lofty thoughts," Winston said, "writing about our Founding Fathers — who certainly knew what protecting this nation actually meant. But you've missed the point of all of it!"

Yes, by all means, lecture me about elitism in the private dining room of the Harvard Club, Charlie thought. He took a bite of his chicken salad sandwich. "Boy," he said, chewing, "that Fish trial sounds disturbing. Seriously psychologically disturbing."

Winston Marder ran his tongue against his molars, seemingly more focused on stray bits of steak stuck between his teeth than his son's concern over the damage done years ago to his psyche.

Charlie went straight from the Harvard Club to Pennsylvania Station, hoping to catch the first train back to Washington. He had refrained from drinking with his father, but he went to the club car of the *Afternoon Congressional* train and ordered a bourbon even before the locomotive lurched and jerked and commenced its southward trip. He checked his watch: 2:50 p.m. The lights in the car flickered as they proceeded under the Hudson River through the North Tunnel, chugging under Weehawken and Union City, emerging from the underworld via the portal in North Bergen.

They zoomed through the slums of Secaucus and Jersey City, crossing over the dingy Passaic River for a brief stop at Pennsylvania Station in Newark, then quickly moved off through Elizabeth, Linden, Rahway — the low-income apartments and one-story homes ran together, blurring the entire state into one giant, nebulous town you would never want to live in. The club-car bartender refreshed Charlie's drink as he stood at the bar, staring out the window. He thought about the *This Is Your Life* investigation, the irony of his father sneering at him for not following orders with sufficient obedience when the only reason he was even in New York City was to steal NBC's *This Is Your Life* investigation from his dad, a testament to his being all too willing to do what he had to do. He thought of the irony of the fact that though he had been obsessed with correct usage of the term *irony* as a young man, he had never truly experienced it until today. He thought of the irony of the fact that his father had been the one to drum into his head the proper use of the term after he had wrongly used it as a synonym for "coincidence," and here he was betraying the man who had taught him what it meant. Or was that not in itself ironic? Charlie's head began to ache.

He felt weighed down again. There were the issues that seemed minor in the grand scheme of things intellectually but still felt like bites of his integrity — stealing the NBC Strongfellow dossier, his failed Goodstone fight, guilt about MacLachlan's death, the pending preposterous comic-book hearings, handing off the Boschwitz folder. A lifetime's worth of selling out in just two months.

And then, of course, the young woman, his fears about what he must have done to have caused her death, though there was part of him that still couldn't believe it. He assumed this was a defense mechanism and that sooner or later he would accept that he was behind the loss of a life, but he wasn't there yet.

And underneath it all there was Margaret, or the absence thereof. *Where was Margaret?* God, how he needed her now.

CHAPTER NINETEEN:
WEDNESDAY, MARCH 10, 1954

Nanticoke Island, Maryland

From Charlie's enlistment in 1942 until the end of the war, Margaret had tracked his journey on a map she tacked up next to her bed. Starting in Fort Meade, Maryland, pins were placed on the North Carolina–South Carolina border where Charlie next was shipped for practice maneuvers, then to Fort Benning in Georgia. In October 1942, Charlie and the 175th Infantry Regiment crammed into the ocean liner RMS *Queen Elizabeth* and set sail for England, where they were ultimately given temporary quarters at a former British military base, Tidworth Barracks.

She wrote to him every day; he wrote back as often as he could, although that became increasingly difficult as K Company got closer to the front lines. In his letters, Charlie described Tidworth Barracks as ascetic — just a dozen brick buildings with no central heat, each named for a battle the British had fought in India. The barracks had coal-burning fireplaces at each end, but Charlie's bunk stood in the middle, so very little heat reached him throughout that cold, wet English winter.

Charlie deployed his usual comic detachment when he wrote to her, but Margaret thought the barracks and the daily training routines sounded miserable. The UK was being bombed constantly, so every night blackout conditions were in effect. Any rare moments of R and R were spent struggling with directions to a restaurant or pub without benefit of street or route signs, which the British had removed in case of enemy invasion. Charlie and his fellow troops conducted practice amphibious assaults on local lakes, rivers, and moors until K Company and the larger infantry regiment were transported to Devon to wait to board the tank landing ships in which they would be shuttled to the beaches of Normandy.

"Of everything we've experienced here in England," Charlie wrote while waiting to ship out for France, in a rare moment of candor,

it wasn't the bone-chilling cold of the

desperate English winter that made me most miserable, though there was one night where I gladly would have traded a limb for a bucket of coal. And it wasn't the constant threat of air assault marked by sirens, panic, confusion, and impotence. It was the moors — the dark, dank, foul, freezing, fetid swamps filled with bacteria and leeches and swarming with mosquitoes, a hundred pounds of gear strapped on our backs, pushing us down into the muck, while the slough tricked us with false floors, causing us to stumble and drink in the grime — the experience was akin to dunking my body into a pool of death, that's the only way I can think of to describe it. I cannot say anything more about what we are doing next, but I am sure it will be worse. I don't know if our times in the marshlands prepared us tactically or just barely introduced us to a taste of the horror that awaits on the mainland.

Now, ten years later, standing on her tiptoes on a sandbar in the Atlantic Ocean, saltwater waves splashing into her nose and down her throat, Margaret had some understanding of what Charlie had described.

The previous night, Margaret had made a glorious discovery. Quadrani and Hinman, their counterparts on Susquehannock Island, had found the three ponies that had swum to their island and concluded they were a stallion, mare, and foal — a family. On walkie-talkies, they shared what they'd learned. Gwinnett assigned each of the members of his team night shifts in which they were to surreptitiously watch the sleeping strings to see if any made their way to the beach and then the ocean. They did that for three nights straight, with no results. But then Margaret found a string in a field and patiently waited behind a shrub thicket of marsh elder. Within an hour, just after midnight, she watched a mare lead her family down a narrow path toward the beach. Margaret, crouched over and scurrying quietly behind them, watched as they galloped into the shallows of the surf and onto an apparent sandbar, after which the stallion, mare, and two foals swam out across the bay, the stallion now taking the lead. She raced back to wake up her colleagues and share with them the confirmation of what was something of a revelation in their field — that the ponies, quite unusually, apparently traveled in families, not larger strings, and that the mare, at least in this case, was the driving force to get the family to the water.

Tonight, however, as they watched a new string make the journey, it seemed the foal might prove too weak. A strong wind raised a more pugilistic surf than normal, with trains of swell waves hitting shore. As the stallion and mare boldly galloped into the surf, the foal stumbled, her legs wobbly and spindly.

"She looks off," said Kessler, kneeling in a patch of beach heather behind a dune, where the group had been sitting since dusk.

"Maybe she was premature? Or just a runt," Cornelius speculated.

The foal made her way to the sandbar, which was within a few dozen feet of shore, the waves slapping into her flank as she followed her parents.

"Is she going to be able to handle the swimming part of this?" Gwinnett asked. "I think I saw her two days ago struggling to keep up just on land."

Aiming Kessler's powerful flashlight at the sandbar, Margaret watched the foal stumble and fall behind while her parents set out into the water. Margaret had long been interested in the bond between mares and foals and whether it had an impact on the larger string, but right now, her intense focus was less academic in nature; she realized that at some point the foal would need to begin swimming, and she didn't know if the young pony was up to the task. The foal looked weak but determined, faltering and nearly collapsing before taking a few halting steps, falling farther behind her parents. Margaret held her breath, wondering whether the stallion or, more likely, the mare would opt for nurturing heroism or if more Darwinian impulses would decide the foal's fate.

"Jesus," Margaret said as a wave smacked the foal's shoulder and half submerged her head in the water.

"Maybe best not to watch, Margaret," Gwinnett said, placing his hand on her arm. She twitched instinctively and his hand fell back to his side.

The foal, now ten or so yards behind her galloping parents, continued on her path to Susquehannock Island, but her struggle seemed to increase with each step. She slowed as she waded into deeper water, and she began to disappear. The farther and deeper she went, the harder it was for the team to track her progress.

Margaret snatched the flashlight from Kessler and ran down the beach, trying to get a better view of the foal.

"Margaret, what are you doing?" Gwinnett shouted from behind her.

The slight extra weight in her midsection slowed Margaret a tad as she began sprinting down the beach, trying to catch up with the foal, running parallel to the angular path of the sandbar and into the surf, lifting her knees to avoid being slowed by the breakers.

"Margaret!" shouted Gwinnett. "Margaret?"

But Margaret barely heard him; she was focused on the young pony, who was trying to keep her head above the waves, fighting not to be dragged down. Margaret waded in and then threw the flashlight onto the sand and dived into the water. She had the foal in her line of sight, maybe twenty feet away, still vaguely illuminated by the moon. The water was shockingly cold.

Gwinnett, Kessler, and Cornelius began running down the beach, following Margaret's general direction in the water but remaining on land.

Margaret was maybe ten feet away from the foal, whose ears were all that were visible as the rip current dragged her from the shore. As a wave approached, Margaret inhaled deeply, then dived into the sea, extending her arms as far forward as possible until finally her fingertips, then her full palms, touched the pony, covered in soft, silky hair. She slid her arms around the sides of the foal's body, clasped her fingers under her barrel, and tried to stand. As she straightened her legs, the depth of the water surprised her. She was able to stand, but barely, on the balls of her feet, with her head and mouth just reaching the air above. She found herself trapped in a tug-of-war with the undertow as she and the foal battled against the current.

It was then that she thought, for just a split second, of Charlie and his stories from training for D-Day.

She could hear the men yelling from the shore, but she didn't know what they were saying and she didn't care. The foal couldn't have weighed that much, and given natural buoyancy, Margaret thought she should have been able to quickly float the pony to the shallows, but it proved more difficult than she'd anticipated. The foal's thrashing complicated her attempts to hang on to her as the ocean dragged her out to sea. Soon Margaret could no longer touch the bottom of the ocean. She was athletic enough to keep holding the foal's head above the water, the scissor kick of her legs preventing them from drifting farther, but the result was essentially stasis.

Then suddenly the burden of the foal was

partly lifted, and the mass of their bodies was successfully resisting the undertow. Though the inky black sky and dark ocean had all but merged into one ominous void for Margaret, she could sense that someone else had joined them. At first in her panic she imagined some giant fish or dolphin, some magical sea creature arriving deus ex machina, but after she regained her footing and she and the foal edged their way to a shallower patch where she could stand, she saw that it was a man with them, and he had the foal by her head and forelegs and was helping to carry her while also bringing both of them to safety, and she thought maybe it was Gwinnett but then the man raised his head to look at her and she was stunned to see that it was Charlie.

Chapter Twenty:
Wednesday, March 10, 1954

Maryland Rural Route 32

His sudden trip to Nanticoke Island had been the most impulsive action Charlie had taken in a decade. Behaving erratically energized and emboldened him, allowing him to cast off the chains of predictable adult behavior amid the chaotic swirl of his life these past three months. He had gotten off the train in Baltimore and hired a taxi to take him to the end of Maryland Rural Route 32, the tip of the isthmus, although he had to try eight different cabbies before he finally found one who agreed to do it, for twice the normal rate. Charlie had the cash on hand; part of him must have known he was going to make this rash journey. He told the hack he'd give him fifty bucks if he waited an hour in that same spot.

He arrived at the tip of the isthmus just after eight p.m. There was a narrow footbridge from there to Susquehannock Island, but to get to Nanticoke he would need a boat. The local live-bait store was not yet open for the season, but a young man doing inventory on new rods and reels, nets and lures agreed to rent him a motorboat. He took it to Nanticoke Island and disembarked at the small, shabby dock.

From there, Charlie had walked through a thicket of trees, then to the campsite, which cast the only light he could discern on the island, from a still-crackling fire around which stood four tents. No one was there, but he heard noises from beyond some bushes, past a dune, so he headed to what he presumed would be the beach.

From the dune he saw Margaret in the distance running into the water; he wasn't sure why. He watched in disbelief as the three men made their way to the closest spot to her on the sand but never went into the water. Charlie began running toward his wife and saw her head disappear beneath the waves. Next thing Charlie knew, he was sprinting into the sea, gasping at its frigidity, racing toward Margaret and what he now saw was a thrashing pony. He grabbed the pony around her barrel behind her front legs and eased her and Margaret to shallower water until the two of them were together carrying the pony to the safety of the sand.

Margaret and Charlie locked eyes and gently laid the foal on the beach away from the waves before they collapsed on hands and knees, gasping for breath and shivering in the cold. At last the other men sprang into action; Cornelius tended to the foal, covering her with a towel while he checked her pulse and breathing; Kessler draped blankets over Charlie's and Margaret's shoulders, while Gwinnett checked their pulses. Margaret, in an adrenaline-fueled daze, kept looking at Charlie and shaking her head, whether in disbelief that he was really here or that they had just pulled off this unlikely rescue, he couldn't tell.

After a few more minutes of silence, Margaret stood and approached Cornelius, still ministering to the wet foal. The pony lay on her side with her head in the grad student's lap; he was scratching her chin groove with one hand, patting her muzzle with the other. She had a teardrop-shaped pattern on her forehead, recalling the stallion from weeks before. Her flank was expanding and contracting at a rapid clip, her eyes staring dolefully at nothing in particular until they flickered to Margaret. Against all her scientific training and instincts, Margaret felt a connection, almost an understanding, pass between them.

"She's going to be okay, I think," Cornelius said.

"Well, she's going to live," Margaret said. "But I don't know that she's going to survive without her parents. Maybe we can get her to a local farm."

"Why don't we go to the camp?" Gwinnett suggested. "Warm up by the fire."

Charlie put a tentative arm around Margaret's shoulders and the two headed to the warmth of the fire that Kessler was now feeding with kindling. It was agreed that Margaret and Charlie should get out of their wet clothes, so Margaret went into her tent, and Charlie accepted Gwinnett's offer of a loan to replace his soaking-wet pants, shirt, and socks.

The group stood around the fire warming themselves, and finally Charlie spoke. "With Margaret's permission, I'd like to take her home. She can come back after a little rest, I think. Yes?" He turned to Margaret and she nodded.

"You sure about that, Mags?" Gwinnett asked. She nodded again.

Charlie shook Gwinnett's hand with a firm grip and looked him in the eye. The message was clear, he felt: *I've got it from here, fella.*

"Okay, we can leave your camp set up," Gwinnett said. "We'll be here until the first week of May. Come back as soon as you can."

"We can move your tent and gear to Susquehannock in two weeks," Kessler added, "or bring it to you in DC in a month."

The Marders walked through the brush and to the dock. Charlie guided Margaret into the motorboat he had rented, and they headed to the mainland, where the cabbie was waiting. They were spent, so they asked him to take them to the local motel, Polly's Lodging. The two barely spoke as they were driven through the dark, though Charlie's hand eventually found its way to Margaret's.

Margaret recognized Polly from her last visit to the island in January, when she'd borrowed the motel phone, but the woman gave no sign of remembering her. She informed Charlie that they had plenty of rooms and offered them what she referred to without a trace of sarcasm as the honeymoon suite at no extra charge if they indeed would be staying only one night. He looked at Margaret, who squeezed his hand. With his briefcase and her leather satchel between them, they walked to room 20 and Charlie locked the door behind them. The clock by their bedside said 1:05.

"Well," said Margaret, sitting on the bed and exhaling loudly, "that was something."

Charlie pulled up a chair and tried to think of what to say.

"I've really missed you," he finally blurted out.

"I'm right here."

"Are you?"

She sniffed, still cold from the ocean, and reached for a tissue. "Yes," she said.

"We haven't talked in forever."

Margaret pulled an elastic band from around her wrist and put her blond hair up in a ponytail. "Truth Train?"

Charlie smiled. His parents' wedding present to them had been a round-trip train ride on "the most famous train in the world," the *20th Century Limited,* from New York's Grand Central Terminal to Chicago's La-Salle Street Station, a trip they took in the summer of 1947. It was not the easiest time in their marriage, as Charlie was struggling with war memories and what seemed to him a shallow and silly civilian world. After a couple of cocktails one evening, Margaret came up with the idea that while they were on the train, they could speak only the 100 percent truth to each other. The result was shockingly effective — the truths one revealed and explored were usually about one's own bad behavior — and for the next year or so they would use the term *Truth Train* to temporarily reinstate those rules. It had been at least five years since either had invoked it.

"Truth Train," Charlie agreed.

"We haven't talked in forever because I've made it clear I didn't like what you had to say."

Charlie grimaced; she was so much better at Truth Train than he was.

"I know," he acknowledged.

She sat waiting for him to offer a contribution.

Finally he told her: "I've been doing the best I can. This hasn't been easy. You and the baby. Everything is so new, and Washington is such a messed-up place." He heard weakness in his voice and cursed himself for it; he wanted to be honest, but he didn't want her to think he couldn't handle the pressures of their new life.

Margaret's face was stony, unreadable. She leaned back on the bed. "I'm assuming there's much more going on here than those insipid comic-book hearings. And part of me doesn't want to know more. But that's selfish." Her face softened. "I think I've been afraid to find out more."

"You don't want to hear that I'm not the man you thought you'd married." Charlie took her hands in his. "I didn't think you did." He looked down at the floor and shook his head. It was hard to meet her gaze knowing everything he had to tell her.

Margaret squeezed his hands sympathetically. "You sound just a bit self-pitying there, honey."

He winced, then smiled. "I forgot how turbulent the Truth Train can be."

"I want to help. But I have to know what's going on."

"That's why I came here. I can get through this, but not . . . not without you."

He was surprised to see her eyes glistening with tears. She patted the bed next to her. He obligingly crawled onto it and sank against the pillows. Margaret propped herself up on an elbow and turned to him, all trace of emotion replaced by her usual inquisitive and methodical manner. "All right, darling. I want to hear everything."

So he told her.

Hands clasped behind his head, Charlie found it easier to look at the motel ceiling than at Margaret as he unburdened himself. He began at the beginning: Why he had the congressional seat. Congressman Van Waganan's death might not have been as neat and tidy as it seemed. At least, not according to Congressman Christian MacLachlan, who was now also dead, shot by Puerto Rican terrorists.

"What was Mac suggesting happened to Van Waganan?" she asked.

"Nothing specific. Just vague allusions to how nothing was what it seemed, how Van Waganan had kept up the fight against companies cutting corners."

"I thought Van Waganan committed suicide."

"Me too, but Street says he was found in a hotel with a prostitute. They were both dead."

Margaret's face settled into an expression of confused disbelief as Charlie told her about the odd note he found in the desk that was once Van Waganan's: *U Chicago, 2,4-D 2,4,5-T cereal grains broadleaf crops.*

"You remember my perky intern, Sheryl Ann Bernstein, she came to the house that time?" Margaret nodded with a slight roll of her eyes. "Her brother's at Northwestern so she asked him to go see what that meant, but he hit a dead end. A woman at the University of Chicago said the study was subject to wartime secrecy laws."

"War's been over for a decade," Margaret observed.

"Yes, so I've read," Charlie said. "Strong-fellow's on House Armed Services so he explored it at the Pentagon but also didn't get anywhere."

She wrinkled her brow. "This is all just so bizarre."

"It gets stranger. Because now Mac is dead," Charlie said, "and on his deathbed, the last thing he said to me was 'under Jennifer.' "

She scrunched up her face in confusion, and Charlie nodded. "We had no idea who Jennifer was, but then Sheryl Ann came up with a smart theory." He started telling her about Maryland delegate Daniel of St. Thomas Jenifer, but Margaret held up her hand to stop him.

"I need to write all this down," she said. She opened the drawer of the nightstand and withdrew a pad of paper and a sharpened pencil. *Mac,* she wrote at the top of the pad, followed by other reminders of related threads. This was how they had worked together while he was writing *Sons of Liberty;* he would research and share his discoveries, and then she would take notes and categorize every item until they could come up with coherent narratives.

"Congressman Street and this girl, Sheryl Ann — how much do they know about your predicament?" Margaret asked.

"Sheryl Ann knows a little, about the broadleaf-crops note and about Daniel of St. Thomas Jenifer, obviously," Charlie said. "Isaiah knows everything."

"Okay, what else?" she asked. "What ever happened with your main mission? To stop funding for Goodstone?"

Charlie shook his head. "I thought I'd achieved it. Carlin told me it was out of the bill, we voted, everyone was patting me on the back —"

"Did you read the bill?" she interrupted.

"I did," he said. "There were no references to Goodstone. That section had been deleted. But then . . . well, Conrad Hilton was throwing a party — a celebration of the migrant bill passing. So we were all at the penthouse of the Mayflower and Carlin was there. The night got away from me a bit. Strongfellow and Bob Kennedy were there. Roy Cohn too. We got into it about Ike and patriotism, and I got hit with the Cohn crazy spray. But more to the point, eventually I ended up drinking absinthe with Carlin, Strongfellow, and some others. La-Montagne."

"Oh . . ." Margaret tapped the pencil against her cheek thoughtfully. "This must have been the morning you came home reeking like a distillery rag."

"Correct."

"Boy, I hated you that morning."

Charlie remained silent, knowing she had every right to resent him. And he hadn't even gotten to the worst of it yet: the car accident. He told her about Carlin cackling when he said, "I screwed you on Goodstone," and, to be fair, because he was nothing if not diligently so, about Carlin's argument that businesses such as Goodstone and General Kinetics needed to thrive as much for national security as for national economic advancement.

"It's so odd that he told you about it," Margaret said. "Why not just do it and go on about his life?"

"Clearly he doesn't like me," said Charlie, who had given the matter some serious thought. "He didn't appreciate my original protest of the funding. And, look, he's a hardscrabble, pull-himself-up-by-his-own-bootstraps kind of guy from Snake Skull, Oklahoma, and to him I must seem like an entitled establishment New Yorker who breezed into Congress without any right to be there."

Margaret kept writing. Underneath *Carlin* she added a note about the chairman's request that Charlie co-sponsor the farm bill with him.

"This is all about controlling you," Margaret observed. And it was difficult to argue with that, though Charlie told her that when he'd asked Carlin to block the General Kinetics plant from Harlem, Carlin had said he would.

"Carlin screwed you on Goodstone because it would hurt General Kinetics," Margaret noted. "Do you assume he's going to follow through with the Harlem plant?"

"I don't know. Maybe, now that he thinks I'm playing ball?"

It was after two o'clock in the morning but neither wanted to stop talking, and the work was almost beside the point. On a page Margaret labeled *Miscellaneous,* a list of names and events grew long: *Carlin, Strongfellow, Cohn, Kennedy, Kefauver, poker night, comic-book hearing.* She designated the next page *Odd,* and that list included Margaret Chase Smith's suggestion that Charlie use the special members-only collection at the Library of Congress to do more research on Ben Franklin and the Hellfire Club ("Why do you think she made such a point of recommending that?"). And although Charlie wasn't sure if or how it related to his ongoing troubles, she insisted on adding his father's drunken luncheon lecture and the unsettling revelation about the Coney Island incubators.

She came to the end of the page and looked at him expectantly. "There's more, isn't there?"

That she knew him so well was both perilous and the whole point. Charlie nodded grimly and took a deep breath.

"So LaMontagne gave me a file full of dirt against a guy at Zenith, Ira Boschwitz. A competitor. About him being a Commie. I went back and forth on it, but ultimately I did what LaMontagne told me to and gave it to Bob Kennedy for the McCarthy Committee. I saw in the paper three days later that he'd been called before the committee and that he'd been fired."

She sat silently for a minute, her head tilted to one side. Were all these compromised decisions just part of adulthood? She knew of no such corruption of her martyred father, but was that only because she didn't really know about his life? Or because he had been killed so young? Now that she thought about it, was his participation in that mission without blemish? The captain of the USS *Shenandoah* had seen that thunderstorms would be on the flight path and urged command to wait them out. He'd been overruled, and fourteen men, including her dad, had been killed. Surely they had all known of the bad weather, yet they went along with their orders. Was that so dissimilar from the difficult orders Charlie faced?

"I could see that decision not being so simple," she finally allowed. "I mean, what if he ends up being a Communist and it comes out that you sat on the file? It would be easy for me to judge. But who knows if it's wrong or right? It's not as if there aren't Communists infiltrating the world of defense contractors."

Charlie nodded slowly. "Yeah, that's how I rationalized it, but it wasn't a proud moment. And I don't trust LaMontagne."

Margaret was less understanding when he told her about McCarthy asking him to steal the file on NBC's investigation into Strongfellow from his father's study.

"Why on earth would you do that?" she asked.

And that was when he had to tell her the worst of it: the car accident. He didn't know who knew what, and he was terrified to disobey anyone lest that person ruin his life.

As calmly and clearly as he knew how, Charlie recounted the events of that awful night — those he remembered, at any rate. He watched his wife's face closely as she tried to understand what he was telling her: waking up in the mud, LaMontagne's arrival, the discovery of the dead woman, LaMontagne carrying her corpse to the car, Charlie refusing to take part in it but also refusing to stop it, the two of them driving off, how he'd collapsed later that morning from the guilt of it all, his terror that he might have killed an innocent woman.

When he was finally done, the tiny room was silent. Outside a chorus of crickets chirped.

Margaret looked at her husband with an expression that suggested both shock and revulsion, and then, without a word, she stood up from the bed, walked to the door, opened it, and took in great gulps of fresh air. The crickets' refrain grew louder and seemed almost taunting to Charlie.

He sat, helpless, while she stood ramrod straight in the doorway, her arms folded across her chest, her chin thrust out defiantly.

He feared he had lost her, that this had been a bridge too far. Had telling her been a selfish decision? Had he blown up his marriage in the name of saving it?

Charlie didn't know what to say. His heart pounded with desperation.

"I know you're disappointed," he said. "I

am too. I know I should have stopped him and called the police."

Margaret stared up at the sliver of moon. She was silent.

"All I can say is that at the time, I was toxically drunk. And in some sort of shock. And when I finally understood what had happened, the thought of leaving you and the baby on your own seemed atrocious. That's not an excuse and it makes me sound as if I think I'm some selfless hero, but you have to believe it's not like that at all. I am disgusted with myself."

"I'm actually bothered about something else more than that," she said.

Uh-oh, thought Charlie. *Jesus. I shouldn't have told her.*

"How did you drive the car?" Margaret asked.

Charlie was taken aback. "What do you mean?"

She turned around and faced him, standing in the doorway. "You were blackout drunk. Strongfellow told you later that you were knocked out."

"Right."

"Charlie, you don't just shake off that sort of thing and go drive. That's not you. You go full coma. You're impossible to wake up from something like that. I can't even get you to stop snoring. And that's from mere martinis, forget absinthe."

"What are you saying?"

"I'm saying I don't think you were driving the car. I don't think you killed that young woman. And then LaMontagne just happens along? And now you're indebted to him? I mean, really?"

Charlie looked at her eyes, as clear and green as emeralds, her expression as sincere as a child's. She meant this. And in her certainty, he began to believe it might be true. It hadn't even been a full week since the crash, but it felt like six months. He'd carried the guilt of that night with him as a constant companion; the thought that he might not have been responsible was something he barely allowed himself to consider, to hope for. He started to offer a protest, but Margaret, silhouetted in the doorway, silenced him with a stern shake of her head.

"There's just no one who knows you like I do, Charlie, and I'm telling you that you weren't responsible for that car crash. Not for any moral or ethical reason; I mean, just pure metabolism."

She reentered the room and shut the motel door behind her.

"I think it was all a setup," she said.

■ ■ ■ ■

At nine that morning, Isaiah Street's 1952 green Plymouth Cranbrook pulled up in front of their motel room, its brakes screeching and gravel spraying.

Charlie had called him a few hours earlier. He knew it was a big favor to ask, but he believed that Street had some idea of how high the floodwaters were rising around him, a sense confirmed when Street immediately agreed.

The Marders were waiting and ready when Street arrived, giving him no need to honk or even turn off the car as they climbed inside, Charlie up front, Margaret in back. Street nodded his appreciation: "No reason for someone like me to be in one place for too long in rural Maryland," he said drily as he made a U-turn out of the parking lot and got back on Rural Route 32, keeping five miles an hour under the speed limit, as always.

"I'm guessing you went faster as a Tuskegee Airman," Margaret joked.

"All I had to worry about up there was the Luftwaffe," Street said.

Street turned the radio dial to news: the statehoods of Hawaii and Alaska were being put on a single Senate bill, against the wishes of the Eisenhower administration.

"Why does he want them separate?" asked Margaret.

"Hawaii's a Republican state, Alaska's Democratic," Charlie said. "Ike is more keen on adding the Republican voters and senators to the rolls."

More news from the Marshall Islands: The Atomic Energy Commission was about to acknowledge that more than two dozen Americans and hundreds of natives had been exposed to radiation during the recent testing of an atomic bomb. Next, stunningly, the army had issued a report charging that McCarthy and Cohn had threatened the military if it didn't provide preferential treatment for one of their former investigators, Private David Schine. McCarthy and Cohn had wanted Schine to get an expedited promotion and be stationed at West Point with a cushy job. After those requests were denied, Cohn threatened to "wreck the Army," sources said.

"What a little creep," Margaret said. "Attack-attack-attack, threaten-threaten-threaten. How did Cohn make it to adulthood without learning how civilized people behave?"

"Civilized people such as whom?" asked

Charlie. "Such as Joe McCarthy?"

"Him too," Margaret said. "This is not normal."

Street chortled.

"Speak up, Isaiah," Charlie said. "You're among friends."

"I'm sorry, but the things commonly said about Negroes not only in polite company but on the floor of the House and Senate . . . you don't know what being uncivilized is. Imagine a world full of Cohns and McCarthys accusing all people with your skin color of every crime imaginable, of being subhuman. Not for our ideology, not for being a Red — whether true or not — but for how we were born. Imagine statues of these accusers lining the halls of Congress. I mean, my people have been facing McCarthyism since before McCarthy! 'Are you now, or have you ever been, a Negro?' "

He shook his head and silence filled the car.

"It's a fair point," Margaret finally said.

"These are the things I typically don't say in front of white folks."

Another silence. Charlie looked toward the backseat, to Margaret, who smiled at him regretfully.

"I suppose there are no secrets among us anymore," Charlie said.

"I would hope not," said Street. He looked at Margaret in the rearview mirror. "Your husband told me all about the predicament in which he finds himself."

"That's right," Charlie said. "You're the only two who know everything."

"Not everything," Margaret noted. "Tell Isaiah about New York. About McCarthy's request." So Charlie told Isaiah about McCarthy's menacing demand that Charlie obtain the Strongfellow file from his father's study and that he'd complied.

Street drove them through the rural hills of Maryland, which, though they were only ninety minutes or so from Baltimore and two hours from Washington, DC, looked like they could have been in Alabama or Indiana. A small town would pop up around a turn — pharmacy, diner, doctor's office, hardware store, gas station, school — then quickly vanish after two blocks, the landscape going back to forests or farms. They sped by immense empty fields where corn would soon grow, roadside produce markets advertising asparagus, tomatoes, and squash that did not yet exist. As they rode, they discussed the murky swamp in which Charlie had found himself wading.

"I think for now, you've got to go along to get along while we figure out what to do next," Street said. "Maybe you can cease to be of any use to them? Get a new committee assignment? Instead of Appropriations, maybe try to get on Veterans' Affairs. God knows it should be easy enough to get a seat — not exactly a meal-ticket committee assignment."

Margaret lit a cigarette and rolled down the window. Wearing black sunglasses and a sheer scarf wrapped around her head, she looked like a movie star trying not to be recognized.

"Let's just try to keep a low profile, though, Charlie," she said. "You don't need to be going out to cocktail parties or poker nights. Just go to work and come home."

"I agree with that, except the poker-night part," Street said.

"Me too," Charlie said grimly.

Charlie sank in his seat. Street found a jazz station on the radio, and none of them spoke until the car crossed the brand-new Chesapeake Bay Bridge, which, at 4.3 miles, was the third-longest bridge in the world. The structure seemed endless to Charlie, and there was part of him that hoped they might never have to return to land.

CHAPTER TWENTY-ONE:
TUESDAY, MARCH 16, 1954

Washington, DC

When Charlie met Cohn at Filibuster's on Constitution Avenue the following Tuesday, the lawyer stood and greeted him with a smile, then sank back into the leather club chair at the corner table and summoned another Manhattan with a word and a flick of his hand in the direction of the bar. Charlie placed the manila folder containing NBC's dirt on Strongfellow in the center of the table.

"You take a peek?" asked Cohn.

"No."

Cohn rolled his eyes while he lit a Lucky Strike. "Need a towel there, Pontius?" He opened the folder and inspected its contents.

They were sitting below framed faded photographs of once-powerful legislators whose names might prove elusive to anyone but the most devoted student of congressional arcana. While Cohn read the NBC memo about Strongfellow, Charlie glanced idly at the men on the wall. He thought of the Howard Chandler Christy painting of the signing of the U.S. Constitution, about how only three or so of the delegates might be recognizable even to members of Congress. *Will anyone know about me?* he wondered. His congressional career to date would hardly merit a spot on even a monument to obscurity.

The waitress brought Cohn's Manhattan and took Charlie's drink order.

"You have no interest in what I'm reading?" Cohn asked without looking up, his eyes keenly focused on whatever incriminating information lay before him.

"Of course I'm interested," said Charlie. "That doesn't mean I think it's my business. And Strongfellow's a friend."

"Friend?" Cohn said. "You're a sweetie pie."

"Why do you need dirt on Strongfellow?" Charlie asked.

Cohn closed the folder. "We need to know what's out there about him so we can protect him," he said. "If NBC Entertainment knows damaging information about a congressman, then NBC News might report it. They probably won't, but still. Strongfellow's on the team; we need to be prepared to protect him."

"Protect him? He was in the OSS and can barely stand because of the injuries he sustained at the hands of the Nazis. If there's a tougher son of a bitch in Congress, I have yet to meet him."

Cohn barked a short laugh. "For a professional historian, you're pretty gullible. I wouldn't believe everything *This Is Your Life* tells you."

"You think I'm a gullible historian?" Charlie attempted a smile. "Maybe it's a good thing I've changed careers."

"Funny you'd say so." Cohn looked at him sternly. "There are some Democrats planning to run against you, as you might expect. Your father and I spoke about setting up a campaign committee. With your permission, of course."

"You spoke with my father?"

"Sure," Cohn responded, as if there were nothing odd about that. "Carlin asked me to. You have no reelect set up."

Head down, Charlie told himself. *Act like this is all fine with you.* "That's a flattering offer and I appreciate it. I haven't even officially decided if I'm running for reelection."

Cohn raised an eyebrow as the cocktail

waitress deposited a glass of Jack Daniel's in front of Charlie.

"Why wouldn't you run?" Cohn asked. "Granted, a certain group of us are well aware that you have no idea what you're doing, but to the wide world out there, including most of the morons in this town, you're a comer."

"I haven't even discussed it with my wife yet."

Cohn reached into the inside pocket of his jacket and withdrew his checkbook and a pen. "Allow me to make the first contribution, assuming you do run," he said. He opened the checkbook, scribbled something, and then handed Charlie a check for five hundred dollars made out to him personally.

"Shouldn't this be for the Vote for Charlie Marder Committee or something?"

"You can always transfer it to that committee after I have it set up for you. If you'd like me to take that step?"

Head down, Charlie thought. He nodded glumly then caught himself, smiled, and raised a glass to his new campaign treasurer as he felt his body sinking slowly into an imagined pit of ooze.

"The makers of Camel Cigarettes bring the

391

world's news events right into your own living room," proclaimed the announcer before a black-and-white film montage of a prize fight, a battleship, the U.S. Capitol Building, and a bathing-beauty contest. "Sit back, light up a Camel, and be an eyewitness to the happenings that made history in the last twenty-four hours."

Renee Street never missed an episode of NBC's *Camel News Caravan.* She looked forward to her nightly reward after a long day spent tending to the twins, whose lives were interrupted five times a week by the sound of John Cameron Swayze's opening line — "Let's go hopscotching around the world for headlines" — a Pavlovian trigger for them to remain silent and out of trouble. With a flower in his lapel and a folksy, direct gaze, Swayze conveyed an air of charming authority.

Renee Street was such a fan, in fact, that she had been one of the first in line at the Woodward and Lothrop department store to purchase Swayze, a news-trivia board game from Milton Bradley. She might have been the wife of a congressman, but she never felt closer to the news and matters of importance than when she was playing Swayze. Which was how Charlie, Margaret, Isaiah, and Renee came to be sitting around a table at the Streets' house two Thursdays after Street picked up Charlie and Margaret from Polly's Lodging, rolling the dice and debating whether the answers to the news quiz were correct.

Isaiah was the first to raise an objection. Margaret had asked, " 'To which country did the U.S. send aid and manpower in the 1950s to help support democracy?' "

"I know the card is going to want me to say Korea," Street said. "But there are really any number of countries that applies to — Albania, the Philippines, Germany."

"Guatemala," said Charlie.

"Iran," Street added.

"British Guiana," said Charlie. "Vietnam!"

"But he means troops," protested Renee defensively, as if John Cameron Swayze had written the questions personally. "That's why it says *manpower.*"

"CIA are men," said her husband. "And they're in Saigon. And all over."

"Poorly worded, Swayze," Charlie teased.

Renee shot him a look of mock offense.

"The card does say Korea," Margaret said. "So go again."

Since returning from New York City and Nanticoke Island two weeks before, Charlie had done everything he could to keep his

393

head down. He'd dutifully, if unhappily, handed the *This Is Your Life* investigation to Cohn, agreed to co-sponsor the farm bill with Carlin, and prepared for the comic-book hearing on behalf of Kefauver. All of it filled him with regret but there was some consolation in Margaret now knowing and understanding that this was what he had to do until they figured out some escape plan.

At work, he seldom left his congressional office except for a hearing or a vote; Leopold kept close tabs on him and seemed pleased with his new attitude, as it made for fewer complications in her professional life. After discovering nothing particularly noteworthy about Daniel of St. Thomas Jenifer, Bernstein retreated to her more secretarial tasks; their banter continued but it was less charged, more benign. He wished he could explain to her the strategy, such as it was: Charlie had retreated from DC socializing and was spending any and all free time with Margaret, dining or seeing movies, and, twice now, staying in with the Streets.

" 'In what town did Senator Joseph McCarthy first reveal the presence of two hundred and five members of the Communist Party in the United States State Department?' " Margaret read.

The Streets conferred. Isaiah thought it

was Charleston, West Virginia; Renee was certain it was Wheeling.

Charlie took the card from his wife's hand and read it silently. "I would note," he said, "that the card suggests that McCarthy's ever-changing number of Reds at State is a factual accusation. When it says he *revealed* the presence."

"What should it say instead?" Renee asked.

"I dunno. *Claimed? Invented?*"

"You yourself have said there are Communists in the government, Charlie," said Isaiah.

"Of course," Charlie said. "But we all know by now that McCarthy and Cohn were making up these numbers. I don't think they've actually nailed down one Red in the State Department. They just concocted a story."

"Don't reporters do that too?" asked Margaret.

"Do they?" asked Charlie.

"I don't think John Cameron Swayze makes anything up," said Renee.

"I read articles about the Puerto Rican guerrillas that got everything wrong," said her husband. "There are a few solid reporters here and there, but it seems like too much of what's in the news media is spoon-fed to journalists by various government factions with agendas. Anti-Communist, pro-GOP, pro-Stevenson, pro-McCarthy, whatever. I don't know what to believe anymore."

"Not these cards," said Charlie. He lit a cigarette.

The next morning, as he walked through National Statuary Hall, Charlie noticed a small floor tile honoring James Polk, the eleventh president of the United States and the only former Speaker of the House to have made it to the top job. The tile marked where Polk's desk had been from 1835 until 1839, when he was Speaker and the House Chamber was located where Statuary Hall now stood. Charlie had walked past or even on this tile countless times without giving it much thought; now he paused to examine it. Polk was an incredibly consequential president most Americans knew nothing about, he thought. Politics was a cruel gig.

Charlie's early days in DC had been exciting (probably too exciting, he knew), but as the novelty wore off and the realities of political life became more oppressive, he found himself missing the less flashy, more substantial work he'd left behind at Columbia. He'd loved the quiet thrills of research and discovery, and if he was being completely honest, he missed the acclaim that came with his bestselling book.

He returned to his office, greeting Leopold with an absentminded nod as he sank into the chair behind his desk. Before him sat a collection of letters and documents as well as two books that had been sent to him: early proofs of Hermann Hagedorn's *The Roosevelt Family of Sagamore Hill* and the latest from his friend Paul Horgan, *Great River: The Rio Grande in North American History*. He sighed. What was he doing? He recalled Mac and then Margaret Chase Smith suggesting he check out the special members-only collection at the Library of Congress; Smith had specifically urged him to look into Ben Franklin and the Hellfire Club he had briefly mentioned in *Sons of Liberty*. Beyond the welcome distraction and the possibility that another book might provide him with a clearer path forward, Charlie felt excited at the prospect of research and access to rare documents. He called Margaret to tell her he'd be late getting home.

"Five thirty. Right on time," Bernstein said, looking at her watch. She'd been waiting for him in the Jefferson Building of the Library of Congress. Above her, in the semicircle over an arched window, hovered a painting of Johannes Gutenberg with two assistants at his printing press. Nearby were other painted tributes to the evolution of scholarship: a cairn, hieroglyphics, a cave painter, a monastery scriptorium.

"Come with me," Charlie said, not breaking stride.

Over the past few months, he and Bernstein had developed an easy friendship and even an affection, and while he wanted to encourage her scholarship, he also felt the need to establish some firmer boundaries so as to avoid any misunderstandings. Bernstein, looking a bit wounded by his brusque greeting, scurried after him as he proceeded up the stairway to the east end of the Great Hall's north alcove, to the office of the Librarian of Congress.

"So?" she said.

"So."

"So . . . what are we up to here?"

"Oh, right," said Charlie, reminded that other people existed. "Why are we here. Both Mac and Senator Smith told me about this members-only section of the library."

"Right. And?"

"And Smith suggested that there might be more information about the Hellfire Club.

Do you remember from my book?"

"Of course! Ben Franklin and his lecherous adventures in England. I'd read a whole book on that subject alone."

"The problem was I couldn't find any more about the Hellfire Club when I was working on my book. I tried. Maybe this special collection will have more. In any case, I thought you'd be interested in joining me to see what they have."

Charlie didn't say it aloud, but beyond his curiosity, part of him was contemplating a return to academia — and a potential project of note might ease the path back to the Upper West Side.

But for now his path was to the office of the Librarian of Congress. The previous holder of that position had left to work for the UN, and President Eisenhower had not yet nominated a replacement, so the task of escorting the congressman and his comely young aide to the members-only section of the Rare Book and Special Collections Reading Room in the Adams Building of the library fell to Stuart Sneed, an earnest and deferential junior librarian who soon appeared at the office of the librarian and apologized for being thirty seconds late. He walked Charlie and Bernstein down to the basement, along a long hall, and then, once they were in the Adams Building, up two flights of stairs. He unlocked a heavy oak door and escorted them into the expansive Special Collections Reading Room, where a half a dozen scholarly types sat in silence in armchairs or at well-lit desks studying various books and documents. Sneed offered Charlie and Bernstein a cursory tour of items on display behind glass cases: the library's Gutenberg Bible, published sometime around 1454; German cartographer Martin Waldseemüller's 1507 *Introduction to Cosmography,* where it was first suggested that the New World be named America; two pairs of spectacles, a pocketknife, a five-dollar bill, and other items President Lincoln had had on his person that fateful night at Ford's Theater.

"Spooky," Bernstein said with a slight shudder.

"But other than that, how was the library, Miss Bernstein?" joked Charlie.

With a deferential tilt of his head, Sneed indicated that they should follow him. At another door at the far end of the room, he extracted an enormous key ring, shuffled through all the possibilities, and finally arrived at one that had been marked with red nail polish. He grinned triumphantly and inserted the key with a flourish. Opening

400

the door created a sound of suction; the members-only collection was obviously tightly controlled for both climate and security.

"When was the last time anyone visited this collection?" Bernstein whispered.

"A couple months ago, I believe," said Sneed. "It's seldom used. Not too many members of Congress take the time to see the antiquities. If they want something from us, it usually concerns information about what's going on today, and we have a page bring whatever is needed right over."

The room inside was cozy, with an ornate Oriental rug, a large sofa, two plush armchairs, and wall-to-wall bookshelves and wooden file cabinets. Sneed pinballed around the room, turning on lamps, explaining how the various papers and letters in the collection were categorized, offering white cotton gloves and tweezers to Charlie and Bernstein for the handling of any document sealed in plastic. He also provided them with a binder detailing all of the various collections in the room and where they might be found.

"Library closes at ten," he said, after which he disappeared and left them to begin exploring the caverns of ancient letters, in search of information about Benjamin

Franklin and the Hellfire Club. They quickly found five folders of deeds, proclamations, books, drafts, newspapers, speeches, and correspondence to and from Franklin, and they divided them into two piles.

Two hours into the documents, Charlie threw his hands up in frustration.

"Still nothing?" Bernstein asked.

"No. A few mentions of his trips to England, but zero about the Hellfire Club, or the Medmenham Monks, as they called themselves. I guess I should have known better than to expect something to just be sitting here, waiting to be discovered."

Bernstein sighed sympathetically. He'd asked her to look in the section on England in the 1700s for mentions of Sir Francis Dashwood, the founder of the hedonistic society. So far, all she'd found was information having to do with his duties as postmaster general in England.

Charlie stood and stretched and looked at his watch; time to get home to Margaret. "Let's call it a night. Tomorrow, we'll brainstorm about what to do next. Maybe there's something in that binder detailing all the collections that we can study in the meantime. Can you ask Sneed to make a photocopy? Pretty sure the library has a Copyflo."

"A what?"

"A prototype photographic copy machine. You know, xerography."

"I have no idea what you're talking about, Congressman."

"New technology. Have you really not followed this? Haloid Company? Xerography? Photographic copies of documents? It will be huge. You should invest in it if you have any money."

"I don't."

"Seriously, though," Charlie said, collecting his belongings, "don't you read the business pages?"

"Not really," Bernstein admitted. "I prefer to focus on the politicians, not the CEOs."

"And who do you think," Charlie asked, walking toward the door, "is telling those politicians what to do?"

CHAPTER TWENTY-TWO: TUESDAY, APRIL 20, 1954

Georgetown, Washington, DC

Charlie exhaled one last satisfied breath to both begin the process of bringing down his heart rate and signal his immense satisfaction.

"Indeed," Margaret said.

Their clothes strewn about the living room, the couple lay naked on the couch. In the weeks since they returned from Maryland, they had been reconnecting — first as friends, now as husband and wife, her expanding abdomen no impediment.

"Second trimester is a bit more fun," he observed.

"Hormones seem to be working for me, not against me, now."

He stood and looked around the room for his underwear.

"On the lampshade, darling," she said.

"Only you could make that sound classy."

"Will you get me a cigarette while you're

up? They're in my purse. By the closet."

They'd had an early dinner, during which they'd talked about the baby — Margaret's appointment with the obstetrician earlier that day had gone well — and Charlie regaled her with tales of the more scandalous members of the House of Representatives: the sot whom the police had saved from drowning after he passed out in the Lincoln Memorial Reflecting Pool; the senator who fancied himself a Lothario and who had hands like an octopus and the breath of a warthog; the young man who'd essentially inherited his congressional seat from his father, though the boy was so dense he could barely write his name in the sand with a stick. They'd laughed together for the first time in months.

Now he lit cigarettes for both of them and handed one to her as she sat naked on the sofa. She reached for a throw pillow to cover herself, but he plunked down next to her and gently stopped her from doing so. She looked at him. He leaned in for another kiss.

"I'm going to ask you to do something for me," she said.

"What is it? Anything."

"I want you to get the hell out of here," she said with a smile.

He didn't understand.

"Charlie. Ever since that night on Nanticoke Island, you've been wonderful." She grasped his shoulders with a gentle squeeze, lowered her forehead to meet his, then pulled away and said, "But I must tell you — right now I feel exhausted. And I feel guilty."

"Guilty?"

"Because I know you loved those poker games and Renee told me there's another one tonight, even though it's Tuesday. I'm going to make some tea, read my book, and fall asleep almost certainly before you do. Why don't you go have fun? It will make me feel so much better."

And so it was that Charlie returned to veterans' poker night, only to learn that LaMontagne had become a regular attendee. He obviously wasn't an elected official, but as a veteran who seemingly had connections with every member of Congress, he had wormed his way into the group.

"Congressman!" LaMontagne greeted him with a Cheshire Cat grin, gleaming and pearly, everything else about him fading away. Charlie wondered if LaMontagne's handshake, firm to the point of pain, was meant to send a message. He faked a convivial enthusiasm as best he could, then looked around to see if anyone else had noted LaMontagne's phony hail-fellow-well-met routine. No one had. In Washington, Charlie thought, insincerity was the air they breathed. It made him occasionally feel like Holden Caulfield. Which, in turn, felt immature.

LaMontagne leaned close to Charlie's ear. "Listen, I spoke with Cohn and we may need you to do something with the Strongfellow dossier. Get it to the press. Do you know any national columnists?"

Charlie shook his head, more in wonder at the man's nerve than in response. In a roomful of Charlie's fellow members of Congress, LaMontagne had just brought up one of the most sensitive subjects of his professional life and assigned him yet another unethical task. Moreover, he'd proceeded directly to the logistics of it all, bypassing whether or not Charlie was even willing. "I don't know anyone, really. In the press."

"We'll talk," LaMontagne said confidently, patting Charlie on the shoulder. "I have some ideas."

Charlie grabbed LaMontagne's wrist and pulled him closer. "You said 'we' need this favor. There's something that none of you have ever explained to me: Who is 'we'?"

LaMontagne smiled. "In due time," he

said. "Senator Know-land!" he called jovi-
ally across the room. He winked at Charlie
as he walked away. Charlie watched him and
realized any escape he'd imagined for
himself was just that: imaginary. He went to
the bar cart and quickly downed a scotch.

"Easy with those, soldier." Street appeared
at his side. "You don't want your poker
judgment impaired."

Strongfellow turned on his radio, and
Perry Como's voice came over the airwaves:
*A jury may find her guilty, but I'd forgive her if
I could see . . .* Two dozen veterans broke
into small groups, and the room filled with
the sounds of decanters clinking against the
rims of tumblers and the fizzing of flat- and
cone-top beer cans being cracked open.

Charlie sat with Street, and Strongfellow
joined them and began dealing a traditional
game of straight five-card poker.

"Weird not having Mac here," Charlie
noted.

"Yep," said Street.

"Well, *this* is turning into a fun night,"
remarked Strongfellow. The other two
chuckled. "As long as we're being all
serious-like, I had the weirdest run-in last
week with Abner Lance."

"Who?" asked Street.

"The Carlin aide," Charlie said.

"That freaky *Nosferatu*-looking guy?" asked Street. "Where? Two cards."

Strongfellow replaced Street's castoffs. "So there's a small town in my district, Skull Valley. Five years ago, a pesticide plant opened up there and everything was fine. But maybe six months ago, thousands of sheep started dying. No reason anyone could see; ranchers just walked outside and found the entire herd was hooves-up."

"Jesus," said Charlie.

"One of my staffers wrote to the interior secretary, McKay, to try to get some money for the ranchers and make sure it was safe for, you know, actual people to live nearby."

"How many sheep total?" Street asked.

"Six thousand," Strongfellow said. "Literally six thousand dead sheep. We got a form letter back from Interior assuring us that we had no business inquiring any further. Saturday night I was in Georgetown at a restaurant, waiting for a table, and Abner Lance shows up out of nowhere and tells me to drop the matter."

"To *drop it*?" Charlie asked.

"Yep."

"That's madness," said Charlie.

"Think about what they're manufacturing," said Street, "a spray to kill millions of insects. A weapon. To commit genocide against a species. So sheep dying is not surprising. My wife's family in Louisiana had to deal with something similar with local chemical plants. And we had dead *people* there, not sheep. But just colored folks, so who cares."

They sat silent until Charlie, to clear the air, took drink orders and headed for the bar cart, listening to the room's buzz about the tensions of the world:

All I'm saying is, if Eisenhower looks at Indochina and sees a row of dominoes, then what the hell is the USSR? A Mr. Potato Head? The metaphor is infantile.

Oppenheimer could well be a Commie spy, but he built the bomb for us, so he might also be a pretty bad one.

Before McCarthy loved MacArthur, he was smearing him. Before he endorsed Ike, he was smearing him.

I'd give my left nut to have Palmer's swing. He's going to kill when he goes pro.

If you're going to bad-mouth Hank Aaron, keep it down so you-know-who can't hear.

But it wasn't McCarthy who revoked Oppenheimer's clearance! It was Ike! That's my point!

You really think the Democrats can take

410

the House back? You're drunk; we're going to be in power for a generation.

Charlie returned to the table to find La-
Montagne in a fierce poker face-off with
Street, Strongfellow having folded early.
Street had learned the game Texas hold 'em
from a fellow Tuskegee pilot from Dallas;
he had made a second living playing cards
during the war.

"Trying to think of what you might have
there to make you confident about this
garbage flop," LaMontagne said, motioning
generally to the three faceup cards in the
middle of the table.

Street, expressionless, looked at LaMontagne. He didn't blink.

LaMontagne smiled ear to ear. After a
beat, he reached into his back pocket,
withdrew his wallet, and removed a ten-
dollar bill.

"Okay, Street," he said.

Street matched the ten dollars in the pot,
then drew the fourth card in the string of
shared cards, the turn card. Two of clubs.

"Trash," said LaMontagne. "As shitty as
the Warren Court."

Street's eyes darted to LaMontagne's at
the mention of the Supreme Court chief
justice who was expected to end segregation

in public education any day now.

"Oh, that's how to get your attention!" said LaMontagne. "Noted." He reached into his billfold again. "You might not make much of that two of clubs, but I'm a man who gets good cards. You can ask anyone in this town." He threw down another ten.

Charlie wondered what Street had as his hole cards. It wasn't unimaginable that La-Montagne had, say, two queens or the king and ace of diamonds and would be gifted with a jack of diamonds when the final, or river, card was revealed — leaving him with a winning straight flush. If LaMontagne was dealing, Charlie would indeed bet on that happening, and if he'd managed to get his greasy paws on the deck before Street began shuffling, who knew if LaMontagne literally had an ace up his sleeve?

Expressionless, Street met LaMontagne's ten with ten one-dollar bills that he pulled from a roll in his inside jacket pocket.

Street tossed the river card from the top of the deck. It was the king of diamonds.

On the table, the flop: the ten, queen and king of diamonds, the two of clubs, and the three of hearts.

LaMontagne smirked with satisfaction. He took out the wad of cash lining his billfold and counted it. "Hundred and twenty," he said, placing it all in the pot.

Charlie glanced at Street, who looked angry, even sulky, about getting himself into this spot.

"Care to call?" LaMontagne asked. "I'm sure Charlie can spot you a loan if you don't have the dough on you."

Charlie nodded, but Street, stony-faced, said calmly, "I'm fine, thank you."

"A personal check will be acceptable, assuming it's from a reputable bank," LaMontagne said. But Street took the wad of cash in his pocket and proceeded to count it. Behind the ones were fives and tens, and quite quickly he plucked a hundred and twenty dollars from the pack, which left him with only two stray bills. He grudgingly threw them down on the table.

"Call," Street said.

With exaggerated fastidiousness, his pinkie extended, LaMontagne carefully revealed the first of his hole cards: the ace of diamonds. Combined with the ten and the queen and king of diamonds, there was a chance he had a royal flush. Then he revealed the second of his holes: the jack of hearts.

He had nothing.

Street flipped his cards: two kings. He had three kings, three of a kind, which certainly beat garbage.

Charlie looked at Street, who was allowing himself to smile. "Jesus, I didn't see that coming," Charlie said.

"You're not supposed to," Street said.

"Too bad about that jack of hearts, Davis," Strongfellow said.

"Fucking jack of hearts, the illegitimate son of the one true king," said LaMontagne good-naturedly, watching Street pick up the cash from the pot.

"The illegitimate son," Charlie said to himself. Street shot him a questioning look.

"Gentlemen, as delightful as this has been, I must bid you adieu." LaMontagne stood, shook hands around the table, and made a beeline for the exit.

"Nice bluffing, Isaiah," said Strongfellow.

"The angry Negro ruled by his emotions and unable to overcome his inferiority," Street said, counting his winnings. "It's a role white folk are always casting black people in."

"He sure left in a hurry," Strongfellow observed.

"Not enough of a hurry." Street chuckled.

Charlie stood up abruptly and turned to Strongfellow. "Can I use your office phone?"

Charlie had phoned his new friend Sneed,

the junior librarian, and wasn't surprised to find him still at his desk after nine p.m. After placing two other calls, Charlie walked back to the library, where Sneed opened the door of the Thomas Jefferson Building to him, Margaret, and Sheryl Ann Bernstein.

"Thanks for doing this," Charlie said, offering the librarian ten bucks.

"It's fine, I'm usually here late anyway," he said, rejecting the money.

Led by the librarian's flashlight, they made their way through the dark empty halls of the enormous building, their steps echoing on the marble. Sneed took them down to the basement so they could walk underground to the Adams Building, where the members-only room was.

"Presumably you're going to explain why we're here, honey," Margaret said.

"I didn't get much of an explanation either," offered Bernstein.

"We were playing poker and Davis La-Montagne referred to a wrong-suited jack as an illegitimate child of a king," Charlie told them as they walked briskly through the library. "That reminded me that when Franklin went to England, he learned of the existence of Temple Franklin — his illegitimate son's illegitimate son."

"That's right, and he eventually took

custody of him and brought him back to the colonies," Bernstein added.

"His illegitimate son had an illegitimate son?" asked Margaret.

"Some of the Founding Fathers took the term quite literally," Charlie said drily. They had reached the Special Collections room in the Adams Building, and now they stood aside while Sneed unlocked the door.

"Some fascinating stuff in here, honey," Charlie said to his wife as they made their way across the cavernous room. "The contents of Lincoln's pockets the night of the assassination."

"Spooky," Margaret said.

"That's what I said!" Bernstein told her.

Sneed unlocked the door to the members-only collection and stood aside to let them pass. "We officially close at ten, but you can stay here until midnight," he said. "I have to shut the whole library down then."

They waited for the door to close behind him. Bernstein thumbed through the photocopy she'd made of the collections binder, stopped, placed her finger on a page, and glanced up at Charlie. "So we're looking for Temple Franklin?" He nodded. "Because there's a file here under that name."

CHAPTER TWENTY-THREE:
FRIDAY, JUNE 5, 1772

West Wycombe, England

Sir Francis Dashwood sent a special red gondola to collect Benjamin Franklin and other notables and whisk them up the Thames River to his estate in West Wycombe, thirty-three miles northwest of London. Franklin had no caretaker for his ten-year-old grandson, Temple, so he brought him along; others from the elite class — the Earl of Sandwich, the lord mayor of London, Prime Minister Frederick North, and the Prince of Wales — brought sons and entourages of their own.

Later in life, Temple would seek to fill in the blanks of his memories of the events there. It was from this attempt at a narrative that Sheryl Ann Bernstein now read, a fifteen-page description Temple Franklin had written recounting the experience, a mini-memoir. Charlie listened with rapt attention and Margaret took notes.

Benjamin Franklin, Temple's grandfather, had first met Dashwood through letters, literally and figuratively. As postmaster of the colonies, Franklin corresponded regularly with Dashwood, the postmaster general in London. After a few formal exchanges, as each learned more about the other, they began letting their guards down. Dashwood knew that Franklin was a Renaissance man and a font of innovation; Franklin knew that Dashwood was a man of great influence and power. Moreover, rumors had made their way across the pond about Dashwood's embrace of a life of debauchery and his secret club of the well-connected, where every desire was indulged. This was the group that Dashwood called the Friars of St. Francis Wycombe, or the Medmenham Monks — what some in the upper classes referred to in whispers as the Hellfire Club.

Their friendship blossomed during Franklin's visits to England, first in 1757, when he arrived as a diplomat representing the Pennsylvania General Assembly, then in 1764, when he came to petition the king to make Pennsylvania a royal commonwealth, though his stay stretched for years.

Temple Franklin had memories of Dashwood greeting them all at the docks in June 1772 and informing them of the secret society's password: "Do what thou wilt." Afterward, Dashwood escorted him and his grandfather around the ornate grounds of what was once Medmenham Abbey but now had been converted into something quite ungodly. A meticulously maintained garden revealed itself to be, from the top of a tower, an enormous representation of a naked woman, with milky water spurting from the red flowers on the tips of two mounds, and water pouring from a shrub carved into a triangle. Ten-year-old Temple Franklin laughed heartily at that one, as did his grandfather, a brilliant man who nonetheless found humor in the ribald and scatological.

Other areas on the grounds hovered in Temple's fainter memories, ones that he later investigated as an adult. Dashwood had, in fact, had a cavern carved out of a hill; he jokingly called it the Cave of Trophonius, the architect of Apollo's temple, whose legendary mythical grotto was a place of nightmares. The den and everything about the estate was designed to provide pleasure, lust, and laughter, not fear; the garden grounds were crowded with sculptures of gods such as Venus and Hermes, with exaggerated emphasis on their more private parts.

Over the entrance of the former abbey, the Medmenham Monks — as they called themselves — carved their password in French: *Fais ce que voudras.* On one side of the entrance stood a stone statue of the Roman goddess of silence, Angerona, while the Egyptian god of silence, Harpocrates, stood on the other side. Both held their fingers to their lips, urging visitors to keep all the secrets that they would soon witness and partake of.

Inside the atrium hung twelve stained-glass windows depicting the apostles in various obscene poses; in the opulent living room, a pornographic fresco had been painted on the ceiling. *Hospes negare, si potes, quod offerat,* announced the carving above the entrance to the Roman Room: "Stranger, refuse, if you can, what we have to offer." That room was crowded with silk-upholstered couches and decorated with paintings of naked fornicating couples, many of them kings of England disporting with notable contemporary prostitutes. Adjacent was a library devoted solely to books about either faith or copulation, from the *Queen Anne Book of Common Prayer and Psalter* to *Fanny Hill,* from the *Koran* to the *Kama Sutra.* Downstairs, a vast wine cellar abutted a pantry stocked with fine meats and freshly baked desserts.

During his childhood visit, Temple Franklin was shipped off to the main Wyndham estate a few miles away with a teenage girl hired to mind him so he could be sheltered from the activities within the abbey. Only later in his personal investigations did he learn what his grandfather must have experienced.

There were officially only twelve Friars of St. Francis Wycombe, plus Dashwood, who in their mock religion was the Christ to their Apostles. The abbot of the day selected the wines, arranged for the catering of the meals, and had first pick of the "nuns" available for coitus. As a guest, Franklin joined the fifty or so lesser members of the club who were permitted to participate in the revelry though not the ceremony.

The night that Temple Franklin missed, he later learned from one monk, was particularly drunken and debauched — an evening of pure urge and indulgence without restraint — not to mention blasphemous: A chapel ceremony was a dark and obscene parody of a Latin Mass, with a toast to Satan and the powers of the world beneath. With incense burning and black candles casting a purplish light, cultists had approached the body of a lovely nude young woman spread out on the altar and drunk sacrificial wine from her abdomen.

From there, everyone proceeded to the Roman Room, where Medmenham Monks and friars could have their pick of various masked women dressed in nuns' habits. The women came from all over — there were prostitutes from London, of course, but friars and monks brought mistresses and girlfriends and even wives and sisters, and once a monk brought his stepmother. Local women would also join in the fun, enjoying the naughtiness under the cloak of anonymity and appreciating the opportunity to share intimacies with the elite and possibly even a member of the royal family. Couples or larger groups would use the couches, individual rooms, spots in the garden, and, of course, the Trophonius cave.

The Hellfire Club was more than just a haven of depravity, Temple Franklin would write years later to his half brother; it had tremendous social and business benefits. The bond of the shared illicit and secret experience was one aspect, but more powerful was the knowledge that you could ruin an ally with these secrets — and that he could do the same to you. It meant that one member would do almost anything for the others because they would do the same for him; no one had a choice. Sir Francis Dashwood labored mightily to fund the colonies before the American Revolution, Temple noted. He did everything Ben Franklin wanted him to do. And Franklin was a great supporter of Dashwood's in every conceivable way.

The flip side must have been true as well, Charlie realized as he listened to Bernstein. Members of the club were prevented from retaliating against one another as they might have done otherwise, not unlike the modern geopolitical concept of mutually assured destruction. The men of the Hellfire Club were thus bound together forever. A member's secrets were safe but only because everyone knew a betrayal would mean the indiscreet betrayer would soon see his secrets spilled as well.

Which was not to say that the monks of the Hellfire Club of the eighteenth century all got along famously. Lord Mayor of London John Wilkes and John Montagu, the fourth Earl of Sandwich, loathed each other. But they had to limit the damage they inflicted, since treading too far beyond an insult at a tavern might result in the full force and fury of the club striking them down. They were all to be protected. Temple Franklin mentioned pages who had disappeared after attempts at blackmail and prostitutes whose pregnancies were taken care of via mysterious means.

"So the Hellfire Club was about much more than pleasures," Margaret said. "It was about alliances."

"Oh my God," Charlie said.

"What?" asked Bernstein.

Charlie gazed at Margaret and then at Bernstein. "There's a Hellfire Club in Washington, DC — today. And I went to one of its parties."

He explained how many oddities he'd witnessed that night at Conrad Hilton's penthouse that had to have been traditions handed down from Sir Francis Dashwood's perverse clubhouse. From Strongfellow using the password "Do what thou wilt" to gain entrance to the library to the two small stone statues holding fingers to their lips outside its doors, there were far too many similarities for it to have been anything else. The engraving *Hospes negare, si potes, quod offerat,* the stained-glass portrayals of important men posed pornographically with naked women, the portraits of presidents and prostitutes — it was a twentieth-century version of what Temple Franklin described in West Wycombe, England.

"Good Lord," Margaret said.

"I don't know anything about this party," Bernstein said.

"It was last month, a wild affair," Charlie said. "Everyone was there. McCarthy, Cohn, Carlin, the Kennedys, Strongfellow, Allen Dulles . . ."

"So you're saying they're all members of this deviant club?" Bernstein asked.

"Not necessarily," said Margaret. "Because Charlie's not a member and he was there."

"I assume most there weren't actual members. Just as in England, Ben Franklin wasn't a Medmenham Monk, though he enjoyed a lesser affiliation in the club, since he was trusted to keep his mouth shut. There were twelve monks plus the Christ figure, right? Maybe it's the same here? I didn't even know what I had walked into."

"Some of those guys must be monks, though," Margaret suggested.

Charlie massaged his temple, trying to recall details. "The room Strongfellow knew the password to get into, the library. Maybe that was where the monks were? Carlin was there, and McCarthy. Um . . . Whitney from General Kinetics. Dulles from Central Intelligence. Sam Zemurray from United Fruit was there. They had the stained-glass portraits and such, though I didn't recognize everyone in them, and to tell you the truth, I was pretty drunk and didn't really study them."

"That's a lot of powerful people in that library," Bernstein said.

The three sat in silence, a ticking clock the only noise in the room.

"Okay, this is now officially kind of scary," Margaret said.

"Why?" asked Bernstein.

"Charlie's getting a lot of pressure from this group to do whatever they want him to," Margaret said. She squeezed the bridge of her nose and thought about the notes she'd made that night at Polly's Lodging when Charlie had divulged everything. Pressure from a shadowy, powerful group. That was what Charlie was experiencing. And with what she knew about Van Waganan and MacLachlan, he likely was far from the first to have been so squeezed.

"Well, it's a good thing LaMontagne called the jack of hearts the illegitimate son of the one true king," Bernstein said, always looking for bright sides. "You had your brainstorm and from there all I had to do was look under William!"

"Under William?" asked Charlie.

"Under William Temple Franklin," she said. "First I looked under Temple but then

I remembered that wasn't his actual first name."

"Ah, right," Charlie said.

"Under William," Margaret said.

"Yes, under William," Bernstein said.

"Under William," Margaret repeated, almost to herself.

Charlie looked at her expectantly. "Yes?" he asked.

"She said 'under William.' "

"Right. What are you getting at?"

" 'Under Jenifer,' " Margaret said. "Isn't that what MacLachlan said to you? 'Under Jenifer'?"

Charlie and Bernstein registered what Margaret was suggesting, and then they sprang into action. Bernstein again opened the collection binder, found the listing for Daniel of St. Thomas Jenifer, and pointed Charlie toward a vintage wooden file cabinet in the corner. Charlie opened the first drawer and began rifling through the papers.

"There's one here under Daniel, but it's just a deed for some land," Charlie said, his voice sinking in disappointment. He checked in the drawer again, more thoroughly. "Nothing else."

"Look under Jenifer," Margaret suggested. " 'Under Jenifer.' Isn't this collection in alphabetical order?"

"This file cabinet appears to be," Charlie said. In the second drawer he looked, he found James Madison; James Wilson; Jay, John; Jefferson, Thomas. "Weird filing system," he muttered.

And then he saw it, right after Jefferson, a crisp manila folder, unlike the mahogany-colored binders that held the rest of the collection. "Hold on," he said. He removed a thick new folder from the drawer with Mac-Lachlan's name written on it.

CHAPTER TWENTY-FOUR: WEDNESDAY, APRIL 21, 1954 — MORNING

Washington, DC / New York City

Charcoal thunderclouds darkened the skies above Washington, DC, as Margaret pulled up to Union Station to drop off her husband. The MacLachlan dossier they'd discovered the previous night was tightly bound and tucked inside Charlie's briefcase, which he gripped as if it contained the nuclear codes.

After the discovery of the folder, Charlie convinced Sneed to once more let them use the brand-new Haloid Company photocopy prototype machine, the Copyflo, reserved for Library of Congress staff, and they made two photocopies of the ninety-eight-page dossier, a process that took two hours. Margaret took one photocopy to hide in the house, and Sheryl Ann Bernstein had the other one, along with instructions to get it to Congressman Street first thing that morning.

Charlie and Margaret had only the beginnings of a plan. They had information but no idea how to use it to extricate themselves from the tentacles of the Hellfire Club. They now knew that the errands Charlie ran for the Hellfire Club were trifling; however, what MacLachlan had discovered and diligently documented was shocking and consequential. They had come up with an idea to signal to the Hellfire Club that they were not willing to be pawns moved around on the chessboard any longer, and they surmised from Van Waganan's example that Charlie needed to be at least somewhat public about it so as to cast a protective spotlight on himself. And more important than their own welfare, of course, was to begin to warn the world about what Mac-Lachlan had discovered, which imperiled hundreds of thousands of innocent people if not more. Before Charlie headed north to participate in the comic-book hearings — inauspicious timing, but just the latest example of nothing being in their control — they had decided that Margaret would drive in Charlie's car to Susquehannock Island, where Gwinnett's team had relocated from Nanticoke. She would be busy there, and safe, with no one in the political world interested enough in her research to have any idea where she conducted it.

Margaret kissed Charlie good-bye and wished him luck. The seven-thirty Morning Congressional would get him into Manhattan with just enough time to make the noon hearing. "I want you to destroy comic books. I want you to be like Lex Luthor with a ray gun, just disintegrating superheroes."

Charlie grimaced. "You laugh while I head to my doom. At least Sheryl Ann did some decent research; I have a good line of questioning that should get us where we want to go."

"The world will be watching."

"Please, don't remind me." Charlie leaned across the seat to kiss Margaret good-bye one more time. "Say hi to the ponies."

After Charlie got out of the car, Margaret lightly honked the horn and exited onto Massachusetts Avenue, veering left toward Maryland to make her last research trip before their baby was born.

Catherine Leopold had arranged for the Senate Subcommittee on Juvenile Delinquency hearings to be held at the Foley Square Courthouse, but Charlie wasn't aware until he walked through the door just how poorly suited the building was for the task. The courtroom was the largest one in the building, but it was a closet compared to most Senate hearing rooms; desks had been jammed in at odd angles in order to accommodate everyone. Scattered throughout the room stood bulky television cameras; their multiple power cords, thick as theater rope, converged like tentacles near the door before snaking down the hall. Charlie spotted his place card on a side table alongside the subcommittee's counsel, staff director, and the court reporter recording the proceedings.

At the center of the main table sat Senator Kefauver. He looked in his element; happy to be in the mix again three years after his successful crime hearings and two years after Democratic bosses stole the presidential nomination from him in a back room of the International Amphitheater in Chicago. On one side of him sat a fellow Democrat, Senator Tom Hennings of Missouri, and on the other side the subcommittee chairman, New Jersey Republican senator Bob Hendrickson. Hennings whispered something to Kefauver, who smiled and patted his arm collegially as the clock struck twelve. A TV producer signaled to the senators as if he were a third-base coach; a light atop the primary TV camera blinked on, and Hendrickson gaveled the proceedings to a start.

"This meeting will now be in order," Hendrickson harrumphed. "The United States Senate Subcommittee Investigating Juvenile Delinquency, of which I am the chairman, is going to consider the problem of horror and crime comic books. By comic books, we mean pamphlets illustrating stories depicting crimes or dealing with horror and sadism. We shall not be talking about the comic strips that appear daily in most of our newspapers."

Charlie hated congressional-speak; it reeked of pomposity and self-importance and was utterly disconnected from how actual citizens talked. He'd observed its powers of intoxication: the longer a senator spoke, the more sure of himself he seemed to become. Hendrickson proceeded with long-winded bluster, assailing "horror and crime comic books peddled to young people of impressionable age" while making certain to underline that the subcommittee fully understood the importance of freedom of the press.

He was followed by the subcommittee's counsel, who took ample time to praise the chairman for his remarks before citing statistics that to Charlie proved nothing so much as a problem in search of someone to blame. Dr. Wertham was soon called to the witness table, where he made his earnest and angry presentation about the damage being done to his patients in Harlem and, indeed, all over New York City — no doubt throughout the United States of America. He was followed by other witnesses, all of them, it seemed to Charlie, associates of Wertham's or blue-haired types dead-set on the need to eliminate any reading more fun than the cleaner parts of the New Testament. As in Wonderland, with the Queen of Hearts' demand of "Sentence first, verdict afterward," the initial part of the hearing was devoted to establishing as fact its premise. After the late and eventful night before, Charlie felt his eyelids weighing heavy; he made repeated efforts, some successful, to stifle yawns.

After an hour, Hendrickson called for a ten-minute break, and Charlie stood, stretched, and headed for the restroom, where he ran into Kefauver.

"You have some questions for our witnesses, Charlie?"

"I do, sir," Charlie said. "My staff and I have been preparing. We think Danny Gaines would be a good witness for me to question, if that's okay with you."

"Wonderful," Kefauver said, zipping up. "Be ready for me to call on you."

Danny Gaines was called as the first witness, and from the very beginning he seemed a hostile one. After swearing to tell the truth, the whole truth, and nothing but the truth, he identified himself as the CEO of IC Comics, which published gory tales of true crime and macabre stories of horror. He then offered the committee a host of snorts, derisive sighs, and exaggerated, disapproving shakes of his head while Hendrickson, with the help of enlarged copies of faded comic-book pages, spent twenty minutes educating the room about how inappropriate IC Comics's material was for the children who consumed it. Among the featured stories from the IC oeuvre: an adorable little girl kills her strict father and frames her mother, who is then sent to the electric chair; a priest uses candy to tempt children into a haunted house, where he murders them, after which their ghosts seek revenge in the most gruesome way; a man rapes and then chokes a woman to death on a rowboat, only to trip and drown after several vengeful frogs seek justice.

Outraged stemwinder concluded, Hendrickson turned to his witness with an arched eyebrow. "Is there anything you can say, sir, to help us understand why your company believes this material is suitable for children?"

"You could ask the Brothers Grimm the same question," Gaines said. "Or Aesop. Or Walt Disney! The hag in *Snow White* is absolutely terrifying. Bambi's mom gets blown to bits. *Dumbo* is one of the most abjectly bigoted films I've ever seen. When are you hauling Mr. Disney before this august committee?"

"Surely, Mr. Gaines," Kefauver said, "you cannot be comparing *Snow White* with this comic book." Kefauver held up *Gruesome True Crime SuspenStories,* issue number 22, whose cover featured a woman's severed head held by its hair by a man wielding a machete. "Do you think this is in good taste?"

Gaines tilted his head at an angle, regarding the image. "For the cover of a horror comic book, it's in fine taste," he said. "If we were aiming for bad taste, perhaps the murderer would be holding her head a touch higher so that blood would be dripping more dramatically from her neck. Or maybe we could see more of her body, to see the bloody neck —"

"There is blood, though, Mr. Gaines.

Coming out of her mouth," interrupted Kefauver, outraged.

"A little," Gaines said, to a smattering of titters in the crowd.

"I apologize for interjecting, Mr. Chairman," Kefauver said, turning to Hendrickson.

"That's quite all right, I yield to you, sir."

But before Kefauver could proceed, Gaines asked for a moment of time. "Senator Kefauver, I would like to correct the record on something Dr. Wertham said about one of our comics earlier today. He cited one of our comics as extolling bigotry. Nothing could be further from the truth."

"When was this, Mr. Gaines?" asked Kefauver.

"Earlier he testified that we had a comic using ethnic slurs for Mexicans, as if we were promoting prejudice. We were not. The story in question, which ran in *Criminal Comics* issue number one hundred and seventy-three in August 1951, was making the point that bigotry was evil and stupid. The racist boss is the clear bad guy, while the braceros who rise up against him are the heroes."

"I see," said Kefauver.

"Mr. Chairman," said Charlie, "may I ask a question or two of the witness?"

437

"If the senator from Tennessee is willing to yield," said Hendrickson.

"With delight," said Kefauver.

"Mr. Gaines, I'm Charlie Marder, the congressman from this district."

"I recognize the name. You were recently appointed to the seat. Your dad helped get it for you."

Charlie could hear some quiet gasps from the audience and some rude guffaws, but he smiled indulgently.

"That's me!" Charlie said, prompting some appreciative laughter. "Perhaps you can help me understand something."

"Perhaps," said Gaines.

"You say that children who read your comics won't be swayed by the demonstrations of evil and gore since they know it's just a story."

"Correct."

"No impact on them at all, these lessons of how to kill your father and frame your mother because they won't buy you the doll you want."

"None whatsoever."

"And yet you say definitively that the lessons you preach against prejudice in those very same comics are absorbed by children."

"We believe so, yes. These are basic lessons of morality."

"So help me understand: Why would the good lessons be heeded and the bad lessons ignored?" Charlie asked.

More murmurs erupted from the audience. The television cameraman pushed his lens closer to Gaines's face to catch the dramatic moment as he realized that he had just acknowledged that his comics had an influence on the behavior of children.

"Very clever, Mr. Marder," he finally said. "But none of this hides the fact that this whole hearing is a sham."

"It is?" Charlie asked.

"Yes, it is!" Gaines said, growing agitated. "It's a sham because children are being raised in poverty and squalor, and instead of focusing on the very real issues of prejudice and the historical legacy of slavery, you're looking at comic books."

"We are looking at comic books, you're right about that," Charlie said. "And while I don't disagree that juvenile delinquency is a multifaceted problem, some of it, maybe even most of it, rooted in the conditions you just named, let us focus on the issue at hand. If one of the court clerks can please deliver this to Mr. Gaines."

Gaines briefly examined the paper a clerk handed him, then raised an eyebrow.

"And?" Gaines said, irritated.

439

"This is a page from your *True Tales* comic book from January 1953, issue number two hundred and thirty-seven, correct?"

"I don't have the title page in front of me," Gaines said.

"Oh, I'm sorry about that," said Charlie. "Here's a copy of the comic book itself. Let's pass this over to Mr. Gaines. I have an extra."

"Thank you," Gaines said, in a tone that was anything but grateful.

"The first story in the comic is a nine-page tale of a boy using common household products to hurt an intruder."

"You don't begrudge a child in a work of fiction defending himself, do you, Congressman Marder? Surely you wouldn't prefer a comic where the intruder savages an innocent child?"

Charlie chuckled. "I wasn't aware those were the only two options, Mr. Gaines." The audience laughed. Charlie stole a quick peek at Kefauver, who was grinning like a proud papa.

"For those of you in the pews here," Charlie continued, prompting more chuckles, "or those of you at home," he added, pointing with his pen to the camera lens, "let me share some details about this comic — but unlike Mr. Gaines, I shall be judicious about what I share, since children might be watching. In one panel the child combines two drain cleaners to burn the eyes of the intruder. With another common cleaning item, a polish that's very flammable, he sets the intruder on fire. These are barely disguised household products you likely have in your closets or underneath your kitchen sinks. I believe my wife and I have these in our home. In light of the irresponsibility of publishers such as Mr. Gaines and IC Comics, I would recommend that all the moms and dads out there either lock up household cleansers or put them on high shelves where children cannot reach them."

The crowd was hanging on Charlie's every word. Gaines appeared confused, as if he were trying to figure out how to respond.

"My wife is pregnant, Mr. Gaines, and God willing, we will have more children after this one, and God willing we will be able to figure out ways to prevent them from falling victim to your recklessness."

There was silence, followed by a smattering of applause, but Gaines interrupted it.

"High and mighty," Gaines said. "High. And. Mighty. You want to talk about chemicals that are dangerous to children, Congressman Marder?" Gaines shifted in his seat and paused dramatically. "Let's talk about chemicals dangerous to children. What about the General Kinetics plant being built in Harlem? Are those chemicals harmful to children?"

Hendrickson banged the gavel. "Mr. Gaines, Congressman Marder is not a witness here!"

"Am I the only one under oath?" Gaines shouted back. "Why are our elected officials not required to tell the truth, the whole truth, and nothing but?"

"It's okay, Senator, I can answer the question," Charlie said, secretly delighted that Gaines had taken the bait. Knowing of Gaines's membership in the local NAACP and his outspokenness against the proposed General Kinetics plant, Charlie had had a feeling the comic-book publisher would bring a conversation about chemicals right to this very place.

"You don't need to, Charlie," said Kefauver.

"It's fine, Senators. Mr. Gaines: Many of us have been working hard to prevent construction of the General Kinetics plant proposed for Harlem, precisely because of the concerns you just raised."

Gaines was clearly unprepared for his bombshell to be defused so swiftly. He said nothing.

"In fact," said Charlie, "as long as we're holding this hearing to protect the well-being of the American people, I should note that I recently came into possession of a dossier that once belonged to a friend of mine, the late Congressman Chris Mac-Lachlan." He reached into his briefcase as the senators at the main table conferred with one another, powerless to stop Charlie given the presence of the television cameras providing live coverage. "The dossier details a number of pesticide-producing chemical plants from Maine to Utah, from California to Florida, that are either controlled or owned by General Kinetics and around which local populaces over the previous twenty years have experienced unusually high rates of cancer, nerve damage, and other severely debilitating illnesses."

The three rows of reporters covering the hearing were fiercely taking notes while citizen observers began buzzing among themselves. Kefauver rubbed his forehead; Hendrickson's face turned a shade of purple.

"MacLachlan was investigating this matter until he was tragically killed on March first, and on his deathbed he entrusted this information to me. This file contains memos and research proving that the pesticides being produced around the country to help this great nation grow its amber waves of grain — supported by taxpayer dollars via the farm bill I just co-sponsored — are poisoning Americans. Which explains everything from tumors in Mossville, Louisiana, to the thousands of dead sheep in Skull Valley, Utah."

Kefauver grabbed the microphone. "Congressman Marder, I'm sure there is a more appropriate time and place for this disclosure."

"No, sir," said Charlie. "This is a good time, in front of these cameras, to provide the American people with the unfiltered truth."

Hendrickson banged his gavel loudly.

"We're going to take a break now; this hearing has veered wildly off course," he announced. "Ten minutes. And when we return" — here he glared pointedly at Charlie — "we will address the issue for which this hearing was called."

The audience groaned. "How is this not the people's business?" shouted a reporter from the back bench. Hendrickson didn't respond and stood to leave.

Charlie grabbed his papers and rushed through the crowd and out the door. Pale journalists sporting fedoras and loud ties hounded Charlie down the hall and out the courthouse door like dogs pursuing a fox, seemingly oblivious to the pouring rain, shouting after him for copies of the documents he had wielded, for more information about General Kinetics, for a second of his time for an interview. He ignored them all and hopped into a black sedan idling in front of the courthouse steps. The driver, his father's chauffeur, smoothly and swiftly swerved away from the curb before the reporters could begin rapping on the windows.

Charlie took a moment. The first blow had been struck. Now he needed to figure out how best to release all the damning information MacLachlan had dug up about the chemical plants — and find a path to escape the retaliation that would inevitably be coming his way.

CHAPTER TWENTY-FIVE:
WEDNESDAY, APRIL 21, 1954
— AFTERNOON

New York City / Susquehannock Island, Maryland

The White Horse Tavern stood at the corner of Hudson and Eleventh Streets in the West Village. Inside huddled beatniks and musicians, Columbia grad students and NYU coeds and self-styled working-class poets, all of them enveloped in a San Francisco fog of cigarette smoke. Each new arrival was announced by the ringing of a bell hanging above the door, followed by the sounds and winds of the thunderstorm barreling through Manhattan. The room reeked of soaking-wet clothing and hair. It was afternoon, but it might as well have been two a.m., given the carousing and degree of inebriation in the crowd. In the back, on a stage illuminated by one hanging lightbulb, a disheveled, hirsute young man in a corduroy jacket was reciting a poem he'd written; he paused to let the room appreciate his rhyme of *ghetto* and *Geppetto.*

Charlie was at the White Horse for one simple reason, and it wasn't its bohemian chic: the tavern was a place where he could sit and chat with a black friend without any hostile looks or comments.

"Were you followed?" Charlie asked as Isaiah Street took off his wet hat and overcoat and hung them on a hook next to their corner booth.

"Not sure," Street said. "I might have had company on the train."

Charlie waved down the waitress, who promptly took their orders, two bourbons on the rocks, plus club sandwiches.

"Listen, I have some great news for you," Street said. "I mean, really great."

"What? God, I could use some great news. Or even mediocre news. Anything other than horrible would be welcome."

The waitress brought their drinks.

"To Dylan Thomas," Street said. " 'Death shall have no dominion.' "

Charlie raised his glass. "Where better to toast him than in the place where he drank himself to death?"

They allowed their first few sips to settle.

"Did you get a chance to talk about the MacLachlan dossier at the hearings?" Street asked. "Bernstein told me that was your plan, but in the cab just now, on the radio, I didn't hear anything on the hearings."

"And you won't," boomed a nasal voice. Abner Lance, Chairman Carlin's right-hand man, loomed above them.

"Jesus, it's Count Orlok," said Charlie.

"There isn't going to be any press coverage of your lies and innuendo, Congressman," Lance told him.

"At least take a seat, Lance," said Street, "before you make a further spectacle of yourself."

Availing himself of an unoccupied chair at an adjacent table, Lance joined them. "Quite a stunt there, Congressman," he said to Charlie.

Charlie shrugged. "I was asked a question. I answered."

"With a stolen dossier of classified information," said Lance.

"With data about the manufacture of pesticides that cause nerve damage and cancer," said Charlie. "To Americans."

"Why isn't this on the news, Abner?" Street asked.

"Because nobody wants it to be on the news. Not the Republicans. Not the Democrats. Not Wall Street. Not the unions. No one. And when no one wants a story to be on the news, it has a way of not being on the news."

"A lot of reporters wanted to talk to me," Charlie said.

"They did," said Lance. "And now they don't." He reached down to the floor for his briefcase. He opened it and withdrew a folder. "Speaking of seeing print," he said, dropping the folder on the table in front of Charlie.

Charlie's heart sank.

"I assume you know what these are," Lance said. "Photographs of you behind the wheel of a wrecked car. Apparently, a young woman was in your car with you, and she fell out as you recklessly and drunkenly careened the vehicle into a ditch."

Charlie felt as if his nerves had seized up, as if he were trapped in a body he couldn't move. He remembered having this feeling once before, for just a moment, during the war, when he listened to reports of Companies A and B of the First Battalion, 116th Infantry Regiment of the Twenty-Ninth Division, landing at Omaha Beach and getting mowed down by Germans, like wheat cut by a scythe. Charlie and his men would soon enough be sent right into that same spray of death, he'd realized, and he sat as still as a statue until his first lieutenant snapped his fingers in front of his face, bringing him back. Eleven years later, sitting in this smoky Greenwich Village tavern, Charlie snapped himself out of his shock.

"Do you want to see the photographs?" Lance asked.

Charlie eyed the folder apprehensively, formulating a response in his head. His mouth was as dry as a desert. He had chills; he wasn't sure if anyone else could see him shaking. He kept his hands on his lap to hide any tremors.

Before he could speak, Street produced a file of his own. He dropped it on the table dramatically, then leaned back in his chair and exhaled a plume of cigarette smoke.

"Maybe you should take a gander at *my* photographs," Street said. "I took these myself."

Lance scoffed and made a show of unconcern, but he moved quickly to snatch the folder out of Charlie's reach, and as he shuffled through the photos inside, his face grew darker and the wrinkles in his scowl sank deeper, almost as if he were aging before Charlie's eyes. Carlin's top aide was already an odd-looking man on the best of days, with his red face and white-blond hair, a swollen bullfrog neck and fang-ish eye-teeth; his current shock exacerbated the ugliness.

Charlie desperately wanted to know what had sent Lance into such a rage, but he looked on placidly, betraying no sign of a heart beating fast enough to give Gene Krupa a run for his money while a stifling heat built up inside his shirt collar. Charlie felt a heightened awareness of his surroundings. Somewhere, a waiter dropped a tray of dishes. The door opened, and the rain hitting the pavement sounded like a herd of porterhouses sizzling on the grill. The new customer passed their table, a peaty smell of wet wool wafting behind him. Charlie glanced at Street, who sat calmly, looking for all the world like a man holding a royal flush, waiting for his opponent to recognize defeat.

Finally, Lance was finished with the photographs. He placed them gingerly on the table, facedown, and then covered them with the folder. Charlie looked at Street, who could barely contain his smile. Lance stood.

"Very well, Congressman," he said. "I hope you've given full consideration to what this might mean."

"What it might mean?" asked Street. "You can't blackmail Charlie for something he didn't do. And those photographs prove the whole thing was a setup. You and LaMontagne arranged it all." He took a final gulp of his bourbon. "Good thing the Three Hundred Thirty-Second Fighter Group of the United States Army Air Forces taught me night photography." He smiled benignly at Lance, whose face had turned a new shade of red.

Charlie was stunned and starting to feel an ignition of fury. This whole time Street had known that Charlie was an innocent man, and he hadn't bothered to tell him? But any resentment dissipated when Lance angrily sat back down.

"You little shits have no idea what you're doing or who you're dealing with," he said, his tone hushed and menacing. "You think it's cute that Charlie just alerted the Reds about our defoliation program, which we will need to protect allies and our own troops in the coming decades? You think you're heroes? You're not heroes. You're treasonous."

Charlie reached across the table to Street's pack of Pall Malls. He shook the box, loosened a cigarette, and lit it with his German lighter. He exhaled into Lance's face.

"Your chemicals are killing Americans, you insufferable worm," Charlie said. "Americans. In Utah and Appalachia and Mossville, Louisiana. They're poor Americans, and colored Americans, so maybe you and Chairman Carlin and your friends at the club don't care. But I care. Isaiah cares. The guys we fought with in Europe — they care."

"Spare me the sermon, Eugene Debs," Lance spat. "If you want to go live in a socialist workers' paradise, feel free to fly to Moscow right now — you'll probably get a hero's welcome."

"You're just sore because we figured it out," Charlie continued. "And it was all right there in front of us."

He withdrew a piece of paper from his wallet and tossed it in front of Lance: *U Chicago, 2,4-D 2,4,5-T cereal grains broadleaf crops.* "That was in my desk when I moved in. Or, I should say, in Van Waganan's desk. And it took me a while to piece it all together, especially since the University of Chicago wouldn't share the information about Mitchell and Kraus's study. But as soon as we got hold of the General Kinetics dossier we figured it out. Two, four–D is a fairly common herbicide. It kills weeds around cereal grains. No real mystery there. Until you combine it with two, four, five–T — used to defoliate broadleaf plants — and the rest of what Van Waganan found."

Lance pointed his finger at Charlie as if it

were a sword. "Destroying brush where Communist guerrillas hide will save lives," he said.

"And is that all the army had discovered in its testing at Fort Detrick? And Eglin Air Force Base?"

Lance once again stood. "We're done," he said. "I hope you have a good lawyer. And I hope your wives aren't home alone."

He left the table and the tavern with the speed and determination of a demon out of hell. Charlie and Street looked at each other, threw down money for the tab, and rushed to Pennsylvania Station to get to their wives as soon as possible.

At the precise moment Lance was vaguely threatening Margaret, the rain, brutal and unrelenting, was beating down onto the tarp of Margaret's tent, and she was wondering how long the canvas would be able to withstand the assault. When she'd driven to the tip of the Maryland isthmus, parked, and then crossed the bridge to Susquehannock Island by foot, she'd wondered if the weather would render the trip pointless. But she had no way of reaching Gwinnett, and she didn't want to disappoint him yet again; almost five months into her pregnancy, this would be her last outing.

Margaret had jogged across the bridge as quickly as she could with her slightly protruding abdomen, which meant she was soaking wet before she reached the halfway point, raincoat notwithstanding. She had guessed that by now Gwinett, Kessler, and Cornelius would have moved to this new island, and she was right. They'd even moved her tent here.

She felt thoroughly alone, unconnected to the researchers in the other three tents who didn't know yet that she had rejoined them, hundreds of miles away from her husband, with no way to reach him, isolated from the world. She could vanish right now, on this spot, and no one would realize it for hours, if not days. A few months ago she might have reveled in that independence, but now, newly aware of menacing forces, she felt vulnerable. Her internal voice told her not to be so melodramatic, but then she reminded herself that these men in the Hellfire Club had tried to frame Charlie by killing a young woman and were, at the very least, indifferent to the poisoning of Americans in the name of some greater struggle against the Communists. They might even have killed Congressman Van Waganan, for all she knew.

She felt like Elizabeth Proctor in *The Cru-*

cible, which Charlie had taken her to see shortly after it opened on Broadway. It was as if the whole world had gone mad. People who were normal, even friends, could be revealed as enemies, even evil. What was that line she had so liked from the play? *Remember, until an hour before the Devil fell, God thought him beautiful in Heaven.*

She looked at her few belongings in the tent, transported over and tossed inside: a small suitcase, a sleeping bag, a journal, her night-vision binoculars. She was surprised to see the specialty binoculars in her tent, and she picked them up and held them. It felt like years since she'd left the Birder Emporium with them. Before this knowledge of everything Charlie was caught up in; a lifetime ago. Under the hiss of rain hitting the pines and the deeper-pitched sizzle of the spray pounding the ground, a faint murmur of conversation made its way to her ears. One of the voices — Gwinnett's — was considerably louder than the others. She tried to focus, ignore the other noises, so she could make out what was being said, but to no avail.

Without knowing exactly why she was being secretive, she walked stealthily, heel to toe, toward the sounds coming from Gwinnett's tent. The soil, a combination of hard-packed sand and dirt, had largely absorbed the water for hours, but saturation was now setting in, and small streams began swirling and trickling throughout the campsite. Twice a sustained gust of wind was strong enough to require Margaret to push her body against it to proceed on her path.

"No sign of her yet," she heard Gwinnett say. "We're frankly not sure if she's coming back. Maybe not with this weather."

She heard a gravelly but fainter voice now, sounding as if it was coming over a telephone — the shortwave radio Margaret had heard Gwinnett mention he had in case of emergency. "That's fine, just know that the mission has now changed. Get us that dossier."

"Understood. And where is he?"

"Last seen in Manhattan."

"What about her?"

"We were tailing him, not her, so we lost visibility after she dropped him at the train station."

The sharp crack of a bolt of lightning hitting somewhere on the island startled Margaret, though she was careful not to make a sound. Thunder growled deeply.

"I can't even believe I can hear you with this storm," Gwinnett marveled. "Weather must be helping."

"Just get the girl . . . folder," Margaret made out. The transmitter crackled with static and the next words she could make out were "now top priority."

"Of course," Gwinnett said. The noise of the transmitter ended abruptly. Margaret strained to hear Gwinnett's lowered voice. "Go to the bridge and keep an eye out for her."

"Got it," said Cornelius.

At the realization that Cornelius, too, was in the tent and any second would be coming to find her, Margaret turned and fled.

CHAPTER TWENTY-SIX:
WEDNESDAY, APRIL 21, 1954
— EVENING

Susquehannock Island, Maryland

Margaret had trusted that Cornelius would follow orders and head right for the bridge, so she ran in the opposite direction. She knew it was a short-term solution; Cornelius would get to the bridge, cross it, and see her car parked nearby. As she'd anticipated, within three minutes of his leaving the tent, Cornelius returned from the bridge to the mainland and briskly walked right to Gwinnett and someone else — was it Kessler beneath that raincoat? — presumably to tell them that she might be on the island. The three began looking around; she guessed they were searching for her.

That was four hours ago.

Margaret lay on her side in a field of brush, sopping wet, watching the campsite, waiting for an idea or an opportunity. Gwinnett had returned to the campsite and now stood there with binoculars searching for

Margaret in the distance. She heard him instruct Cornelius and Kessler to run in opposite directions around the island, which they did, though so loudly that it wasn't difficult for Margaret to avoid them both. She was grateful the other two researchers, Quadrani and Hinman, were no longer there.

At first Gwinnett and his assistants attempted to appeal to her as if nothing was wrong.

"Margaret, where are you?" they shouted, as if she'd gotten lost.

As hours passed, however, and their frustration grew and the raging winds turned raindrops into pinpricks, they abandoned the pretense.

"Margaret, come out!" Cornelius yelled. "There's nowhere for you to go! Kessler is at your car!"

And then: "You're going to die in this storm, Margaret! What worse could we do to you?"

She had slowly and silently negotiated the marsh and the wetlands. Fierce winds pushed ashen, billowing thunderclouds across the sky without a break in sight. Night was coming, which complicated matters for both hunter and prey — they would not be able to see her, and she would not be able to see much beyond the lights of their camp.

Every inch of her was wet, and she was knee-deep in the bog. She had never been so cold; her jaw started to tremble, her teeth hitting each other. But it was too risky to move. Thank God she had been absent-mindedly holding her night-vision binoculars when she walked to Gwinnett's tent, she thought. They might save her life.

Charlie and Street just made the train — the five-fifteen *Evening Congressional* from New York to DC — climbing aboard as it was starting to chug out of the station. Traffic had been especially bad in the rain, the line for tickets was long, and the salesclerk expressed skepticism that they'd make it. But they ran to and then alongside the slow-moving train until they found an open door and jumped on. Sweating, panting, they slowed their pace and found seats in the club car. After a waitress took their drink orders, Charlie finally asked the question.

"So those were photographs of me? Of that night?"

"Correct," said Street.

"What did they show?"

"Lance driving you to Rock Creek. Some other guy had already purposely crashed

461

the car and placed the dead body by the side. He and Lance carried you to the spot and left. You woke up and LaMontagne showed up — he was cued to do so, I'm sure. The photos make it clear you weren't driving the car. That it was a setup."

The waitress returned with their drinks, and Street bought a pack of cigarettes. Charlie stared out the window at industrial sites and trash-filled vacant lots, trying to take in all that he'd just learned.

Street lit a cigarette and exhaled loudly. New Jersey swampland rushed past the window, and Charlie could see his reflection; he felt as if he'd aged ten years in the past week, and he looked it too.

"How long have you known this?" Charlie asked, irritated. "You said you took the pictures?"

"I don't know who took them," Street replied. "I *said* I took them, but that was a lie. Your dad gave them to me just before I met you at the White Horse Tavern. He had —"

"My dad?"

"Yes," Street said. "I don't know where they came from, but thankfully someone was tailing you that night." He lit another Pall Mall. "I don't know who took the pictures. For all I know, the Hellfire Club did it so they'd have leverage over Abner Lance and LaMontagne if they needed it. This is a weird and screwy group. And there appears to be a struggle going on within the Hellfire Club. Hoover and McCarthy and Ambassador Kennedy are on one side, the Dulles brothers and some other Ike allies are on the other."

"And what exactly is your role in it, Isaiah?" Charlie asked. "And why are you just now telling me about these pictures?" He was trying to control the anger in his voice, without success.

Street raised both hands in mild protest. "Listen, I didn't know they even existed until this morning. Neither did your dad. I was going to tell you at the White Horse Tavern, but Lance showed up before I had a chance. Your dad called me first thing this morning and told me he'd managed to secure photographs that would be exculpatory. He said he was having them delivered to him this morning and I needed to come to his house to get them. He knew I was already coming up at your request. I met him, got the pics, then came to you. Ever since you told me about your predicament, your dad and I have been trying to figure out how to save you. Thank God his connection worked out."

Charlie looked down at the floor. Street took another drag from his cigarette.

Charlie was silent, squinting at Street as he worked to piece things together. Outside, the rain beat down on another set of train tracks, beyond which leaned the shacks of the slums of Newark, New Jersey.

"So you're like — a spy for my father?"

"No, no," Street protested. "You and I are friends. That's real, Charlie. But your father and I are . . . affiliated. And we talk. About things that have nothing to do with you."

"Affiliated how?" Charlie asked.

But Street only shrugged. "That's not for me to say right now."

Charlie stared at him, then he stared out the window again. The train sped by a parallel roadside where signs, white on red and lit by individual lamps, had been hammered onto telephone poles: DON'T TAKE / A CURVE / AT 60 PER / WE HATE TO LOSE / A CUSTOMER / BURMA-SHAVE. The sky was a ceiling of black and gray clouds. Thick sheets of rain looked like ink stains in the distant horizon. A bolt of lightning flashed and then crackled several miles away, making the cloud behind it glow a bright yellow, as if it were a pinball-machine TILT.

"We're all on the same side here, Charlie," Street finally said. "Your father should be the one to tell you anything more. He'll be furious at me if he finds out that I told you even this much."

"You haven't told me anything!" Charlie exclaimed angrily.

Street shook his head. "I'm sorry, I just cannot say anything more right now. Just know there are good people looking out for you."

At this point Charlie wasn't sure if there was anyone he could trust other than Margaret. Even his father had been withholding information.

The train continued on its southern path to Baltimore, with Washington at the end of the line.

The cloak of night had fallen on Susquehannock Island; the only light emanated from a flickering lamp inside Gwinnett's tent and the two dim flashlights Cornelius and Kessler held at their hips. But through her night-vision binoculars, Margaret could see just enough: Cornelius stood on the bridge to the mainland; Kessler stayed in the wooded area between the bridge and the camp.

She was grateful she had the binoculars, though all they accomplished right now was to highlight the extent of her predicament.

Short of swimming off the island — which in this storm was too great a risk — she was trapped, unless she could get them to move. Which would require a diversion. But what?

Determined not to give in to her fear, she tried to remain focused. Her only option was to get off the island before the storm subsided and the sun rose. She began moving west, to her left, crouching low to the ground, trying to be as quiet as possible, though her sloshing in the bog was drowned out, even to her own ears, by the roil and thunder of the storm.

She stood slowly, taking cover behind an elm, and used the binoculars to follow the green glow of Gwinnett's body heat as he walked from the tent to the bridge. The other two men had turned off their flashlights, but she could still make them out in the distance. She considered running to her tent, where she knew she had a knife in her supply kit. Could she make it there and out without them seeing her? It seemed too great a chance.

She sensed something to her right. It started as a feeling, then she heard a sound. She turned the binoculars away from the men and saw a giant glowing green mass speeding toward the researchers. It was barreling through the rising waters that had formed in a field of salt-marsh cordgrass; it took Margaret a second to make out the individual parts of the immense shape.

The ponies.

It was impossible to get a precise count but there were maybe a hundred of them, all galloping from the wooded part of Susquehannock Island toward the men standing near the bridge. The stampede had started for no discernible reason beyond a storm that had been raging for half the day.

Gwinnett shouted something Margaret couldn't make out in the tempest, and through the binoculars she saw the other two green shapes turn to see the ponies running toward them, and then the men began to run in three different directions.

With the stampeding ponies several yards to her right, Margaret — her agility and speed compromised by the pregnancy — jogged alongside them, running through the brush and onto the northern shore as the ponies continued their charge. The storm, while steady and intense, hadn't noticeably increased in the past few minutes; panic was the only explanation she could imagine. She jogged behind a scrub pine tree, then looked around for any sign of a human as the last of the herd — foals, mainly, accompanied by their mothers — galloped past her.

Margaret realized that the distraction of the stampede might be her only chance to escape the island. She was about to sprint toward the bridge, when she saw Gwinnett emerge from behind a shrub thicket maybe ten feet away; she didn't need her night-vision binoculars to see him. He was close enough that she could see him scowling at her, with a look of menace she'd never seen before. She stopped in her tracks and unconsciously reached under her shirt to pat her abdomen, to reassure herself that the baby was okay and also to calm herself. Her swollen belly felt perfectly fine, but the shock of her ordeal caused her to shake. A wave of nausea hit her and as she gasped, she was stunned by a bright strobe of light and, one second later, a loud crack.

She thought lightning had struck. But the lightning bolts that had struck the sea and the island over the previous few hours had been clear bolts zigzagging from the sky with deliberate speed. This was just a circle of light that flashed from the bridge, and it was followed by Gwinnett falling limply back into the thicket.

Then she saw: someone was on the bridge with a gun.

Margaret squinted as the beam from a powerful flashlight blinded her.

"Don't move!" a voice commanded.

A woman's voice.

The streets outside Baltimore's Pennsylvania Station were being pounded with torrential rains, and taxicabs were scarce. When Charlie finally found one, the grizzled hack wouldn't consider any sum to make the drive all the way out to the bridge to Susquehannock Island. "Never," he said, chomping on his cigar. "And you ain't gonna find no one willing to do it in this weather. Not no one." The prediction proved correct, and soon enough Charlie was at the local Hertz auto-rental office, where he was offered a black 1951 Studebaker Commander.

The last time I was in a Studebaker was that night in Rock Creek, Charlie thought. And then he corrected himself, since he now knew he hadn't been in the car that night at all.

When he was here a month ago, the journey via taxi had taken an interminable three and a half hours. Driving himself, he could theoretically drive faster and more recklessly, but with accidents and flooding from the storm, it took him five hours — an insufferably frustrating trek that reminded Charlie of a recurring nightmare he'd had in high school in which no matter how hard he tried, he couldn't reach an object that he desperately needed to.

As he neared the bait shop, he saw in the distance not only his car, which Margaret had driven there, but three others parked on the shoulder between the store and the footbridge. One car had its lights on and was still running. Charlie turned off his lights and pulled over to the side of the road.

At first Margaret didn't recognize the woman. Her head was shrouded in the hood of a dark poncho; she looked like a sinister nun. But then the woman lowered her lamp and came closer, and Margaret realized who had just shot Gwinnett.

"Make sure he's dead," Catherine Leopold said.

Stunned, Margaret obeyed, hustling to the thicket where Gwinnett had fallen. She reached into the brambles and pulled him up by the back of the neck. His head was heavy and lifeless. No breath, no movement, no pulse. She gently released him back into the bush.

What on earth is happening? she thought. *Why is Miss Leopold holding a gun?*

"He's dead," Margaret said, still reeling from the intensity of the night, all ending with the shock of seeing Leopold. She was of course relieved that Gwinnett was no longer chasing her down, but why did Leopold shoot him, and who was she with?

Leopold turned to two other figures standing behind her, men that Margaret hadn't focused on until now. "Go find the others," she told them, and they hustled past Margaret onto the island.

From under her poncho, Leopold produced a cigarette, but she struggled to light it in the rain. She finally ducked completely into the poncho like a turtle and then reemerged with it lit.

Margaret braced herself to ask. "Why —"

"He was a threat to you, your Dr. Louis Gwinnett," Leopold interrupted, exhaling her cigarette smoke. "He wanted the dossier, of course. Where *is* the dossier, Margaret?" No more "Mrs. Marder"; such formalities were no longer called for, apparently.

Margaret had so many questions.

"At the house," she replied. "The dossier is at our house. We made a photocopy; Charlie has the original."

Leopold nodded.

It all seemed impossible, this scene: Catherine Leopold holding a gun while they stood there soaking wet, minutes after the ponies stampeded. Gwinnett, who just hours ago had gone from seductive to menacing, dead in a bush just feet away. Margaret tried to make sense of it but couldn't. She tried to appeal to Catherine, figuring it was her only chance.

"Thank you for saving me, Catherine," she said. The rain poured down on her face as if she were standing beneath a fire hose. "He and his . . . goons were chasing me all over the island."

"Gwinnett was a Communist agent," Leopold said. "Did you know he was a Communist?"

"Yes. No. I mean, I suspected he had those sympathies from comments he'd made here and there. But frankly, it's not all that unusual in academia. I never thought he took any action. But then a few hours ago I overheard someone on a radio telling him to get the dossier and to get me, so I ran and hid."

Leopold took a deep drag of her cigarette.

"We've been following him for the past month, since we picked up shortwave radio chatter about you," she said. "You must have heard some of that as well."

" 'We'?" Margaret asked. " 'We've' been following him for the past month?"

"Hoover," she said. "I should be more

precise. The FBI. Hours ago they picked him up talking to a Soviet agent; he was told to get the file at any cost. The Feds put out an APB for him, and of course Chairman Carlin and the others were also alerted. Through the club. I knew his whereabouts because we've also been monitoring you. And your house."

"Can we get out of the rain?" Margaret asked. She shivered.

"In a minute. We need to wait for them to finish the job."

They stood there in the darkness, rain beating on them relentlessly. Leopold flicked her cigarette into the brush. "You put yourself, your husband, and your country at great risk today." She stared at Margaret with her enormous blue eyes, which right now conveyed fury. "I don't mean to sound harsh, but you are a very foolish woman."

From a distance came a bang and then the echo of a gunshot. Then another one, seemingly from the other side of the island. Margaret was terrified; her mouth was dry and her limbs felt heavy. Worried about her baby, Margaret touched her abdomen underneath her shirt again. "I don't understand," said Margaret, trying to keep the conversation friendly, trying not to sound alarmed. "All three of them were Communist agents? I thought Kessler and Cornelius were just grad students."

Leopold shrugged. "The Bureau has been monitoring Gwinnett since the late 1940s; he'd been recruited years before, likely by Hiss. He'd been recruiting and had also been tasked with pursuing, er, friendships with susceptible young women in proximity to power. Your father-in-law was the long-game target, we assume, but then Charlie was appointed to Congress and your star rose even higher." She gestured with her left arm, indicating the landscape. "This entire research project was funded by Mother Russia so Gwinnett could get close to you while Charlie was in Congress."

"But why? Charlie's just a freshman."

"The Reds have tentacles throughout the government. Everywhere. And Charlie's been the focus of a lot of groups. Clubs and associations. The Commies, the Hellfire Club, other competing interests. Folks want to be close to the son of Winston Marder. And when Charlie tried to stop the funding to Goodstone, he showed a certain egoism, a selfishness, early on that Chairman Carlin and others in the club knew needed to be stopped."

"Can't have too many folks trying to do the right thing, I suppose," Margaret said.

"You and your idiot husband wouldn't know the right thing if it bit you squarely on the nose," Leopold said. "You think you're keeping us safe? From what? The engine of our economic boom? From the makers of weapons that will protect us and prevent Communism from spreading here? I know your kind. You sneer at Joe McCarthy while he ferrets out the traitors in our midst. You turn your nose up at the workers who slave away at General Kinetics plants, but you enjoy their products and the safety they afford you and your unborn baby."

Margaret felt her heart skip a beat. *Is this really Catherine Leopold? A trained killer?* She wondered if Leopold's smiling, efficient, aging-beauty-queen persona had ever been legitimate. Margaret tried to appeal to her vanity by treating her like an expert.

"Why would the Reds even want the dossier?" Margaret asked. "Why would Gwinnett be chasing me down like that? I don't understand."

"We don't know if they intended to leak the information to their lackeys in the press or, more likely, whether they were planning some sort of combination of espionage and sabotage, learning as much as they can about the chemical plants and destroying them when need be. The Soviets' ability to recruit spies has been depressingly efficient."

"I want you to know I appreciate your trying to help Charlie, trying to steer him away from this madness," Margaret said, hoping her ploy to appeal to her captor wasn't too obvious.

"I did for him what I tried to do for Van Waganan. I gave him advice on how to succeed on Capitol Hill and do right by the American people. Neither one took my advice, with predictable results."

The two men she'd sent off hustled back from their tasks. "Should we go?" one of them asked Miss Leopold.

"Indeed. Put Margaret here in the backseat. Tie her hands and have her sit between the two of you. I'll drive."

At the sound of the first gunshot, Charlie had instinctively crouched into soldier position as if he were back in France. Except, he immediately realized, he was without a weapon.

He ran to the left, to the bank, as far as he could to escape from the beam of the one idling car's taillights, and then slowly walked toward the bridge. He saw shapes on the island, barely illuminated by the car's headlights, dissipating in the downpour. There were three figures, two larger men and one smaller shape. The two bigger shadows suddenly ran in opposite directions out onto the island, one to the left and the other to the right. Charlie took his chance and scurried under the bridge.

The footbridge from the mainland to Susquehannock Island spanned roughly five hundred feet, short enough to swim at a normal time but too far now, given the swift current. Charlie held up the flame of his lighter to inspect the underside of the bridge; a stabilizing beam ran its length, with perpendicular bars roughly every ten feet. He could probably have made it across when he was at peak army fitness, a decade ago, but attempting to complete such a challenge today seemed mad.

And yet, what choice did he have?

Charlie put the lighter back in his pocket, then took off his overcoat and suit jacket and dropped them on the muddy bank under the bridge. He rolled up his sleeves and jumped up to the first perpendicular bar, which he was relieved to find was relatively dry. His grip was firm and felt steadier than he'd anticipated. Good. He swung himself back and forth like a trapeze artist until his body was parallel with the ocean and he could hook one leg around the long beam that undergirded all five hundred feet of the bridge. With his back to the ocean, he began to shimmy across.

About halfway along, he could faintly make out two women's voices, one of them Margaret's, though their tones were too low for him to discern what they were saying. As he continued, he heard a gunshot, and he froze, suspended above the churning waters. He started moving at an increased pace and soon heard another blast of gunfire. After what seemed like an eternity, he heard his wife speak again. As he approached the island, one set of heavy footsteps clomped on the footbridge above him, then a second set, then more. He heard Margaret's voice as she crossed the bridge above his head.

When Charlie arrived on Susquehannock Island, he jumped to the ground, poked his head out, and saw four people walking briskly in the other direction, returning to the mainland. In the light of the car, the outlines of the men revealed their guns. As did the woman's. She spoke, and Charlie recognized Leopold's voice. Her gun was resting at the small of Margaret's back.

Chapter Twenty-Seven:
Thursday, April 22, 1954 —
Early Morning

Capitol Hill

A few hours after he got home, Isaiah Street was almost relieved to be awoken by the pounding on his front door, even though, according to his watch, it wasn't yet five a.m. He'd been in the grasp of his recurring nightmare, reliving the time the Tuskegee Airmen of the 332d Fighter Group lost some of the B-24s they were escorting on a bombing run. Struck by German bombers flying in formation, eight of the B-24s were hit by Luftwaffe fire over Nîmes, France; three crashed. From his cockpit he'd watched two of the planes go down; he saw only three airmen able to secure their parachutes and jump.

Renee murmured something inaudible; Street pulled the covers over her shoulders and reached for his bathrobe, then jogged to the door to stop the knocking before it woke the twins. Eye to the peephole, he wasn't entirely surprised to see Charlie, disheveled, with a panicked expression discernible even through the tiny distorted lens. Street opened the door, stepped out onto the front stoop, and closed the door gently behind him.

Charlie dispensed with greetings. His face was a study in pure terror. "They have Margaret."

Street gripped Charlie by both shoulders. "Stay calm." He could see Charlie's panic rising. "It's the only way to help her." Street shook him gently. "She's going to be okay. Just let me get dressed."

"I'll be in that car," Charlie said, pointing to the black Hertz Studebaker Commander parked in front of Street's modest town house, revealed by a street lamp. "If you have a gun, bring it."

"I have two," Street said.

Three minutes later, Street was dressed and in the car. Charlie hit the gas and raced through the remnants of the storm. He told Street about the events of the night: After Leopold and her two thugs had driven away with Margaret, Charlie had run across the bridge to his rental car. Headlights turned off, Charlie trailed them for miles, a task made a bit easier by the storm, which kept Leopold from driving as fast as she no doubt would have otherwise.

"I followed them all the way back to Washington," Charlie said. "Around the Bay Bridge, there was enough traffic for me to turn my lights on and blend in."

Charlie turned left onto Pennsylvania Avenue Southeast. The street was dark and empty, the sun not yet risen, the disquieting hour before dawn when it feels as if no one else is alive. The stillness was interrupted by the click-clack sound of Street loading an odd-looking pistol that resembled a flare gun, with room for bullets in the pistol grip. Street caught Charlie's uneasy glance.

"What the hell is that?"

"It's an FP-forty-five Liberator," Street told him. "The only guns I have here. I have others back in Chicago. It's designed to look like a flare gun, but it ain't. Mainly used by OSS during the war."

"You were OSS? Clandestine services?"

"I'm a Tuskegee Airman, you know that," Street said.

"Okay, but were you also OSS?"

Street paused and then said, "Yes, I was, and I'm also still in a branch of former OSS who continue to serve, in our way. We can talk about that later — where are we going?"

Charlie raised an eyebrow at his friend

481

and was ready to press him further but was distracted by the view of the immense black dome looming five blocks ahead.

"I saw them take her into the Capitol," he said.

The attack by the Puerto Rican nationalists was apparently not enough to warrant increased security before dawn, since only one Capitol Hill Police officer roamed the grounds outside the Capitol Building. Charlie and Street saw him off in the distance, on the Senate side, as they pulled up. The cop briefly turned and considered their car — Charlie's rented Studebaker — but then seemed to recognize Charlie as he exited the vehicle and looked back in the other direction. Members of Congress were given a wide berth to do whatever they wanted.

Street discreetly handed Charlie one of the two OSS guns he'd brought. Charlie tucked the dossier on General Kinetics at the small of his back under his shirt, and with the gun in his right hand, he led the way into the Capitol.

They first entered the Rotunda Crypt, a round room on the first floor containing thirteen statues representing historic figures from each of the original colonies. Red light from an exit sign exposed Robert E. Lee's mournful gaze as Charlie and Street ran between the Doric columns in the center of the room, then took a left to exit the crypt. They rushed past a giant bust of George Washington and softly hustled their way up a curved stone staircase to the second floor.

The Rotunda was dimly lit by small lamps built into the circular wall. Normally daylight flooded the room through the dome windows a hundred and eighty feet above them, but at this early hour, with cloud cover, visibility was dim. Charlie knew that twelve statues of various Founding Fathers and former U.S. presidents stood like guards throughout the room, but all he could see were their immense looming shapes. The details of the eight paintings displayed — enormous renderings of explorers from Columbus to Daniel Boone — were all but invisible.

Charlie and Isaiah stood silently for a second. The Senate side of the Capitol was to their right, the House side to their left.

Street leaned close to Charlie. "Do you have any idea where they took her?" he whispered.

"No," Charlie said. "I saw them go through the door we just came through, and then I went to get you."

"Smart soldier," Street said. "Let's split

up. Meet back by this doorway in fifteen minutes. You go to Statuary Hall, I'll head toward the Senate side."

"Roger," Charlie whispered.

Street fell back and disappeared into the darkness.

Charlie drew his FP-45 Liberator and held it with two hands. He walked carefully along the walls of the Rotunda, heel to toe, making as little noise as possible. After passing by the statues he believed to be Thomas Jefferson and Theodore Roosevelt, he took a left out of the Rotunda and into National Statuary Hall.

He had been holding his terrors about Margaret at bay, focused as he was on his mission to save her. In this, he instinctively relied on the muscle memories of his days as an army captain in war, the ability of a soldier in life-or-death situations to cram unhelpful emotions in a box. But the war was nine years ago, and he was a different man now. A softer man. He started to tremble as his fears for Margaret crept into his consciousness.

Suddenly aware of his shaking legs, Charlie made himself stop short. There was no time for such indulgences, for fear or self-pity. He needed to finish this mission.

Statuary Hall was better lit than the

Rotunda, and Charlie could make out some of the faces on the vast array of sculptures, men whom he and Street had been arguing about just a few months ago: Georgia governor Alexander Stephens, the vice president of the Confederacy; Mississippi's Jefferson Davis, its president. The men containing multitudes. Charlie shook his head as he recalled making that remark.

He walked softly on the black-and-white-checkered marble floor as he moved along the edge of the room, stepping on the tile dedicated to James Polk. The faces of the statues, shrouded in shadow, were doleful, like guests at a funeral. He wondered what Street was finding. How much time had passed? He checked his watch: only five minutes. He quickened his pace, making his way out of the room and into the hall that went to the House Chamber. As he approached a narrow stairwell leading downstairs, he suddenly felt a metal object poking his back as he heard a voice.

"Hello, Charlie."

His heart skipped. Phil Strongfellow was behind him. With a gun, presumably, one whose muzzle was now nestled firmly against his back. Charlie raised his hands in the air.

"Hi, Strong," Charlie said.

485

"What is this you've got? A flare gun?" Strongfellow asked, half curious, half mocking, as he took it from Charlie's hand.

"It's an OSS gun, Strong," Charlie said, turning his head to the right to try to see Strongfellow behind him. "Designed to look like a flare gun, but it's not." Strongfellow didn't react. "Odd that you wouldn't know that," Charlie said. "I mean, given your illustrious history in the clandestine services. According to *This Is Your Life,* I mean."

Charlie felt Strongfellow shove the butt of his gun more sharply into his back.

"Fuck off, Charlie," he said. "Move. We're going downstairs."

Charlie proceeded slowly down two flights of stairs, turning his head to get a look at Strongfellow, who, he noticed, still had a limp but was no longer using crutches. "Where are your crutches?"

"Shut up, Charlie," Strongfellow snapped. "You wouldn't want to risk me getting agitated. I might trip, causing an accidental discharge of my firearm."

In the basement of the Capitol, Strongfellow guided Charlie through a labyrinth of unlit hallways.

"Where are we going?"

"To your wife. If you're lucky, they'll let you swap the dossier for her."

"Why would they let me live?" Charlie asked. He didn't expect an answer and he didn't get one.

They passed storage rooms and the occasional maintenance closet, went down one hall, then another. They came across a stairwell leading them down an additional flight, though Charlie hadn't known until then that there was a floor lower than the basement in the Capitol Building. At the bottom of that stair, Strongfellow guided them to the right, down a long hall so dark all Charlie could see were the two closed oak doors at the end of it. Their footsteps echoed above the dull hum of the generator as they finally arrived at their destination. On one of the wooden doors was written STORAGE.

"Open it and keep your hands up," Charlie was told, and he obeyed.

The expansive room was filled with statues, fifty or more. In front of one honoring Confederate congressman John Tyler — a former U.S. president who'd backed the wrong horse in the Civil War — stood Margaret, her mouth gagged with a cloth, her hands tied behind her back with a rope, her pregnant belly moving rapidly in time with her breathing. To her left, leaning against a sculpture of Aaron Burr, stood Chairman

Carlin, his arms crossed. To her right stood Leopold and the two thugs Charlie had seen out on Susquehannock Island.

"Honey, you okay?" Charlie asked Margaret.

"She's fine," Miss Leopold answered for her. "For now."

"Congressman Marder, you've proven to be quite the irritant," Carlin said. "Phil, did you check to see if he has the General Kinetics dossier with him?"

"Not yet," said Strongfellow. He approached Charlie from behind, frisked him, and easily located the dossier under his shirt. Strongfellow removed and inspected it, then handed it to Carlin. The chairman looked at the dossier, then raised his eyes to meet Charlie's.

His voice was low, the menacing tone unmistakable. "Do you have any idea how much damage you could have done to the security of this nation?"

"By exposing pesticide plants that are literally killing your fellow Americans?" Charlie asked.

"Might as well tell him, Mr. Chairman," someone behind Charlie said. "If he's not ever going to leave here, maybe he should know just how out of his depth he's been this whole time."

Street's voice.

Charlie looked around and saw his friend lighting a cigarette, his gun in one hand, as casual as a summer breeze.

"There you are, Isaiah," said Carlin. "I was wondering when you were going to show up."

Chapter Twenty-Eight:
Thursday, April 22, 1954 —
Early Morning

Capitol Hill

"Oh my God," Charlie said, and he looked to Margaret, whose eyes widened in disbelief.

Carlin and Leopold chuckled. The two thugs stayed silent. Strongfellow looked as if he wished he weren't there.

Street ambled casually into the room, cigarette in one hand, OSS gun in the other. He stopped next to a statue, looked up, and regarded the likeness of Confederate general Nathan Bedford Forrest, the first grand wizard of the Ku Klux Klan. He smirked and pulled himself up to sit on the statue's marble pedestal, then ashed his cigarette on General Forrest's boots.

"You want to know why," Street said, looking at Charlie.

"He's not entitled to know anything," Leopold said.

"I want to know everything," said Charlie,

turning his gaze to Carlin. "And start at the beginning: Did you have Van Waganan killed?"

"You don't have to tell him, Franklin," Leopold said.

"Franklin?" said Charlie, noting the unusual use of Carlin's first name.

"Go ahead and explain it, Mr. Chairman," Street said. "We never meant for Charlie to get tangled up in any of this. And certainly not Margaret."

"Of course not," said Leopold. "I did everything I could to try to steer him in the right direction. But you wouldn't listen, Congressman."

"Martin Van Waganan had figured out what you're doing," said Charlie. "That's why he's dead, isn't it?"

"Martin Van Waganan is dead because he was even more treasonous than you!" Carlin spat. "Someone at the Pentagon told him about the University of Chicago study by Mitchell and Kraus, how a defoliant could be used as a weapon against the Reds. And then he started looking into all of it. He had all these connections at the Pentagon and in corporate America that he'd picked up on the Truman Commission. Thankfully, *our* connections quickly told us what was going on and we positioned one of our

Hellfire Club nuns right next to him so she could keep us abreast of everything the whole time."

Leopold nodded, lips pursed.

"That's correct," she said. "And just like Congressman Marder, Congressman Van Waganan ignored me and thought he was somehow above it all and that all of those working so hard to save this country from the Red Menace were its enemies."

"Which reminds me, Charlie," said Carlin, "you owe Miss Leopold and our security team here a thank you for saving your wife's life. Louis Gwinnett had orders from his Soviet friends to do whatever he needed to get those files on the General Kinetics plants. I have no doubt he would have killed her."

"As you're about to," Charlie said.

Carlin shrugged. "At least this way you get to say good-bye."

Charlie glanced at Margaret, who looked terrified.

"What do you mean, good-bye?" Strongfellow asked.

"By that, Chairman Carlin means that he intends to kill Charlie and Margaret," Street said. "Or have them killed by you or me or those two meatballs over there." He pointed at the two thugs next to Leopold, who shot

Street angry looks. "Speaking of which, bring me my gun, the one you took from Charlie." Street hopped down from the statue and held out his hand.

Strongfellow looked around the room in disbelief. He walked slowly toward Street and handed him the OSS gun he'd taken from Charlie. "Let me see yours too," Street said.

Strongfellow handed over his .38. Street opened its chamber, clicked it back in place, and felt the weight of the piece in his palm.

"I've seen the Smith and Wesson Chief's Special before, but I've never fired one," Street said to Strongfellow as if he were at a cocktail party. "Feels good."

"You'll get to use it in a second," Carlin said.

"Lyes rubyat, shchepki letyat," Leopold said to Charlie. "That's what Lenin said. 'To chop down a forest, splinters will fly.'"

"Or in American, 'You can't make an omelet without cracking some eggs,'" said Carlin. "Forgive Catherine, she loves to show off how much she learned when she was undercover for military intelligence in Moscow."

Margaret tried to speak, but they couldn't understand her through the gag.

"What's she saying?" asked Strongfellow.

"Go ahead and remove that, Catherine," Carlin said.

After Margaret swallowed, she spoke: "Love the notion of an anti-Communist quoting Lenin," she said.

"Should I put the gag back on?" asked Leopold.

"Margaret's right; it's perfect," said Charlie. " 'To chop down a forest, splinters will fly.' So they'll fly into me and Margaret, right, who cares. But how many splinters are flying? General Kinetics is manufacturing this pesticide to spray all over insurgencies around the world — and the people and livestock dying here in the U.S. are just collateral damage? That's what this is about? Is this pesticide really worth it?"

"You half-wit, these aren't *pesticides,*" Carlin snarled. "We're making *chemical weapons.*"

"You really think all of this is about *defoliation?*" said Leopold. "This is about the next century's worth of warfare. Nukes probably won't ever be used in our war against the Soviets or the Chinese. We will fight conventional wars, and we cannot afford another loss like in Korea. So we need a better way to fight."

"Chemical weapons were outlawed after World War One," Charlie said.

"Which is why a chemical weapon disguised as a defoliant is so brilliant," said Leopold.

"You're sick," said Margaret. "You're sociopaths. Innocent people might die."

"They already have," said Street. "It's going on in Malaya right now. Vietnam might be next. Wake up, Margaret."

"It's simply astounding to me that people like you can literally almost be killed by Reds one minute and the next minute you're essentially defending them," Carlin said.

"You're the ones reciting their mottoes," Margaret said.

"We're not defending Communists," said Charlie. "We're objecting to you killing innocent people. Whether in Malaya or here in the States."

"None of the problems here in the U.S. are intentional," said Strongfellow. "At least, the livestock incident in my district, in Skull Valley, was an accident. Chemical spill."

"Oh, dear, sweet Strongfellow," said Street. "None of this is an accident. They're testing how effective these poisons are. On animals in Utah and on poor folk, whether blacks in Louisiana or whites in Appalachia. No one introduces a product to the market without vigorous testing."

"We've told General Kinetics to change that," said Carlin. "They're moving the testing to Mexico and India."

"So the Hellfire Club had Van Waganan killed before he could come forward with any of this, Charlie," Street said. "He was starting to figure it out. What they didn't know is that Van Waganan and MacLachlan were working together, and after Van Waganan was killed, Mac kept going."

"But didn't the Puerto Ricans kill Mac?" asked Strongfellow, clearly the most confused person in the room.

"Don't be a fool," Carlin said. "It's not as if we wanted him dead and got lucky. There's no such thing as lucky. There's what we do and what we fail to do."

"I don't understand," said Charlie.

Street chuckled. "So, Charlie, let's imagine that Chairman Carlin is a powerful member of a secret society, an association that includes the FBI director as a member. An FBI director with paid informants everywhere — one who might have inside knowledge of the Puerto Rican nationalists' plot to shoot up the Capitol ahead of time. And then let's imagine that in the midst of that shoot-out, a congressman who is a thorn in the side of this secret society, who is threatening to expose a company run by another member of that club, just happens to get shot. And killed."

Carlin shook his head admiringly at Street. "I'd have to be some kind of goddamn genius to pull off what you're insinuating!"

"See now?" Street said with a smile. "You're not so modest after all. It's too bad they don't give Pulitzers for assassinations."

"All the things we do to keep this nation safe from the kinds of Reds who tried to kill Margaret just a few hours ago," Carlin said. "And still these idiots don't get it."

"We get it," said Margaret. "But General Kinetics is killing Americans in the process."

"Look," said Carlin, "in retrospect, could our friends at General Kinetics have exercised more caution, spent more money on safety measures and such? I suppose, but it would have slowed down production. Like with the need to rush gas masks to the front lines. As we said — omelets, eggs. You know."

"I do indeed," Charlie said grimly, fists clenched at his sides.

"And who won the war, Charlie?" asked Carlin.

"Those of us who actually fought in the war didn't have this in mind," Charlie said.

Carlin frowned theatrically, looking doubtful. "Oh, really?" he said. "Street fought in that war. Strongfellow fought in that war."

"You sure about that?" Charlie asked.

"Aha!" Carlin said, almost pleased. "So you're not a perfect angel. You read *This Is Your Life*'s investigation into Strongfellow here! The one you stole from your father!"

"What?" Strongfellow asked.

"The file we have on you proving that you never served with the OSS," Carlin said. "Charlie purloined that from his father. His dad is a lawyer, does work for NBC, and they found out right before your episode of *This Is Your Life* aired, the one that shared the story of your glorious, if entirely concocted, heroism. They buried it. Charlie's dad had it. Charlie stole it. And here we are!"

"You son of a bitch," Strongfellow said to Charlie. "That true?"

Charlie winced and turned his head around to look at Strongfellow.

"I did it for the same reason you're presumably doing this," Charlie said. "I thought they had dirt on me. Turns out it was all a setup, that I didn't do what they told me I'd done. But in any case, yes, I swiped the NBC investigation from my dad's office."

"Ooo-eee," exclaimed Street. "What does it say?"

"It goes into detail about how for the

498

entire war, Strongfellow was a machinist. Stateside. There's a letter from Dulles stating he was never OSS. Letter from the Pentagon saying he was never overseas."

Strongfellow appeared to be grinding his teeth.

"Why'd NBC run the episode, then?" Street asked.

"You'd have to ask them why they sat on it," Charlie said. "I assume ratings. Currying favor with Republicans. Are the presidents of the networks in the Hellfire Club?"

Carlin turned to Street and waved a hand in Charlie's direction. "We need to wrap this up, Mr. Street."

"That's fine," said Street, "but I'm not going to clean up any messes."

"Of course not," Carlin said.

"That's what Catherine's henchmen over there are for," Street said, drawing angry glares again.

Charlie looked straight ahead at Margaret, her arms bound behind her back, her face a mask of pure panic.

"At what point does your construction of this Potemkin village start undermining your ability to build the actual village?" Charlie asked. "If your leaders are frauds like Strongfellow and demagogues like McCarthy, at what point do they supplant real leaders? At what point are you killing and hurting more Americans than you're saving?"

"Be quiet," instructed Carlin. "You hold no cards here."

"So who else is in the Hellfire Club?" asked Margaret.

"They're just stalling, Frank," Leopold said.

"Mr. Street?" Carlin said. "Ticktock."

Street gripped Strongfellow's .38 with two hands and began to raise it.

"Mr. Chairman?" Charlie asked. "Can I at least kiss my wife one last time?"

"Oh, sweet baby Jesus," said Leopold. She took a gun out of her jacket pocket. "I'll shoot him if you need me to." The two men standing with her took their guns out of their jackets, presumably in case their services were required as well.

"Go ahead and kiss her, Charlie," Street said. "Make it quick."

Charlie raised his hands in surrender and slowly walked over to Margaret, looking at Carlin for the okay. Carlin nodded. Her eyes were wild with fear and fury. "Charlie!" she said. "They —"

He lowered his hands and silenced her with a kiss, feeling her angry resistance until he broke away to whisper in her ear.

She swallowed and nodded.

They kissed each other again, tenderly.

Charlie then turned to Street, his hands back up near the sides of his head.

"Okey-doke, Isaiah," he said.

Street nodded. Aimed the gun at Charlie.

"Okey-doke, Charlie," Street said.

"Roger," Charlie said.

"Shoot him already," Carlin said.

"Three . . ." said Street.

"Oh, good Lord," said Leopold.

"Two . . ." Street continued.

"Love you, honey," said Margaret.

"Love you too, baby," said Charlie.

"And . . ." said Street.

At the last second, Charlie and Margaret dropped to the ground while Street simultaneously turned his aim from Charlie toward the two thugs standing with Leopold. Two shots were fired, and the two thugs dropped to the ground. Leopold gasped; Carlin exclaimed, *What the fuck?*" and jumped behind a sculpture of Crispus Attucks a split second before Street turned a hundred and eighty degrees and shot at him.

Lying on her back on the floor, Margaret pulled the hoop of her bound arms under her rear and her legs to bring her hands in front of her. It was a struggle, given her pregnant belly, but her adrenaline and flexibility made it work.

Leopold fired at Street. She missed, but she got his attention. He returned fire and Leopold ran behind a statue of Charles Lindbergh holding an America First banner.

Leopold, using the statue for cover, fired at Street from the far side of the tribute to Lindbergh, and Margaret crawled around the other side. Focused on Street, Leopold didn't notice Margaret creeping up and looping her arms over her head and around her neck. Margaret pulled back with all her might; Leopold gasped for air and dropped her gun as she struggled to insert her hand between Margaret's bound wrists and her own neck.

Charlie ran to Strongfellow and squared up against him, but before he could punch him, Strongfellow kicked him in the groin. Charlie fell on the ground in agony. Strongfellow began kicking him in the gut — his legs very obviously perfectly functioning. The image of Margaret and their baby sprang into Charlie's head. He lunged for Strongfellow's legs and knocked him down. Strongfellow's head hit the floor hard as Street ran over and began kicking him in the stomach.

"Isaiah!" Charlie yelled.

Carlin was pushing a statue of General George Custer onto them. Charlie shoved Street out of the way; the statue hit Charlie's back. Custer's arm broke off its body and smashed into Strongfellow's head, knocking him out. Charlie cried out in pain.

Margaret was still locked in battle with Leopold, her wrists still bound and around Leopold's neck. Leopold, demonstrating surprising strength as she struggled mightily to free herself, began bucking like a bronco, first pulling Margaret forward and lifting her off her feet, then suddenly running backward and ramming Margaret into a statue of Supreme Court justice Roger Taney. Margaret was terrified but couldn't let go since her wrists remained bound, and the more Leopold battered Margaret, the tighter Margaret hung on, strangling her.

Street checked on the two thugs to make sure they were dead, then raced to Charlie's side to help him, but Charlie, teeth clenched in agony, shook his head. "Go help Margaret!" Street did, but not before slamming his OSS gun into the palm of Charlie's hand.

Street turned toward Margaret as Carlin emerged from the crowd of statues, bent down to the base of a figure of Continental Army general Charles Lee, and tried to topple it onto Charlie. Lee teetered, and Charlie managed to push himself out of its way a moment before the stone mass fell onto the space he had just occupied. Hands on his knees, gasping, Charlie found the OSS gun on the ground and aimed it right at Carlin.

"That's a single shot, Charlie," Street called. "You can't miss!"

Charlie aimed for Carlin's head.

Carlin's eyes widened. "No," Carlin said. "Wait, Charlie, listen to me —"

Charlie fired, but the Liberator was a gun for emergencies, and Charlie reverted to his basic-training mistake of flinching as he anticipated the gun's recoil. The bullet whizzed past Carlin's head and hit the statue of Crispus Attucks.

Carlin jumped forward onto Charlie and grabbed his throat, then tried to shove his thumbs into Charlie's eyes. Charlie pulled at Carlin's wrists, trying to stop the pain. Carlin's obvious desperation seemed to empower him, but he was also much older and weaker than his adversary. Charlie, in pain, kicked Carlin in the groin, then twisted Carlin's wrist and slammed his forehead into the older man's nose. Carlin coughed and released his grip; Charlie threw him to his right.

Carlin grabbed at Charlie's arm and bit it. Charlie screamed as Carlin's teeth broke the skin.

Feeling a white-hot jolt of fury, Charlie grabbed Carlin by his shirt collar and lifted him off the ground, then turned his body to the left and slammed the man's head into the sharp corner of the base of the Crispus Attucks statue. It might as well have been the edge of an ax.

The marble edge was now marked with a deep crimson stain as all fight left Carlin's body. He groaned and his eyes rolled back in his head.

It was at precisely that moment that Leopold succumbed to Margaret's bound hands around her neck. She dropped to her knees, then fell onto her face, dragging Margaret along with her.

Charlie stood, ran to Margaret, extricated her from the death trap she had fastened around Leopold's neck, and embraced her.

The room was suddenly still, the only sound Margaret, Charlie, and Street breathing heavily. They were surrounded by their fallen enemies: one unconscious, one dying, three dead.

"I told you I was on your side," Street finally said.

CHAPTER TWENTY-NINE: THURSDAY, APRIL 22, 1954 — MORNING

Capitol Hill

Three men in suits, Colt .38s in hand, walked into the storage room. They all looked alike: brown hair, mid-thirties, trim builds, dark suits. Secret Service, maybe, or FBI; their exact affiliation was unclear.

"Nice timing," said Street, hands braced on his knees, dripping with sweat and breathing like Jesse Owens after a wind sprint.

"Is everyone okay?" one of the men asked.

"We're fine," said Charlie, holding Margaret, his hand on her pregnant belly. "Everyone's good." Margaret's face was buried in his chest.

"You should vamoose," the third man said to Street. "We'll take care of it from here."

Street nodded and motioned to Charlie and Margaret to follow him. They reached the hallway and paused.

"Who were they?" Charlie asked.

"The good guys," said Street.

"Do you know the way out?" Margaret asked.

"Out of the basement? Or this situation?"

"Either," she said.

"Basement, yes."

"And the situation here? Three dead bodies and two sitting congressmen knocked out, all in the basement of the U.S. Capitol?"

Street shook his head. "That one's a little trickier."

Outside, a bright dawn was breaking as if the sun were proud to be seen after days hiding. Charlie heard mourning doves coo and could smell the earthy, loamy scent of spring. A bus drove up Constitution Avenue; the city was starting to stir.

A red Cadillac Coupe de Ville sat in the Capitol driveway, its engine running.

Charlie peered in and saw Senator Kefauver behind the wheel, a grim expression on his face. Winston Marder was in the backseat.

"Get in," Winston said. "Margaret, honey, you sit up front."

"Please hurry," said Kefauver. "We need to git."

"I love it when you pretend you're a

hillbilly," gruffed Winston.

The three piled into the Cadillac, and Kefauver hit the gas and took a right out of the Capitol driveway onto Independence Avenue. The atmosphere inside the car was tense; they rode in silence for a few blocks, Kefauver and Charlie scanning the surroundings for a tail. Finally Margaret turned around from the front seat to face the men.

"That's all going to be cleaned up?" Margaret asked Winston.

"Area will be secured and cleaned," he said.

"We left behind maybe four dead bodies, including the House Appropriations Committee chairman," Charlie said.

"However many you left behind, and whoever they are, it will be taken care of," said Winston. He turned to Street: "Four dead bodies? Including Carlin?"

"Yeah, it got ugly," said Street, who took a few minutes to explain everything that had happened since he last saw Winston a day before in Manhattan. Margaret filled in other blanks, describing Gwinnett's menacing hunt for her and how Catherine Leopold killed him.

"Good Christ," Winston finally said. "I'm so sorry, Margaret. I never wanted you to get caught up in any of this. I never wanted

Charlie to get caught up in it."

"Then why arrange for me to get the congressional seat?" Charlie asked, a note of irritation in his voice. "Or at the very least, why not tell me about everything that was going on so I could have a better way to protect Margaret and the baby?"

"We didn't know, Charlie," Street said.

"I can defend myself, Isaiah," Winston said.

"I know," Street said, "but Charlie, you need to understand, we've only been about a half step ahead of you. We didn't even know about the car accident until you told me."

"I had no idea you were going to be pulled into any of this when I got Dewey to give you the seat, and I certainly didn't know you were going to pull that foolish stunt at the comic-book hearing," Winston said. "That's what escalated everything. Until then, the Hellfire Club thought they had you where they wanted you. And until then, Estes and Isaiah were keeping me abreast of everything. We all were doing everything we could to steer you *away* from the Hellfire Club."

"Except for telling me about it, of course," Charlie said.

"You were supposed to just do your job,"

Winston said. "You weren't supposed to take on the whole goddamn system or screw with Carlin. Or steal papers from my goddamn study."

"You knew about that?" Charlie asked.

"After the fact," Winston said. "Dulles told me. That poor miserable son of a bitch Strongfellow is going to be ruined. Not by me. By the club. Especially now, tied to this mess. Poor sap probably thinks he's in the clear."

"Wait — you're going to let him loose after he tried to kill me?"

"That's how this works, Charlie," Winston said. "We don't call the police on one another. We bribe the police to stay out of it. The FBI or Secret Service swoops in and cleans everything up. Our organizations don't play by the normal rules."

" 'We'? What organizations besides the Hellfire Club?" Margaret asked. "Who is 'we'?"

"The, ah, loose association that I'm in," Winston said. "And Isaiah."

"What is this 'loose association'?" Margaret asked. "Central Intelligence? FBI? I don't understand."

"You will soon enough, but I've said all I can," Winston said.

"Margaret, surely you realize that clandestine services in the U.S. are made up not only of organizations you know about, but also ones you don't," Street offered.

They stopped at a red light.

No one spoke. The light changed and they drove on in uncomfortable silence.

"I assume you can tell us about the Hellfire Club at least?" Margaret asked. "Who are they?"

"We don't know anything for sure," Winston said. "We think its monks include Carlin, Hilton, McCarthy, the Dulles boys, Hoover, Ambassador Kennedy, um . . . Who else?"

"Duncan Whitney from General Kinetics," Street said. "We don't know them all. You got closer to the club, Charlie, than I ever could."

"And what do they do?" Margaret asked.

"Control almost everything," said Kefauver.

"Make a lot of money," Street said.

"They all have networks of people who owe them favors or people they've compromised," Winston said. "And yes, they're getting rich but they're also fighting Commies."

"They contain multitudes," Street said, smiling at Charlie.

"Charlie, after your run-in with McCarthy

and Cohn at Connie Hilton's party, we think you had an even bigger target on your back," Winston said. "Carlin was already chomping at the bit to get you in line. But that was to control you, not kill you."

"And that was the night Charlie was set up," Margaret realized.

"Indeed," said Winston. "Carlin got his henchmen to arrange that whole thing — the knockout drug, the staged accident. But we didn't know any of that until just recently. I begged Allen Dulles for help. Turned out he'd had you tailed that night and had the photos that cleared you."

"But we didn't find out until yesterday," Street said. "Right before I brought them to you."

"Allen's a cagey bastard and he wouldn't just turn anything over. Now I owe him."

"What do we need to do to make sure they don't try to kill us again?" Margaret asked.

"That was just Carlin and his team," Winston Marder said. "Not the whole club. But you need to drop the General Kinetics thing."

"Drop it?" Charlie said, alarmed.

"We think the club is in factions right now," Street said. "They're being torn apart over McCarthy. Kennedy brought McCarthy into the club in 'forty-nine. He got

McCarthy to agree not to campaign against Jack during his Senate run three years later. They've all been allies."

"But McCarthy since then has gone nuts," Kefauver added.

"There's a struggle going on in the club," Winston said. "They all see McCarthy is out of control and needs to be stopped before he takes on Ike in 'fifty-six. The Dulles brothers and some of the generals and CEOs are looking to end the problem. It may prove easier for him to be hoisted with his own petard."

"We suspect a few defense-contractor CEOs are monks or second-tier abbots," Street said. "They want the enormous defense contracts to proceed, and McCarthy's focus on the army is causing them huge problems."

"McCarthy smeared General Marshall back in 1950; they thought he was going to stop there?" Margaret asked.

"Gotta hit the rat on the head the moment he pokes his head out of the sewer," Charlie agreed. "But that holds true for General Kinetics too, Dad."

"That's nonsense," Winston said angrily. "The chemical weapons program is vital. The Hellfire Club isn't wrong about that."

"The Reds *are* a menace, Charlie," Street said.

"Look at how they manipulated Margaret, sending that zoologist to get close to her with me and you as targets," Winston said. "You need to stop being naive about the Reds. There are forces at play here that are much bigger than your ideals and the way you think the world should work."

"But you're playing by the same corrupt rules as the Hellfire Club," Charlie said. "You agree with those rules?"

"That's like asking if we agree or disagree with oxygen," said Winston. "Or the tides."

"This is how it works," Street said. "I'm quite certain I like it even less than you do, but these are the realities."

"General Kinetics is going to change the way they do business," Winston said. "And you need to keep your mouth shut. That's nonnegotiable."

They sat in silence. Kefauver took a left onto Rock Creek Parkway. Margaret looked out her window at the circular Doric temple that stood just off the road, dedicated on Armistice Day 1931 by President Hoover as a tribute to the men and women of Washington, DC, who had given their lives in "the Great War." As if there would never be another. Simpler times, Margaret thought.

"It's just stunning that this whole time, you and my dad have been working together," Charlie said.

"It's even more stunning that he convinced Carlin that he was working for him," Winston observed.

"That's actually a good point," Margaret said, turning to look at Street behind her. "How did you win the trust of . . ." She searched for the words.

"Of a bunch of old white bigots?" Street finished for her.

"It's a smart question," Winston said. "My daughter-in-law possesses much more intelligence than her husband."

"I gave them just enough information to trust me," Street said. "Intelligence comes from people of all colors; they might be bigots, but they know that much. Intel comes from Arabs, Africans, Jews, Chinese . . ."

"You realize, Charlie, Isaiah was working on trying to learn more about the club long before they set their sights on you," Winston said.

"It was your dad's idea originally," Street said. "When I came here in January of 'fifty-three, I pretended to be a willing source for them. Given my background in the OSS, they were interested."

"I brought it up to Dulles, who mentioned it to Hoover," Winston said. "They wouldn't have invited Isaiah over for supper, but they were happy to take his information. Or have him be a button man to kill you two."

Kefauver sighed impatiently and turned on the radio. "Y'all talk too much," he said to himself.

"*. . . showdown between Senator McCarthy and the U.S. Army,*" the announcer said. "*McCarthy claims the army is behind a conspiracy to discredit him . . .*"

"And he's right!" Kefauver laughed. They fell silent, listening to the news. Kefauver left Rock Creek Parkway and worked his way to Dent Place in Georgetown, through tree-lined streets where young lawyers and secretaries briskly walked to bus stops.

"Here we are!" Winston said, clearly relieved to be pulling up to Charlie and Margaret's town house.

Winston patted his son on the knee.

"Remember what Falstaff said, my son," Winston said. " 'The better part of valor is discretion.' "

"But I still have a lot of questions," Charlie said. "The other day we stumbled on these documents about the Hellfire Club in England in the eighteenth century. So Ben Franklin brought it to the U.S.?"

Street chuckled. "Charlie, we're still trying to figure out everything going on in the club *today;* we don't even know who all the members are *now.* We damn sure haven't traced its genealogy."

"Legend is that Franklin replicated the club once he returned to the colonies," Winston said. "But we don't really know. We're only just now getting a handle on this, thanks to Ike."

"Why thanks to Ike?" Charlie asked.

"You'll see," Winston said. "Now, please let us go so I can phone Dulles and we can clean this all up."

Margaret opened the car door. "It was nice to see you again, Winston," she said drily, as if they were coming from a mixer and not a fatal shoot-out. "And nice to see you again, Senator Kefauver. It has been way too long since you were kind enough to take us to see *The Pajama Game* — we need to repay the favor, have you over for dinner." Kefauver laughed.

She stepped out of the car and straightened her blouse. A passerby would have no idea of the chaotic, bloody night she'd just survived. She leaned toward the passenger window.

"And Isaiah, you and Renee need to come over soon," she continued, a caricature of a

Georgetown hostess. "Tell her I'll call her. Toodles!"

Street grinned. "Your wife is crazy," he said to Charlie.

She stood on the sidewalk and looked expectantly at Charlie, who remained in the crowded backseat.

Charlie nodded at her but first turned to his father and said in a low voice so Margaret wouldn't hear, "Are we safe?"

Winston hesitated. "I . . . I don't know. I don't know who wanted you gone other than Carlin. I assume Hoover and Dulles want this sorry chapter over. You will have to keep your mouth shut about General Kinetics. That's not negotiable. You need to burn any copies of the Van Waganan dossier, the info on the chemical plants. You do that, and maybe we can put this all behind us. I'll make some calls as soon as we get to Kefauver's house."

Street opened the back door and stepped out, followed by Charlie. They shook hands.

"We'll talk soon," Street said.

"I owe you," said Charlie.

"I have a feeling I'm going to get a chance to collect," Street said.

Charlie patted Street on the shoulder, then bent down and looked at his father and Kefauver. "Thank you," he said.

"You don't need to thank me," Kefauver said. "All I did was give the son of an old friend a ride home from Capitol Hill."

Charlie and Margaret walked up the stairs to their front door as Kefauver drove off. Down the street, they could see Senator Kennedy leaving his brownstone, with Jackie fixing the lapels on his sport jacket and kissing him on the cheek. The senator saw Charlie and Margaret, waved, and got into his car.

An hour before Charlie and Margaret returned home, LaMontagne was picking the lock of their town house, thinking about how much he didn't like killing.

The act of ending a life was unpleasant. It was sometimes a physical chore requiring significant exertion and it was often messy, whether from blood or struggle or end-of-life bodily expulsions. It ticked him off that he'd had to kill the redheaded club cocktail waitress to set up Charlie. Why him? Hadn't he paid his dues by now? Enough already. It made him even angrier when Carlin ordered him to murder Charlie after his stunt at the comic-book hearings. LaMontagne thought it beneath his station at this point in his career. Sure, he'd risen quickly in DC by being a Mr. Fix-It, but he expected to have graduated from this kind of task by now.

LaMontagne had no idea what had happened to Carlin and Leopold in the previous hours, and he was unaware of the saga on Susquehannock Island. All he knew was that the day before, Charlie had been on national television alluding to national security secrets that the Hellfire Club had already killed two congressmen to conceal.

Van Waganan had been easy. LaMontagne hid in the backseat of the congressman's car, then as soon as he got behind the wheel, out came his Ruger Single-Six, bang, a shot to the head. With the help of Abner Lance they'd staged a murder-suicide with a local prostitute. The cops had been on the scene for only five minutes before Hoover's agents arrived and guaranteed the crime would remain unsolved in perpetuity.

Offing MacLachlan had been more challenging, given Carlin's scheme to blame it on the Puerto Ricans. One of Hoover's Puerto Rican informants tipped off the Bureau about the attack, and the night before, LaMontagne had planted a rifle under a bench in the House gallery. During the House debate on Mexican migrants, Abner Lance had walked up to the gallery and waited. As soon as the *"Viva Puerto Rico libre"* chant started, Lance — a sniper in the

Korean War — aimed at MacLachlan and fired. Amid the chaos, and with every eye focused on the Puerto Ricans on the other end of the gallery, no one saw.

The tumblers on the lock gave way. La-Montagne slowly turned the knob and stepped in.

Once inside Charlie and Margaret's foyer, LaMontagne closed the door softly and reached to the small of his back to retrieve a pistol he used for these special occasions: a Welrod Mk IIA, developed by Station IX of the UK Special Operations Executive during the war specifically for assassinations; quiet, reliable, with no markings. Fewer than three thousand Welrods had been manufactured. LaMontagne had acquired his through a British friend, a fellow expert in wet work.

The house was silent and dim, the curtains still closed against the daylight. LaMontagne poked his head around the doorways of the downstairs rooms, confirming that they were empty, and then put a tentative foot on the bottom stair, wary of creaks. Cautiously he ascended, placing his weight on the balls of his feet, pausing on each step. He would need to look around the house for a place to hide.

■ ■ ■ ■

Charlie unlocked the door and stepped back to let Margaret enter. Exhausted, they trudged up the two flights of stairs to their bedroom, where Margaret began taking off her flannel and chinos, which had gone from soaking wet to crusted and uncomfortable.

Charlie's nostrils flared. Something was wrong. He quickly peered into the walk-in closet and then the bathroom. He dropped down and looked under the bed.

"Something wrong, honey?"

Charlie approached Margaret and whispered in her ear. "I think Davis LaMontagne is here."

"How —"

"Shh. I smell his cologne."

There was no other explanation for the faint whiff of Cuir de Russie in the air.

"He's probably downstairs," he whispered. "Act normal and let's be ready."

"It was good to see your father," she finally said aloud.

"Yep," Charlie said. "Hey, honey, I'm going to take a shower." He walked into the bathroom and turned on the water.

She thought she heard something from

the first floor. A step? The creak of a door-knob turning?

"Honey, don't use all the shampoo," she said, struggling to come up with small talk. She tiptoed into the bathroom and whispered to Charlie: "I have an idea."

"So do I."

Hiding in the basement, LaMontagne wondered if this had been Charlie's fate from the moment he'd tried to organize the veterans in Congress to defy Carlin over the Goodstone funding. Powerful vectors crush obstructions; the laws of physics are not dissimilar from the rules of man.

He could hear Charlie and Margaret talking in their bedroom. LaMontagne began creeping upstairs. As he stepped lightly on the stairs from the ground floor to the second, the oak beneath his foot emitted a high-pitched creak. LaMontagne froze in place. No one upstairs said anything.

Had they heard him?

The clanging of pipes and the sound of the shower spray suggested they hadn't. Margaret uttered something. LaMontagne continued his slow trek to the Marders' bedroom.

The door to the bedroom was slightly ajar.

He pressed himself against the hallway wall and peered carefully into the empty room. Slowly he nudged the door open with his foot and eased his way inside. In the adjoining bathroom to his right, the shower was running. To his immediate left was a door to a walk-in closet.

The bed was unmade. LaMontagne steeled himself to kill both Charlie and Margaret. He would make it look like a burglary gone wrong.

"Honey, what's the dress at this luncheon?" Margaret's voice suddenly bellowed from behind him, in the closet. She sounded odd, muffled. Maybe she was pulling a shirt over her head.

He would dispose of her first. LaMontagne turned around.

The door to the walk-in closet was partly closed. He pushed it open with his left hand, his right hand holding the pistol, ready to shoot Margaret where she stood.

But the closet was empty. And too late he realized the sound he'd heard was from the baby monitor he'd given them, placed inside the closet; he had been fooled, and that meant Charlie and Margaret —

Heat, intense heat. His head, his hair, and his skin were on fire.

He wheeled around and dropped the gun

to grab his head with both hands, as if that could quell the pain.

Margaret was ten feet behind him, squirting two different containers at his neck and head; when the chemicals interacted, they formed a weapon that burned LaMontagne's skin. Charlie was to his right, torching him with what felt like a flamethrower, spraying a furniture polish he ignited with his German lighter.

LaMontagne was in agony; his body was on fire. He couldn't think past the pain.

Margaret opened their bedroom window and Charlie hoisted him out of it. LaMontagne fell three stories and landed on his head.

Charlie looked out the window and down onto the brick sidewalk where LaMontagne's body lay, twisted and still and on fire.

Charlie leaned against the windowsill, his heart pounding. "Okay," he finally said. "That worked well."

After they'd called the police, they went to the kitchen and tried to calm down. Charlie boiled water to make them tea; he laid out a small plate of butter cookies, which Margaret began devouring.

"Where did you learn that?" she asked.

"With the drain cleaners? How did you know that they would be so dangerous if you combined them? Or that the furniture polish was flammable?"

"The comic-book hearing!" Charlie laughed. "Good thing for us the nation's comic-book publishers offer courses to America's children on how to turn household products into horrific weapons. But it was your idea about the baby monitor that gave us the upper hand."

"Well, I've been thinking quite a bit about the baby," she said, smiling and patting her stomach.

He put his hand on hers.

"It took us a little while, but I think we're finally figuring out how to survive in the world of politics."

EPILOGUE:
FRIDAY, APRIL 30, 1954

Washington, DC

Washington was in mourning.

Five days before, a small plane had crashed in the Blue Ridge Mountains of Virginia and taken the lives of the chairman of the House Appropriations Committee, Representative Franklin Harris Carlin, Republican of Oklahoma, as well as several others, including Charlie's own office manager, Catherine Leopold, and two unknown men, presumably the pilot and copilot. Their plane had disappeared on the way to Oklahoma. After locating the wreckage, authorities said the bodies had been burned beyond recognition.

That was what everyone was told, at any rate.

The funeral aired live on local television in Washington, DC. A camera inside the National Cathedral panned across the faces of the more illustrious guests at the service:

527

Vice President Richard Nixon and his wife, Pat, and, in the pews behind the vice president, Senators Kennedy, McCarthy, and Kefauver. House Speaker Joseph Martin and Democratic leader Sam Rayburn had also been given prominent seats.

Charlie watched the proceedings on the television in the West Wing lobby foyer. Originally he'd planned to attend the funeral, as insincere as that might have been, but an early-morning phone call from Ann Whitman, President Eisenhower's personal secretary, forced him to change plans.

The funeral made him uncomfortable, not because Charlie had killed Carlin, but because the oratories eulogized an evil and manipulative politician. Then again, Charlie knew, Carlin wouldn't be the first or the last politician so falsely memorialized.

"Pretty creepy to hear all that praise," Bernstein whispered to him. He had brought her for the company, because neither of them had ever been to the White House, and because her internship was soon going to end. In May, she would be heading back home to Los Angeles for a summer job at UCLA. In the fall, she would return to Georgetown for grad school, but it wasn't yet clear if she wanted to continue working in Charlie's office. Her experience had been

528

quite a bit more than she'd expected, and a return to normalcy sounded enticing.

The West Wing lobby was filled with men and women darting in and out of offices for appointments with various officials, some sitting on leather chairs and sofas to be greeted, others with special badges, walking around determinedly as if this were Penn Station. Charlie's eyes went everywhere but the television — to fellow visitors, to the black-and-white-checkered marble floor, to the paintings of American history. The work most clearly in his line of sight was the oddest and most disconcerting one in the room: President James Garfield, post–assassination attempt, suffering through his last miserable days on earth before the infection from the bullet took his life. Snatches of conversations of aides walking by urgently filled the room:

If Secretary Dulles doesn't say Indochina is in the security interests of Southeast Asia, then France will know we ain't sending even one soldier.
The networks should be paying McCarthy. I hear ratings are through the roof.
The veep gets *one* o'clock shadow. They don't make enough makeup.
So Toscanini freezes. He forgets all the

music or something. And the network
panics. They cut away; they didn't know
what to do.
At least now no one has to pretend that
Margaret Truman can sing.

He'd already read every article in the
Washington Post on the coffee table in front
of him, including the exposé on the front
page, below the fold, "The Curious Case of
Phil Strongfellow," in which it was revealed
that the U.S. government had no record of
the Utah Republican having ever been in
the OSS or any other clandestine service. A
spokesman for Strongfellow stated that the
congressman would be directly appealing to
the Eisenhower administration for his war
records to be released.

"So what's going to happen to Strongfellow?" Bernstein asked.

"He's over and done," said Charlie. "You
see the unnamed Republican congressional
aides quoted in the story saying the party
leadership is looking around for someone
else to run for the seat in November?"

"Why did he lie?"

"I don't know," Charlie said. "I don't
know if he'd be able to explain it either."

Charlie wondered whether the Hellfire
Club had leaked the information to the *Post*

or if it had been shared by his dad or his associates, whatever they called themselves. The *Post* story depicted Strongfellow as either delusional or criminally mendacious. There really wasn't any acceptable explanation; even the most benign version suggested serious emotional problems.

Ann Whitman appeared at the far end of the lobby and spoke to the receptionist, who motioned to Charlie. In her forties, trim and attractive in a no-nonsense way, the president's secretary strode purposefully toward him.

"Congressman, we're ready for you now," she said.

"You should probably get a cab back to Capitol Hill," Charlie said to Bernstein as he got up to follow Whitman. "I don't know how long this is going to last."

Bernstein nodded, stood, and smoothed her dress. She seemed to want to say something, but no words came out.

"It's okay, Bernstein, we'll talk more when I get back to the office," he said. She nodded, and Charlie followed Whitman out of the reception area and down the hall to the Oval Office.

Charlie had met Eisenhower once before, back in 1948, when the retired general and hero of World War II had been president of

Columbia University. Attending a reception honoring students and faculty who had served in the military during the war, Charlie was one of many who stood in line to shake the hand of the former supreme commander of the Allied Expeditionary Forces in Europe. At the time, Charlie was pursuing his PhD in American history, and Eisenhower, then fifty-eight, was just beginning what would be an ill-fated tenure at the Ivy League school. Their interaction lasted maybe thirty seconds — handshake, information about the company Charlie had served with and where, photograph, "Thank you for your service."

"Come in," the president said now when Whitman knocked on the Oval Office door, his voice as flat as the Kansas plains where he'd been raised.

Eisenhower hadn't changed the Oval Office decor much after moving in a year and a half earlier. The walls were gray and the rug was a blue-green; he'd even stuck with the Teddy Roosevelt desk that Truman had brought out of storage. At the opposite end of the room, an immense floor globe stood before the fireplace, on the mantel of which were thirteen miniature flags. To the president's left sat a smaller version of the famous *Seated Lincoln* sculpture.

The only touches from the new resident of the office hung on the wall: photographs of a clean-shaven Abraham Lincoln and a uniformed Confederate general Robert E. Lee were displayed to the president's right, Lincoln slightly higher than the man he had defeated. Across from the president, adjacent to the fireplace, were oil paintings by John James Audubon, one of a woodpecker and one of an oriole. Over the mantel hung a painting of a pueblo village in New Mexico. Charlie noticed that one painting by the door — a mountain landscape — was signed *DE,* the artist no doubt the man behind the desk, who was busy signing a stack of papers as Charlie walked in.

At the edge of Eisenhower's desk was a small display case featuring twenty-four stones, each taken from a place where he'd once lived, from Fort Sam Houston to Gibraltar. Next to that was a glass block on which was inscribed the Latin phrase *Suaviter in modo, fortiter in re* — "Gently in manner, strong in deed."

"Have a seat," the president said without looking up. An aide standing next to him handed over and retrieved document after document. "Just need to finish signing these, whatever they are."

Charlie regarded the man, who seemed

much older than the last time he'd seen him in person. His charisma and likability were unmistakable, but his body was more slope-shouldered, his appearance now more grandfatherly than fatherly. He had defeated Hitler and Hirohito but he was no match for Father Time.

Eisenhower completed the documents, and the aide waited for Eisenhower to dismiss him, which he did, quickly and politely.

Now it was just the two of them in the room. Eisenhower took off his glasses and placed them on his desk, then stood up and shook Charlie's hand.

"I'm told we may have met before. At Columbia?"

"Yes, sir," Charlie said.

Eisenhower nodded and walked from behind his desk to take a seat on the deep red couch; he invited Charlie to join him in a chair across from him.

"They're about to build a putting green out there for me," Eisenhower said, waving a hand toward the windows. "You golf at all?"

"Poorly and infrequently."

"Ah. Well, the rest of us do it poorly and frequently. Your way is probably better."

Charlie grinned. Eisenhower had been his

commanding general in France and his college president at Columbia, so he was having difficulty escaping the feeling that he'd done something wrong and had been called to the principal's office.

"Your father tells me you're thinking of returning to academia," the president said. "That it's been something of a bumpy ride here."

Charlie chuckled and then, aware that the president might not understand why, said, "You'll forgive me, sir, but I'm not quite sure how much you know about the past four months."

"I know more of it than you probably think I know," he said. "I know you got caught up in this silent war we're in. Not the Cold War, though that's part of it. But these factions and associations and clubs. Hellfire and such. Not to mention the Communists, of course."

"I did, sir. *We* did, rather. My wife, Margaret, and myself."

Eisenhower looked down at the coffee table, then back up at Charlie.

"I heard of the nasty business with that lobbyist breaking into your house," the president said. LaMontagne's fall onto the Georgetown street had been impossible to contain or conceal; the Marders had immediately called the police and reported an intruder. Local newspapers covered it as a DC businessman gone mad and then the FBI took over the investigation.

"And of course I know about the Reds going after your wife," the president added. Two days earlier, the National Park Service had discovered the decomposing bodies of Gwinnett, Kessler, and Cornelius floating in the ocean. The FBI's official conclusion was that the three academics had drowned because of the powerful storm; they neglected to mention the small detail of the bullet wounds.

"Yes, we've been getting it from all sides," Charlie said.

Eisenhower looked at him thoughtfully.

"You fought in France," he said.

"Yes, sir."

"Our allies in that war very quickly became our enemies. The Chinese snatched half of Korea. The Soviets did the same with Germany. Blink of an eye, everything turned. On my desk when I first walked into this office, back in January 1953, was an appeal for executive clemency for the Rosenbergs. Which I denied. There are spies: Alger Hiss. Truman's number two at Treasury, Harry White. Dr. Fuchs over in England. I mean, they're there. We don't know how many. Of course, McCarthy is fighting Communists in the most un-American way. But the threat is real."

"I know it's real," Charlie said. "The Communists tried to kill my wife. And then a few hours later, some anti-Communists tried to kill me and my wife."

"And my guys saved you two."

"Yes, sir. Your guys."

"Charlie, what do you know about the intelligence establishment?" Eisenhower asked.

"Just the basics, sir. Need for intel during the war created the OSS, which is now Central Intelligence."

Eisenhower chuckled. "Well, there's a bit more to it than that. You know, we had practically nothing when I went to Europe. Years before, Secretary of War Stimson had even ended what we had, a tiny code-breaking office. 'Gentlemen don't read each other's mail,' he said. Cripes. Can you imagine that? 'Gentlemen don't read each other's mail.' " Eisenhower chuckled forlornly.

"Yes, sir. That sounds hopelessly naive."

"No one was a fiercer opponent of the OSS continuing after the war than the isolationist wing of our own party. Except maybe J. Edgar Hoover, who didn't want the competition. But by now, we have a growing intelligence apparatus out there, run by Allen Dulles. I'm confiding in you now. But the truth is, I don't trust how much it's grown. So I, personally, have my own network of folks keeping track of what's going on. Reporting to me. Those are my boys. My advisory group, I call them. They don't exist on paper anywhere. They're solely mine. They tell me everything. Your dad is one of them. Street too. There are three dozen of them, and they all have their own sources and methods. It's invaluable. Matters are in many ways getting out of hand."

Charlie was quiet for a moment, then said, "When you say matters are getting out of hand, I'm not sure if you're referring to McCarthy or the Hellfire Club or the Reds . . ."

Eisenhower greeted Charlie's questioning pause with a stern look.

"Well, let's discuss these one by one," the president said, "since I am now assuming you will be serving on my advisory board. On the first matter, soon enough McCarthy won't be a problem. We already see in public opinion polls that his popularity is plummeting. By the end of this year, it will no longer be McCarthyism; it will be

McCarthy-*wasm.*"

"Permission to speak freely, sir?" Charlie asked.

The president smiled. "Permission granted, soldier."

Charlie collected his thoughts. Watching the U.S. Army–McCarthy drama had been nerve-racking; it felt as though the nation's tolerance for indecency and lies would never reach a limit. He had watched as senators he'd previously respected pretended that the unacceptable wasn't becoming the status quo. He feared McCarthy would keep rising in popularity and status, leaving in his wake the complete destruction of basic societal norms. The historian in him intellectually suspected that something at some point would stop McCarthy; all great tyrants experience downfalls. But he couldn't see it coming for Tail Gunner Joe. He tried to take some small comfort in the president's confidence that the end was near, but he needed to know more.

"Sir, how can you be so sure?"

The president took a second to consider his reply. "I am sure because I am confident in the idea of the United States of America, Charlie," he finally said. "I believe that the combination of checks and balances and a free press and our democratically elected

representatives ultimately will expose charla-
tans. I believe in the good sense of the
American people, and I know in my soul
that truth will win out."

"Permission to speak freely again, sir?"

"Granted," said Eisenhower.

"That's a nice speech, but I assume there's
more to it than your faith in the American
people."

"There is," Eisenhower said. "We've set a
perfect trap for him, just as we did the
Germans with Operation Fortitude. I am
convinced that the only person who can
destroy McCarthy as a political figure is
McCarthy himself. And he has many weak-
nesses. One of them is drink. Another is
Cohn. And Cohn's weakness is Private
Schine. McCarthy and Cohn demanded
special treatment for Schine last year. It was
denied. So now McCarthy is going after the
army. That's a fight he cannot win. And it's
a fight we are prepared for. He will not walk
out of the hearings on the army unscathed."

Charlie considered what the president was
saying. He would have to take it on faith.
"There are others, of course, who are rip-
ping apart our country in the name of
preserving it," Charlie said. "It's not just
McCarthy."

Eisenhower looked away, toward his painting of a mountain landscape. "The main characteristic of the seven years between V-E Day and my moving into this office has been the steady consolidation of power in two blocs facing off against each other," he said. "With a growing arsenal of enormously destructive weapons on both sides."

"Chemical weapons being one facet of that," Charlie said.

"One of many." Eisenhower frowned. "Part of understanding everything at play in Washington right now is understanding the birth of a multibillion-dollar industry. Do you know that the amount of money our government spends on military security every year is greater than the net income of all U.S. corporations? It's astounding. We need a strong defense, of course. But I'm concerned about the conjunction of an immense military establishment with this large arms industry. It's new in the American experience. The total influence is felt everywhere. Every town, every village — every congressional vote."

"The arms manufacturers won't make as much money if we're at peace," Charlie noted.

"Precisely. When our wars are determined not by the threat of Nazism or fascism or Communism but by the influence on policy-makers of those who stand to reap financial benefits from the use of these arms — that, Charlie, is my biggest fear for this country. We have, for the first time in the history of this great nation, a war-based industry that exists even though we are not at war. Officers leave the military and take jobs in this industry and influence policies. We don't want to become what the Communists say we are."

He stared at Charlie, his ice-blue eyes projecting seriousness and concern.

"And that's one of the reasons why I need you to stay in Congress, Charlie," the president continued. "Because you understand both the threat of the Communists and the threat of those who would destroy the United States in order to save it."

There was a knock at the door and Mrs. Whitman poked her head in.

"Just give me two more minutes, Annie," the president said.

He stood and walked back to his desk.

"Sir?" Charlie asked.

"We need men like you, Charlie. The Republican Party does, Congress does, and, more important, the nation does. I need you working for us the way that your dad and your colleague Mr. Street do. For me. As my eyes and ears. One of my soldiers."

As Eisenhower sat, Charlie stood.

"Soon the nation will be waging wars just to bring up stock prices," the president said. "The Hellfire Club, as you well know, has been around for centuries. And they've generally kept their business private. But recently, its members have been flexing their muscles in ways that are getting people killed. Look at the Banana Man, what's his name, from United Fruit Company —"

"Sam Zemurray," Charlie said.

"Right," said Eisenhower. "In Guatemala, I can't tell what I'm being pushed to do because of the Communists and what I'm being pushed to do because Zemurray doesn't want to pay his banana pickers a living wage. And while he's not a member — the Hellfire Club doesn't admit Jews — he wields huge influence with a few of the monks. Allen Dulles and Foster, both. So I need my own eyes and ears all over the place. I trust Allen Dulles, but I need to know what he's up to. If he and his brother are continuing to take money from Zemurray, for instance."

Now Charlie felt less reassured. If even Eisenhower was this confused about agendas, what hope could he possibly have of understanding it?

"Don't give up the fight," Eisenhower

said. "We need brave people like you — and your wife — people who are willing to do the right thing. Heroes. Heroes like your dad and Congressman Street. That's how we defeat enemies, foreign and domestic. With men — and women — of character."

All Charlie could think about were the moments since he'd come to Washington when he was not brave, when options were put in front of him and he had decidedly not done the right thing. He hadn't gone to the cops immediately after waking up in Rock Creek. He'd passed the Boschwitz file over to Bob Kennedy. Swiped the NBC documents about Strongfellow from his dad's office and handed them over to Roy Cohn. He had done what was most comfortable and advantageous for himself, nothing more. Here was the president suggesting he was on the path of the righteous because midway through it, he'd snapped out of his stupor and worked with Margaret and Isaiah on a plan to rebel, and somehow they'd all survived.

He wanted to ask Eisenhower about this. Did all heroes feel like such frauds? What had Charlie done, after all? Killed Carlin and helped Street save Margaret. She was healthy and would soon give birth, and the doctor reported that the baby looked great too, and that was the most important thing. But the CEO of General Kinetics was fat and happy manufacturing his poisons, and the Hellfire Club was down one monk but still thriving and pulling strings. Nothing had really changed except he and Margaret were not immediately being threatened. But McCarthy and Cohn and Abner Lance were still out there. His father had told him that Allen Dulles had sworn that Charlie and Margaret were safe for now, but how long would that last?

"I feel as though I have failed this nation more than I have fought for it, sir," Charlie said. "Since coming here to Washington, anyway."

Eisenhower looked grimly down at his desk. "Charlie," the president began. He stood and stared out the window. "In October 1952, I was campaigning in Wisconsin. Milwaukee. I was going to give a speech. And in it, I planned to stand up for my friend General Marshall. McCarthy had been smearing him as a traitor for the better part of a year. I was very excited; I had a section in this speech vouching for my friend's patriotism. And I would do so in Milwaukee with McCarthy onstage. It would be a moment I could feel proud of."

He exhaled, and the life seemed to go out

of him. He turned and put his hands on the back of his chair. "Then the governor got his hands on a copy of the speech, and he convinced my aides that they should take out that section, that if I stood up for George Marshall, I might alienate McCarthy, which could cost me Wisconsin's electoral votes."

There was another knock at the Oval Office door, and Mrs. Whitman once again poked her head in. The president turned to her. "One more second," he said. She closed the door. Eisenhower paused, apparently trying to find his place in the story.

"So what did you do after you heard that the governor told your aides to take out that section?" Charlie asked, attempting to help.

"I had them take it out of my speech," Eisenhower said. "I wish I hadn't. And this ended up, of course, not being the last time I had to defer to the egoism of this demagogue. McCarthy kept coming and coming and coming at me. My secretary of the army has been trying to accommodate him; that hasn't stopped him. He is incapable of stopping, even when it's in his own interests. Smearing and lying. It's what he does. One cannot appease the insatiable."

"And, as it turned out, you didn't need Wisconsin's electoral votes," Charlie noted.

"And it turned out I didn't need the electoral votes," Eisenhower agreed. He smiled at Charlie. A sad smile, tinged with regret.

"Okay, soldier, dismissed," Eisenhower said, extending a hand to shake Charlie's. "Take care of that pregnant little lady of yours."

Charlie thanked the president and walked out of the Oval Office and the West Wing. It was a gorgeous spring day, sunny but with a cool breeze rising from the Potomac River. Grape hyacinth and tulips decorated the North Lawn; men in dark suits and skinny ties and young women with tight blouses and high heels walked with determination to and from the building.

Outside the White House grounds, across Pennsylvania Avenue, Margaret sat in the driver's seat of the parked car, waiting for him. He walked around to the passenger side and got in.

"So where to?" Margaret asked. "Capitol Hill? Back to Manhattan? Somewhere else entirely?"

Her face was glowing with possibility and trust and partnership. She grinned at him expectantly, her eyes sparkling with joy. Charlie put his hand on Margaret's swelling belly and smiled.

"Wherever you want the road to take us," he said.

SOURCES

To state the obvious, *The Hellfire Club* is a work of fiction. That said, I did rely on numerous nonfiction accounts to write this book, ones to which I am indebted.

As a general note, David Halberstam's *The Fifties* (New York: Ballantine Books, 1994) was a great resource. Jack Lait and Lee Mortimer's *Washington Confidential* (New York: Crown, 1951) provided a severely flawed but otherwise revealing and muckraking account of the sleaze in the nation's capital in that era.

Chapter 2: For details about the life of Senator Estes Kefauver, I relied on Joseph Bruce Gorman's *Kefauver: A Political Biography* (New York: Oxford University Press, 1971) and Jack Anderson and Fred Blumenthal's *The Kefauver Story* (New York: Dial Press, 1956).

I took some liberties regarding Charlie's appointment. In real life, vacant House seats remain vacant until an election (special or otherwise). Governors appoint senators in case of an unscheduled vacancy, and resident commissioners for Puerto Rico can be appointed in such cases, too. First-term members of Congress were not considered for Appropriations until the 1970 reforms. But this is a work of fiction.

For plot purposes, *The Pajama Game* is shown premiering in DC in January of 1954; while the show did have tryouts in other cities before it opened on Broadway that spring, DC was not one of them.

Nixon's poker skills were documented in Chuck Blount's "How Playing Poker in the Navy Transformed Richard Nixon," *San Antonio Express-News,* February 21, 2017. Nixon talked about his poker skills with historian Frank Gannon on February 9, 1983; the interview is available at the University of Georgia website.

Chapter 3: The wild ponies of Nanticoke and Susquehannock Islands are loosely based on the actual wild ponies of Chincoteague and Assateague Islands. You can read more about the wreck of *La Galga* at the National Park Service website https://www.nps.gov/asis/learn/nature/upload/

wildhorses-%20In%20Design.pdf, and you can read more about the ponies in general in Ronald Keiper's *The Assateague Ponies* (Atglen, PA: Tidewater, 1985).

Chapter 4: For details about Fredric Wertham and his work, I relied on his own *Seduction of the Innocent* (New York: Rinehart, 1954) and David Hajdu's *The Ten-Cent Plague: The Great Comic-Book Scare and How It Changed America* (New York: Picador, 2009). The website http://www .lostsoti.org is also a great resource.

Chapter 5: Charlie's general war experiences were based on the actual heroics of the very real men of the Twenty-Ninth Infantry, many of whom shared their stories at the wonderful Twenty-Ninth Infantry Historical Society website (http:// www.29infantrydivision.org/). Some other details were taken from William R. Buster's *Time on Target: The World War II Memoir of William R. Buster* (Lexington: University Press of Kentucky, 2001).

Street's time as a Tuskegee Airman was based on the actual experiences of those heroes detailed at http://www.tuskegee.edu as well as Dr. Daniel L. Haulman's "Misconceptions About the Tuskegee Airmen," Air Force Historical Research Agency, July

551

23, 2013.

Chapter 6: New York Yankees pitcher Bill Bevens did indeed get put on the DL after a reaction to a smallpox inoculation, but it took place in 1947, not 1941, as it appears here. (And Bevens didn't join the Yankees until 1944.) See James Dawson, "Yankees Release Medwick Outright — Reynolds Will Oppose Browns Today with Bevens Ailing from Vaccination," *New York Times,* April 30, 1947.

Chapter 7: The crash of the USS *Shenandoah* on September 3, 1925, has been written about; see http://www.airships.net/us-navy-rigid-airships/uss-shenandoah/ and Tony Long, "Sept. 3, 1925: Shenandoah Crash a Harbinger of Grim Future," *Wired,* September 3, 2009.

Chapter 8: The Chase Smith conversation with McCarthy is recounted in her book *Declaration of Conscience* (New York: Doubleday & Company, 1972).

Kefauver was upset about this story: "Rival for Senate Assails Kefauver; Sutton, House Member, Runs in the Tennessee Primary, as 'Ultra-Conservative,' " *New York Times,* January 24, 1954.

Ambassador Lodge's speech and some of the details of the Alfalfa Club event that night were taken from "Lodge Wins

'Nomination' for President Alfalfa Club," *Courier-Journal,* January 24, 1954.

Chapter 9: Information about baby monitors in this chapter and throughout the book came from Rebecca Onion, "The World's First Baby Monitor: Zenith's 1937 'Radio Nurse,' " *Slate,* February 7, 2013. Also see Roger Catlin, "After the Tragic Lindbergh Kidnapping, Artist Isamu Noguchi Designed the First Baby Monitor," Smithsonian.com, December 20, 2016.

McCarthy hearing testimony taken from transcript for March 10, 1954, in *Executive Sessions of the Senate Permanent Subcommittee on Investigations of the Committee on Government Operations,* volume 5, Eighty-Third Congress, Second Session, 1954.

Chapter 10: Poems are "The Lodestar" by Wilfrid Wilson Gibson and "I Have a Rendezvous with Death" by Alan Seeger. The information that the latter was a favorite of John F. Kennedy, who often asked Jackie to recite it, is from the John F. Kennedy Presidential Library and Museum website.

Chapter 11: Congressman Taulbee being killed by a reporter is true; see Peter Overby, "A Historic Killing in the Capitol

Building," *Morning Edition,* National Public Radio, February 19, 2007, https://www.npr.org/templates/story/story.php?storyId=7447550.

The ghosts that haunt the Capitol were described by Bootie Cosgrove-Mather, "Haunted House on the Hill," Associated Press, October 31, 2003.

Debate on the Mexican Labor Amendment to the Agricultural Act of 1949 is taken from the House debate as recorded in *Congressional Quarterly Almanac* 1954, 10th ed., 02-128-02-129 (Washington, DC: Congressional Quarterly, 1955), http://library.cqpress.com/cqalmanac/cqal54-1360893.

The March 1, 1954, attack on the House of Representatives had five very real victims (the fictitious Congressman Chris MacLachlan not among them). Details about the incident were taken from Manuel Roig-Franzia, "A Terrorist in the House," *Washington Post,* February 22, 2004; Leada Gore, "In 1954, an Alabama Congressman Was Shot in the U.S. Capitol's House Chamber: Here's What Happened," AL.com, August 24, 2016; J. Michael Martinez, *Terrorist Attacks on American Soil: From the Civil War Era to the Present* (New York: Rowman and Littlefield, 2012); memo by House Parliamentarian's Office employee Joe Metzger, as entered into the *House of Representatives Congressional Record* on March 1, 1994.

Chapter 13: Details about the Howard Chandler Christy painting of the signing of the U.S. Constitution came from the website of the Architect of the Capitol, https://www.aoc.gov/art/other-paintings -and-murals/signing-constitution.

When Senator Herbert Lehman, Democrat from New York, claimed during that Senate debate that one hundred Communists were crossing into the U.S. from Mexico every day, he was quoting the Acting Commissioner of Immigration: "It was recently discovered that approximately 100 present and past members of the Communist Party had been crossing daily into the United States in the El Paso area; also that the number of present and ex-members of the Communist Party residing immediately across the border from El Paso number about 1,500, and it has been established that there exists active liaison between the Communist Party of Mexico and the Communist Party in the United States." *Senate Congressional Record,* March 8, 1954, https://www.gpo.gov/fdsys/ pkg/ GPO-CRECB-1954-pt2/pdf/GPO

-CRECB-1954-pt2-21.pdf.

The racism of Representative Howard Smith, Democrat from Virginia, is long established and vile. See Clay Risen's "The Accidental Feminist: Fifty Years Ago a Southern Segregationist Made Sure the Civil Rights Act Would Protect Women. No Joke," Slate.com, February 7, 2014.

The people of Mossville, Louisiana, have indeed been victims of the very real problems caused by chemical plants in their midst. Some of the details for this book were taken from Bernard H. Lane, "The Industrial Development of Lake Charles, Louisiana 1920–1950" (Louisiana State University and Agricultural and Mechanical College, January 1959); Tim Murphy, "A Massive Chemical Plant Is Poised to Wipe This Louisiana Town Off the Map," *Mother Jones* (March 27, 2014).

Details about Congressman Adam Clayton Powell Jr. were taken from his own memoirs *Adam by Adam* (New York: Dial Press, 1971) and *Keep the Faith, Baby!* (New York: Trident Press, 1967) and from Wil Haygood, "Power and Love," *Washington Post,* January 17, 1993. Some of the information about the Senate debate comes from "Power to Recruit Mexicans

Is Voted; Bill Authorizing the Admission of Migrant Labor Goes to White House," *New York Times,* March 4, 1954.

Chapter 14: Roy Cohn was vividly brought to life in Nicholas von Hoffman's *Citizen Cohn: The Life and Times of Roy Cohn* (New York: Doubleday, 1988). Cohn's own book about his mentor, *McCarthy* (New York: New American Library, 1968), is also quite revealing.

That Joseph Alsop did work for the CIA was revealed by Carl Bernstein in "The CIA and the Media," *Rolling Stone,* October 20, 1977.

Yes, Joe McCarthy would eat a stick of butter when he drank! At least according to Jack Anderson and Ronald W. May's *McCarthy: The Man, the Senator, the "Ism"* (Boston: Beacon Press, 1953). Roy Cohn's speech in chapter 14 about why McCarthy would be a good president is taken from comments made by Urban Van Susteren (Greta's dad) about McCarthy in that book. More about the Nazis he defended can be found in Gabriel Schoenfeld, "The Truth, and Untruth, of a German Atrocity," *Weekly Standard,* June 19, 2017, and the *Malmedy Massacre Investigation, Report of the Subcommittee of the Committee on Armed Services of the United States*

Senate, Eighty-First Congress, October 13, 1949.

If you're interested in reading more about Sam Zemurray and the relationship of the Dulles brothers to United Fruit Company, please check out Rich Cohen, *The Fish That Ate the Whale: The Life and Times of America's Banana King* (New York: Picador, 2013). One interesting excerpt: "John Foster Dulles, who represented United Fruit while he was a law partner at Sullivan & Cromwell — he negotiated that crucial United Fruit deal with Guatemalan officials in the 1930s — was Secretary of State under Eisenhower; his brother Allen, who did legal work for the company and sat on its board of directors, was head of the CIA under Eisenhower; Henry Cabot Lodge, who was America's ambassador to the UN, was a large owner of United Fruit stock; Ed Whitman, the United Fruit PR man, was married to Ann Whitman, Dwight Eisenhower's personal secretary. You could not see these connections until you could — and then you could not stop seeing them. Where did the interest of United Fruit end and the interest of the United States begin? It was impossible to tell. That was the point of all Sam's hires."

Chapter 15: Yes, night-vision technology

existed in the 1950s; see "Black-Light Telescope Sees in the Dark," *Popular Science* (March 1936). (But no, there were no night-vision binoculars available commercially.)

Information on John F. Kennedy, especially about his health, comes from Ted Sorensen, *Kennedy* (New York: Harper and Row, 1965), and Evelyn Lincoln, *My Twelve Years with John Kennedy* (New York: David McKay, 1965).

Chapter 16: Details about Communism in academia were gleaned from Ellen Schrecker, "Political Tests for Professors: Academic Freedom During the McCarthy Years," University of California History Project, October 7, 1999, http://www.lib .berkeley.edu/uchistory/archives_exhibits/ loyaltyoath/symposium/schrecker.html; David H. Price, *Threatening Anthropology: McCarthyism and the FBI's Surveillance of Activist Anthropologists* (Durham, NC: Duke University Press, 2004); and Samuel W. Bloom, "The Intellectual in a Time of Crisis: The Case of Bernhard J. Stern, 1894–1956," *Journal of the History of Behavioral Sciences* 26 (January 1990).

You can learn more about the saga of Clinton Brewer in Hazel Rowley's *Richard*

Wright: The Life and Times (Chicago: University of Chicago Press, 2008) and Jerry W. Ward and Robert J. Butler, eds., *Richard Wright Encyclopedia* (Westport, CT: Greenwood Press, 2008).

Chapter 17: Some basic details about trains in the 1950s came from Mike Schafer and Joe Welsh, *Classic American Streamliners* (Osceola, WI: Motorbooks International, 1997). Also see "The Congressional Services" at https://www.american-rails.com/congressional.html; "Pennsylvania's Congressional, 1952–1967" at http://www.trainweb.org/fredatsf/cong52.htm.

Chapter 18: Details about the history of the Harvard Club of New York were taken from its website: https://www.hcny.com/.

The story of Martin Couney came from Claire Prentice, "How One Man Saved a Generation of Premature Babies," BBC, May 23, 2016.

There are many fine books and articles that detail how pesticides became what is commonly referred to as Agent Orange. Among them: Alvin Lee Young, *The History, Use, Disposition and Environmental Fate of Agent Orange* (New York: Springer, 2009), and *Biologic and Economic Assessment of Benefits from Use of Phenoxy Herbicides in the United States,* Special

NAPIAP Report Number 1-PA-96, United States Department of Agriculture National Agricultural Pesticide Impact Assessment Program in cooperation with Weed Scientists from State Agricultural Experiment Stations.

Chapter 21: Before it was Xerox, it was the Haloid Company. Background on the photocopy machine is from Alfred Zipser, "Printing System Speeds Drawings: Xerox Machine Can Make Copies of 10 Different Plans a Minute," *New York Times,* October 26, 1958. Other information about the history of xerography comes from the Xerox.com website.

Chapter 22: The incident with sheep at Skull Valley, Utah, happened in 1968. For more, see "Nerve Gas: Dugway Accident Linked to Utah Sheep Kill," *Science,* December 27, 1968; and Jim Woolf, "Feds Finally Admit That Nerve Agent Was Found Near 1968 Sheep Kill," *Salt Lake Tribune,* January 1, 1998.

Chapter 23: Details about the actual Hellfire Club were taken from two excellent books on the subject: Evelyn Lord, *The Hell-Fire Clubs: Sex, Satanism and Secret Societies* (New Haven, CT: Yale University Press, 2008), and Daniel P. Mannix, *The Hellfire Club* (Lake Oswego OR: eNet Press,

1959). The details of the club during the eighteenth century are directly from those two books.

Chapter 24: Some of the testimony was taken directly from the transcript of the *Hearings Before the Subcommittee to Investigate Juvenile Delinquency of the Committee on the Judiciary, United States Senate, Eighty-Third Congress, Second Session, April 21, 22, and June 4, 1954.* Danny Gaines of IC Comics is based on William M. Gaines of EC Comics, and the comics described are based on ones that the juvenile delinquency subcommittee focused on in the actual hearings.

Epilogue: Phil Strongfellow is fictitious but Douglas Stringfellow was indeed a real Utah Republican congressman profiled on *This Is Your Life* who apparently lied about his heroic war record with the OSS. You can read more about him in Lee Davidson, "Scandalized Utah Congressman Believed His False War Stories; Douglas Stringfellow's Autobiography Says He Preferred Being Seen As Lying About WWII Service and Not 'Crazy,' " *Salt Lake Tribune,* December 30, 2013, and Vern Anderson, "For Politician Who Concocted a Tale of Heroism, the End Began on TV," Associated Press, October 30, 1994.

Descriptions of Eisenhower's Oval Office came from Anthony Leviero, "President Hangs 7 Office Pictures," *New York Times,* March 25, 1953, and Bess Furman, "The Oval Room: Eisenhoweriana," *New York Times,* November 30, 1958.

Eisenhower's views of the military-industrial complex were taken from his farewell address as well as from Charles J. G. Griffin, "New Light on Eisenhower's Farewell Address," *Presidential Studies Quarterly* 22, no. 3 (Summer 1992): 469–79. Eisenhower's views on McCarthy were taken from his own *Mandate for Change, 1953–1956* (Garden City, NY: Doubleday, 1963), as well as from David Nichols, *Ike and McCarthy: Dwight Eisenhower's Secret Campaign Against Joseph McCarthy* (New York: Simon and Schuster, 2017). Much of the notion of Eisenhower setting a trap for McCarthy was inspired by that informative book. Eisenhower's relationship to the intelligence community is detailed beautifully in Stephen Ambrose, *Ike's Spies: Eisenhower and the Espionage Establishment* (New York: Double-day, 1981).

That said, let me reemphasize that this is a work of fiction.

ACKNOWLEDGMENTS

This book could never have happened without the faith, wisdom, and partnership of my editor and publisher, Reagan Arthur, whose guidance and support were invaluable. I am also deeply indebted to my attorney Bob Barnett, who steered this project from the very beginning.

At Little, Brown, Maggie Southard and Shannon Hennessey have been enthusiastic boosters in publicity, as have Pamela Brown and Ira Boudah in marketing. Pamela Marshall, Marie Mundaca, Mary Tondorf-Dick, and Tracy Roe made it all sing and flow. The artistic gifts of Allison Warner and Chelsea Hunter have been so thrilling to watch, while Joseph Lee and Leslie Armstrong have helped in myriad other ways too numerous to detail. I also want to offer a deep thanks to deputy publisher Craig Young and digital and paperback publisher Terry Adams.

Early on in the writing process, Judy Sternlight helped me take an idea and give it a narrative structure and framework that turned it from a vision to reality. My pal Matt Klam provided editing love and attention early on that took the book to a new level — I'm lucky to benefit from the friendship of such a gifted writer. My dear friends Josh Flug, Lisa Cohen, Paulette Light, and Alana Fishberg offered keen insights and observations.

Thank you to all the amazing people at CNN, headed by the inimitable Jeff Zucker and including my wonderful team. Deepest appreciation to Jay Sures at UTA.

That I was fortunate to have been born to parents who instilled in me the belief that I could and should try to accomplish any endeavor almost goes without saying, and lucky me, but they also offered support and suggestions, as did my supportive stepmother. I have the best brother in the world, and he too had lots of interesting thoughts and constructive suggestions.

Lastly, my wife, daughter, and son were always understanding and of course are fundamentally the reasons I do anything, really. And it is my wife to whom this book is dedicated. I love you, honey.

ABOUT THE AUTHOR

Jake Tapper is CNN's chief Washington correspondent and the anchor of *The Lead with Jake Tapper* and *State of the Union.* Tapper has been a widely respected reporter in the nation's capital for almost twenty years. He is the author of four books, including the *New York Times* bestseller *The Outpost: An Untold Story of American Valor.*

The employees of Thorndike Press hope you have enjoyed this Large Print book. All our Thorndike, Wheeler, and Kennebec Large Print titles are designed for easy reading, and all our books are made to last. Other Thorndike Press Large Print books are available at your library, through selected bookstores, or directly from us.

For information about titles, please call:
  (800) 223-1244

or visit our website at:
  gale.com/thorndike

To share your comments, please write:
  Publisher
  Thorndike Press
  10 Water St., Suite 310
  Waterville, ME 04901

Also by the Author

Selling Money

The Outlaw Bank